BREAKAWAY

ALSO BY JOEL SHEPHERD

CROSSOVER
A CASSANDRA KRESNOV NOVEL

KILLSWITCH
A CASSANDRA KRESNOV NOVEL

JOEL SHEPHERD

BREAKAWAY

A CASSANDRA KRESNOV NOVEL

an Imprint of Prometheus Books
Amherst, NY

Published 2009 by Pyr®, an imprint of Prometheus Books

Inquiries should be addressed to
Pyr
59 John Glenn Drive
Amherst, New York 14228–2119
VOICE: 716–691–0133, ext. 210
FAX: 716–691–0137
WWW.PYRSF.COM

13 12 11 10 09   5 4 3 2 1

Library of Congress Cataloging-in-Publication Data

Shepherd, Joel, 1974–.
    Breakaway : a Cassandra Kresnov novel / Joel Shepherd.
        p. cm.
    Originally published: Sydney, Australia : Voyager, an imprint of HarperCollins Publishers, 2003.
    ISBN 978-1-59102-742-3 (mass market paperback)
    ISBN 978-1-59102-540-5 (paperback : alk. paper)
    1. Androids—Fiction. I. Title.

PR9619.4.S54B74 2007
823'.92—dc22

                                                        2007001854

Printed in the United States of America

For Nathan,
who in many ways
is still taller than me

"Look at the size of that," Ayako breathed, gazing down at the seething mass of people along central Patterson. "Looks like eighty thousand plus."

"Peanuts," said Ari with studied disinterest, eyes fixed to the navscreen on the dash, "Patterson's got half a million and over four hundred thousand stayed at home. It's an apolitical city, everyone says so. Get us a direct approach, the circuit wastes time."

Ayako punched keys, uplinking directly to central traffic control through CSA Headquarters. Ari spared the protest a brief glance as it faded behind looming towers, a flood of humanity beneath a white, spotlit glare, air traffic hovering in close attendance, most roads blocked by police vehicles. Everyone hoping the mob stayed quiet this time, no one wanted a repeat of the Velan protest with its two hundred and fifty comatose rioters still filling space in the nearby hospital. But what option did police with no riot gear have but neuralisers when confronting rioters? Tanusha, the apolitical city, was woefully unprepared for such events.

". . . no," Ayako cut into some unheard transmission, "this is Googly, we're CSA One, I have priority override . . ." and broke off at an interruption, throwing Ari an exasperated look.

"I've got it." Ari pressed the speaker button.

"... *live perimeter*," the voice was saying, "*we have no record of your authorisation, this is an unscheduled incursion* ..."

"Fuck you, you little piece of shit," Ari said calmly. "Do you know what CSA One means? Authorise this." Uplinking mentally he triggered his best attack code. Static burst from the other end as the attack software took control of com frequencies and shoved the CSA Priority ID into the uncooperative guard's visuals.

"Lot of traffic," Ayako said nonchalantly into the pause that followed, eyeing the display ahead, and the airborne ID markers that blipped about their inward trajectory. "Going to have to bump someone down a space."

"Do it, the damn suits can wait for once ..." Authorisation flashed to green on the navscreen as the local heavies cleared them through. "Thank you," he told them, loud with sarcasm. And to Ayako, "Jesus Christ, if I have to fight through another fucking turf war in the next thirty minutes I'm going to use my gun."

"Change that silly codename," Ayako said mildly. "No one believes CSA One Ops would use that codename."

"I shall do no such thing." Scanning at maximum capacity through his scanning linkups, additional airspace data from central filling in the three-dimensional space around the termination point of their flightpath— Kanchipuram Hotel. The whole tactical picture hung clear and tactile in his inner-vision, even as his eyes gazed through the windshield.

"Googly. What on earth is a googly?" Ayako steered the cruiser through a gentle approach bend past the West Patterson towers, the nighttime cityscape looming up on the left as they banked. Blazing light, towers, traffic filled streets, all blissfully free of protesters.

"Cricket, you poor philistine Asiatic person—it's a deceptive, spinning delivery ..." Ari's scans came up empty. He didn't trust them. "The cornerstone of all true civilisation—first there was upright bipedal motion, then there was language, then there was cricket."

"Oh," said Ayako.

The hotel lay ahead, a broad, neocolonial sprawl of floodlit pillars and arches, seriously retro-Greek architecture and seriously five-star, on the perimeter of a broad park, tree-filled and dark with shadows. The infonetwork showed security everywhere. "Snipers," said Ayako as she followed the display course, bringing them about and descending.

"No kidding." Ayako's vision enhancement was better than his. Ari preferred network capability, Ayako liked her physio-perks.

Another few seconds and he could see them himself, armoured figures crouched on the broad roof above the driveway that passed beneath the front pillars. Limos and vehicles everywhere. There was no shortage of grounded air traffic on the nearby lander either, mostly big official cruisers, with the occasional four-engine flyer, armoured and expensive, drivers waiting around the open doors.

"Too damn many," Ari muttered, hopping from site to site as his software jumped along the security perimeter, sorting files and searching those of attendees. It was the usual messy overlap of local, private and government security, too many layers in some places and too many holes in others. "We're going to have to wait until we get inside."

Ayako set the cruiser to auto-approach, the windshield display indicating the gleaming route ahead as she took both hands off the controls to check her weapon and belt interface. Ari did likewise, absently, staring intently through the right-hand windows as they came in past the front pillars. Hotel staff and security clustered about the unloading space before the main doors—various well dressed importances still arriving, a throng of over-long vehicles with tint-out windows and accompanying security with dark suits and broad shoulders.

The airpark was temporary, a hotel staffer was waving them down in the wash of the cruiser's forward light. Ayako killed the glare with a control button as Ari holstered his pistol at his side, frowning as a pair of suited security came jogging their way from back near the main entrance. The cruiser touched, doors powering upward even as Ayako activated the standby sequence. They got out and left the cruiser to complete its own wind down, the hotel staffer protesting loudly that this was a temporary space and if they wanted to park permanently they'd have to move to the visitor's park . . .

Ari ignored him, walking even as Ayako jogged around the car to catch up. The two security agents, moving fast to intercept, had to change direction abruptly.

"Can I see your ID please?"

Ari flashed it, walking fast with Ayako in tow, headed back along the hotel front toward the clustered activity at the main entrance. They paused as the security man internalised both his and Ayako's vis-seal, no doubt sending back on uplinks to reverify for himself. Ari spared the front hotel gardens a brief scan as they walked. Broad and green in the wash of light, obviously wired end to end with sensor gear. Groundcars flashed by beyond the perimeter fence. Beyond rose the clustered towers of Patterson central, a pair of mega-rise soaring skyward in a blaze of light, flanked by smaller buildings. Several near-stationary aircars, circling slowly amid the usual airborne flow—official or media, he guessed, no doubt monitoring the protest.

Above the gentle, familiar rush of traffic noise, Ari fancied there was something else in the air. Not a sound, not a sight, nor a smell. A feeling. An urgent, prickling buzz in the air, like electrostatic charge. Tension. It was everywhere. The city was alive, with commotion, nervous energy and outright fear. A resident of Tanusha all his twenty-eight years, Ari could never remember having felt anything like it. Even New Year's celebrations, notorious events in party-mad Tanusha, felt nothing like this. The old happy complacency was gone. The universe had descended upon Tanusha. In some senses, literally.

"How can we help?" the security asked, falling into step alongside Ari. Ayako edged herself past in annoyance, taking place at Ari's side.

"You've been branched," Ari told him. "I have a very

reliable information source telling me that there is a potential code-red security threat present in the hotel, probably among the guests. You can get me whoever's in charge of security here and full access to the guest and staff lists, minus the usual privacy censors."

"You could have just told us that, we can handle it."

"Branched is branched, pal, your networks aren't secure. And I know who I'm looking for, you don't." Several more security were looking their way amid the procession of newly arrived guests and vehicles before the main entrance. At a signal and inaudible transmission from the first guard, one headed inside at a fast walk. Ayako skipped ahead onto the sidewalk, off the road as a departing ten-metre-long limo accelerated past, her smaller steps hurrying double time to keep pace with Ari's stride.

The guests at the main entrance ignored them as they entered the huge, gleaming lobby, all Tanushan importances being inclined to ignore the ever-present security these days. A huge staircase ascended past reception to the main ballroom, late arrivals climbing in tuxedos and a glitter of fancy gowns that caught the light and pastel shades of the walls and cavernous ceiling. A broad African man in a suit emerged through the crowd to meet them halfway.

"Takane," he introduced himself, hard and businesslike, "S-3. What's the problem?" S-3 was Parliament security. Ari knew there were three senators present, and one Progress Party backbencher . . . but no way did S-3 have this many personnel spare for the presence he saw, and certainly not for the snipers on the roof.

"You've been infiltrated," Ari repeated, reflashing his badge. "Who's your joint cover?"

"Infiltrated by whom?"

"Dangerous people."

Takane scowled at him, eyes narrowed. "What's your source?"

"Can't tell you."

The eyes narrowed further. "This is S-3's patch, *Agent*, I'm not going to allow some hotshot ghostie just to come in here and shoot off on his own private pursuits. If you've got a trace, you hand it to us and we'll take care of it."

Ari's gun holster suddenly acquired an attractive, tempting weight beneath his jacket.

"Callsign Googly," he said instead. Takane blinked. His security clearance was high enough, evidently, to know the significance. "Give me full access or there'll be trouble."

Receptor software kicked in, a pressure on Ari's inner ear, as internal visual graphics overlayed schematics across his vision. It registered Takane's own abrupt transmission, and the reply reception, confirming his own codes. But he didn't need the enhancement to tell that Takane was rescanning his own datasource, looking for visual confirmation. Three seconds later . . .

"Get them full access," Takane said to a nearby heavy, "do what they say, keep it quiet." And he stalked off. Ari and Ayako followed the heavy up the broad staircase.

"*I trust that's the last silly crack at the callsign?*" Ari formulated on their private, encrypted frequency.

"*For now.*" Ayako didn't change her mind easily. "*Their joint cover is all separated. I checked their systems, they're integrating on an MP5 tac-grid, local net, standard encrypt.*"

"*That's about as safe as primed plastique . . .*"

"*No shit.*"

The main ballroom was broad and extravagant, filled with expensive guests sipping champagne and snacking from tables beneath gleaming chandeliers. Red-gold leaf decorations covered the broad ceiling. The band was African, guitar and drums, strictly background music. Hardly a techno rage, Ari reflected, gazing about as they followed the security through the milling crowd and mingling perfumes, and up a side stairway that climbed the ballroom wall. The balcony ran in a big U across the ballroom's far and side walls, descending to the floor via the staircases on each side. Uplink graphic unfolded across Ari's internal vision, showing him the meeting rooms and auditoriums that lay beyond through the corridors that sprawled across the lower floors of the hotel. Dark suited security stood at intervals along the balcony, covering the doors that led back into those hallways. Observing the guests with dark, intensely scrutinising stares.

"Wait here," Ari told Ayako, before following his guide down a corridor that led off one side of the balcony. Headed past hurrying hotel staff and caterers and caught a brief glimpse inside a room through a closing door. Well-dressed people inside seated about broad display-equipped tables, deep in discussion. This, quite obviously, was where all the real business was taking place, away from the chattering masses of the ballroom—high-powered meetings between high-powered Tanushan and off-world elite, complete with five-star catering. Another corner, more security suits, and an innocuous side door. It opened onto banks of mounted displays, three security monitors seated before them, uplinked and visored, scanning all rooms, corridors and network monitors simultaneously in a multilayered rush of sensory data.

An uplink was available by a mobile unit. Ari took the chair, slipped on the visor and connected the input socket to the back of his skull behind the right ear—wham, the uplink hit him, vision glaring across the visor, datalinks and modules in colourful three dimensions. He selected, scanned, then picked out the correct links, sorting through the oncoming rush with practised skill.

"Ayako, give me a feed." Flicker and bloom, and a second, real-world visual scan overlayed his schematics, a first person's view over the ballroom—Ayako's view of the milling crowd. "Good . . . I'm going to run you a sort-and-match, give me as much resolution as you can, show me those upgrades were worth the money you spent."

"*I'm government now,*" Ayako replied smugly, "*the CSA pays my bills.*"

"Yeah, ain't that a laugh." He hooked the feed to the datasearch and let it run on auto. Guest names ran by, files, associated links, connections. The scan raced across the net, branching out from the hotel across Tanusha and Callay beyond, searching for incriminating data and matching faces in the room. The database continued to compile, and the list of suspects ticked slowly downward.

"Why not just use the ballroom security scanners?" asked one of the seated security techs, watching his progress with curiosity.

"Not safe when the system's been branched," Ari replied distractedly, "you can't even trust that the monitors will show you the right face if they see it." The sec-tech blinked in astonishment.

"Realtime graphical replacement? I didn't know even the CSA can do that?"

"Hey, it's Tanusha. The biggest network geniuses don't work for the government, you know." Not until he'd joined, anyway.

Ari, meanwhile, switched attention to the back rooms. Seven meetings were in progress through the various hotel suites he counted, and several others that didn't look so formal. Two of the senators and the Progress Party rep were in the second floor executive suite above the main kitchen on the floor below. Security there was super tight. The other senator was just two rooms down from this security hub. He switched to local visual and got an internal view of one of the rooms—five people, seated and standing, sipping drinks and deep in discussion. The display screen was running, someone was demonstrating a stats schematic of some business model or other.

He scanned the faces, zooming for closeup. The senator was Allesandra Parker, Progress Party again. All of them were Progress Party, plus the rep. Curious indeed. Parker, Ari knew only too well, was a good friend of high-tech industry, didn't care much for social policy, and hobnobbed frequently with the corporate movers and shakers. Pan to the man conversing with her . . . Ari recognised him too without effort, Arjun Mukherjee, Bantam Technologies CEO. Big-time infonet company, very big recent moves into implant interface software. It made waves because the interface modules themselves were threatening to override what the neuro-researchers were calling the brain's natural "load capacity," or the amount of digitally generated information it could handle without augmentation. Neuro-augmentation was of course a touchy subject in Tanusha. It warranted much discussion amongst policy makers, and they with their constituencies. Allesandra Parker's position was well known. Mukherjee's went without saying. The potential profits involved were, as always, colossal.

The auto-scan abruptly fingered a possible and Ari switched scans back to the ballroom, finding that an Asian woman in a glossy red dress had been highlighted. Too old, and wrong background, a few seconds' further pursuit showed him, especially considering who he thought he was looking for. But still, an unannounced breach . . .

"Who's this?" he said to the room at large, and flashed them the image on general freq.

"Um . . ." The woman in the seat behind did a fast scan. ". . . not on the main list, must be one of the sublist invites . . . hang on, I'll check."

"Sublist?" Ari frowned. Spun his chair about to stare at the young security woman. She looked barely twenty-two, S-3 were recruiting them young these days. "What sublist?"

"Oh . . . A-list guests had the option of selecting their own invites, security vetted them, of course, full checks . . ."

"Which security?" A very, very bad feeling was building in the pit of his stomach. As bad feelings went, this one rated among the very worst. "S-3?"

"Of course."

"You double-checked the IDs? Counter-forgery?"

Frown from the puzzled young woman. "No . . . should we have? They were all selected by A-list, security-cleared guests . . ."

"Who submitted the list?"

"Mrs. Tatiana Chernomirsky, she's public liaison for the Government Trade Department . . ."

"Get her here, now!" In a tone of voice that turned the young security woman pale and wide-eyed as she rushed to comply. Ari switched frequencies, heart thumping, his mouth abruptly dry as all his previous contingencies went up in smoke. "Ayako, there's a sublist of guests submitted by some damn Department woman, they didn't run checks for shifters . . ."

"*Oh shit,*" Ayako summed up succinctly, "*you never trust civil servants with security, I thought everyone knew that!*"

"Okay, that could mean any number . . . we might need backup here. Be ready, there's overlapping security concerns here, we don't want to trigger a panic or they might end up shooting each other, for all I know . . ."

"*I've got a good view here, if we evacuate it'll be spotted and that could be a trigger. Let's just stay cool and find them first.*"

Ayako was keeping her head, Ari noted with relief. Probably better than he was. Dammit. He wiped sweaty palms on his thighs.

"Sir," said the young security tech, "Ms. Chernomirsky's on her way, she was just about next door." A monitor screen showed a well-dressed woman walking up the nearby stretch of corridor. Ari unhooked from the monitor, went out the door and met her halfway.

"Oh hello," said the rather attractive civil servant, blinking pleasantly, "you must be Mr. . . . ."

"I need your sublist of invited guests. It's not on database. I want full attachments and I want it immediately."

Confused blinking. "Of course, it's on my personal datacomp . . ." turning back the way she came, ". . . if you'll just follow me . . ." Ari followed, heart thumping, pushing vision enhancements into multi-light, the corridor turning to a wash of red and gold before him. ". . . is there some kind of problem? I'd swear I followed all the protocols . . . what we're given, actually, is a standard form. CSA issued them to all government departments just last week, I believe, and we're all trying to follow them as closely to the letter as possible . . ."

People passed in the corridor, hotel staff, mostly, and a guest on his way out of the men's bathroom, wiping newly dried hands upon a handkerchief. Ari's hand itched to reach for the gun holster beneath his jacket, but he did not want to start an alarm yet. He monitored his position in the back corridors, passing another smaller function room as they turned into a wider thoroughfare. Big double doors, an electronic noticeboard pronouncing a guest speaker at some earlier hour, attendees still milling around discussing the recent presentation. Adjoining double doors from the next presentation room up ahead, a security man on duty, doors opening to admit another guest from within . . .

"Oh look," said Ms. Chernomirsky, "there's Mr. Carvuto now. He's one of the sublist invitees, perhaps he can help us . . . Mr. Carvuto!" Walking eagerly toward him as the dusky, clean cut young man turned to look . . . his eyes missed her completely, and locked on Ari, trailing a step behind. His eyes widened. Ari's did.

Carvuto ran, with Ari exploding past the startled Chernomirsky in pursuit, ripping the pistol from its holster . . . no time for silent formulation . . . "Ayako, got one. Track him and watch for responses!" Carvuto slammed a pair of guests screaming to the ground, smashed a stunned security agent with a well-placed running elbow and vanished about the next left corner. Ari hurdled bodies and ducked, rolling around the corner . . . shots exploded overhead, blasting chunks from the walls, Ari rolling up, pistol tracking as Carvuto kept running, firing back past his side. Security appeared in front, Carvuto changed targets real fast and blew him messily in half. Ari fired from a tight crouch against the wall, three quick shots precisely between the shoulder blades . . .

The explosion blasted him backward, flaming wreckage and shrapnel shredding the hotel walls like paper . . . Ari rolled, arms over his face as the secondary explosion decimated the walls further up.

"Ayako!" he yelled on open channel amid the crackling flames, hissing fire retardant and screeching emergency alarms, "it's fucking suicide rigs. They've got themselves primed to blow! Don't shoot them with people around, the blast'll kill everyone!"

"*Ari!*" Frightened and bewildered amid what sounded like the outbreak of mass panic in the ballroom. "*Are you okay?*"

"Get the sublist off Chernomirsky's database!" he yelled, rapidly getting drenched by fire retardant as he heaved himself up on one knee, aware of flames crackling dangerously close and noxious fumes in his lungs. "It's on her personal datacomp, rip the codes to pieces if you have to, just get it out. I don't have time! Get anyone who came in with a guy called Carvuto . . . it was Hector Iglasio, the fucker recognised me . . ."

"*Iglasio! That's Vanguard. I bet Yueman and Christophson are here too . . . Wait, I don't need any sublist, I know what the fuckers look like . . .*"

"Great, good, go!" He staggered upright, cursing himself for not thinking as straight as Ayako in a crisis. He knew Christian Vanguard's main goons as well as any underworld hack . . . Found himself being roughly grabbed by the arms and dragged stumbling around the corner . . .

"You okay?" shouted a man over the noise of alarms and fire . . . Not even security, Ari noted—the man holding his arm was a guest. Where the fuck were security? Uplinks rushed in as he accessed, racing across the local network . . . oh, of course, *that* was where they were . . . "Sonny, you hearing me? Oh hell, your arm's hurt . . ."

He stared down, and found the jacket sleeve of his left forearm pierced in several places. A considerable amount of blood was seeping out. Human bombs. Shrapnel, ball-bearings. Recalled the wall being decimated beneath a hail of exploding metal . . . God only knew how it'd missed him, maybe being set off accidentally had triggered it wrong . . . It should have hurt, but of course the enhancements took care of that too.

"I'm okay," he gasped, his lack of breath surprising him as he steadied against the corridor wall. "I'm CSA, you'd all better get out that way." Pointing unfeelingly with his damaged arm. "There're exits on the other side of those rooms . . ." His uplink-map showed him so. ". . . don't try to get out the main doors. There's important senators and stuff that way, security everywhere . . . they're the targets, you get me? Keep away from them, the bad guys aren't interested in you, only senators."

And beat his way clear, off down the thoroughfare, shoving and weaving past screaming, panicking guests emerging from side rooms or looking wildly about for lost friends . . . Uplinks showed him the way, a staircase ahead and main corridor leading back to the ballroom on level one. All the security were up here on level two where the senators were, but the underside was vulnerable . . .

"Ayako, see anything?"

"Nothing, everyone's panicking, there's a mad crush headed for the exits . . ." A brief flash to visual channel, Ayako's overlayed view of the ballroom from the level two balcony. Crowds of running guests swarming toward the main staircase and entrance hall . . . *"Anyone could be right under me and I couldn't see them, I'm going to get down there . . ."*

The staircase descended left and Ari hurtled down it, leapt the last seven steps and hit the ground running, avoiding major collisions through good luck and agility . . . The ballroom doors ahead were ajar, hotel auto-safeties activated for evacuation, and most people were running in the same direction he was. Ari roughly collided with someone on the point of entering, bounced off breathlessly, staring around the huge, increasingly empty ballroom. Tables overturned, glasses and food platters strewn and broken across the floor, instruments abandoned . . .

Gunfire crackled from out beyond the grand staircase, accompanied by an explosion of warning yells over general frequency . . . Security broke and ran across the ballroom, hurdling debris. More yells for help and backup . . .

"Come on!" came Ayako's yell from the right-hand stairway leading up to the balcony above, a small figure in a long-tailed leather jacket pelting down the steps . . . Uplinks showed the firefight outside, someone in the gardens by the side exit way, pinned down and spraying fire. Another, they thought, might have gotten in through that exit, though cover was now on the way . . .

"Wait!" he shouted at Ayako as she hit the bottom

step. She spun, frustrated, security racing out down the main steps beyond. Ari stared blankly ahead, only marginally sighted on her or the ballroom. Ayako's eyes widened. She recognised that look.

"What? You think . . . ?"

"Senators are that way." Pointing back and upward to the corridors leading back from the balcony above. "Security just went that way." Pointing out at the main entrance. "That's not right."

"Shit, how powerful are the bombs?" She strode quickly his way, angular Intel-issue pistol comfortable in her small hand. Ari shook his head, racing full speed through the uplinks, scanning all available hotel schematics and getting way too many blanks . . . the blast had taken out half the hardware network. The inner convention centre was effectively network blind.

"Powerful enough. I'd guess someone's chem-lab plastique, directional shrapnel front and back. It went straight through the walls back there . . ."

"Would it go through floors and ceiling?" And saw at close range . . . "Oh shit, your arm . . ."

"It'll last ten minutes." Distractedly. "I'd be almost as worried about the firearms. He had an Ubek-5, he was taking out whole pieces of wall back there. That's the HE-shells—if someone's got AP mags, he wouldn't even need to blow himself up, he could shoot through the floor." The volume of gunfire from beyond the main entrance had increased to steady, irregular bursts—covering fire, Ari figured from the schematics before his eyes, pinning the infiltrator down while someone moved around for the killshot.

Another rush-scan through the nearby rooms . . . S-3 had only enough personnel for level two, not enough for top and bottom. He determined several signals on S-3 frequency that showed agents in blocking positions about the ballroom level, but there were plenty of gaps, especially with half the network hardware missing . . .

"Take that side," he said to Ayako, pointing across to the other doors in the ballroom's rear wall, beneath the overhead balcony. "I've got this one . . . remember if you have to shoot, shoot for the head, these things could be uplink triggered."

In which case there was no guarantee, he reckoned, as he darted back up the corridor he'd come from, that blowing the bomber's brains out wouldn't also trigger the explosion. Took the first right into a small meeting room. Comfortable chairs set about a central table, doubtless for comfortable covert meetings between various involved persons. His uplinks got no reading on the room through the open doorway beyond. He flattened himself against the side wall, darted a quick look around, then followed, with gun levelled one-handed. Rear corridor, much smaller than the mains. Staffroom down one way, dead-end door with no-admittance notices. Closed. They shouldn't be closed with the auto-emergency systems opening everything for evacuation. He edged sideways down the corridor, pistol trained the opposite way, covering his more vulnerable side. Uplinks gave him nothing beyond the closed staffroom door either.

He spun and kicked in one smooth motion, pistol searching as the door smashed open . . . there were lockers, cabinets and drawers for various staff things in rows, narrow aisles between for access. No sound, beyond the echoing wail of emergency sirens, and the background crackle of reports, gunfire and schematic audio in his ear. The room smelt slightly stale, telling of less than perfect ventilation, and too much shoe polish and body spray . . . and something else.

He crept forward, darting a quick look into each aisle between the big storage rows . . . and was little surprised by the dark-suited body lying face down in the third aisle, head bent around at an unnatural angle. S-3 monitored each other's vitals, was his immediate thought. But the network was chaotic, damaged, and various encryption channels weren't working at all. A quick attention to his uplink schematics showed where the next obvious hole in the perimeter would be.

He turned and walked, briskly, weapon ready. Running was too dangerous now. In this proximity, he needed time to react. Down the narrow corridor into the broader thoroughfare and turned right where the main traffic would continue straight ahead—that was carpeted, with wall signs pointing toward convention rooms. The way right was bare floor, and the open doors down the end revealed wide steel benches for food preparation.

Ari entered the kitchen sideways, back to one side door, weapon ready. Switched quickly across to the other side. The kitchen was broad, divided by several long aisles, benches, microwaves and other kitchen stuff between . . . Ari didn't know, he preferred takeaway most nights. He rolled quickly behind the near benches, and crawled.

Heard muffled activity, close by, like someone rearranging gear. A clatter that could have been a weapon on a steel counter. Whoever it was was in a hurry. He reached the end of the bench and rolled fast to his feet, pistol levelled. "Don't move."

The man froze. He'd been standing on a counter, out of sight of the main kitchen entrance behind the tall storage units, now side-on to Ari's position. Attempting to stuff something into the space between the big storage cupboards and the ceiling. He was wearing formal pants and shoes like any number of guests, Ari noted, but his jacket was lying on the counter alongside his feet, and his plain shirt bore crease marks in unusual places. The bundle he was attempting to stuff into the gap between cupboard and ceiling dangled harness straps, close-fitting, low-intensity magneto locks, undetectable on basic security scan. God knew how they'd gotten the charge past the detectors, though.

"Hello, Claude," Ari said. The pistol fixed an unwavering sight upon the blond-haired young man's left eardrum. That was where the uplink transmission would come from. With his own systems at full-max, Ari reckoned he'd detect anything serious in time. Human encrypt formulations weren't exactly millisecond fast, and personal bombs would require serious encryption to avoid them going off in random traffic. "Change your mind about the 'suicide' bit, did you?"

"Ariel." With jaw-tight frustration. "I might have known. Did you kill Hector?"

"Hector killed himself. His death was pointless and achieved nothing. Yours will be too unless you deactivate that stupid thing and step down here. You can't penetrate the floor with that explosive, anyway, it's too thick."

A blatant lie . . . at least he had no real idea of the truth. But Claude had the position spot on, directly beneath the room now holding the senators. He'd done his homework. And, at this range, Claude had enough uplink capability to detect if Ari made a transmission to warn them. Ari knew he had that capability, it was on file—a file he himself had written. If Claude tried the trigger, Ari knew he'd have to shoot to kill. And Ari wanted a live interrogation. This much of a security breach warranted some serious analysis.

"Hector's death was *not* pointless," Claude retorted, clenched jaw trembling. Not looking Ari's way. "He has gone to a far better place. As will I. You, however, Ariel, are in question in this regard."

"You're running around the city blowing people up, and you question *my* Godly virtue?" Damn these guys were funny. His arm was suddenly throbbing. "That's . . . that's creative, Claude, really."

"Ariel . . . Ariel, in the Lord's name," Claude burst out in frustration, glaring with wide, trembling eyes in his direction, "you're a smart man, can't you *see*? Can't you see what's going on? This . . . this is lunacy!" Waving a hand about, encompassing the kitchen, the hotel, the entire teeming city of fifty-seven million.

"You're damn right it is." Thinking furiously. He couldn't patch-and-disable Claude's uplink trigger by remote, Claude could mistake it for a warning transmission and blow them both to pieces. He needed to knock him out cold, but carried no stunner. Dammit. Last time he made that oversight.

"Ariel, I know about you . . . most of my friends know about you. Opinion is divided but I, *I*, Ariel, I alone believe you to be a decent person. But you serve the wrong side, why don't you *see* that? These . . . these people, Ariel, they believe in ungodly things, they would vote for things that would forever warp and . . . and distort all of humanity in evil ways, and they would use this vote in the houses of power, Ariel, and life for all God's children would never be the same again!"

"Claude," Ari said, with what he thought was commendable calmness, "I respect your beliefs." Holding up a placating free hand. The arm was definitely throbbing now. It made concentration difficult. And holding one's temper. "I respect your beliefs, and I respect your right to hold them— and to voice them to whoever may choose to listen. But there are other ways to voice your beliefs than to go about killing people . . . 'thou shalt not kill,' Claude, does that ring a bell?"

"Like they're killing us?" Eyes blazing. "Like they're wanting to turn us all into some . . . some damn synthetic machines for their *profits* and their *portfolios* and their grand corporate empires!? Like they're wanting to kill our *souls*, Ariel? Dammit, man, how can you be so naive? You know better than anyone how the system works, you're a part of it! You know the politicians are in the corporate executives' pockets! And you're protecting them, you're protecting the whole, twisted, immoral system!"

Like it was such a horrible, sinful thing to do. Well, Ari'd heard that one before. And from saner people than Claude Christophson. He pursed his lips in exasperation.

"You know, Claude . . . you've nearly convinced me. Really. Why don't you put that explosive vest away, and rather than blowing yourself and all your very convincing rhetoric into very small pieces, you can live on, and stay here in Tanusha . . . You'll get a trial, it'll probably be public, with all the civil rights attorneys who'll no doubt do your case for free because of the publicity . . . You'll get a planet-wide broadcast podium, everyone will be listening, and then you can tell them all what you've just told me and everyone will believe, and then everything will all be right again. What d'you say?"

Too sarcastic, was his immediate thought. It was his usual flaw. But Claude actually hesitated. Ari could see it in his eyes, the faint uncertainty, the pause for thought. And maybe, just perhaps, that little voice of self-preservation whispering in the background, looking for excuses, reasons to be listened to. Religious loonies always believed their truths were universal. That there was such a thing as truth itself. It was their weakness.

A blue flash lit the air. Claude jerked and convulsed, then fell from the bench.

Reflex overcoming initial surprise, Ari leapt forward, awkwardly catching the falling body one-armed, the other ready in case the vest tumbled from its hiding spot . . . it didn't. He dumped the young man's limp body upon the floor between stainless steel benches and checked his vitals. Racing heartbeat, but he was still breathing.

"CSA give you that too?" he asked, searching Claude's pockets.

"Of course," said Ayako, coming down the aisle and repocketing her stunner. "You can get them through the underground, of course, but they're too expensive."

Ari found the sidearm, an Ubek-5 again, and plenty powerful for a concealed weapon.

"That Claude?"

"Yeah . . . I think he's the last. There's at least two outside. Four's the absolute limit I'd have thought could get in. The rest of it looks pretty well covered."

"And you left someone alive to question this time." Ayako sounded impressed. "You're evolving as a CSA operative, Ari."

"First guy who gave me a choice," Ari replied, finishing with one leg, then the other. There was a light thump as Ayako leapt onto the counter behind, and started to gingerly remove the explosive vest from up against the ceiling. "You know," he added, "I always picked Claude for a nutter, but suicide vests are just a bit extreme."

"The future of the human race is something that tends to make them a bit upset." After disarming the vest, Ayako pulled it down. A simple contraption, a basic vest with flat, body-hugging pockets, a few wires and a trigger switch. Too slim to be visible under an evening jacket. "You know, if this keeps up, you're going to lose all your lunatic friends very shortly."

"Oh no." Ari gazed down at the young terrorist's calm, sleeping face. "I can always make new friends. Plenty more where these came from."

CHAPTER 2

The swell was large today.

Sandy sat on her board, part submerged in the heaving sea, and watched the churning curl of the last wave pass, thundering on toward the beach. Breaking, a muffled roar of collapsing water, headed for the distant shore. A surfer emerged from the churning wash, nose first, and resumed paddling. Lost, momentarily, as the swell took her down again, and moving dunes of water rolled between, glittering in the pale light of an overcast sky.

The wind was changing. Sandy turned to face into it, brisk and salt-smelling from the southeast, blowing leftwards along the north-south coastline. And tending now to onshore, she thought, as it whipped at careless strands of salt-wet hair, narrowing her eyes as it chopped the heaving seas to a broken mess. Soon it would be completely onshore, and the scudding patches of low cloud would turn to thick, blackening thunderheads, dark with the lateness of autumn.

Another swell lifted her, and suddenly, she could see a long way. The long, thin line of coast, stretching away to the southern distance. Nearby to the right, Lindolin Heads, a flaring mass of dark rock and sprawling reef, the surrounding sea flat with white, broken wash. Further out, the breakers pounded, exploding white spray along the outer reef. Beyond, a pleasure boat was cruising a rolling, bounding course through the roughening seas. Back on the near beach, the small figures of people, watching from the shore.

The other surfer continued out on a different angle, briefly hidden by the rolling swell. It was no one she recognised.

Weather for serious surfers, she thought idly, scanning the surrounding sea for other dark, wetsuited figures upon the broken surface. There were several, widely spaced across the broad stretch of beach front.

A faint smile played at her lips. So she was a serious surfer now. Vanessa thought so. Vanessa had wanted her company at lunch, with friends and family. Vanessa hadn't understood how a weather report could make that impossible. A serious surfer was surely someone who, given several hours' respite from the worst security crisis the planet had ever seen, would grab her board and wetsuit from her CSA locker, hire a flyer from a regional hire company and head out to the coast. Most agents spent such precious timeouts sleeping, or, like Vanessa, catching up with friends and family, mostly unseen for the last few weeks. Lacking family, not needing much sleep, and her attention consumed with the surf report, Sandy's priorities were different.

The swell loomed up in front, not quite the correct angle of face. She let it go, a giant heave and rise over the lip, then sliding down the back. Roar and crash as it broke behind her, churning on toward the beach. A wonderful sound. The last opportunity she'd had, on a precious rotating weekend off, she'd camped overnight on a beach near this. Vanessa had been with her that time. Lying in the dark, wind rippling the canvas tent walls, they'd talked about many things, and looked out the window mesh at the stars, while the waves had pounded and roared out in the dark.

Meteors that night, she remembered, reseating herself upon the board, facing the wind. Shooting stars, Vanessa had called them. Another of those strange civilian terms, unconnected with reality. Yet all the more charming for it.

Sandy gazed out into the freshening wind, beyond the lumpish horizon of sea in motion, and remembered the most spectacular meteor storm she'd ever witnessed. Nothing natural could rival the aftermath of a trans-orbital battle. Wreckage that burned in brilliant flares, flaming pieces that lit the sky in their multitudes and turned a moonless night to noon-day glare. Yet another difference between her perceptions and those of the people around her. She had stopped counting long ago.

Further out, another dark swell was looming ... and another behind it, she saw, as another rise took her higher ... even larger than the first. She thought it looked very nice, very promising. And felt a flare of excitement, watching that first, looming wall of water grow. Rode it all the way up, a fast ascent, then plunging over the lip as she saw, to great delight, that the second had indeed been worth waiting for. Roar as the first broke, rushing away. She lay flat and turned the nose of her board back toward the shore. Behind her, the mountain rose, dark and glistening.

And then it was on her, several sharp thrusts from her arms to accelerate as the board tilted forward, and the massive wave lifted her clear of the flat surface ... then plunging forward, upward shove from tightly gripped hands, and a smooth swivel got her feet under her. Firm grip of bare skin on the roughened board as she plunged and bounced down the huge, racing wave face. Decelerated at the bottom and cut hard left, back up the face, shooting upward and slicing back ...

... and for an exhilarating, flying moment, she hung upon the vertical face, high above the flat sea below ...

... and plummeted down, a rush of wind and racing water, a mad vibration of board on water that jolted through her legs. Sudden explosion of foam everywhere, half the lip collapsing behind as the wave broke, and she cut left again, aiming to keep ahead of the surging mess. Up and racing at double velocity across the face. Flat sea below, balanced midway up a rushing, vertical wall that roared with howling, salty wind and spray.

She laughed out loud, soundless against the roar. Trailed the fingertips of her left hand along the racing wall-face, and at that hurtling, shuddering velocity, it felt solid as concrete. Spray erupted along her path as she zigzagged madly up and down the vertical face. And then, with heavenly grace, the lip curled over to fall like a giant curtain on her right, and she was in a tube.

Time slowed. Encircled by rushing, shimmering water, everything echoed. The curl of arcing sea above her head was possibly the most beautiful thing she'd ever seen. The world turned green and shimmering blue, refraction of moving light and water. It was eerie, and heavenly, and utterly exhilarating.

And suddenly ending, as she shot into open sky amid erupting spray from the blowhole effect, the wave collapsing further ahead. She cut back hard right, falling downslope, and sensed the rest of it falling in behind her, like a cliff-face collapsing. Everything exploded, with massive force, blasting her forward . . . within which she held her balance, inhumanly, and came back down on her feet . . . except that the board was no longer under her.

Wham. Roaring silence, everything churning over. Muffled thunder. A few exploratory strokes, to test resistance. Direction. Up from down. Felt herself rising, as the foam passed, and stroked in that direction.

She broke the surface, a rush of light and sound. Hauled her board in by the leg strap, grinning uncontrollably, and looked around for the next set. There was another one out there, rising nicely and coming her way. What a day. She threw herself jubilantly back onto the board and began paddling back out to sea.

Frequency alarm—a sharp register in her inner ear. She frowned, still paddling, and accessed. Click and response, a merging tune into frequency . . . a shielded line with priority code, but no message. A specific recall, just for her. Someone wanted her back at work. She swore, loudly. Several more strokes and she decided that she had to stop paddling. Dammit. Ahead, the next wave exploded into towering whitewash, and she was nearly too annoyed to bother rolling under.

She emerged from the water several minutes later, board under one arm, bare feet trudging over rough, shell-strewn sand. Wiped dripping hair from across her face. Refused to hurry, the recall would have told her if it were urgent. More damn procedural rescheduling. Some politician had probably slipped in the shower and twisted her pinky. To hell with politics, didn't they know the surf was up?

She walked along the shore, sand plastering her wet feet, and headed for the ranger's bungalow on stilts that overlooked the beach from the height of a neighbouring dune. Surfers gathered about. Boards, clothes and towels, and carry bags for a day trip or longer. She walked among them, dripping, getting looks from many of the men as she went. Broad shouldered and somewhat less than tall, she was hardly the long, leggy, wandlike surfie-girl ideal. But broad shoulders came with broad hips, and compact, lithely muscular curves, pronounced enough, as Vanessa said, to take your eye out.

Sandy knew very well what she looked like in a wetsuit. She'd been told often enough lately. And in a city where the predominant skin colour was brown, and the predominant natural hair colour was black, attractive blonde Europeans got more than their fair share of attention.

She reached her bag where she'd left it on the sand, shouldering it without bothering to check the possessions—here among the surfer community, no one worried about rare urban concepts like common theft. Besides, no one stole stuff in Tanusha. The very idea was beneath majority criminal contempt. There were so many infinitely more valuable things to steal in Tanusha than the contents of surfers' carry bags.

From the beach it was a fifteen minute walk through scrubby dunes and along a pressed-earth road to the small park designated for flyers. Groundcars parked haphazardly along a roadside that was definitely not equipped for autocontrol, wearing ruts off the road shoulder. Sandy recalled one of the locals saying recently that the council had wanted to build carparks to accommodate all the traffic, but the locals wouldn't stand for it. Scrub turned from low bushes to trees as she walked along the roadside, board under one arm, and the most hi-tech thing she could see was the solar panel atop the public toilet, near the mouth of the path that led to the camping ground. Sandy had long decided she liked it better this way, all natural bush and sand, a fresh breeze blowing and the roar of surf upon the air. But she kept a careful eye upon the occasional groundcar that rolled past on its way to or from the major western freeway ten kilometres off—out here, all cars drove on manual, a skill Tanushan drivers rarely practised. Despite the onboard computer assist, away from the urban central network several still managed to end up nose first into trees.

The flyer sat upon a rectangular, grassy clearing off the roadside behind a line of tall trees, one of an angled line of other flyers. It was already humming in the preflight mode she'd initiated with a mental uplink. She stowed the board and climbed to the driver's seat without bothering to remove the wetsuit from her lower body. Engines thrummed within the nacelles, and the ground fell away below . . . the field with its row of parked flyers, the road to the beach, then the white, rippling dunes, a pale line before the turquoise ocean, broken in white, frothing lines . . . all laid out below, the short distance she had walked, maplike.

Sandy gazed regretfully at the ocean for several lingering seconds, at the churning white froth of a break, at a big swell looming further out, a glimpse of a surfer, plummeting joyfully along that advancing wall of ocean swell . . . She reangled the thrust and banked away from the ocean, heading inland and gaining altitude.

Rajadesh passed below, a single main street, some basic buildings and side streets, holiday accommodation and not much else. Beyond, and all about, the trees grew thick, green and profuse. To the left, the glittering tangle of waterways that made the Shoban River Delta. At a further distance to the right, the looming peaks of the Tuez Range, a bare, rocky spread of tall, broken landscape. Above, the broken grey cloud seemed near enough to touch, scudding by at noticeable speed as she angled the nacelles to cruise. Spread before them, and seeming quite close at even this low altitude, was the forest of tall, reaching towers that was Tanusha. Like a forest of gleaming sticks beneath a dull and broken sky. It spread for many kilometres to either side, towers too numerous to count. One of the greatest, monolithic civilisations in all human history. Home.

The skylane brought her into Tanushan airspace at .86 kilometres, four hundred metres above the uniform Tanushan height for mega-high-rise. Towers sprawled in clusters in every direction, central regions fading to suburbia and back again, and the sky was alive with a profusion of air traffic. Sandy recovered her makani juice from the little refrigerated glovebox where she'd been saving it, and took a long sip. Offhandedly decided to interface through a local connection, high bandwidth receiver. A fast reception and in, zooming through a section of regional infrastructure network as her eyes and hands effortlessly followed the lane ahead.

Scanned on a range of securitied levels, searching for telltales, anything with that certain scent about the codes . . . sipped again at the makani juice, flying one-handed as she waited. Rush of data, freeform and tangible, network branches sprawling in an orderly, tangled mass . . . click, right there. She zoom-scanned and focused, there was a feeder-monitor of some description attached to one of the central control relays, part of the air traffic grid. Put there to monitor something, obviously. Small system, to escape curious attention. A fast probe showed it as official. Illegal to hack, not to mention difficult. A quick push further, through linkages open only to her . . . and caught the active trace . . . there was something about the diversion flows, the way each key linkage was siphoned off through fancy accesses . . .

Which meant . . . she did a further quick break-and-enter, using a series of coded combinations that would have frightened certain security types if they'd known she possessed them . . . and found the connection, and the data trail, and the spot to which it all pointed.

She turned about in her seat and looked. Could see, a brief glimpse through the rear-side window past the nacelle, a small spot among many such spots, cruising innocently on a parallel skylane. A fast flash-zoom through the gap between nacelle and window-side—a Chandara Falcon, large cruiser, darkened windows. A type commonly used by government agencies. Three point one kilometres away, with a clear monitor-fix upon her flyer.

It annoyed her no end. She accessed another, more familiar code, and awaited an answer. Got one, several seconds later.

"Sandy?"

"Hi, Ricey," she said, racing ahead on a separate link, checking out her assigned flightpath. "Are you on call?"

"I just got out of my car. I'm at the apartment, thought I'd better change. What's up?"

"I'm in a flyer on the way back from Rajadesh Beach, and I'm being followed. Chandara Falcon, no identifying marks, just over three clicks away but they've got a jobby monitor somewhere in the local airgrid infrastructure. It's feeding to them direct."

"Official?" Vanessa sounded concerned.

"It looks that way, but I can turn orange if I decide I'm a pumpkin. I was wondering if I should run a trace."

"Hell no. Run a fix and throw it priority over to Ops. They'll nab him and ask some questions."

"Even better." She smiled, doing that in a flash, full position and fix data, straight into CSA Ops, where the traffic rider ought to be receiving some very interesting information right about . . .

"Hello, Snowcat, this is Ops," spoke a formal, unrecognised voice in her inner ear. *"Your queried vehicle is black-flagged. Do you require further assistance?"*

A "black flag" meant government. More than government, it meant official, authorised, and not to be messed with. Sandy took in a deep breath through flared nostrils. The texture of golden light upon a gleaming tower shifted shade to pale—heat-light amid a darkening curtain of infrared. Independent movement highlighted, cruising aircars, a beckoning awareness, precursor to targeting-vision. The vibration of engines thrummed with enriched texture upon her eardrums, unveiling whole new shades and levels of sound and complexity.

She thought about taking it higher. Thought of contacting Ibrahim and putting the question to him directly. He'd told her the SIB were watching her. She hadn't thought it meant a tail on her surfing trips. She hadn't thought it would include a tail this blatant at all.

But there was a time and a place for such inquiries. Her instinct told her that this was neither.

"No. Thank you, Ops." She changed frequency, upped her encryption, and reconnected the old hookup.

"Sandy? Shit, is this another of your key-grade encryptions? This stuff gives me a headache."

"Tough. Ops says it's a black flag." Pause on the other end. Sandy's own readings showed the Falcon still with her, feeding off the air-grid fix. Her right index finger felt jumpy, the strain feeding through her hand, back up her arm. The redness had not left her vision.

"Well, you did kind of expect it," Vanessa pointed out.

Sandy made up her mind, reflexively slipped half-tranced into attack mode, and infiltrated the air-grid monitor through her connection.

"That I did," she replied shortly, eyes unsighted as she found the trailing aircar's defensive barriers. Broke them with her best combination and released a killer-cell, military-level code destroyer, a selective virus that fed on complicated software. Many years of League military ingenuity did their job and the Falcon's civvie ID beacon gave a shrill, panicked screech, and died.

"But," she continued, seeing a clear wobble show up

on her nav-scan, "I've decided that I've had enough of being tailed. It's a clear security risk to me and my broader circumstances, don't you think?"

"*Obviously*," Vanessa agreed. "Someone unofficial could imitate a black flag, or use their surveillance as a cover. You want me to talk to Ibrahim?"

"Not necessary." The Falcon, Sandy registered through her own links, was being queried by central flight control as to their lack of ID beacon, and their erratic flightpath. The Falcon gave their flag ID. And announced a flight emergency. Flight systems failure, massive systems malfunction. Backups operational, they were headed . . . somewhere. It didn't register on the flightpath. Sandy reckoned that with their systems down, she might be able to infiltrate far enough to find out that one, too. But she didn't want to push her luck. "I just nuked them."

"*Subtle*," Vanessa said dryly. Then, "*Shit. Oh well, makes things a bit exciting, I suppose.*"

"That's the Dark Star concept of surveillance, Ricey. If you don't know where the bastards are, send them a mail bomb and watch where the smoke rises."

"*This is a flammable environment, Sandy. Everything burns.*"

"Not me," Sandy told her, taking another sip of her drink. "I'm resistant. Didn't you know?"

"*I could have guessed.*" Still dryly. "*Since you're airborne, you want to give me a lift?*"

Vanessa came jogging across the landing pad to the rear of her apartment building, two gearbags bundled under her arms. Tossed both in through the open rear door, and climbed in the front, up beside Sandy.

"Hey-ya." Looked at Sandy's wetsuit-clad lower half, loose arms tucked between her back and the seat. The doors closed, and Sandy fed on the power. "Good waves?"

"Excellent waves." Throbbing vibration, and the flyer heaved off the pad. The rooftop awning flapped in the downdraft, above empty rows of car space. Sandy noted Vanessa's government cruiser, alone in her spot. Next to

Sandy's vacant space. Rows of garden ferns rippled and waved, dropping away below as they gained altitude. "They ought to be just about perfect right now."

"Oh well, we all have our sacrifices to make." Vanessa stretched. And silenced the blinking panel light by buckling her seatbelt. The apartment building's approach lane began to turn horizontal, and Sandy angled the engines once more. The rooftop slipped away below, giving way to now familiar neighbourhood roads beneath a spreading canopy of trees.

Further down Tago Road were the stores at which she now did her shopping, and got takeaway when it suited her. Further on still, beyond the Leung Street intersection, was the Santiello swimming complex, rectangles of blue water in a break in the trees, surrounded by decorative green gardens. In the opposite direction, Romanov Park, sports ovals about a central garden of lakes and drooping native willows. Beyond, the Subianto Stadium, grandstands looming in the middle distance.

Suburban Santiello. Vanessa had lived here for the past four years, and liked it. The only serious highrise was over to the southeast corner, where the Lantou Tower loomed skyward, and the crossstreets converged into full-on megadensity downtown. But mostly, Santiello was mid- to low-density suburbs, residential living, and an eclectic mix of architecture that largely did what it pleased. Some complained of a lack of ethnic-chic . . . but for the odd mosque or church . . . but Sandy thought it little to complain about. And Vanessa declared that she did not want to live in a postcard.

It had been Vanessa who had suggested Sandy take an apartment near her own. In the same building, as it turned out, that being specialised for government employees. And it had made certain official, bureaucratic types happy that the reliable, security-approved and "rising star" (a term she hated) SWAT Lieutenant Vanessa Rice was living next door, and taking care of her. Making sure, Sandy had supposed, that she did not assault the occasionally noisy neighbours, disembowel the somewhat coarse-mannered grocer on Tago Road, or, as Vanessa herself had suggested, bring home bevies of pretty, innocent Tanushan boys to molest in her apartment at her leisure. God save her from bureaucrats. And social conservatives in general. And representatives from the Ministry of Social Justice and Welfare. Those most of all.

"How did lunch go?" Sandy asked, remembering. The airlane climbed toward a merge with a lower altitude lane. The flyer cruised ahead, engines fully swept, as towers loomed in a sky scattered with traffic.

"Awful," said Vanessa, quite pleasantly. "Just awful. I've never been so glad to receive a callback in my life." Vanessa, Sandy had noticed, was prone to exaggeration. "I swear, I have the most obnoxious relatives in Tanusha, did I tell you?"

"Many times."

"My aunt-in-law . . . good grief, ninety-four years old . . . is suing her surgeon for some pointless hearing enhancement she had done two weeks ago—she claims it's given her insomnia. She can hear the bats squeaking to each other in the trees outside the bedroom."

"I can," said Sandy.

"Hearing enhancement, at ninety-*four*! Cost her half her savings . . . she doesn't eat well as it is. She thinks she'll make a hundred and thirty on enhancement alone. Doesn't believe she still has to worry about trivial things like diet and exercise . . . spends half her life on immersion hookup . . . you seen that adreno-glactic sim?"

"I have." Turning the music volume up, still soft enough to talk over. The engine noise was a gentle thrumming, erasing all higher tones to Sandy's ear—she had to tune consciously through it to grasp higher sounds. Not all GI sensory enhancements were perfect.

"What'd you think? Cheap junk?"

"Direct immersion VR doesn't work on me, Ricey. I don't have a reflex hook-in, it's all conscious."

"I'm telling you, I tried it, it's crap. It's like bad sex, you get all excited only to be let down."

"Now bad sex," said Sandy, "that's an oxymoron."

"*You're* an oxymoron," Vanessa retorted, grinning. "*Three* hours a day on adreno-glactic, six hours for that crummy magazine she works for, that's nine uplinked hours a *day* . . . And she calls friends direct, won't talk to anyone who uses a phone. People like her are what's scary about infotech, you can spend your whole life plugged into a machine and not realise the alternative . . ."

"Ricey," Sandy said, smiling, "you're bitching."

"Of course I'm bitching. That's what friends are for, they bitch to each other. Only you don't bitch anywhere near enough, it's got to be unhealthy. So I bitch for the two of us . . . it's quite an effort, you should appreciate it. You're seeing a master bitcher at work. It's an honour and a privilege for you, if I do say so myself."

"You *talk* for the two of us," Sandy corrected. "If you'd occasionally shut up, I might get some more practice." Vanessa ignored her, wincing and flexing her left shoulder. "Damage?"

Vanessa nodded, rubbing with a hand and grimacing. "Feedback. I still haven't gotten that suit adjustment right." Sandy reached over with her right hand, keeping her left upon the controls. Took a firm hold of Vanessa's shoulder, and probed.

"There?"

"Further up." The hand moved further, and Vanessa winced, wriggling the shoulder. "More. More. AH! Just there . . . oh yes." Sandy applied gentle pressure, and felt thumb and fingertips digging in. "Ouch! Not so hard, you'll rip my arm off."

"Complainer." She massaged, gently. Was careful not to exceed the reflexive tension generated by the feedback through her fingertips. It was an accustomed reaction, around straights, and as with all hardwired reflexes, it was difficult to shake. It wasn't at all likely that she would hurt Vanessa. But she *could*, hypothetically at least. It was a con-stant concern, and she was *never* careless. Never.

"Oh yeah . . ." Vanessa leaned her head back, eyes

closed and smiling. Soft, dark-brown curls fell about her brow. Slim, fine features. Beautiful, Sandy thought. Delicate. And living proof that some qualities went no further than skin deep. She massaged with careful fingers along the offending length of muscle, probing the collar bone along that slim, small shoulder. "You're good at that."

"I'm good at everything, remember?"

Vanessa's dark eyes opened slightly, and fixed her with a lidded, contemplative gaze. "If it weren't the truth, you'd be insufferable." Sandy smiled, steering them through another gentle bank one-handed, massaging Vanessa's shoulder with the other. Armour strains were always a problem . . . although not so much for herself. But she, of course, was the all-time leading consumer of massage time in the entire CSA, hands down. And Vanessa was the one who usually got stuck with the duty. She never missed a chance to even it up a little.

Vanessa wriggled the shoulder again. "That's much better. You've got it. I'll have to put you up for loan, charge by the hour. I'll make a fortune."

Sandy smiled. And worked her hand carefully up the shoulder toward Vanessa's neck. Vanessa grinned, and lowered her head, allowing Sandy's fingers to press and rub at her neck muscles, generating effortless, powerful, careful pressure.

She watched Vanessa's expression in her peripheral vision, and enjoyed making her wince with pleasure. It was such an easy thing to do, with her fingers on Vanessa's neck. It amazed her that it should feel so good to do so. *That's what friends are for*, Vanessa had said, about her bitching. With perhaps no real idea of the warm feeling that such a simple comment should provoke. It was unexplainable. Like the fingers on her neck, gently massaging. Like the smile it provoked upon Vanessa's lips, and the occasional low groan in her throat. Friend, she supposed. Perhaps that was all there was to it.

She smiled to herself. Nearly wishing, whimsically and not for the first time, that she herself was bisexual, like

Vanessa. That would have been interesting indeed. And sometimes, just sometimes, she suspected that Vanessa wished something similar, if only from curiosity.

But she wasn't. And try as she might, she just couldn't conceive of it. Her ever-curious mind did, it seemed, have its limits, however hard she tried to push her thoughts beyond the realm of the comfortable, or the familiar. Vanessa was beautiful. But she wasn't *attractive*, not to her. Women weren't, never had been, and never would be. Not sexually. It was almost disappointing to realise. It was an experience that she would never have. And sex with a person she merely liked was one thing . . . sex with someone like Vanessa . . . well, that would have been something else. Something she'd had so rarely in her life. Something meaningful.

She sighed. And thought, just then, that she recognised the wry, contemplative smile upon Vanessa's face, eyes closed with calm pleasure. It was their private joke. That a massage was as close as they would get, in that respect. A substitute. And she was suddenly certain, in a way she rarely was with civilians, and straights in general, that she knew what Vanessa was thinking, right at that moment.

"It's not cunnilingus," she ventured, "but I bet it's pretty damn good."

Vanessa's smile grew to a grin. And she broke up laughing, doubled up against the restraining belt. Sandy stopped massaging, hand on her friend's back as she shook with laughter. Grinning broadly herself at Vanessa's controlled hysterics.

Finally Vanessa recovered herself. Wiped her eyes and leaned back in her seat. Sandy put both hands back on the controls, still grinning.

On an impulse, Vanessa unhooked her belt, leaned over and kissed Sandy firmly on the cheek. And leaned back, in the corner between the seat and the door, to contemplate her.

"No," she sighed, "it's not as good as cunnilingus." Grinned. "But what is?"

"Penetration," Sandy retorted playfully.

"Nonsense. You've got a phallocentric brain."

"No, I've got a phallocentric vagina."

Vanessa found that hysterically funny, and laughed for another twenty seconds straight.

"Which is kind of a pity," Sandy ventured further, once Vanessa had stopped. Vanessa sighed.

"Yes, your phallocentric vagina is rather a pity. I feel sorry for it."

"Please don't, it has too much fun."

"I know, I can hear it laughing." Grinning broadly. Vanessa gave Sandy a rough shove on her shoulder. "Don't you go feeling sorry for me, Sandy. Me breaking up with Sav isn't the end of the world, I'll find someone else to keep me happy. Or someone else's."

"I wasn't feeling sorry for you," Sandy retorted, "I can't imagine a one-man life, anyway. Leaving Sav is the first thing I'd have done."

"Gee," Vanessa snorted, "thanks for your concern."

"I was thinking," Sandy pressed on, "that I like you just about enough to want to make you happy by screwing you senseless, but the catch is that I don't find you the slightest bit attractive sexually. Which is a pretty big catch."

"Yeah," Vanessa sighed. "You'd be as much fun as a cold trout. But thanks for thinking of me." With amusement. "That's what makes you such a cool friend, Sandy, you don't know the rules yet. No other girlfriend I know would have brought it up."

Sandy snorted. "Well, hell, what would I know? I'm just a glorified kitchen appliance, after all."

"I said I *like* that about you, you moron," Vanessa retorted. "Don't change."

"Hmmph. That'll be a task."

"Yeah," Vanessa sighed. "Yeah, it sure will." Silence for a moment. Headquarters was approaching. Another minute ahead, and the designated lane began angling downward.

"You want your neck done again?" Sandy suggested brightly. Vanessa grinned.

"No thanks. It was making me horny."

CHAPTER 3

Central Briefing was a fair walk from the Doghouse—as the SWAT compound was known. Not much on design, Sandy reckoned, gazing about as she reclined in the leather cushions about the long central table. There were no windows, for one thing. Most un-Tanushan. But then Central Briefing was neighbours to Central Ops, deep in the bowels of the Central admin complex. "Central," she reckoned, was a word in danger of being over used in these parts.

"Least the chairs are comfortable," Vanessa murmured, mimicking Sandy's reclining posture. A typical pair of SWAT grunts, they were, reclined and lazily informal among the gathered high ranks and senior suits. Though, these days, Sandy had noted, everyone was looking a little more rumpled than usual.

Twenty-three people in all, a large gathering by any measure. Assistant Director N'Darie sat at the far end to the left, leaning her small frame forward on the table, hands clasped, in serious conversation with Assistant Administrative Director Fung. Intel Director Naidu leaned against the wall by the doorway in conversation with two junior Intels. Others talked, scanned desktop monitors, carried out uplinked conversations or otherwise made use of the time. Only the two SWAT grunts sat and waited.

It was, of course, about the previous night's commotion at the Kanchipuram Hotel . . . it was the lead story on the news networks for the moment, the broader debate of Article 42 supplanted for now by the more exciting events of a major assassination attempt gone wrong in a very public gathering. There had been an alarming number of such cases lately, and the CSA was catching hell for it.

The door opened and Director Ibrahim entered. Directly behind, and continuing a conversation from the hallway, were a lean young man and a smaller woman. Both wore nonregulation clothes, with a predominance of black. Conversation about the room paused, attention shifting to the new arrivals.

"You think they shop at the same store?" Vanessa murmured, eyeing the Director's two companions. She spoke barely loud enough for Sandy to hear unamplified, but the woman fixed them both with an immediate, direct stare from narrowed oriental eyes. A flare of recognition, and the gleam of a smile. "Nice jacket," Vanessa added, volume unchanged and utterly unfazed. "They make synthetic leather look so real these days, don't they?"

The woman (Japanese, Sandy was guessing the ethnicity) gave a slight, gracious nod as the Director took his empty chair by the end of the table, and people about the room made for their seats. Gave a faint twist as she took her own seat, showing off the gleaming black jacket. Sandy watched on with amusement . . . very, very serious hearing enhancement for a straight, to hear Vanessa's low tones across a room filled with conversation. That, plus the clothes, gave her some clue as to who the two arrivals were.

"Ruben and Kazuma?" she asked Vanessa with similar volume. No matter if they were overheard. She knew something about these two and their ilk. She in particular was safe with them.

"The temperature up the far end just dropped a few degrees," Vanessa affirmed. Sandy looked at her. Vanessa's eyes flicked down to the table's far end . . . Sandy looked beyond, and saw that Fung and several admin colleagues were glowering silently down the long table. Assistant

Director N'Darie, too, looked far from thrilled. Sandy looked back at Ayako Kazuma, whom she knew only by reputation. Kazuma's return smile was sly, eyes fixed on Sandy in particular, as if pleased to see her. She looked, Sandy reckoned, like trouble. Trouble seated only one place away from the Director's right hand.

Immediately at the Director's right hand was Ari Ruben, Kazuma's occasional partner ... informality in operational arrangements went with the territory with agents like these, she'd gathered. The dark sleeve of Ruben's jacket bulged at the left forearm where the reports had said he'd been injured last night. He had short, thick dark hair, heavy-lidded dark eyes, and prominent black eyebrows that gave his gaze a certain serious intensity. Handsome, was her immediate, predictable conclusion. Not fashion-model handsome. Boyish, off-the-wall, intelligent handsome.

"*How old is he?*" she asked Vanessa on their private channel. Enhancement, of course, made age difficult to tell ... but there was something about Ruben, particularly, that suggested youth. Kazuma, she wasn't so certain of.

"*Oh, he's just a wee lad, most of the new ghosties are barely more than kids. That's part of why some of their elders are so little pleased to see them.*"

Sandy frowned. "*I didn't think anything in Tanusha worked on a seniority system?*"

"*It doesn't. But that doesn't mean people have to like it. Ari's a kid, he's from a whole different world, and he's real damn good at finding trouble. Like last night. Some people aren't sure if he's finding it, or if it's finding him.*"

"*Ibrahim doesn't appear to have a problem.*" Watching the ongoing conversation between the CSA's chief and the young, upstart agent.

"*No,*" Vanessa agreed. "*Ibrahim's never minded trouble.*"

It had, Sandy knew, been Ibrahim's idea. Tanusha had a massive resource in the many thousands of largely self-employed netsters, hackers and network jockeys who constituted the city's enormous techno-underground. Anti-authority and anti-institution, they were a force unto themselves, and were said by most to have a firmer finger on the pulse of Tanusha's swirling confusion of tech politics than CSA Intel.

For a man of Ibrahim's pragmatism, the conclusion was obvious—such skills would serve the interests of the CSA better on the inside than without. And so, as of two years ago, Ibrahim had ordered a recruitment drive through the underground, with special terms for anyone showing the skills, and willing to make the commitment.

Most had laughed at the offer. But a small few, for their own reasons, had accepted. Ruben was the most prominent of these, and in the two years since his full-time inclusion in CSA's ranks, his star had risen at enormous velocity. Ibrahim, it was rumoured, gave him jobs to handle personally, Director to agent. Such intimate access to the Director was yet another reason the CSA old guard disliked him. That and the fact that he was an independent, young, intelligent know-all who was part of an anti-authority grouping well-known for its dislike of the CSA and government in general, and with whom he continued to associate in shady, under-cover ways that only made the old guard even more nervous.

"*He's good, though?*" Sandy asked.

"*Sure. As Intels go.*" As if Vanessa, a SWAT grunt, would either know or care. "*Word is Kazuma's the guns, Ari's the brains.*"

Kazuma, Sandy noted, was still watching them. A moment's concentration, and Sandy could detect the active scan from across the room, monitoring the fact of their silent conversation if not the words. Contact, as Kazuma registered Sandy's counter scan. Smiled again, curiosity gleaming in narrow, dark eyes.

"So, people," Ibrahim said, and all conversation abruptly ceased. Ibrahim never spoke loudly. His quiet, impenetrable cool and effortless authority ensured that he never needed to. "You've all seen the prelims and studied the details. Let's get to the business. Agent Ruben."

"Um . . ." Ruben rubbed his brow with his good hand,

a nervous, energetic mannerism. "... fine. Okay. The um ..." Another rub, and a twitch at his smart collar. "... the group at the hotel were Christian Vanguard. They were formed about six years ago, breakaway from an independent sect that in turn broke away from the main Tanushan Mormon Church three years before that ... that's the, um, Central Mormons, not the East Delta Mormons ..." Another fidget at his collar, confronted by blank stares and frowns. "... I know, it gets confusing, I swear they pick up their bad habits from the Hindus."

"Which bad habits would they be, Agent Ruben?" came Personnel Administrator Tirupati's interjection from down the table, a raised eyebrow wrinkling the red spot upon her brow. Ruben looked up directly for the first time, a sudden, unapologetic fix of intelligent dark eyes.

"Fragmentation, disorganisation and general ideological chaos." Deadpan, but Sandy got the distinct impression he was pulling Tirupati's leg. "It catches, you know. Every religious organisation that has arrived on this planet from the founding has split itself at least four ways over the subsequent period ... it's a very Hindu state of affairs."

"Typical Indian shambles," someone else commented. Tirupati realised she was being made fun of, and smiled benignly. Sandy did a fast mental count, and arrived at seven Indians or part-Indians around the table. Minorities making fun of the majority, she'd gathered, was acceptable sport. Only when it turned the other way around did the risk of offence become serious.

"Now, I and ... my colleagues," with a nod to Kazuma, "have been watching Christian Vanguard for some time now. Their threat assessment was always quite high. Their leader, Claude Christophson, has been a regular on the cult-net for the last three years. Psych had him tagged as a risk almost immediately ..."

"Psychopathic?" asked Intel analyst Pangestu. Ruben's eyes registered mild surprise.

"Um, no, actually. Cattalini insists he's borderline sociopathic, but I think that's a stretch in a heavily religious society already suffering this degree of delusional removal. Most of these guys are just linear thinkers with a persecution complex. But then I think that pretty much sums up Christian radicals everywhere . . ."

Uncomfortable shifting in several of the seats down the long table. "Or Jewish radicals, for that matter, Mr. Ariel Ruben," added N'Darie from the far end, with telling emphasis.

Ruben coughed, and scratched at the back of his head. "My people don't, um, have a persecution complex, Assistant Director. It's just that everyone's always out to screw us." Some people grinned. Some did not. Ruben barely appeared to notice. "The point is that while the type is pretty rare, it's not so rare that you won't get a lot of them in this city's population profile among fifty-seven million people."

"Your critique of the SIB's last SCIPS on the matter was considerably more robust than *that*," Pangestu reminded him. A SCIPS, Sandy recalled, was a Statistical Crime Intervention-Prevention Survey. Typical analyst's jargon-ese, ignored by all but those who compiled them. Ruben restrained an exasperated half smile, it turned into a wince.

"Abi, I've seen more attempts to statistically quantify this city's predilection for various kinds of criminal activity than I can remember . . . I mean, religion doesn't even matter much to most people. South Asian theology is mostly inconsistent, anyway, the interactions between various ethnic groups, language groups, philosophies, religions, histories, generation gaps, backlashes, historical nostalgia, politicisation . . ." He shook his head in exasperation. ". . . you can't quantify it. You'd be nuts to try. If I deal in broad generalisations, it's because any attempt to quantify the minutiae will immediately be contradicted.

"Now . . . Vanguard are right on the fringe, the far lunar-right, but they're not crazy. They're just extreme. It's an extremist culture we've got here, in some sections. The diversity ensures it, the fragmentations just bounce off each other, push each other further to the brink, and of course infotech means everyone's a fucking expert . . ."

"Why that gathering?" Ibrahim interrupted calmly. "Why Progress Party? Why those senators?"

"Article 42," said Pangestu immediately. "Killing two Progress Party senators and a Progress rep would put a big dent in the pro-breakaway numbers."

Ibrahim looked at Ruben, who was shaking his head.

"No, that's not how they think. They're not thinking of the numbers. They don't like the system and they're not prepared to play that game. They don't like it, don't trust it, and don't really understand it. It's a statement. Allesandra Parker was there, Arjun Mukherjee was there . . . all the people who represent high-power, big-business biotech, all the people who'd most like to see the biotech restrictions lifted. It was a big, moral statement. They think they're doing God's work to smite the evildoers and save humanity from the corruption of unnatural technologies and soulless machines."

Flicked a brief glance at Sandy. Sandy gazed back, eyes unblinking.

"How can you be so sure?" Pangestu appeared in an argumentative mood, his stern, angular Indonesian features etched in a serious frown. "Like you said, these groups aren't stupid. The infiltration and assault as outlined by your own report was expertly done and suggested some serious expertise. If they can do that, why can't they figure out the present state of the Article 42 debate, figure the numbers required by either side for the prereferendum vote, and work out who they need to kill in order to affect the outcome? It's a conscience vote, Ari, the politicians aren't just going to vote along party lines, so we can't just count on Union Party's numbers carrying the day as usual . . . that means some of the core Progress Party people become convenient targets. Kill a few Progress Party pollies, you lessen the breakaway vote dramatically."

Sandy watched Ruben as he listened, chewing absently on a fingernail. He had, she noted with interest, a curiously absent, unflappable demeanour. A purposeful blandness. But too purposeful. As if hiding an implacable intellectual drive that burned just beneath the surface. And he shook his head to Pangestu's assertions, abandoning the fingernail.

"No, no, if they kill senators or congressmen, there's an immediate by-election . . ." Tapping the table with a fingertip for emphasis. "It'll only put the vote back a few weeks and they haven't finalised a date yet anyway, no big deal. Plus the politicians' vote is just a preliminary on whether or not to submit it to a popular Callayan vote and under what terms . . . it's the popular vote that determines the final outcome. Christophson's not stupid, he knew that. He was just doing the good old-fashioned terrorist thing— scaring people into voting the way Vanguard wanted. Or as he saw it, reminding them of God's wrath."

"The by-election could cause a constitutional crisis, it's all untested under emergency legislation," Pangestu retorted. "That could hold up the vote itself. What makes you so sure that has nothing to do with it?"

"He told me."

Pangestu didn't reply immediately. No one did. His frown grew deeper.

"Who told you?"

"Claude Christophson." Very mildly. "Old buddy of mine, we go way back. About a month ago, just after Article 42 was tabled for debate, he told me that any attempt to directly alter the technical process of the vote by violence would be pointless, that the only thing that could work would be to appeal to people's greater moral instincts, the aspects of people's humanity that transcended the technicalities of the process."

"Claude Christophson made a direct threat against this world's elected representatives a month ago," N'Darie said disbelievingly, "and you neglected to tell anyone?"

"He didn't make a direct threat, he was speaking hypothetically." With utter disregard for the Assistant Director's bluntness. "And I did tell someone, I filed a report."

"Lost among how damn many hundreds of Intelligence reports . . ."

"If people don't read my reports, I can't help that." Meeting her gaze calmly down the full length of table, N'Darie glared back. "People who value my reports tend to prioritise them for reading. Those that don't . . . well, they can set their own operational priorities. I'm in no position to dictate to them what they ought to find important."

"And if we prioritised every report about every person who threatened violent action against Article 42 . . ." Kazuma spoke up for the first time, ". . . you'd all be swimming in them up to your ears."

"Already there," someone muttered.

"Ari," Intel Director Naidu intervened, "what's your risk assessment of the religious extremist groups in general at this point? And what do you think we can learn from this attack?"

Ruben nodded thoughtfully for a moment, as if mildly thankful to receive what he considered a useful question.

"Umm . . . unfortunately the risk is pretty high right now, ninety-five percent of them are all hot air, but considering how many groups there are, five percent still adds up to a lot of trouble. Mostly they're focused on the public supporters of advanced biotech, or anyone deemed sympathetic to League causes . . . most high-level stuff should be safe, though. There's not much expertise out there in hard-target infiltration, just the kind of bureaucratic screw ups we saw at Kanchipuram."

"How many more attacks do you think we could see?"

"From nutter-wallahs?" Which was Hindi-English slang for religious loonies these days, Sandy had gathered. "I'd guess two or three a week at present." Silent disbelief from around the table. "Infotech and tape-teach mean it's real easy for your average Mr. Citizen to make bombs and reasonably sophisticated trigger mechanisms these days. That's the main concern, plus acquiring the skill and knowledge to assemble and use them. And, of course, with the end of the League-Federation war a year ago, there's suddenly a surplus of guns on the black market."

"So what do you think is the best proce—"

"Wait, wait." Ruben cut off the new question, as if abruptly troubled by something. "I think I have to say at this point that most of this stuff is just pointless nonsense, a few crazies taking their Messiah-complexes out for a spin around the block ... I don't think we can afford to lose sight of the main game here, whatever the media want to get upset about."

"I'd say firefights and suicide bomb attacks in major industry get-togethers is a fairly serious occurrence, Mr. Ruben," N'Darie said incredulously.

"What is the main game, Ari?" Naidu asked calmly, ignoring the Assistant Director, as he usually did.

"The main game," Ari said, with an emphasis that might have been sarcasm, "is Article 42. Politics. Big, humungous, colossal, mind-blowingly huge politics ... It's not every day that Callay has a vote on whether or not to break away from the Federation. We're a powerful world in the scheme of Federation economics, everyone's upset by this. That's why they're all here, why we've got representatives from every damn planet, political organisation, major corporation and media network in Federation space cramming up all the five-star hotel rooms in Tanusha of late, holding all these talkfests all over town that stretch our security so thin we'll soon have knuckle-dragging gorillas from every pea-brained 'fuck the government' organisation strolling through the front doors with auto-cannon slung over each shoulder.

"A few loonies who think Jesus Christ wore camouflage is nothing compared to all that. They're just a circus show for the usual fireworks on the evening news. They're a ... a cultural pressure valve, just letting off some steam. The main concern is what they're talking about at all these damn parties—just now I saw Allesandra Parker and Arjun Mukherjee in the same room together. You want to guess what they were talking about in there? Business deals and insider trading—Parker tells Mukherjee all she knows about where her political opponents might be vulnerable, Mukherjee uses contacts and financial influence to twist the arms of their support base. Everyone's looking for opportunities to blackmail everyone else into voting the way they want them to vote, or to influence the direction of the ongoing debate—even if the vote goes against them, the breakaway faction are still going to put a lot of influence into what they want the shape of a new Callayan constitution to look like . . . or even a new Federation constitution. That's been gaining strong ground lately. Given how badly the Feds showed they can screw any member world they like lately, there's now a push going on to rewrite the entire Federation system.

"This kind of thing is where the real action is, and with things so chaotic right now, my main concern is that we'll miss some piece of subtle foul play that will affect the outcome of the vote. Then if further investigations reveal the foul play, confidence in the entire voting system will be undermined, and whatever conclusion was reached will collapse—through the lack of a perceived mandate—and then we're all really in the shit."

"He's right," Director Ibrahim said calmly before anyone else could respond. "Whatever the outcome of the vote, the public both here and throughout the Federation must be able to have faith that the outcome is both fair and accurate. All the camel trading and shady deals going on right now are not conducive to producing such faith."

"We should lock them all up and feed them dinner through a slot," Vanessa muttered. Some laughter and wry smiles from around the table. Some of it, Sandy reckoned, a touch patronising of the pragmatically minded SWAT lieutenant who always thought of the most brutally direct solution to every problem.

"I had considered enforcing something similar," Ibrahim replied in total seriousness, "but neither the CSA charter, nor Callayan law, nor indeed Callayan public opinion, will allow it." The smiles faded. "Ari is correct in his general assessment that there is far more at stake here than the lives put at risk by various radical parties. The future of the Federation is in question. It is to influence that outcome that the radicals are motivated in the first place—they are reactive, not proactive. They do not determine the agenda. The people who do determine the agenda—the politicians, business leaders and other VIPs—they are the focus. The better we understand those processes, the better we can predict the reactions of the radicals."

Sandy flicked a wary sidelong glance up the table at N'Darie. The expression on her round, African face was sour. Ibrahim was agreeing with Ruben. Not everyone around the table, evidently, found that to their liking.

The meeting went for another half hour, with much discussion of underground organisational structure, the cultural scene in general, and the latest shifts in funding, rumours and tipoffs. It was so very complicated, and there seemed no way any security organisation could seriously expect to monitor it all, let alone contain it. Just figure the general flows, and concentrate on those bits that were most important. And that, Sandy guessed, was Ruben's speciality. He knew the whole underground scene so well, and appeared to have contacts everywhere. It seemed a very unorthodox method of operation, for any government operative. But at the Kanchipuram Hotel, at least, it had worked.

"Agent Kresnov," Ruben said as the meeting was dismissed, and people rose from their chairs, "can I have a word with you?"

She was not particularly surprised. Given his reputation, it was somewhat surprising that he had not introduced himself earlier.

"Um . . . I gotta get back," Vanessa told her with a flat glance at Ruben. "Tac drill in forty-five remember, don't be late."

"No, mother." Which she'd thought would be funny, but Vanessa gave her a very strange look. Then slapped her on the arm and left, following the rest of the agents out the main doors. Ruben and Kazuma remained behind.

"So you're, um, getting invited to general briefings these days?" Ruben looked and sounded a little nervous, she reckoned, with mild surprise. Leaning on the back of the Director's seat at the end of the table, as if pleased to have that occupying his usually expressive hands.

"It was Naidu's idea," she replied, mirroring his pose behind her own chair. Not so much of a lean, from her smaller height, just a loose folding of arms upon the headrest. "Ibrahim backed it. And Vanessa's pretty much head SWAT behind Krishnaswali now, so she'd have to turn up anyway, but it's still nice to have her here to explain things to me."

"And do you, um, still need that? Explaining?"

"Occasionally." Watching him with expressionless curiosity. Unblinking. Some straights, she knew, found that intimidating. Which she was discovering to have its advantages. Particularly when she wasn't sure what someone wanted of her. Someone, in this case, whom she suspected of having a very strong agenda of his own. "What did you want to speak to me about?"

Ruben licked his lips, dark eyes darting briefly away.

"He's just looking for an excuse to meet you," Kazuma said lazily from the other side of the table. "He's just like all these technogeeks in Intel, he's got a huge crush on you." Sandy raised an eyebrow at her. Ruben's look was more incredulous. Kazuma just leaned against the wall and smiled, hands thrust deep into the pockets of her sleek leather jacket.

"Thank you, Ayako," Ruben told her, "helpful as always." Kazuma inclined her head, gracefully.

"Do you?" Sandy asked him. Ruben grinned. A faint shade shift of facial temperature showed her his blush. Only faint, though.

"I don't have your photograph stuck to the inside of my locker, if that's what you mean . . ."

"I could tell you a few Intel geeks that do," Kazuma interrupted, "and it's not stuck there with adhesive, I can tell you."

"Ayako," Ruben said with his usual quizzical sarcasm as Sandy repressed a grin, "do you have to make a complete and total mess of every conversation I try and start?"

"Oh, you were trying to make *conversation*? I'm sorry, I thought you were only discussing insignificant things like the end of civilisation as we know it . . . *conversation* is far more important. I'll shut up then."

Ruben cleared his throat, loosening his collar with an exaggerated twist of his head.

"This is the, um, extent of our working relationship, you'll note . . ." Strolling closer to Sandy. ". . . it's, um, very difficult to work with someone with such a trouble-some birth defect as that, um, gaping black orifice beneath her nose . . ."

Sandy glanced at Kazuma. Kazuma sighed an amused, long suffering sigh, eyebrows raised and lips firmly closed. Looked back at Ruben, who leaned against the chair one place away.

"So how *are* you fitting into the CSA?" Ruben pressed, curiously from this closer range. Taller than her, though most men were. And very handsome . . . yes, that too.

She shrugged. "Fine. I'm still technically attached to SWAT Four under Vanessa's supervision, but Intel are bor-rowing me a lot these days. I've been given free rein to play around with the security infrastructure across the entire government network, so that's an interesting hobby."

A corner of his mouth curled up in delighted enthu-siasm. "Wow. Considering what a piece of fine Swiss cheese the overriding protocols are in this place, that should be a pretty big job, even for you."

Sandy smiled . . . Swiss cheese, yes, that certainly fit. Ruben evidently knew the networks pretty well.

"I could spend years on the details. Luckily they just want an overview. That takes up most of my spare time, otherwise it's SWAT drill and training, or active patrol—we go out in pairs. There's just too many targets to allow for full teams, we need to maximise coverage."

"Combat drill must be a bit of a drag," Kazuma remarked. "Considering your capabilities?"

Sandy shrugged again. "This is a civilian city, there's a ceiling on threat levels. They get the job done."

"And if more GIs drop in?"

Sandy frowned at her. "Are more GIs dropping in?"

"Would you be disturbed if they did?" Ruben replied.

Sandy turned to fix her frown upon him, his proximity forcing her to tilt her head a little.

"Disturbed?" What the hell kind of a question was that? "If they're here meaning no good, of course I'd be disturbed."

"You're not meaning no good. Neither was your friend Mahud."

"He damn well was," she retorted coolly. "He planned a raid that would have killed the President if I hadn't been there to stop it. GIs do what they're told, that's the tragedy of it."

"You don't."

"I damn well do. I do what Ibrahim tells me, just like you do."

"To what ends?"

She stared at him for a moment, arms folded. Nerves or not, he was very calm and level when getting to a point. A point that she reckoned had better be coming real soon.

"To do good. What else is there?"

"Good matters to you?"

"Good matters to everyone, Ruben. The FIA think they're saving the sanctity of the human species. Governor Dali thought he was serving the best interests of the Federation. Hell, Adolf Hitler thought he was creating paradise on Earth. Everyone's motivated by their own personal definition of 'good.' It's just a pity that 'good' is such a subjective term."

Ruben smiled agreeably. "Please, call me Ari. My headmaster used to call me Ruben. It brings back some . . . very bad memories. Years of counselling."

"Poor man, he must have suffered." Ari grinned crookedly. Sandy's patience exhausted itself. "Ari. What's your damn point?"

"Point?" With an incredulous smile. "I don't have a point. Jeez, how anachronistic. I'm just curious to see what you think about this whole mess. Being the lone GI in a huge political argument that basically revolves around advanced, GI-related biotech."

"And why does my opinion matter?"

"Because you're involved. The politicians are already using you as a reference point . . ."

"You mean a target," she interrupted.

"Same thing. They're the ones driving all this, Sandy. That's what I was concerned was being overlooked just now in all this diversion over fringe group lunatics. What the politicians can get away with, and . . . and the stances they take, is all driven by the mood of their various support groups. That's politics."

"That's populism."

"Same thing again." Again the crooked smile, but more intense this time. As if enjoying himself. "Everyone knows you exist now. You're an issue. Thankfully they all know about how you saved the President's life a month ago, and that you played a big role in eliminating the FIA infiltration, even if the details aren't clear yet . . . but most people still assume you only helped out of duress. The anti-GI xenophobia is still pretty damn extreme. So the politicians have made you a target in the Article 42 debate, an issue they can use to play to their ideological constituencies. But no one ever bothered to ask what *you* thought. I thought I'd be the first."

No one ever bothered, Sandy reckoned, because she wasn't allowed to go public. No CSA field agent was. Transmission of identity or personal information was illegal. Several individuals had been caught doing that so far, and shut down just as fast. Which suggested a leak; someone in the usually impenetrable techno-underground was feeding information to the CSA. One of the main sources of which, she guessed further, was standing directly in front of her, protecting her anonymity. As for *his* motivations, however . . .

"How do you know I didn't just act out of duress?" she asked him pointedly.

Ari blinked. "Did you?"

"Ari, look." She fixed him with a very firm stare, making very sure she had his complete attention. Where men of Ari's disposition toward her were concerned, she generally found it wasn't very difficult. "I know where you're from. The only reason this city's techies are helping keep me anonymous instead of spreading classified government data like they usually do is that they've got this strange notion that I'm some kind of 'white witch.' I'm not the implacable killing machine the conservatives and the religious Right think I am, but I'm not some kind of glorious superhero either. And I sure as hell don't want to get drawn into that kind of League-sympathetic politics . . . hell, I left the League, remember? I think League ideology is morally bankrupt. If it all collapsed tomorrow and forced a re-amalgamation with the Federation, no one would be happier than me."

"I'm not a League sympathiser."

"Really? Do you agree with the biotech restrictions?"

"No, of course not. Economic reality will knock them over eventually, and even if there were an economic niche for artificial humans beyond military roles like your own, they'll never match organic humanity for reproductive efficiency, and that puts them at a huge economic disadvantage compared to us straights. But just because I believe that doesn't mean . . ."

"And yet you've just quoted me League policy word for word. You're Jewish, right? Do you go to a synagogue regularly?"

A deeper frown. "No, neither do a lot of Jews these days. What does that have to do with anything?"

"But you consider yourself Jewish? You have some interest in the cultural heritage, the beliefs and customs?"

Pause to look at her in puzzlement. "Not particularly. My mother would have kittens if I didn't marry a nice Jewish girl, but she may just have to deal with that, because the vast majority of beautiful women in Tanusha aren't Jewish . . ."

"And there are just so many priorities beyond ancient cultural traditions that are no longer relevant in the modern societies being constructed beyond the bounds of old, irrelevant mother Earth." Looking at him very flatly. Understanding dawned in Ari's eyes.

"Look, okay, I'll concede I have some sympathy for some basic League-ish positions . . . religion gets a lot of people killed, Cassandra. Those people at the Kanchipuram Hotel most recently among them . . ."

"The biggest ideological death toll lately came from the League insistence on self-determination away from old-fashioned Federation ideology. Self-perpetuating ideologies are all the same, Ari, the intolerant, self-righteous ones all end up getting people hurt—atheism's just as bad as religious zealotry in that. Look at the League, or twentieth-century communism for that matter. It's only those societies that embrace diversity and alternative points of view that have a good chance of long-lasting peace and stability. I think the old cultural antiques in cities like this one play a damn important role, they make diversity an unavoidable part of the cultural and political landscape so that people just accept diversity as second nature.

"After the League, I can't tell you what a goddamn relief that is . . . they've gotten so impressed with their scientific capabilities and logical thought processes that they've almost managed to take all the fun out of life. And they're so fucking convinced that their way is best that they're unable to spot their own failures, even when they're right under their noses . . . they're nowhere near as self-critical as the Federation is, Ari. That's why they lost the damn war. They just assumed that the use of GIs would give them such an extensive personnel advantage, and they completely failed to realise the shortcomings of GIs, with their limited imaginations. Not to mention the enormous economic cost of having to *make* soldiers instead of just recruiting them . . ."

"Wait wait wait a second . . ." Ari waved both hands, shaking his head. Sandy stopped. He looked at her incredulously. "You *agree* with Federation biotech restrictions? Bans on artificial humanity in all forms?"

"Would that surprise you?"

He blinked rapidly, still looking amazed. "As civilisation's most advanced artificial human yourself, yes, that would surprise me."

Sandy sighed. "Ari, don't get me wrong, I like you and your kind of people." With a nod at the silently watching Kazuma. "I've found most of you smart, funny and interesting—and Tanusha needs people like you to even out the balance. But please, don't classify me into some kind of political or ideological group just because of what I am. I get enough of that from the radicals without having to contend with it from the people who actually like me."

Ari outright grinned at her. Ran both hands through his thick dark hair, the med-cast showing transparently within his left coat sleeve. Sandy stood with her arms firmly folded, hoping he'd got the message. He needed to, for everyone's sake. A sideways glance at Kazuma showed the small Japanese woman watching with silent intrigue.

Ari exhaled sharply. "Jeez," he said, with wry, flat humour, "you make it sound like I'm trying to recruit you for something."

"Aren't you?" Ari looked offended. "N'Darie doesn't like you. I've found her very consistent where League-ists are concerned, she doesn't like any of them. And your kind of Intel work is all about contacts, isn't it? I bet you could use a contact like me. With what I know about League-side, I mean."

"You know, you are *very* suspicious." Fixing her with a mock-hard stare and jabbing a finger at her chest. "I'd heard you were an idealist."

"I am, I'd ideally like not to get mistaken for something I'm not. Everyone in this city seems to, one way or another."

"We do important work, Cassandra." Kazuma interrupted for the first time in the argument. Sandy looked across at her. She looked very sincere, and totally unbothered by the whole thing. "Not just me and Ari, but our friends too. There are things that go on in this city that the CSA has no jurisdiction over. Officially. That's where we come in. If you ever need our help . . . and I have a feeling that you probably will at some point . . . you only need to ask. No favours, no return promises, just ask. We'll help."

Sandy targeted the other woman with her most penetrating, merciless stare. Kazuma never flinched. "Trusting," it occurred to her. She wasn't sure she liked that. Unconditional trust. It didn't seem any more safe or reliable than unconditional hate. And she didn't understand either very well at all, as far as this city and its politics went. Neither group knew who she was. They only knew *what* she was, and based their tenuous understanding upon that.

"Look," Ari sighed, "Cassandra." And to her disbelief he stepped forward and placed a hand upon each shoulder, looking down at her face. She wasn't sure she liked that, either. The "military spec ops officer" part of her brain objected quite strongly. "You're operating in a civilian environment now. I know you must find that disconcerting."

"You're a shrink too?"

"I can understand why you're so suspicious," he continued, ignoring her. Which she *definitely* didn't like. "I respect that you don't like to be categorised, and that your opinions and politics are yours alone and none of anyone else's business . . . but like Ayako says, we're your friends. We *do* share a lot of common concerns. I just wanted to let you know that no matter how badly things gang up against you, you do have some friends in this city. That's all."

Sandy stared up into his handsome, sincere dark eyes, and found it was all she could do to keep herself from grabbing his other arm and twisting until it hurt, and warning him never to forget what she was. And that she wasn't half as pretty on the inside as she was on the outside. She didn't trust the sincerity for a moment . . . he believed it, obviously—the prospect of a natural, self-evident alliance between like minds in service of like causes. But "just friends"? No return commitment?

No way. Whatever else he was, Ari Ruben was too smart for that, and far too dedicated. Dedicated to what, she hadn't figured out yet. But she reckoned she would, sometime soon. And she was damned if she was going to get caught up in his agendas without knowing exactly what they were in advance.

"I'm a soldier, Ari," she told him, "not a politician."

"Oh sure, and soldiers aren't political in the League either." He jabbed her casually in the chest with a fore-finger. "*You* need a support base. We're it." Clapped her on both shoulders, and smiled at her cheerfully. "Think about it." And he turned and left, his smaller, similarly black-clad partner swaggering jauntily in tow, sparing her a sly, parting smile as she left.

"I'm not his damn cuddle-bunny," she muttered to Vanessa a half hour later in armament prep, deep in the bowels of Doghouse Testing and Training—T&T, in SWAT lingo. Doing a fast reassemble on a KT6 multi-function close-assault weapon, hands sure and rapid as barrel, stock, sighter, comp and magazine slotted quickly and efficiently back into place. B Range echoed with the hard-alloy clack-ker-chack! of weapons coming apart and going back together . . . SWAT Seven had C Range, SWAT Four's usual haunt, but schedules were tight and messy these days, and no one complained.

"Should have flattened him," Vanessa said helpfully, peering down the sight of her own heavy pistol. Aligning armscomp electronics between targets on the far range wall, the pistol in her uplinked right glove, and the headset eyepiece strapped across her brow and uplinked to the insert socket in the back of her skull. "Usually works for me, people have this idea that because I look like a cross between a stuffed baby animal and a teenage bikini slut, everyone can line up and have a pat. I find a short, bone crushing left jab to the solar plexus usually does the trick."

"Look, sorry, LT," said Johnson from Sandy's left, reading armscomp diagnostics off his booth screen, "you need tits to be a teenage bikini slut."

"You'll need a windpipe to keep breathing," Vanessa replied, sighting calmly. "You think he's just hot for you?"

"Damn, I wish," Sandy muttered. "Thinks I'm a fellow techie-geek—long live the march of rational scientific progress. I don't need it." Finished the reassembly, activated armscomp and shoved her right hand into the sighting-glove. Pulled the headset off the hook on the wall of her booth, slid it on, inserted the connection beneath her increasingly unruly hair (she'd never had it so long), flipped down the eyepiece and raised the gun.

She didn't need all the gear, she had enough direct interface crammed into her unadorned skull to make a far cleaner shot than the armscomp link could possibly calculate. But it was weapons check, and so she was checking weapons, gear included, the basic SWAT rule being that everyone checked everyone else's gear too, not just their own. Sighting down the open, eighty metre, low-ceilinged space, the targets showed bright and clear on comp-vision, a range of holographic spheres and highlighted trajectories across the range's virtual imagination. Lowered the short, snub-nosed rifle, a mental deactivation of comp-viz, and the long, empty underground range turned blank and dull once more, lit only by the reinforced inset glow-lights for depth perception down the length.

Warning call down the row of booths, and then someone fired, four short, staccato bursts that assaulted the eardrums with a familiar rhythm. Clusters of vicious dark holes erupted in quick succession across four solid target outlines on the far wall, like swarming black insects. Echoes racketed, then silence. The riddled targets replaced themselves.

"Not bad," called Hiraki's voice, a softer echo after the gunfire. "Uneven rhythm, third out at point two, fourth scattered, adjust recoil, target acquisition down and left point four. Sandy?"

"Trigger tension down five," she yelled down the line of booths, "RPS up one. Comp it and watch the recoil on your transition, that Panchi-3 kicks like a horse. Use a bigger mag if you like, keeps the nose down."

"Gotcha, Sandy." Zago's voice, deep and strong. No one ever questioned her fire analysis, she was quite literally the walking armscomp on such things. She had no idea how straights saw it, though even augmented straights seemed to struggle. How were these things difficult? Trajectories in a three-dimensional space . . . it was only data. Data was easy. Visual, graphical data in particular. And of course if there was a firearm in League or Federation space she hadn't seen, tested, stripped and written field reports on . . . she would have been surprised.

CSA SWAT weren't as good as her old Dark Star team at such basic things as shooting, and of course no GI ever had to worry about recoil all that much, but they made up for it in other areas. Like lateral thinking, forward planning, and the ability to avoid walking into traps because of things called "hunches" . . . all very alien to the vast majority of the League GI soldiery. And so she adjusted, and tried to accept their weaknesses while playing to their strengths.

"So aside from the fashion sense," Vanessa continued, "what's the problem?"

"I don't like being used. Besides which, my resources aren't sufficient yet to do a proper threat analysis. Never walk into a firezone without one."

"You know," said Johnson, still reading from his screen, "for such a big shot spec ops commander, you can be a real pussy sometimes."

"You seem to know all the cliches, Steve. Don't make me repeat the one about old soldiers and bold soldiers."

"How did that go again?" Vanessa asked.

"There ain't no old bold soldiers," Johnson announced.

"Ah, that's right, I could never remember how that one went."

"So you're an old soldier, are you, Sandy?"

"Fifteen," Sandy told him, allowing the armscomp to adjust itself on auto as she fed it corrections. "In GI years, that's ancient."

"I'm thirty-two," Johnson told her. "You're a baby."

"Compared to the crap I've seen in my life, Steve, you're a fetus."

"My, how competitive," said Vanessa. "I suffered the traumatic dismemberment of my pet bunbun at the age of ten when my cousin Pierre shoved a live wedding firecracker up its arse. Do I get points for that?"

"Cool!" said Singh from Vanessa's far side.

"What's your mental age?" Johnson challenged Sandy, taking his eyes from the screen for the first time. "There's gotta be a psyche profile for GIs, there's one for damn everything else."

"Hell, they gave you one," Vanessa agreed, "that's sure the thin edge of the wedge."

"Vanessa," Sandy stated with commendable pleasantness, "you're not being very helpful."

"I'm the unit CO, that's my job."

"Tell me about it," said Singh.

"You can't measure mental age on GIs," Sandy told Johnson, only too aware that Vanessa habitually ridiculed those conversations she thought were headed in unhelpful or even dangerous directions. "Mental age is a rough approximation of mental development, which is hugely accelerated with League advances in developmental and foundational tape-teach. GIs never really go through 'infancy' as you'd understand it, anyway. The childlike emotional state is specific to straight humans, GIs skip it entirely. There's just developed and less developed, though GIs internalise information in their early years at a similar pace to a straight human child. It's a very rapid learning phase. Mine just continued six or seven years, most GIs only need about three . . . and regs only about one and a half."

"But you don't remember any of it?"

"Almost nothing . . . memory-wise, everything that happened to me before about nine years ago is very fuzzy."

"Weird life," Singh remarked.

"I was in combat much of that time . . ." She shrugged. ". . . they're not memories I miss. And I don't think I would have liked myself much, back then. Mentally I'm a different person now . . . which is why I don't remember much from then. My psychology's changed so much it's like a computer trying to access data stored in a different, out-of-date format. My brain today just doesn't recognise it. It surprised the hell out of my minders, they'd never had a GI mature over such a long period before."

"So are you going to remember stuff from today in ten years' time?" Vanessa asked. Giving her a concerned look from her booth, weapon temporarily lowered to safe-hold against the rim of the booth.

"Definitely," Sandy assured her with a faint smile. "I plateaued about seven years ago, the rest was just normal learning, like anyone learns . . . my memories from about seven or eight years ago are crystal. It's just beyond that it gets progressively more fuzzy. But, I mean, age is a tenuous guide for anyone, it depends how you spend your time. Twenty formative years spent partying or on uplink VR won't create as much mental maturity as twenty years spent reading books and practising concertos."

"Or practising combat drill and killing things."

"No, that's character building."

"Sure, if you want the character of a chainsaw."

"Jesus, Steven," Vanessa exclaimed, exasperated. Sandy only smiled. Steve Johnson was what Vanessa called a typical SWAT male. Women, Vanessa opined, tended to join organisations like SWAT because they wanted to achieve something, be it personal, political or ideological. Men tended to join because they liked blowing stuff up. Sandy hadn't noticed any lack of enthusiasm during Vanessa's combat drills, but she had to concede the basic point, however much it puzzled her.

"And you're wondering why I'm so soft and cuddly instead?" Armscomp found the correct alignment and she locked it in. Deactivated the safety, selected to single shot, yelled, "Live fire!" to the range, and sprayed a split second burst across the row of sixteen targets with index finger depression alone. Range-comp read back sixteen bull's-eyes, straight through the centre.

"Hah!" Kuntoro shouted back. "Number thirteen is one point three centimetres from centre. You're slipping, Sandy."

"One point four," Sandy replied calmly, ejecting the magazine and stripping the weapon back down. "Round thirteen misfired, KT series tend to do that every twenty rounds or so. There's something erratic between the mag feed and the ignition charge. That's why I don't use them."

"They're not meant for single fire, though," someone objected. "You put 'em to full-auto and there's nothing in the range bracket that's got the firepower."

"Like I said," Sandy replied, "that's why I don't use them." They all knew Sandy rarely used full-auto weapons, rapid-fire was a compensation for human inaccuracy. Sandy could place individual rounds in a thirty-round-per-second burst to within fractional millimetres over a hundred metres or more, provided the targets weren't too far apart and all in some kind of straight line, and her index fingers moved just as fast as most hand weapon auto-fire mechanisms, military-grade electro-mag excluded. Of course, in real combat, targets were rarely so obliging, but it was good practice nonetheless. Compared to what she could accomplish in single-fire, auto-fire was crude and imprecise. Sometimes necessary, it was true, but not in many situations she expected to encounter in a civilian city.

"Fuckin' hell," Johnson said, grinning and shaking his head as the targets replaced themselves. "I've been seeing that for close on a month now, and it's still the most fuckin' incredible thing I've ever seen."

"Just data, Steve," Sandy said, hooking the weapon's exposed comp insert to the booth hardfeed for direct diagnostic. "Data's easy."

"How does anyone ever kill a GI, anyway? If *they* can shoot you, *you* can shoot them." With a meaningful nod at the sixteen bull's-eyed targets in a row.

"You could probably shoot the balls off a gnat from a hundred metres blindfolded, just going by the sound," Singh remarked with a similar over-enthusiastic grin.

"GIs make stupid mistakes," Sandy told them. "Like I've already told you a hundred times." They just loved to talk about it regardless. When it came to blowing stuff up, she was the undisputed master. She supposed this was why famous holo-vid stars got sick of talking about their work—to them that was all it was, work, and nothing particularly remarkable. But casual acquaintances found it fascinating, and bombarded her with the same predictable questions, to the point of exasperation. "You gotta get creative."

"But that's why they made you smart, right? That never worked on you?"

Sandy sighed. "Nothing works on me, Arvid. I'm fifteen years old, eleven of which were operational. Most GIs in the war didn't make it past three."

Ibrahim was not impressed at being called away from Ops Control to attend to his office, and the desk that resided there. It was his enemy, that desk. A broad, powerful mahogany, made of tiak wood, from regional plantations. Built into its firm frame was the latest communications gear, full interface and multidimensional. It enticed him to sit behind it, and bureaucratise.

Ibrahim did not like to bureaucratise. He liked to work. Bureaucracy was N'Darie's job, and she did it well. Ibrahim preferred to work from Ops, where he could talk to his people, and benefit from their observations. Or from Intel offices, where he could judge firsthand the latest data, rather than briefly view what his assistants would sift for him, secondhand. He liked to feel the gears working, and watch the progress made. He did not want to read about it on his terminal. He did not want to be "informed." He wanted to know, personally and immediately.

But now, he sat behind his mostly bare, infrequently used desk, and waited for his office door to open. The two agents in suits who waited to the side of the room offered no conversation, nor would he have participated had they done so. He merely examined his terminal, and read the latest piece of bureaucratic irrelevance that N'Darie had sent him, and waited. He was not impatient. He merely wanted the door to open. Soon.

Click, and it did so. Kresnov entered. Blue eyes, cool and effortlessly penetrating, immediately flicked to the suited pair. Her stride did not waver as she walked to a particular spot before the desk, and halted there. It was the same spot, Ibrahim had noted, upon which she always stopped. Everyone had one. Familiar coworkers and acquaintances came close. The inexperienced and nervous behind that. The fearful further to the left, so the door was not at their back. Kresnov's spot was unlike all others—a shade back from middle distance, but precisely to the centre, and unconcerned of the door. Her eyes never left the two agents.

Until she looked toward him. Ibrahim pushed back in his chair, studying her. In her dull SWAT-issue cargo pants and jacket, and standing perhaps middle height for a woman, she cut a less than immediately intimidating figure. She looked, in fact, incongruously young, with her wide, attractive features free from makeup, and her penetrating blue eyes framed by increasingly erratic blonde hair that fell loose about her brow. She could have been someone's kid daughter, Ibrahim thought, going through a rebellious streak against the more typical feminine glamour frequently found in Tanusha. Only the military calm in her posture, and the almost inhuman, unwavering steadiness in her gaze, put the lie to that.

It challenged the mind of even the most perceptive person to comprehend precisely what she was. This middle-sized, broad-shouldered, attractive young woman with the mild demeanour was the most dangerous thing on two legs in all human space. If she wanted any single individual within Tanusha dead, with the possible exception of the President, Ibrahim doubted very greatly that it would be beyond her. And even the President could not be guaranteed. No wonder the SIBs were so frightened.

"You wanted to see me." A flat, inexpressive tone. Her stance was more than passingly military, feet apart, hands clasped behind. Ibrahim sighed. Disliking this unasked-for bureaucrat's role even more, at that moment.

"Cassandra." His eyes flicked briefly to the pair of waiting agents, and back again. "These are Agents Bhaskaran and Muller, Special Investigatory Bureau." Kresnov looked at him for a moment longer, eyes narrowing slightly. And looked at the SIBs.

"Ms. Kresnov," said Bhaskaran, "we've been sent here by our superiors because today—merely a matter of hours ago—you caused severe damage to a Special Investigatory Bureau data network, and in fact used a restricted, military-grade attack barrier to assault an SIB cruiser. As a result you directly caused an in-flight emergency to be registered with Traffic Central, endangered the civilian skylanes and potentially placed lives in jeopardy. Do you agree that you did in fact do these things?"

"No," said Kresnov, unblinking.

Bhaskaran frowned. "You deny this?" Her brown features thoughtfully incredulous. It was a superior frown. Ibrahim disliked it.

"I deny that lives were placed at risk," said Kresnov. "I deny that civilian skylanes were endangered. I would correct you in saying that the SIB—since you say that it was the SIB, I had not known that until now—were the cause of any endangerment or damage, and have only themselves to blame. That's all."

"You just said that there was no endangerment," the agent named Muller said mildly. Thinking himself very clever, Ibrahim reckoned, with his semantic games. He disliked that too.

"Given the degree of SIB's incompetence I've witnessed so far," Kresnov replied, "anything's possible. But I can hardly take responsibility for other people's stupidity, can I?"

"What type of attack barrier was it that you used?" Bhaskaran continued, unperturbed.

"It was a Cross-X variant, a five-link series A."

Bhaskaran blinked. "I'm not a technician, Ms. Kresnov," she said, "but our own experts said they could not recognise it. They suspected it was in fact a League construction."

"It was," Sandy replied calmly.

"In which case, Ms. Kresnov, I am instructed to remind you that Section Five, Subsection A of official Security Act 91—that's the act by which you are now legally a citizen of Callay, you may remember—states that your continued inclusion into the ranks of the Callayan citizenry is conditional upon you continuing to behave appropriately. And upon you continuing to refrain from using any of your so-called special skills in any manner that may adversely affect Callay or its institutions. This matter clearly qualifies. Given that the SIB and the CSA are indeed working together on this matter, I am here to lodge a formal procedure with Director Ibrahim directing you to hand over all controller functions for your active cerebral interface mechanisms. This incident clearly demonstrates that your continued possession of such potentially lethal League military-designed codes and code modulators is a danger to the security and well-being of everyone in Callay. Here is the request, we trust that it will be given your utmost attention."

Bhaskaran produced an official plastic folder from her jacket pocket, and laid it open on the table. It contained a single paper sheet printed in official format, along with a storage chip in a separate pocket. Ibrahim looked at the paper, lips pursing with mild consideration. Looked back at Kresnov. Kresnov was gazing at some point beyond his head, out of the window. He doubted she was admiring the view.

"Ms. Kresnov," Agent Muller said in Ibrahim's continuing silence, "do you have any statement you'd like to make about this?"

Kresnov looked at him. It was not the kind of look that most straight humans enjoyed receiving from lethally capable combat GIs of any designation. Muller, to his credit, did not flinch.

"You want my codes?" she said mildly. "Come and get them."

For a long moment, Muller made no reply. He glanced at Ibrahim. Ibrahim leaned back in his big leather chair, steepled his fingers, and looked at Muller. He gave no sign of speaking. Muller looked back at Kresnov, hiding his disconcertedness with practised skill.

"Would you be making a threat, Ms. Kresnov?" he pressed.

"Not at all." Her voice was calm and measured beyond her usual tones. The Kresnov cold temper. Ibrahim marvelled at it. Kresnov did not get angry. She got dangerous. "You want my codes, you come and get them. You'll have to use a serious breaker, since my barrier elements are so tough. And you'll have to use a direct point of access, which means keeping me still while you jack me in. So you'll have to use drugs, and restraints. Which won't be pleasant for me, but don't let that stop you. Where are the troops? Waiting in the corridor?"

"There are no troops, Ms. Kresnov. Under the written act by which you are legally a member of the Callayan citizenry, you will be required to . . ."

"I'm trying to protect the Callayan citizenry, you pointless wanker," she said coldly. "I'm the main key in the ongoing investigations to break down the remnants of the League's undercover biotech ring in Tanusha. You'll remember that—it was the biggest security breach this city's ever seen. It killed a hundred and thirty-two Tanushans that we know of, and so long as the same systemic flaws remain, this entire planet remains vulnerable to further League infiltration.

"That's my job now. It's what I'm paid for. If anyone manages to knock me off, it'll be a big loss to Callayan security, because I can tell you, this place needs a lot of work yet. As such, I'm obliged to defend myself against possible personal security breaches. So imagine my reaction to finding an unidentified cruiser tailing me, hooked up to a sucker bug on the traffic network. If I'd left it alone, I would have been derelict in my duty to Callay, and then some other idiot from some other department would be over here screaming at me for failing to comply with the other bits of that security act."

"You knew very well it was a government vehicle before you attacked it, didn't you?" countered Bhaskaran.

"Would you like me to list the number of ways government codes and facilities can be infiltrated?" Kresnov retorted. "Did you guys learn anything from what happened a month ago? No government operative can afford to get into the habit of being tailed by people of unconfirmed identity. It's a very bad precedent and it clearly interferes with my ability to do my duty to this planet, this city and its people. If you'd like to tail me, give me your identities and location codes first, and I'll track you so I don't confuse you with the bad guys. But I assure you, if I get attacked, I am required by my obligation to the CSA to eliminate all direct threats. If you're tailing me with no ID, that'll include you."

"Mr. Ibrahim," said Bhaskaran, who had been attempting to ignore her for the last several sentences, "can we expect your reply shortly?" Ibrahim looked at her. Fingers remained steepled. His lean, angular face conveyed a great authority. Bhaskaran waited, that being her only option.

"You might not like my reply," Ibrahim said finally. "My agents have standards to maintain. They must be allowed to maintain full security at all times."

"Mr. Director," Bhaskaran began. Took a deep breath. "Ms. Kresnov has detection capabilities far exceeding the security norms of your other agents. We are not requesting that her security be degraded below the standard of others. Merely that it be equalised."

Ibrahim looked at Kresnov. She stood fixed to her spot. Her rigid posture, and the set of her jaw, suggested contempt.

"Without my codes," she said, with a dark, forced calm, "I am vulnerable. I am entirely synthetic. My brain function allows a far greater bandwidth of interaction with any com network than does organic brain function. I integrate at approximately a factor of seventeen beyond what an organic mind can achieve. I am more effective, but as such I am more vulnerable to infiltration. My enhanced capabilities are necessary to protect me from my enhanced vulnerabilities. If you remove them, my safety becomes severely jeopardised."

"We are only talking about your attack barrier function, Ms. Kresnov," Bhaskaran told her. "Your defensive codes will remain entirely intact."

Kresnov looked at Ibrahim. Jaw set and eyes hard, Ibrahim detected that she wished to speak to him. Alone.

"Thank you very much," he said to the two SIB agents. "I'll give due regard to your report and assessments. Good day."

"Thank you, sir." Bhaskaran turned and walked out, her junior partner in tow. Kresnov waited until the door had shut.

"This is nuts," she said after the click. "You're not going to take this seriously."

Ibrahim blinked, very calmly. Kresnov was not prone to rash outbursts. This was as close as he'd seen her come. She was, he judged, severely agitated. By Kresnov's standards, anyhow.

"Cassandra," he said after a moment, "you knew the SIB had you under surveillance. I myself informed you, just twenty days ago, when you returned from vacation." Her eyes darkened, imperceptibly. Perhaps it was the mention of her "vacation," and the memories it stirred. Ibrahim filed it away for later study.

"They're incompetent," Kresnov said shortly. "If they'd done it properly, I might not have noticed."

"Ah," said Ibrahim. Tapped his jaw with a forefinger, short-bearded chin in his hand. "So that's it. You fried them because they were incompetent, and a top flight professional like yourself could not tolerate the dent to your ego."

"I fried them because they were violating my security perimeter," she retorted. "Not to have fried them would have been . . ."

". . . a dereliction of duty on your part, I know." Ibrahim held up a hand, waving the argument away. Scratched at an irritating beard itch. Looked back at her. "You don't think you overdid it?"

"Blasting them from the sky would have been overdoing it. I felt I was being generous."

Ibrahim sighed. "Cassandra . . . I know you find it bothersome, this tailing business. But you should by now have learned enough to know the political necessity." The jaw tightened again. So that was the soft spot.

"I'd had something more discreet in mind," she said coldly. "Some network checks, the occasional tracker . . . But anything that interferes with what I judge as my mission effectiveness, I'll eliminate, within good reason. If you were in my position, you'd do the same."

"Cassandra, the SIB belong to a totally different command structure than the CSA. I have no authority over them, nor even ranking superiority. In some ways, they exist to investigate us, if necessary. They've always had priority in special Senate interests, and right now, whether you like it or not, that means you. The Senate is full of the President's enemies, and it's full of people who would be your natural enemies as well. And you cannot fight them, not with the weapons presently at your disposal.

"Instead, what you've just done is to start a brawl. Certain anti-biotech senators will read this report and conclude some very negative things about yourself, and your place in this society. Right now they want your network codes. Tomorrow, and some new incident, and perhaps they'll demand limiting your freedoms. And although you don't like it, you're going to have to learn that within this system, aggressive confrontation can frequently only exacerbate the problem. You have to be patient. I'm asking you to be."

"You won't fight for me." A flat statement. Her arms were folded, her eyes hard and unblinking.

"I did not say . . ."

"You'd fight for someone else." Ibrahim frowned at her, not accustomed to interruption. "You'd fight for Rice. Damn right you'd fight for Vanessa, if the SIB were hounding her over something. You'd kick their butts."

"That's different."

"I know." With evident sarcasm. "It's so *very* different."

"Cassandra," Ibrahim said, with measured patience, "this is a huge political brawl. I've never seen its like. I hope to never see its like again. It's my job to keep the planet safe. That's a very big, very important task. If I start taking sides in this, politically, it will only make my task more difficult. I have 120 million lives under my responsibility. And I'm sorry, you're not Vanessa Rice, Vanessa Rice is not a GI—you are. And as such, you are very much in the middle of this, whether you like it or not. That is how it stands. I cannot change that fact. You cannot. We can only deal with it as best we can."

"You want my codes?" Arms still folded, staring at him.

Ibrahim blinked. Off guard, for the moment. Kresnov could do that to him, where few others succeeded.

"The SIB Director wants your codes. Several chairing senators want your codes. I don't."

"But you'll give them to them anyway." The hard, blue stare locked with his own sombre brown one.

"I've yet to decide that." Quietly. "My instincts are against it. But the political pressure that can be applied, where your case is concerned, Cassandra . . . is quite considerable. It is a matter of gain and loss. I must balance the scales. It's my job."

There was a quiet silence. Outside Ibrahim's broad office windows, the sky had turned a dark shade of grey. Distant lightning flickered, lighting the overcast in faint, staccato bursts. Soon it would be raining. Hard.

"It's such a load of bullshit," Kresnov said quietly. Gazing out of the window, past Ibrahim's head. Her eyes were suddenly distant. Deflated. "Populist politics running the CSA. Who'd have thought."

Ibrahim was uncertain if it was intended as an insult ... but it was accurate, insult or not. He understood her frustrations. He shared them. But it was an old, long debated topic for him, and he was accustomed to its predictable lunacy. Kresnov, evidently, had yet to adjust.

"Would you be upset" he asked, just as sombrely, "if your attack codes were to be removed?"

"It would significantly reduce my usefulness to you or anyone else," she replied.

"That's not what I'm asking." There was another silence. Then she shrugged.

"I'd feel violated," she admitted. "But what the hell, it's hardly the first time."

Ibrahim sighed. "I'm sorry," he said, with quiet sincerity. "It may not happen. We'll see what eventuates. But in the meantime, please refrain from similar responses, however provoked. There's only so much that I can do for you under the present circumstances, Cassandra. Nothing would please me better than to help you more. Callay and its citizens owe you a debt far greater than most of them or their representatives appear to realise. But you understand what's at stake here. And I know you understand my limitations."

She got out late in the afternoon, after Ops briefing, and waited in the Doghouse personnel landing bays for a ride as the rain hammered down beyond the open outer-bay doors, and thunder rumbled across a rapidly soaking city outside. There was a queue, as always, and she dropped her gearbags to the ferrocrete behind a group of people in assorted admin suits and techie overalls, and another two who'd already changed into civvies. Those closest to her looked at her.

"Hi," she said, with the pleasant smile she'd been practising of late. The admins looked uncomfortable. Wind gusted as a cruiser passed in a low, throbbing hover that echoed within the enclosed ferrocrete hangar, drowning the roar of falling rain. Techs were clambering over a broad-shouldered flyer against the opposite wall, automatic tools clanking and yammering periodically, punctuating the ever-present whine of engines. Another cruiser came in more slowly, approaching on autopilot, a sleekly angular, broad rectangle, its nose and hindquarters a mass of repulsor-lift generation, the seats empty behind aerodynamically angled windows. Doors slid upward as it came to rest, engines a deep, pulsing throb, and the first five people in line got in. And departed, leaving her with two very nervous, silent admin personnel. Desperately short of airborne transport, all CSA personnel, save the highest officials, had been reduced to air-pooling or public transport. It could take a long time to get home with passengers being dropped off in all different parts of the city. But with all the other transport reserved for security ops, lower-priority concerns had to make do with whatever they could scrounge.

"Where do you guys live?" she asked the two admins.

"Mananakorn," one said quickly.

"Denpasar," the other.

"Mananakorn's right near me, I'm in Santiello," she said. "Easiest to do us two first, don't you think? Sorry, Denpasar's a bit far for a two-person detour."

The Denpasar resident shrugged. "Fine."

"I gotta get prepped for duty tonight," she continued determinedly. "Patrolling till about three AM, there's not enough security to go around for all these parties and talk-fests right now. How about you guys?"

The whine of another approaching cruiser interrupted any reply, the engine note throbbing downwards as the cruiser slowed . . . A lower note than previously. It was a larger cruiser, larger field gens and noisier, indicating an extra weight that might have been armour plating, to judge from the rugged, bulkier appearance. It came to a halt at the curbside barrier that marked the front of the queue, windows entirely blanked out, reflecting like mirrors. Sandy uplinked and found its ID tag before it had consciously occurred to her that it might be a good idea— government ID, Alpha Team. The Presidential bodyguard.

The sinking feeling began almost immediately. Alpha

Team was occasionally used to run personal errands for the President—it wasn't strictly their job, but excess personnel were rare in the crisis, and people improvised. She guessed what they were after before the doors had even opened, and the lean, armed, neat clipped and shaven men inside had gotten out.

"Agent," one said, looking at her, "please come with us." Their stance made her uneasy, one to each side, ready as if prepared for trouble. She looked at them sourly for a long moment. If they thought they could handle any "trouble" she might cause, they were even more stupid than certain unkind CSA jokes reputed them to be.

"Does the President want to see me?" she asked them.

The two admins stood very still and quiet, eyes wide, no doubt wishing very strongly they were elsewhere.

"We're not at liberty to discuss it," said the shorter of the two Alphas. "Please accompany us now, Agent."

"If the President wishes to see me," Sandy continued dryly, "she need only ask. I am obliged by her rank to consider that a direct and immediate command, and would make my way directly to see her at whatever location she requires. I don't need a guard or an escort."

"Nevertheless," said the shorter Alpha stubbornly.

She didn't like it. But it wasn't a good idea to argue with Alpha Team. These Alphas were all new, all volunteers, all ruggedly, unwaveringly dedicated to the point of obsessiveness. Their predecessors had all been killed a month ago. It hadn't deterred the newbies. On the contrary, the defiant self-sacrifice of the original Alphas was now folklore, the veracity of which Sandy could testify to personally, having witnessed the events firsthand. Competition for a coveted position in Alpha Team had increased even more among potential recruits. The look in this pair's eyes suggested that it wasn't a good idea to do other than they suggested. Being young, idealistic and utterly determined to live up to the legacy of their predecessors, she reckoned they might be prone to rashness if pushed. And the President, with her newly discovered soft spot for all her personal security, would be sorely upset with her if she had to rough them up.

"Fine." She picked up her gearbags. They rattled with weapons and ammo, to the admins' further discomfort. "I'll register my complaint in person."

One of the Alphas made to take the bags from her, blocking her way. "No unsecured weapons in the hold." The young man before her was of Chinese ethnicity. His face was impassive, jaw smoothly shaven, and he smelled of aftershave. Her vision caught the faint refractory shift of light in one eye—telltale military-grade enhancement, Vanessa had it too.

"Kid," Sandy told him, "I'll wait here all day if I have to." Meeting his gaze calmly, head tilted, nose barely twenty centimetres from his. Most straights, knowing what she was, melted before such a gaze.

"I'm sorry, ma'am," he said firmly, and grabbed the bag handle. Sandy held fast, her eyes not leaving his. "Ma'am, I have my instructions."

"I am a SWAT agent. These are my weapons. Read your rulebook, kid. You try and remove these from me, I have to stop you."

"Presidential security takes precedence."

"In matters of emergency, yes. Not here." She caught the faint trace of transmission from his partner. The Alpha glanced, once. Then stood aside without further word. Sandy got into the broad rear seats, knowing better than to expect an apology. Doors hummed closed as the Alphas got into the front seats, and she locked her belt harness into place. Less insulted than she might have been—if she were being truly "escorted," one would be sitting in the rear with her. Perhaps they were smart enough to know that if she didn't wish to accompany them, there was damn little they could do to force her. But this was Alpha Team. Appearances had to be maintained.

They cruised to the broad exit, lifting above the open flightyard tarmac beyond and into the pelting rain. SWAT flyers and assorted vehicles sat in parked rows, overlooked by admin offices, grey shadows looming through dimming sheets of water. Bank and climb, gaining altitude, the broad, angular CSA compound dimly visible below in an orderly, regular arrangement of low buildings and humble greenery. It looked a hell of a lot nicer in sunlight than some of the security compounds she'd seen League-side, with their square-edged architecture of ferrocrete blocks and barely a tree to be seen. But it was still a functioning high security zone, scandalously unconcerned about aesthetic trivialities by Tanushan standards, and the several kilometres of trigger-rigged wall that ringed the perimeter was not for show.

"Any excitement lately?" she asked the two Alphas in the front seats, as the course bent again, taking them northwards toward Canas, a small, exclusive suburb not five minutes' flight time from Parliament. The ground faded from sight as they gained altitude, only the dim shadows of towers visible through the downpour, even to Sandy's super-enhanced vision.

"Alpha Team is not at liberty to discuss operational occurrences," was the predictable answer.

"Did you implement Tactical Adjustment B58?"

"Sorry, ma'am, can't talk about it."

"I *wrote* Tactical Adjustment B58," she said dryly. "I saw your predecessors buy the farm in person, I was subsequently asked to critique your operational procedures and where they went wrong at the Parliament Massacre. For all your sakes I hope you implemented it, because I'm not the only one keeping tabs on your operational performance."

Silence from the front. They knew all right. She wasn't yet sure how any of them felt about it. She'd saved the President's life, for sure. Perhaps they felt she'd belittled Alpha Team in the process, achieving single-handed what all of Alpha Team could not. And she certainly hadn't managed to save any of *them*. It was possible she could have. But it would have forced her to strike early, thus lessening her chances with the President by conceding surprise. Strategic objectives just didn't work like that. She'd rarely in all her operational career managed to have her cake, and eat it too. She'd chosen the President. Alpha Team, given their entire reason for existence, surely could not have found fault with her choice. But the fact remained that they were all dead, she could have done more to prevent it, and hadn't.

Welcome to war, boys. Now you know why I wanted to become a civilian.

Canas was exceptionally pretty. The cruiser landed in a yellow-striped security transit zone beside a residential park on the neighbourhood outer perimeter, underside wheels unfolding. Once through the heavy scanner outer checkpoint with its five guards, they were allowed to drive in through the roadway gap in the tall stonework. The outer security wall quickly gave way to ancient-styled brick and stonework buildings, wooden shutters and hand-carved signwork in Spanish, all wet and gleaming in the sunlight now that the black storm clouds were moving on toward the west. Wheels vibrated over road cobbles, the cruiser steering down narrow streets that were little more than lanes, winding mazelike with no regard for orderly geometry. Wood-railed balconies overlooked the street in places, and once a small church, its steeple rising beneath a beautiful spread of native raan-tree canopy, and colourful orange-blossomed creepers spreading over stonework walls.

Canas, of course, was a museum piece, crafted in memory of a particular Earth culture that city planners had thought worth remembering. It was also impenetrably high security, shut off from the rest of Tanusha, lived in only by those Tanushans whose security rating warranted the protection. That meant the President, a majority of ranking politicians, and their closest family. Only public servants, though . . . private sector heads in need of security (meaning biotech CEOs, these days) could presumably afford their own. Politicians, whatever the public cynicism about their salaries, did not make that much money.

The Presidential Quarters were also sometimes called the Hacienda . . . Spanish for house, Sandy had gathered. Or mansion. Not much was visible from the road, by intention. The cruiser rounded a slow, tight corner behind a high stone wall, then up the narrow lane to a heavy metal gate. Pause, while various scanners did their work, and then the gate wound slowly open. A paved roundabout served as a driveway, circling a large fountain draped in lush greenery. Several vehicles were parked by the disembarking apron, all aircars, heavy armoured cruisers crouched low on compressed suspension, several drivers waiting with other armed security, all totally conspicuous in dark suits. They pulled up behind the last vehicle's bulky rear end, Sandy catching all the while the continual flash of encrypted security codings across local airwaves . . . Doubtless there was more she could not catch—direct laser com—vehicles such as these were equipped for such things. Doors hummed upward, Sandy collected her bags and got out.

The Hacienda was big. Exactly how big was difficult to see from this vantage—tall trees and lush, four metre ferns and palms surrounding, all dripping from the recent downpour . . . The fragrance of sodden greenery in the moist air was powerful and delightful. They were parked by the end of a long, rectangular wing, stairs leading up to ornate doors, frame glass windows overlooking, late afternoon sunlight gleamed orange on colourful, sloping roof tiles amid mottled patches of shade. Another such wing showed faintly through gardens lush enough to pass for heritage botanic gardens, glimpses of lovely stonework and arches amid the profusion of gleaming leaves and branches. Not only pretty—it made outside surveillance difficult. Every millimetre would be trigger-tripped and monitored.

"Ma'am," said another Alpha, blocking her way from the cruiser, "please leave your gear in the vehicle."

"I'm not having this discussion again."

"Ma'am, only security-authorised weapons are allowed within proximity of the President. You can keep your pistol, but please leave your bags in the vehicle."

"Do you have a guard room in the premises?" The Alpha's silence said as much. "I'll leave them there. I'm not leaving my gear in a vehicle that could get called away with me not in it."

A moment's silent consultation, uplink frequencies flicking encrypted messages back and forth. Sandy was aware of others standing about. Of the guard station built into the heavy stone wall by the gate at her back. Of any number of possible lethal and nonlethal weapons systems built into the picturesque surroundings. Even she wasn't allowed knowledge of these systems, heavily upgraded as they'd been of late.

"Very well," said the Alpha. And put out a hand. Sandy gave him the bags. Reached inside her jacket, slowly pulled out her pistol in full view, rechecked the safety, dechambered the loaded round, removed the magazine and placed it into her jacket pocket. Pointed the weapon at the ground, clicked the trigger five times to demonstrate it was empty, rechecked the safety and tucked it back inside her jacket. It was politeness. Alphas were employed to be nervous, and any exception made in security protocol was a dangerous precedent.

She followed the Alpha with her bag up the stairs . . . Someone opened the door for them from the inside, admitting them into a long hallway. The Alpha with her bag immediately turned into a near room, and she followed a new Alpha down the hall, another pair bringing up the rear. Her boots squeaked on floorboards . . . wonderful things, floorboards, of all the things she'd thought, prior to becoming a civilian, that one could do with wood, *walking* on it hadn't occurred to her. They stretched polished and gleaming down a hallway of smooth plastered walls, with paintings, decorative potted palm fronds and overhead chandeliers. She gazed about as she walked, security technicalities temporarily set aside, and felt somewhat better about the whole thing. Being in Tanusha, moving among people of power, had its benefits—even when she got in trouble, it landed her in a lovely house like this one, with the smell of polished timber and lush gardens, and never mind the nervous armed escort. It wasn't like they could threaten her anyway.

The hallway ended and they entered into the body of the Hacienda proper, large rooms, ornately furnished, rugs on the floors, offices and people in suits working . . . the President's personal staff and key Administration figures. They worked here when not at Parliament, the President dividing her time between debates and sittings in chambers, and then paperwork, meetings, and strategy discussions here at the Presidential Quarters. Another corridor then, entrance flanked by a pair of permanent Alpha guards, and into a waiting room, the President's personal secretary sitting behind a big desk on the side, locked into his information system with headset and multiple display screens before him. A pair of big double doors beyond.

"Hi, Sandy," said the secretary, Alexei Sarpov. A mild young man with pleasant manners and an unbreakable concentration span. "How are you today?" Like she was a regular visitor. Well, she'd been here twice before in the last month, more than most people could boast.

"I'm fine, Alexei. How are you?" Simple civilian courtesies still sometimes eluded her. It took a conscious effort to remember what was appropriate and polite at what moments.

"I'm doing great, Sandy . . . the President would like to see you immediately, though I do believe she's in the middle of an important teleconference right now . . ."

"I'll stand in a corner and be very quiet."

Alexei smiled. "That would do perfectly."

The lead Alpha opened one of the double doors, and peered through. Opened the door fully, and gestured for Sandy to enter. She edged past, aware that two of them followed her in before closing the door behind her.

The French Office, as it was called, was of course superb. Large and grand without succumbing too much to self-conscious ostentation, it had a somewhat darker, more thoughtful mahogany feel than she'd expected when she'd first visited. The room got its name from the row of french doors that spanned the rear wall behind the main desk, a broad view leading onto a wide balcony that overlooked gardens and trees surrounding a wide, overgrown court-yard. The opposing face of the rear wing spanned beyond, more brickwork and balconies showing through the trees. The office was decorated with the paraphernalia of authority, bookshelves, cabinets, paintings of several famous figures. A comfortable sofa set ringed a coffee table in the centre of the office.

The President sat behind her main desk, her back to the windows, conversing to some person or persons on the display screen before her. She leaned back in her comfortable chair with informal disregard, hands clasped behind the back of her head, elbows out. The windows behind the President made Sandy slightly nervous, her mind on security. But vantage points were limited thanks to the greenery and opposing wing, and all opposing windows and balconies were continually occupied while the President was working. They also allowed her security to watch her at all times. Somehow Sandy doubted President Neiland appreciated that very much. Though no doubt last month's fatal carnage at Parliament had changed her perspective somewhat.

The President saw Sandy over the top of the screen, and waved at her to come forward. She did, with security close behind.

". . . look," the President was saying, ". . . you have to make it conditional on the funding bill. I'm not handing that chairmanship to someone who won't even back us on funding for the very apparatus he's supposed to be advocating. Tell him he gives us the support on the bill or no chairmanship, and his faction can damn well eat him alive, for all I care. None of them have any say on legislation without a seat on the committee and he knows it."

The reply was silent, no doubt uplinked to Neiland's inner ear. Sandy glanced about. There were paper files on the President's desk, a whole stack of them—some documents still circulated in paper, low confidentiality ones. Another small box contained encrypted memory chips for high confidentiality documents. Several thick books sat to one side—academic titles, Sandy noted, from local university presses. And read from the spine of the largest *Interstellar Federation Law: Founding Principles and Practice*. And *Markets of Light: Interstellar Trade and the Physics of Economics*. She nearly smiled. Light reading, Ms. President? The third book was in Hindi, in which all senior Tanushan politicians were fluent by necessity . . . and often Arabic, too. Neiland, she knew, added Bahasa, Mandarin, Spanish and her own native Dutch to that tally. Seven languages was not exceptional in Tanusha, language tape-teach worked better on some people than others, but irrespective of that, it generally reduced the amount of time taken to learn languages from between fifty to ninety percent.

". . . fine," Neiland was saying now, ". . . just get it to him before the next sitting. I don't want to waste time arguing with him myself. Get him briefed and make him fully aware of his position, because I'm not sure he's realised yet what trouble he can get himself into." The screen went off, and President Neiland got up.

"Hi, Sandy." Came around the desk and surprised her with an offered kiss on the cheek, Arabic-style . . . Sandy returned it, repeated on each side. It always surprised her, her instinct was to salute. Neiland pulled back to look at her, hands on her arms in a most friendly manner. There was a faint smile in her sharp green eyes, a lingeringly dangerous amusement. Sandy was surprised at how good she looked. She'd half expected to see a haggard, weary President with dark rings under the eyes, irritable and short-tempered with all around her. Instead Neiland looked bright and alert, red hair neatly bound at the back with a comb and clasp. She had on a green suit jacket that was only moderately formal, a red bow-ribbon at the collar that bordered on flamboyant. Civilians, Sandy remembered the prejudice back in Dark Star, lacking military discipline, tended to get weak and flaky under great pressure. Between the Callayan President and the CSA Director, Sandy reckoned she'd seen enough evidence to cast great doubt upon that reckoning. "How are you?"

"Good." Volunteering more to the President didn't

seem a good idea until she knew what she was here for. Neiland smiled, seeming genuinely pleased to see her. And looked at the two Alphas at her back.

"Thanks, guys, we need to be alone for a moment."

"Yes, Ms. President." And turned to go, offering no argument.

"You didn't give her a hard time, did you, boys?" Neiland called after them.

One turned, still backing to the door. "No, Ms. President."

"You sure?" Playfully. The Alpha kept walking backward while his partner went for the door, apparently well familiar with his boss's mood.

"Very sure, Ms. President. She was most cooperative."

"She could have had you all for breakfast, you know that, don't you?"

"Of course, Ms. President."

"He doesn't believe me." To Sandy. And to the Alpha, "Thank you, Mahesh. Wish your sister happy birthday for me."

"Thank you, Ms. President, I will." And retreated from the room, appearing both pleased and amused despite the stony-faced formality. Sandy couldn't help but feel approval. Neiland, she'd gathered, had never paid her personal security much attention before. Until they'd all been brutally killed, sacrificing their lives against futile odds to protect her. Now she knew all the new Alphas by name, had their important family occasions bookmarked for Presidential well-wishings, and bantered with them in spare moments like a proud aunt to her respectful nephews and nieces. Sandy wasn't sure what the previous bunch of Alphas had actually thought of their President. But it was clear that this bunch would die for her even more cheerfully than the last. Though hopefully it wouldn't come to that again.

"Come on, have a seat," said the President, putting a hand on Sandy's back and ushering her to the comfortable chairs in the centre of the room. As if on cue, another side door opened and a staff member entered, holding a tray with steaming tea and biscuits. "*Were* they a bit rough?"

"No, just confiscated my weapons . . . I know the procedure, it's not me they're worried about, it's any loose weaponry being scooped up by traitorous staff members or visitors. They have to account for every firearm. They do a good job."

"They do, don't they? Been surfing lately?"

"Yes, just today." Sat on the big sofa by the coffee table, Neiland in the single chair to her left. "I had my first half-day off in a week, hired a flyer and went out to Rajadesh for the morning."

"Oh, it's nice out there, isn't it?" Took an offered cup of tea from the staffwoman with a nod. "I used to go beedie foraging on the headlands just a few Ks up from there with my father and brothers when I was a girl . . . you know beedies?" Sandy shook her head, taking her own tea. "Black shellfish as big as your hand, you crack them open with a big knife. The meat's just bite-sized, fry it over an open fire camping by the beach, just heavenly. Tastes all smokey and sweet and juicy. Can't get them confused with banyas, though, those things will kill you. Well, me, anyway, probably not you."

The staffwoman left the tray on the table and departed. Sandy sipped the tea—Chinese green tea, fragrant and hot. She'd liked it last time she was here, she recalled. Neiland must have remembered, and had staff prepare a pot. She wasn't sure if such forethought ought to make her suspicious or not.

"The surf was good?" Neiland pressed.

"Very good. Nice waves at Rajadesh. Good breaks, plenty of tubes, you can ride for nearly thirty seconds on the best ones."

"How long did it take you to master it?"

Sandy repressed a smile, sipping at her tea. A subtle, mild, mellow taste. Amazing. The military food of most of her life's experience was not known for subtlety.

"I don't know if you could say I've mastered it. The best riders are expressive as much as technical."

"But you've mastered it technically?"

"Sure. Took about five decent waves. I was doing most of the moves within a few hours."

Neiland grinned. "You know, anyone else, I would think they were boasting. But not only do I know what you're capable of, I know you're not the boastful type, anyway."

Sandy shrugged offhandedly, and sipped her tea again. She enjoyed Neiland's compliments as much as she enjoyed anyone's, especially as she was very prepared to believe that Neiland genuinely liked her, on a level that went well beyond simple gratitude. She didn't think it wise to be flattered by them, however. Neiland was too good at compliments when it suited her. It was a big part of her job.

"Surfing never occurred to me as a sport," Neiland continued. "I played basketball. Couldn't shoot to save my life, I just liked the energy."

"There's a basketball court at the Doghouse. I tried it once. Hit my first ten shots from six out to twelve metres. Kind of lost its appeal after that."

"That's really sad." With contemplative concern, chin in hand, elbow resting on the chair arm. "It never occurred to me before I met you that being technically perfect would make everything boring. Is there any sport you find challenging?"

Sandy shook her head glumly. "Not really. Only mind games. Chess, sometimes."

"I'd imagine, given your tactical prowess, you wouldn't lose many times at chess either, would you?"

"No. I only play the computer, no one else lasts more than twenty moves. The computer tells me I'm a level below Grand Master, and I've never really played it that much." She shrugged. "It's not much to be proud of, I'm psychologically structured for spatial awareness and numerical sequencing. In chess I just count, memorise and project. Sublevel memory and processing implants carry most of the workload, I just give the directions."

"It still technically qualifies you as a genius."

"By whose standard? I can't write a concerto, paint a masterpiece or turn out a novel. I'm still struggling with chicken fettuccini. I certainly don't have much aptitude for poetry, my language skills aren't much above average, and while I'm good with raw numbers, I'm sure as hell no mathematician. I'm just good at three-dimensional spaces and rapid-track calculation, but much of that is reflex rather than thought."

"You have a specific set of skills, Sandy. When you learn to apply them to other things, you'll discover they work equally well on things other than military strategy and network engineering, I'm very sure. It's only your lack of experience in anything nonmilitary that makes you think you're not good at it."

"Maybe." She sipped her tea. "Or maybe it'll turn out I'm just a mass of trigger-sensitive programmed reflexes guided by an over-large ego with an identity crisis and delusions of grandeur."

Neiland smiled. "So what's the attraction to surfing? Since you obviously don't find it difficult?"

"It's not a competition. It's just me, and the wave. And . . ." She pursed her lips, thinking of how to explain it, what words would be adequate. Sipped her tea, for the inspiration of flavour. "It's like admiring a nice sunset. Or a great view from a mountain top. It's something beautiful, the force in that wave, the sound it makes and the shape as it curls and breaks, and to ride along with it somehow makes me feel a part of that force. I couldn't give a damn how many cutbacks or floaters I pull off, though that's fun. It's a way to appreciate each wave, and get a feel for its different aspects. Technical difficulty's not the point—and it's not much more of a challenge than basketball, really. It's just a beautiful sensation."

Neiland just looked at her for a long moment, smiling at her contemplation, teacup dangled thoughtfully from long, elegant fingers.

"Must give you a good rush of blood," she stated. Meaningfully. "Get your heart rate up. Might take a while for those feelings to fade away after you get out of the water."

Sandy took a deep breath. "I don't think that's got anything to do with how I handled the SIB tail."

"No." Decidedly. "You eliminate all direct threats all the time, regardless of circumstance. It's what you do."

Another deep breath. One learned to be wary of casual chat with politicians and senior officials. One learned that disarming chitchat about weekend pastimes was often little more than the slow circling of a razor shark about a slow and unwary surfer. In deep water and a long way from shore.

"Ms. President, I have been instructed many times by advisors in your own staff, and senior CSA people, not to let the SIB boss me around. I am advised to conduct my affairs as I deem prudent. Security arrangements are largely my job now in the CSA, I couldn't just allow such a blatant violation of my security perimeter. It's a precedent that allows all kinds of direct threats to have that much more chance of targeting myself or those I'm guarding."

Neiland sighed. "Sandy, the political realities were explained to you . . ."

"You wanted my experience." Flatly. "You said my military background and lack of political compromise was what the CSA needed at present, that I'd help close up the loopholes that too much political compromise and lack of resolve had allowed to develop."

"Sandy, you're a soldier." More firmly this time. "A good soldier knows the need to understand her strategic environment, surely. To learn the lie of the land. I'm asking that of you now—learn how things work here, learn how the politics shape everything. Otherwise you'll just walk blind into an ambush like you did today."

"Ms. President, if I'm not allowed to be me, and utilise my strengths, what real use am I to you?"

"Sandy, please, call me Katia. At least in private."

Sandy nodded slowly, accepting that wordlessly. She wasn't sure she liked it at all. She *liked* Katia Neiland, whatever her judgments to the better. She wasn't the slightest bit sure that it was wise to do so. And now, the requested informality was troubling. She could deal with Katia Neiland as a superior. Rank was something she understood intimately, as a founding principle in her life's experience. She knew the boundaries, the responsibilities, what was reasonable and unreasonable behaviour for both superior and underling respectively.

Deal with Katia Neiland as just a friend? Whatever else she was, Neiland was a politician, and a damned accomplished one at that. Nothing she did was without an ulterior political motive. Nothing was *ever* just as simple as "friendship" with such a person. Inexperienced as she was in such matters, she knew enough to know that for a very certain fact.

"Sandy, look." Neiland recrossed her long legs, bare from just above the knee . . . indecorous of an Indian or Arabic politician, she'd gathered, yet tolerated with a decadent European. "This isn't the military. I might be President, but I can't just give orders like an admiral and expect them to be followed—it's every politician for themselves. And they're all beholden to their factions and interest groups . . . even within my own party, be it the religious conservatives on the Left, the moderates on the Right, or the pragmatists like me in the Centrists. And then there's the Senate, which has a different voting system. There are more minor parties, and upstaging the two big parties on populist, ideological issues is what they live for . . ."

"I know, I know," Sandy said tiredly, "and the Senate Security Council includes members of the Rainbow Coalition due to a political trade-off a few years back. No one thought it would matter having a few conservative religious activists on the council—because no one on Callay ever took security issues seriously before now. I have been paying attention, Katia."

"Have you really?" With a pointed expression beneath raised brows. "You do know then that the Senate Security Council sets the agenda for the SIB, and that they value their independence from the CSA and executive power more than just about anything? If I'm seen interfering in that independence, Sandy, it'll be seen as a dictatorial attack upon the Callayan constitution. I have to live with them. That's why they were created, to *force* me to live with them."

"Ms. President . . . I can't think about public relations in operational circumstances. It's against everything I'm trained to be, and every instinct I have."

"You're going to have to learn. Don't think of it as PR. It's just another set of factors to include in your operational parameters, just like any tactical mission . . . I'm reliably informed by Shan and Krishnaswali that you're a tactical genius, Sandy. I'm certain you can do this if you try."

"And leave jobs incomplete, objectives unaccomplished?"

"Your objective, Sandy, is to be effective. If you accomplish your field objective only to cause destabilising political consequences as a result, that's a tactical failure on your part. I'm asking you to see the bigger picture. You can't change this system, no matter how stubbornly you attack it. Your only choice is to work within it."

Sandy took a deep breath. Ran a hand through her hair, and stared briefly out the broad windows of the french doors, across the view of ornate brick walls and gardens beyond. Restrained a grimace with an effort.

"Okay . . . if this is a public relations issue, why not let me go public?"

"Because we need you as a CSA security operative, and that role will be severely undermined if you throw yourself headlong into the media spotlight—your personal information will become fair game, people will know your face, your name, your details. It'll raise more questions for the Administration and the CSA, the whole works. Sandy, people know some good things about you—they know you saved my life, that you played a big part in stopping the Parliament Massacre, that you're an important security asset to this planet. The rest of it, the moral issues of GI technology and the policy ramifications of that . . . it's a hornets' nest, we can't afford it right now, it'd be a massive distraction. It can all just wait for another, quieter day."

"You don't think the mere appearance of my pretty blue eyes and firm breasts in the public arena will improve public opinion?"

Neiland raised an eyebrow. "You could arrange to show them in an interview?"

"I serve at the President's pleasure."

"It's not me who'd get pleasure from it."

"Your suggestive hemline never helped you get elected?"

"Oh sure, my red hair too. Blonde is rare enough on Callay, redheads are downright exotic. My pollsters had taken another five centimetres off my hemline and added five new hairstyles to my repertoire by the end of the campaign. It worked wonderfully." Smiling broadly. "Sandy, public debate on Callay is not exactly advanced at this point in time. I also got elected because people liked my management style and the ideas I had for revamping the legal system regarding network protocols . . . People here know that stuff, it's their everyday lives and business. They *don't* know much about League-Federation politics and have only basic knowledge about the war. Give it time, they're not stupid, just under-informed."

"And the only people doing the informing are the radicals who think I'm going to break into their homes at night and murder their children."

"And whom most Callayans don't take very seriously, Sandy. The political wisdom is that whatever the prominence of religion and cultural values in people's lives, only about a third of Callayans actually vote on those issues, and only a third of *them* are total, close-minded conservatives. But the more ammunition you give the radicals, the easier you make it for them."

Sandy sighed. Took a biscuit from the table and bit it in half. "I just don't like being passive."

"I know. The best form of defence is attack and all that

. . . It's a fine philosophy for a soldier in a war, but things here are different." Neiland sipped her tea. "That's how it is. Please don't antagonise the SIB any more than they already are. Consider that a direct Presidential order. It makes my life difficult."

"I'll try." Neiland gave her a firm look, eyebrows raised. "I'll try very, very hard," Sandy amended. The President looked sceptical. "And that's the only reason you asked me out here?"

"No. I wanted to ask you in person about Governor Dali. And some things I'd rather not discuss over any network."

Sandy nodded slowly, washing down her biscuit with a sip of tea. It didn't surprise her. Dali had been a continuing thorn in the Administration's side ever since his FIA-arranged takeover of government had collapsed a month ago, setting in motion the entire present mess over Article 42 and the proposed breakaway from the Federation. No one wanted to remain a part of a federal system that allowed its shadowy intelligence agency to overthrow democratically elected governments while committing crimes and murder among the populace. In order to make an informed decision about any possibly breakaway, however, people wanted to know just how deep the whole plot with the Federal Governor of Callay had gone, and just who knew what at the highest levels of the Federal Grand Council back on Earth.

"He's still not talking?" she asked, knowing the answer well enough in advance.

Neiland shook her head. "He'd be stupid to. The moment he opens his mouth he risks implicating the entire Grand Council bureaucracy, not just the FIA. But the Grand Council . . ." she shrugged, "Dali's their boy. He came up all the way through the system, from Indian civil service to United Nations to Grand Council officialdom and a governorship. Only, somewhere along the way the FIA got their tentacles into him, like they've got tentacles into a lot of federal governors, we think . . . Eleven member worlds have already begun appointment reviews of their own governors, and are demanding full records and disclosure from the Grand Council. It's caused quite a stir."

"How much power does that give you?" Sandy asked, trying to recall as much as she knew about Federation governments and internal power relations between them. And realised it wasn't all that much, except there were fifty-seven of them, comprising roughly twenty billion people. Earth's population was hovering these days at roughly seven billion. Immensely powerful, by the standards of any individual Federation world or system. But if all the other Federation worlds stood together, even Earth's influence could be countered. Unified cooperation, however, was no more a common condition for Federation members than it had been among League members. "How many of the member worlds are behind you? Behind us?"

"Not enough." Neiland shook her head glumly. "A lot of the border worlds near the League are very hawkish still, very pro-Federation, have always accused worlds like Callay of being too withdrawn and self-interested with the war going on—with some cause too, I think. Others are totally dependent on trade with Earth and good relations. It's too risky for them to stick their necks out before they know exactly who holds what cards. Right now, it's us and about nine governments. Maybe twelve in a pinch. The other forty-five governments are all on the fence to varying degrees."

Sandy exhaled in mild disgust. "Doesn't say much for the 'brave colonial spirit,' does it?"

"No," Neiland agreed, with a faint grimace. "If someone's going to take a hit for this, it'll be us, not them. But if we look like winning, things will change. This is why we need to beat that extradition order so badly. If the Feds get Dali back on Earth, it'll be the last we ever see of him or his evidence. If we can keep him here on Callay, we can try him here under Callayan law and get some answers from him."

"He'd answer?"

"If we're proved right in Federation law, according to Federation statutes he won't have a choice. He's still the

Governor, he's legally bound by Federation statutes. For him to refuse to answer would be incredibly embarrassing for the Grand Council, it raises the question of what good the present Federation system really is if its own appointed guardians won't even play by the rules . . . which is our entire point in threatening to break away. And if he does answer, and we establish once and for all the Grand Council's degree of complicity in this whole mess, then the whole Federation system is discredited before everyone's eyes and all the power swings to us. Dali's the key, Sandy. Trying him on Callay would give us the proof we need. The leverage."

"To do what? Break away?"

"If need be." Neiland shrugged. "We'll decide when we get to it. Any breakaway needs to go to a popular vote, anyway, it's not just up to the politicians. But public opinion would swing enormously if all Dali's evidence were revealed. We'd have the Grand Council and all the vested Old Earth interests wrapped around our finger."

"And what do you want to know from me?"

"What do you think the League will think about the prospect of him testifying?"

Damn. She didn't like being mistaken for an expert on the new League Government. She'd only seen them in opposition, challenging the old wartime guard, and only then from the greatly removed distance of a frontline soldier.

"Ms. President, I don't think I'm the best person to ask . . ."

"Sandy, there's no one else I can ask, everyone else is just as removed as you are, and no one yet knows what to make of the new leadership. Except that you've been there, you've spent most of your life as a soldier in League forces. I don't want accurate intelligence, just gut instincts. You've got more of that than any of the CSA's Intel analysts."

Sandy thought about that for a moment. It made sense. And something else occurred to her. An unpleasant thought.

"Have the League been talking to you? Is their ambassador here?"

Neiland smiled. "I couldn't tell you if they were."

She understood that well enough. League never talked to anyone in the Federation on serious policy matters without the condition of total secrecy.

"I really couldn't tell what they'd think. There are some factions in the League who want to see a divided Federation, member worlds weak and bickering among themselves. Others fear a divided Federation would tear up the ceasefire treaty and cause Federation hardliners to come to the fore. They don't want a new leadership here when they've just made peace with the old one.

"I think the only thing you can guarantee with the League is that if they talk to you . . ." Pause to look at the President with meaningfully raised eyebrows. The President looked serenely back. ". . . it'll be with only one set of interests at heart—their own. The economy's in shambles. They'll be wanting a possible loosening of the trade embargoes, especially if Callay becomes independent and starts making her own decisions on these things separate from the Grand Council. Right now that self interest might go well beyond any concerns about what Dali's testimony might do to the Federation. And thus to Federation relations with the League.

"My guess is the League's had enough adventures for now. They're pragmatists, they'll be wanting a nice, slow, quiet period to rebuild the economy. Any diplomacy they do will be simple little queries, feeling out the possibilities. But, on the other hand, I can't see them missing an opportunity to stick their nose into this present mess and sniff around for a bit." She gave Neiland an accusing look. "They *are* talking to you, aren't they? You wouldn't be asking me otherwise."

"I ask a lot of people a lot of things, Sandy," Neiland said mildly. And smiled at her. "But I appreciate your insight. You really were wasted in Dark Star, weren't you?"

"So I've been told." She sipped at her tea. It was cooling, and she reached for the pot, and a refill.

"And do you feel fully utilised at the CSA?"

Sandy smiled, pouring tea. "I'm happy enough." She settled back, and took a pleasant, hot sip, savouring the mild fragrance. "I am still essentially a grunt, Katia. I always will be."

"And I'll always essentially be a politician. But that doesn't mean I can't aspire to greater things."

"Do you?"

"Sometimes. Then I get over it."

CHAPTER 4

Late evening in downtown Baidu. Sandy jogged briskly along the sidewalk, dodging raincoated pedestrians beneath huddling umbrellas. Rain fell along the wet gleaming street, the mirror reflection of blazing light and neon broken by the hissing passage of passing cars. Streetlights ribbed the roadside far down its length, and colour sprawled from a multitude of huge, designer window front displays.

Fancy fashion labels, Sandy noted as she jogged. Clothes, perfumes, jewellery, luggage, furniture, accessories . . . even in the rain, the broad sidewalk was smothered with shoppers, browsers and strollers, gazing in the windows and wondering at the price. She ducked past another group, leather boots splashing on the pavement puddles, and wished that Vanessa had thought to bring an umbrella. There were no ped covers along the broad main shopping strips of districts like Baidu. It spoiled the neon view.

Another block, another fast illegal sprint over a cross-street, and she finally found the place—Rajastan Curry Heaven, a small sign leading down a sidewalk staircase. She jogged briskly down, squeezed past a pair of customers emerging from the doorway, and went inside. There was a big restaurant floor to the right, with many people seated. And three presently waiting alongside, sitting on benches. Indian decorations everywhere . . . she gazed about, marvelling at some of the designs and patterns, and at the uniquely styled tapestry of elephants about a pagoda on the far wall.

"Yes, Madam," said the man behind the near counter, in thickly Tanushan-Indian accent, "can I be of service?"

"Um . . ." She recovered her attention, wiping damp hair from her brow. "Order for Rice, we called in half an hour ago."

"Oh yes, Rice . . ." The man turned to a nearby counter, stacking containers into a bag. ". . . we were having much trouble, wondering if Rice was just your name or possibly your order too . . ." Grinning at her as he put the bag on the counter. Sandy smiled back, extracting her CSA card from her wallet. "Is this a traditional European name, by any chance?"

"Very traditional." She handed him the card for him to swipe, thinking it lucky that she'd come instead of Vanessa. She didn't want to spend the next half hour fending off a verbal spray about "bloody arrogant Indians." Vanessa, Sandy thought, tended to overreact to such things. "I think we adopted it some time in the 1800s when all of Asia and India lay crushed and helpless beneath our heel."

The Indian man laughed. "My daughter just recently dyed her hair blonde, like you. Small exoticisms from cultural minorities are so fashionable these days . . . before the hair, it was Senegalese gowns and Russian furry hats, whatever they're called, it's so difficult to keep track these days. You're very lucky to be the genuine fashionable article, so to speak."

It was sometimes fun to pretend, she pondered with a smile as she jogged back to the carpark, to be the genuine, ethnic-European that she appeared to be. Not that it was always safe to do so, as so much of the cultural and ethnic baggage in a city like Tanusha remained well beyond her grasp. But reminding an Indian of a time when Europeans ruled all India and Asia held much the same humour as a resident of Rita Prime reminding a Tanushan of a time when RP held sway as the predominant colony in the Federation, and Tanusha was just a far-fetched architects' plan, and a swathe of messy construction sites cutting through the forests of the inner Shoban Delta. Of course, critics—including many Indian cynics—now proclaimed that no one actually governed India, that it was so huge, diverse and powerful that it was essentially ungovernable, and effectively ran itself like some mythical beast with many heads. Which made smaller powers like Russia, Brazil and the USA effectively more powerful (well, relatively) in political terms, because the huge, decentralised Indian system could never agree on anything, and was largely ineffectual. Sandy thought it a small price to pay for sharing global dominance with the Chinese. Who were more politically cohesive than the Indians but, after five hundred years of trying, *still* hadn't managed to close the considerable technology gap the Indians loved to laud over their heads like an unattainable prize . . .

The elevator arrived at parking bay level, where the cruiser was already waiting on the main apron, in a space only a high-level government vehicle could reserve . . . The door whined open as she ran to it and clambered in. Vanessa waited for the door to close, and gunned them immediately out the exit. The retail strip appeared below, an endlessly long, gleaming wet profusion of light and people. Then gone as the exit lane steered them over the smaller building ahead, and into a long, accelerating climb to the right, engines thrumming comfortably through the seat leather. Vanessa clicked on the autopilot and Sandy handed her a container.

"Autopilot activated," said a gracious female voice from the console.

"Blow it out your ear," Vanessa told it, cracking the lid and digging about with the fork provided. Sandy did likewise, and the cruiser interior filled with the fragrance of steaming hot curry and rice. "You know, I've had this ship for three years and I haven't yet figured out how to shut up that annoying voice."

"Easily done," Sandy told her, taking a hot, delicious mouthful. Wiped wet hair from her face with a free hand, gazing out at the sprawling, wet spectacle of nighttime Tanusha. A blurring mass of light through the water streaked windows. Above, the scudding grey cloud glowed palely luminescent, trapping the mass of light below. Everything glistened and shone for as far as the eye could see. "Anything happen?"

"The river party at Tianyang consumed another hundred litres of chardonnay," Vanessa said around a mouthful. That was the Andaman Corporation delegation and associates, one of the Federation's biggest shipping and construction companies. All one hundred and twelve of them, cruising happily down the Pesh, a central-southern branch of the meandering Shoban River Delta. "Three smaller parties broke up and went home, the Tsang meeting is now two hours over time and counting, Swami Ananda Ghosh has rejected CSA cover, claiming that his supporters and 'metric karma' will provide him with all the protection that he needs . . ." She swallowed a portion. ". . . and the new lemmings are still delayed at Gordon Spaceport."

"Lemmings" were what bureaucracy and media alike were now calling the innumerable delegates from the multitude of interested parties who were descending from the heavens to participate in the Federation-shaking debate over Article 42. A mass migration of mindless herd animals into a potentially calamitous circumstance. Lemmings indeed.

It was of course impossible for Federation-wide governments, companies and other organisations *not* to come—communications between Federation member worlds only travelled as fast as the next inter-system freighter, and negotiations could only take place in person. Governments and corporations alike sent out senior delegates with the power to negotiate in the name of the organisation in question. But people who could make up their minds could also change them. Or have their heads blown off by desperate people who didn't like their conclusions.

Lots of security out tonight.

Especially given that half the major delegations from Earth itself were just crawling with Federal Intelligence Agency personnel, armed with "official" Federal passports that CSA Intel had become increasingly good at spotting. No proof, no means of challenging a visa, just clear and all-but-proven suspicion. What they were doing here was anyone's guess. Intel had some ideas. Mostly, Sandy suspected, there were big moves afoot in Tanusha, and the FIA were loath to miss a chance to influence it, or at least to keep very close tabs for their political masters back on Earth. Exactly what they'd do, and under what circumstances, the brightest brains in the CSA could only guess at. But the FIA had not been reticent about interfering in Callayan affairs before. All Earth-based delegations were under particularly close watch tonight—and all nights—especially those multinational institutions such as the United Nations, the Pan-African Union and Earth Gov itself, where joint security was less solid.

The CSA made no attempt to be discreet in their surveillance of such groups. Rumours of rumblings within CSA elements of revenge hits upon suspected FIA personnel had been spread within those delegations, with Ibrahim's blessing. It kept the FIA off the streets, and discouraged them from wandering. Ibrahim apparently liked it better that way. And could not, in all seriousness, give any guarantee that the rumours in question were not in fact true. Sandy had heard some genuine rumours in circulation that indicated otherwise.

She shook her head in disbelief, and washed down a mouthful of curry with her makani juice. "This isn't a diplomatic gathering," she said. "This is a zoo."

"It's a fucking circus," said Vanessa.

Sandy frowned, remembering something. "'Metric karma'?" she said curiously. "What's that?"

"Our certified whacko swami has apparently devised a foolproof method of measuring karma via electronic database. Thus 'metric karma.' I think he's got copyright on it."

Sandy shrugged. "Pretty tame, by Tanushan standards."

Vanessa snorted. "'Foolproof' is a technical impossibility in this city," she replied. "Nothing can be 'proof' from this many fools."

Navcomp skipped them onto an adjoining lane, curving back one hundred and eighty degrees. The main Baidu strip passed below once more, flanked by midlevel office towers. A residential suburb lay beyond, then a bend of river, flanked by taller apartments. Light blazed on the water as they cruised overhead. Small craft made widening trails of wash, and light rain made the air glow yellow with ground light.

Security, she noted while shovelling her way through her meal, was exceptionally tight about Gordon Spaceport, many kilometres out past Tanusha's westernmost edge. The new lemmings that Naidu had told them about at the briefing had not left the terminal. That made them nearly three hours overdue. Whatever the hold-up was, no one had thought to inform a couple of roaming SWAT operatives. No one even knew who the new lemmings were, nor where they came from. No one with her security clearance, anyway.

They cruised for another hour, letting CSA Central plot the cruiser's course with an uplink to the central traffic network. Everything was integrated. Their course, Sandy noted, wound conveniently past a number of ongoing "security concerns" in their particular region between Porcetti and Vanos, from Southern-Central to Central-Southern Tanusha. About one hundred square kilometres of urbanity, alive with remnants of late-weekend nightlife. Of the sixteen "security concerns" within their designated region, only three broke up and dispersed back toward their various hotels, their private security and bodyguards in tow. Still the lemmings had not left Gordon. But then, considering Gordon was a city unto itself, with some of the best duty free shopping within light-years . . . not surprising. The whole thing sometimes seemed more like a giant business junket than an interstellar, political, constitutional crisis.

Another ten minutes, and it was 10 PM. Vanessa got bored with listening to mundane radio traffic, and put on some music—Latino rhumba, a favourite of hers, and infectiously rhythmic, even on low volume. Several sectors away, Parliament traffic picked up, and transmission traffic increased forthwith. The Senate had packed up for the night, from another of their after-hours sessions. No one really knew what went on in most of them—much was security sensitive, and sessions were closed to media. Sandy recalled her meeting with the President, and the alarm in the Senate over her own role within the CSA . . . among other things. In all likelihood they'd been talking about her over there. Well, at least a little.

"You want to go shopping with me tomorrow if we get a spare half hour?" Vanessa suggested. "I need a new outfit. Or two."

Sandy frowned, fingers tapping absently on the dash to the rhythms. "A new outfit for what?"

Vanessa shrugged. "I've got a date."

"Oh," said Sandy. Blinked in surprise.

Vanessa flashed her a sideways look. And grinned. "What, you thought I was going into a prolonged period of post-relationship celibacy?"

"Hey," Sandy replied with a faint smile, glancing back out at the hypnotic view as the cruiser performed a slow bank, "I'm the slut here, remember? Who's the guy?" For a moment, the ground rose up on the cruiser's side, and she could look straight down onto the maze of streets, lights, trees, buildings and parks. A beautiful, relaxing spectacle of colour and detail.

"Girl," Vanessa corrected. "Sylvia Lopez, troubleshooter tech in maintenance. She helps with the suit calibration sometimes, you've met her."

"Yeah." Sandy recalled a tall, attractive, tanned woman with long brown hair. "You ever thought of going out with someone more your own size?"

"No *way*, I like tall, tall's nice. No offence."

"I'm taller than you," Sandy replied with a smile.

"Who isn't?" The cruiser levelled out, a gentle bump and wobble past the blazing side of a tower. "Anyway, I asked her today just before training, I've always liked her."

"How are you going to find time for a date?"

"Oh, I can wrangle a coincidental night off for two people. You've just gotta know who in admin you have to ask to make the schedules match."

"How'd you know she was gay?"

"I just did, I dunno ..." Vanessa shrugged, theatrically. "Just her helping me get a few suit adjustments ..." A sly, creeping smile. "... I could just tell. It's a subtle thing."

Sandy raised an eyebrow, faintly, eyes not leaving the view. "Nothing to do with the bite marks she left on your arse?"

The alarm bleeper combined with Vanessa's hard, backhanded whack on her arm to cut off the sentence. Sandy touched the reception before Vanessa could stop looking annoyed.

"This is Snowcat," she announced.

"*Hi, Snowcat ... is that Cassandra?*" It was hardly proper protocol.

"Yeah, this is Cassandra." With a curious, sidelong glance at Vanessa, who sent a similar one back. The voice was familiar, but the reception quality was not sufficient for identification. A quick mental probe of the link made her suspect that it might have been intentional. "Snowcat is my personal callsign, but tonight it covers a two-man unit. Who is this?"

"*Um, it's Ari Ruben, Cassandra ... do you need a direct interface to receive code?*"

"No." Even more puzzled, though increasingly less surprised. "Why?"

"*Well, then ... I just wanted to see what you made of this. Stand by to receive ...*"

Sandy hooked reflexively into her linkups, and felt the

interface kick in as a transmission code arrived . . . and recognised it immediately.

"That's a sleeper, Ari . . . I don't know if you know that coding, but that's a Blue Sigma, triple lock . . ."

". . . *with intercompatible C-grade interface, yeah,*" Ruben cut her off, "*and it can sing, dance, and cook you an omelette in the morning. What I don't know is how old it is, and I had this idea League software was better at cycle-lapse deterioration than what I've got . . .*"

"This one's been active three hours, twenty-three minutes and fifty-something seconds," Sandy said immediately. "Why's that important?"

"*I think we might have some bats in the belfry . . . hang on, I'll get back to you . . .*" Click, and he was gone. Sandy looked at Vanessa. Vanessa looked at Sandy.

"Bats in the belfry?" said Vanessa, incredulously.

"What's a belfry?" Sandy asked.

"And what's he doing on direct ops, anyway?" Vanessa said. "I didn't think they'd let him in, he doesn't hang around Central much."

"He never said he was in Central." And Vanessa gave her another hard look. Sandy scanned further along her links, breaking down the signal. The further she got, the more complicated it became. "In fact, I can't tell where the hell this is coming from."

"Which, considering that you can track pretty much anything, makes him one slippery little Jewish boy, right?"

"Logical conclusion." She scanned further. They were over Nagpur now, the other side of the winding, gleaming Pesh from Baidu. But if Ruben had contacted her because of her League software, there was no guarantee that his security concerns were located in her region. There was transmission traffic everywhere. Electronic data—mountains of it. More than a year spent living in a civilian environment, and she was still getting used to it.

"Got anything?" Vanessa asked after a moment of high-speed information deluge.

"Not yet." Then, "There's something."

"What?"

"Don't know. Sounds like shielded traffic." She scanned further. Someone's transmissions were running hot. "Private security, it looks like."

"Where?"

"Uh . . . Derry. That's pretty near." It was two districts over, back beyond Baidu.

"It's outside our region," Vanessa replied. Tapped manually through the cruiser's frequencies, frowning as she tried to find what Sandy was monitoring. "We also don't have any official call-in . . . private security don't qualify."

On the horizon, something bright caught Sandy's eye. She looked . . . and her eyes widened. She pointed, and Vanessa looked too. And swore, breathlessly.

"You think that looks serious enough?" Sandy asked mildly, as the fireball climbed into the middle-distant sky. At two hundred metres, it began dissipating. On the frequencies, all hell broke loose.

"Jesus," said Vanessa as the auto-control reverted to manual and she fed in the destination . . . directly at the thick plume of black smoke and raining fragments of small debris, eight kilometres away. The cruiser leapt forward with impressive acceleration, sliding into a new lane with emergency beacons flashing on the navscreen, and traffic ahead sliding out of the way. "Oh fuck, that looks like a couple of kilos worth, oh shit . . ."

She looked pale, Sandy noted with interest.

Incoming traffic was a garbled mess, saying something about boats and water traffic, and fires on a bridge . . . a direct location fix, and she could see it all—a large river boat with its stern section ablaze, and what looked like a large section of river foreshore blackened and scorched, but with very little actually blown away . . .

"Jesus, what'd they do?" Vanessa breathed, staring wide-eyed at her display screen. "It wasn't on the boat, right? Just on the foreshore? That was one fucking huge explosion . . ."

"Amateurs," Sandy told her. Vanessa stared at her.

Sandy continued to scan calmly through her links, observing the new vid-feeds coming in from the explosion site, and racing through the surrounding infrastructure for telltales.

"Oh Christ," Vanessa said, breathlessly, "don't tell me that's not *serious*!"

"No, they were serious. They were just stupid . . . that was basic plastique, backyard stuff, big fireball and no real shockwave, it's mostly flammable chemicals and doesn't generate much punch. You see any crater? No heavy debris in the explosion cloud either." As she spoke, calmly reasoning, shouts and cries for assistance and support were howling over the frequencies, and about fifty media outlets were simultaneously screaming for information on the broader net. "Looks like they took out some of the boat's windows, but those fires are mostly chemical, they won't catch."

The boat was big, perhaps a one hundred capacity. On one vid-feed, there were people in the water, amid patches of flame. A splash, as another jumped, and another. Panicking, thinking the boat would sink. She shook her head in disbelief, scanning further, seeing a bridge overpass with a wrecked car, and more flames. That looked more serious. By the riverside, some trees were blazing like matches. A nearby building was missing some windows, and the gardens were smouldering. She hoped no one had been walking along the riverside when it went off. But the people in the boat should be fine. If the fools didn't drown.

But where did a couple of amateur pyrotechnicians hide when setting off a device that size? Where would they be if, as it seemed, they had been reading the instructions from the side of a box?

In the driver's seat, Vanessa was engaged in a desperate conversation with someone on a frequency. Sandy recalled Ruben's sleeper code, wove it into her most advanced scanner function, and went hunting.

She found a trace almost immediately, in a nearby com relay. She followed it, noting the mutations as it went, allowing her software to adjust for it, tracing the patterns . . . racing through massive, multitudinous relays and network branches, a staggering, sprawling complexity that baffled any visual scan and tried to split the brain into a million different directions at once. She unfocused slightly, allowing the programs to do their job, monitoring on automatic as Vanessa continued shouting something into her voicelink . . . They banked about another towerside, the drifting plume of smoke now clear ahead, flames burning at a broad bend in the river, aircars coming to hover in close proximity—a confusion of multicoloured, flashing emergency lights, flaring off building windows already alive with chemical fires.

"Back off," Sandy said, eyes half-focused on the chaos in front. "Keep us out of the mess. I think I've got something in Lagosso."

A pause as Vanessa broke off her conversation . . . "You think? Lagosso's fifteen klicks in the other direction."

"Just hold off a second . . ." Internally focused as the patterns converged, racing through the mass of network chaos, chasing the thin, repetitive strain of datatrails. A throb of engines declining as Vanessa bled off their velocity, and the navcomp blinked a query . . . Civilian traffic being quickly rerouted, emergency programs overriding to keep the onlookers away, and their airspace was rapidly clearing of company. Another query from navcomp.

"Dammit, Sandy," Vanessa exclaimed, "what d'you want? If we go in now we might get something on the ground."

"There's nothing on the ground," Sandy murmured. "It'll be crawling with suits in a few minutes, anyway . . ." Ahead, an emergency flyer had arrived in a howling downdraft of multiple engines, the fire scene erupted with foaming spray. It smothered crowding civilians on the boat's foredeck, a sea of fending arms submerged by carpeting foam . . .

"Oh good lord," Vanessa muttered. Someone had undoubtedly hacked a surveillance camera by now—

illegal, of course. News media would have this footage. "Oh Jesus."

More people were jumping, more frightened of the foam now than the fire. Vanessa stared through the windscreen, jaw open, hands fastened unthinkingly to the control grips. Aircars were landing, foam blowing every which way from the flyer's downdraft, struggling civilians in the water now whipped with flying spray and rippling chemical fires still alight. Personnel sprinted from landed aircars, leaping head-first into the water after the swimmers. Nearby pleasure craft were manoeuvring closer in to help. Someone was nearly run over. Another slipped and fell from an assisting hand, awkwardly. The flyer lifted away, perhaps warned of the havoc it was creating, and huge billows of greasy smoke blasted all and sundry with lung-choking mouthfuls.

"Oh no." Vanessa's hand had gone to her mouth, her voice weak. Tanushan emergency services. With no real idea of how to handle an emergency. It did, Sandy thought with tired irony, sum the place up rather well. And then she found what she was looking for.

"Vanessa, Lagosso, right now."

Vanessa raised no word of protest, merely set in the coordinates and let the emergency navprogram assign them the fastest course. The cruiser banked steeply as it accelerated once more, up and away from the carnage of entangled, converging police, CSA and emergency units. Still the smoke billowed from riverside fires. Sandy hoped someone would attend to the wrecked car on the bridge.

She cast a sideways glance at Vanessa. Vanessa looked in shock. Her hands were tight on the moulded control grips, turning instinctively to stay within the low-level lane navcomp had prescribed. Their velocity hit six hundred, legal maximum for any trans-Tanushan air traffic, even emergency services. At fifty metres altitude, the tree-covered suburbs were flashing past below at an impressive rate, blurring glimpses of brief, lighted neighbourhoods and traffic.

"I don't think we'll call any backup for this one," Sandy remarked after a moment, over the unaccustomedly powerful multitoned whine of the engines. A slight bank pressed her forcibly into the seat, towers and speeding horizon leaning sideways. "Do you?"

"Shit no," Vanessa muttered. "They'll crash into each other and level a suburban block." She looked pale, in the wash of speeding, swinging light from beyond the windows, a tower rushing by. Levelled out of the slight turn, and the downward pressure eased.

"Hey," Sandy offered, "if it makes you feel any better, I'm not very surprised. They don't exactly get a lot of business here."

"Oh God, I don't want to talk about it." She sounded decidedly shaken. "I was under the impression that I was working within a system that was actually capable of responding to emergencies without turning them into catastrophes. I'm suddenly terrified that this entire city is just one more stupid mistake away from wiping itself out."

Sandy shrugged, observing their high-velocity perspective with interest. Air traffic was about them again, mostly above. Some were heading in the same direction they were, quickly overtaken and left behind at speed, a brief flash of motion to their sides and above.

"It's a big city," she replied finally.

"All the more reason for terror," Vanessa muttered. Glancing at the navscreen. Lagosso was approaching. Fifty seconds. Towers fled past the windows. Faint patches of rain came and went, lit yellow by streetlight. The cruiser's com-link beeped, and Vanessa hit receive.

"Snowcat," she snapped.

"*Snowcat, what are you doing?*" asked Ruben's curious voice.

Vanessa looked at Sandy. And Sandy realised that she couldn't exactly lie to a direct inquiry.

"I think I might have found a trace of that sleeper code over in Lagosso," she said reluctantly. "It might be nothing."

"*Um . . . well that's funny,*" Ruben replied, "*because I*

think I might have found something similar. We'll compare notes later . . . would you like some backup?"

"That depends."

To her surprise, Ruben gave a snort of nervous, tense laughter. *"Oh God,"* he sighed, *"it's a bloody nightmare, isn't it? Um . . . well, fair warning, Sandy, I've already got some people onto it, but there's no CSA available unfortunately. They're all at the bombing or off elsewhere . . . who knows."* He sounded, Sandy thought, as if the whole thing would be quite darkly entertaining if it weren't so serious. She knew how he felt. She wasn't certain Vanessa did.

"Who'd you get?" she asked, with trepidation.

"SIB," Ruben replied shortly. Sandy swore, lightly, surprising herself. It was a very civilian thing to do. *"Please don't hurt me, they were all that's available."*

"What are you doing on Ops, anyway, Ari?" she asked him, somewhat testily. "Don't you have something boring and meaningless you should be attending to?"

"Look, don't pick on me, Sandy, I'm just on work experience . . . hey, I gotta go and mop some floors. Be careful . . ."

Sandy outright grinned, as the connection clicked off. And gave a snort of laughter, shaking her head.

"Since when did he start calling you Sandy?" Vanessa asked tersely.

"I don't care," Sandy sighed. "He's a pain, but he's cute. And he might just be my only chance to get laid, now everyone knows what I am."

"Maybe he's gay," Vanessa muttered unhelpfully.

The cruiser was slowing, bleeding velocity amid a brief, buffeting turbulence.

"I'll convert him."

"That'll be a task."

"I can do it. I'm a sex goddess, didn't I tell you? Turn a gay man straight . . . long and hard in five quick, easy steps . . . Fifty bucks, full refund if unsatisfied."

"Oh God," Vanessa murmured, scanning the way ahead, "you're in a mood again. Bad things happen when you're in this mood."

Sandy turned an appraising blue gaze upon her friend and blinked in mild affront. "I beg your pardon, my dear?"

"That's exactly what I mean. Behave yourself, we're in a civilised place."

"My behaviour has been impeccable of late."

"Tell that to the SIB."

"I did."

Vanessa swore to choke off a treacherous smile, and held her grim demeanour in place with effort.

"Where you wanna go?" she drawled, as the cruiser climbed slightly into a regular skylane, banking low across the Lagosso skyline. The major river bend that was the central Shoban itself, broad and mirrored with gleaming reflections. Another few automatic sorts came clear, and the options narrowed further. And again. "Sandy?"

"Just a second." Eyes unsighted as the cruiser swung above the river bend, violating regular skylanes on emergency privilege as Sandy let her functions run down, flashing through electronic mountains of digital data, recent transmissions. Seeking patterns or variations on that sleeper code . . .

"Sandy," Vanessa warned, eyeing the navscreen, trajectories headed out from Lagosso as the Shoban swung away beneath them. "Sandy, I'm running out of airspace here, even emergency privilege doesn't like me below fifty metres anywhere up here. There's too much highrise . . ." as midlevel towers loomed ahead, around a bend where the Shoban curved back upon itself, luxury apartments overlooking the gleaming waters . . .

"Got it," Sandy said as it came clear, and Vanessa blinked, her navscreen abruptly reconfiguring to a new trajectory, sending instructions to central control, clearing them for a new course.

"Jesus, Sandy," she muttered, swinging them about. "That's spooky, you've got an interface like a damn AI."

"Get used to it. See the building?"

"Yeah, I've got it," Vanessa said, with a narrow-eyed glance through the windscreen, past the faint green lines of holographic HUD. The cruiser levelled out once more, humming at barely forty metres as it headed back along the riverside. Bridges spanned the width, glistening stretches of light across the mirror surface. Sandy fixed her eyes on the building, two blocks in from the riverside up ahead. Lower midlevel residential, just twelve storeys, balconies and broad glass. Inexpensive, relatively . . . for Tanusha. Her mind found the barriers—basic security that gave with barely a nudge—and she was in. Found the room in question, clear traces of code, coming back to a single operational terminal on the left wall by the sliding window to the balcony, ten storeys up . . .

Vanessa banked them in over the riverside, losing velocity as they drew near.

"Tenth floor," Sandy told her, "this one here, overlooking the river . . ." Pointing at the apartment.

"This one?" Bringing them gliding close, and dropping level, engines throbbing on hover pulse, a deep, shifting vibration.

Sandy flash-zoomed beyond the window reflection . . . The room looked empty, unlit, untidy, with plants that hadn't been watered on the balcony and an empty deckchair.

"Got anything?"

"Nothing, looks like they're gone . . ." Scanning further down the links, but beside the single terminal, nothing else registered. "Door please."

Clack-whine, and the door heaved open, panel lights blinking a red indication of safety restraints overridden . . . A breeze blew in, and the abrupt, loud throbbing of the engines, echoing off the building side here at the tenth-storey level, buzzing the balcony glass. The cruiser performed a gentle sideways slide as Vanessa's hands moved on the controls. Sandy unfastened her belt, checked her pistol, grabbed the door rim with both hands and performed a careful, controlled leap. Landed smoothly on the balcony between deckchair and potted plants, a controlled impact with the glass door to stop her. The door was locked—

mechanical lock, nothing electronic that could be hacked. She grabbed with both hands, and gave it a sharp yank. Crack! as the mechanism broke, and the door leapt back on its runners.

The apartment room beyond was indeed empty. Her vision tracked through multiple spectrums about the bare walls, a made bed in the right corner, a dresser alongside with a small interface terminal in the wall . . . She walked over, and stared at it. Strained her eyes to the most sensitive extreme, squinting slightly. There was a faint rectangular mark on the dresser bench, near the terminal. Like someone had used a portable here. Nothing special in that . . . under other circumstances.

She turned around. A cool breeze billowed the curtains, alight with the blinking flare of running lights from the cruiser, a great angular shape hovering just beyond the balcony ledge. The engine whine was nearly deafening, and she tuned her hearing into differing frequencies, taking the edge off it. And saw a clear mark on a wall. A handprint, quite recent, red with residual heat. But there was nothing to indicate the apartment had been lived in. It was small, empty, and mostly undisturbed.

She checked the bathroom, and found it empty. Opened the front door and went out into the corridor. Someone was standing out there, ten metres down.

"Hey!" A man, dressed only in a towel. A big man, Asian, with bulging muscles and tattoos. "That you cruiser? I hope serious, you big trouble, you wake me up, damn noise, huh?" The noise was indeed loud, the man's voice, raised.

"Sorry, CSA." She flashed him her badge as she walked over. He squinted, frowning. "You hear or see anyone using this room just now?"

"That room?" The noise was less loud down the corridor, away from the open door. "Nah. I sleep. You wake. What you do, huh?" He didn't seem particularly helpful, Sandy thought. Loud, big and frowning obnoxiously. And his English seemed almost deliberately bad.

"Do you know if anyone lives there?" she persisted, looking calmly at the broad, frowning face as she refolded her badge and tucked it into her jacket.

Hard shake of the head. His second chin wobbled. "No. No idea." Walked up close and jabbed a finger at her chest. "You get damn car away from building, hey? You make big noise. I call cops!"

"I outrank the cops," she told him mildly. There was a lot of him for just one towel to cover. All that skin smelt funny, at this range. "Are you certain you don't know if anyone lives here? Or are you just being difficult?"

"Difficult? I give you difficult, girlie, you know what I am?" A hand grabbed her shoulder, hard, as he prepared to explain something to her. Sandy took his wrist and gave a twist . . . thud, the big man went down on one knee, face straining in sudden pain as she applied a simple armlock with hands on wrist and elbow.

"No," she told him. "You see, I'm in rather a hurry, I don't really care who you are, and I don't know if you recognised the badge or not, but to you that means 'don't touch,' okay?" Applied a gentle pressure, and the man yelled, protestingly. His once stubborn face was now contorted. And the towel was slipping.

"*Sandy?*" said a voice in her inner ear. "*What's going on?*"

"In a minute," she said, not bothering to formulate an internal reply. And cut off the link. "Now, let's try again . . . Who lives in that room?"

"Not know," the man gasped, shifting about to try and take the pressure off his arm. "You . . . big augment, huh? No do, I sorry. Very sorry. No problem, huh?"

"Sure, no problem." She let him go and he collapsed back onto his knees, grasping his arm. Sandy gave him a disgusted look. "Thanks, friend, you've just wasted my time." And took off running down the corridor, toward the stairs.

"Hey," came the shout from behind, "you know me? I Chai Chong Li! I big fight promote! You want good money, you call, huh? You big augment, I make you good money . . . !"

"*Sandy,*" came Vanessa's voice again . . .

"*Nothing,*" Sandy told her, crashing the stairwell door and leaping down, four at a time at half-falling velocity. "*Just I nearly got recruited to the local underground fight scene.*" She was, in fact, rather amused. And even more so at the thought of the man's expression if he ever figured out who she really was.

"*I won't even ask,*" Vanessa said dryly. "*I read you going downstairs . . . you want airborne cover?*"

"*Just you, Ricey,*" Sandy said, hammering down the fourth flight, rebounding hard off the wall and taking the next just as fast. "*Better keep it away from the windows, you're upsetting the populace.*"

"*Any decent Tanushan would be out getting drunk and laid at this hour,*" Vanessa retorted. "Underground hours," Sandy knew that meant . . . maybe three drug-accelerated hours' sleep per cycle, to be grabbed at all kinds of unusual hours before racing off to work, party, or generally make trouble. The spreading popularity of such irregular hours had doctors and sociologists worried for a multitude of medical and social reasons, but, as of yet, no one had arrived at a totally convincing argument as to why regular, natural rest was superior, when the drugs and enhancements evidently did such a good job. Tanushans were frequently accused of decadence, but rarely laziness, and most Tanushans would evidently rather party than sleep.

Sandy sensed the cruiser's ID beacon shifting further away, out beyond the side of the building. She finished the last flights in a free-fall plunge, accessing the front door security system with her links. Hit the bottom flight and bashed out the door . . . into the lobby, as her links connected on the security camera, overrode the lockouts and raced backward through the last few minutes of footage . . . there.

A young man in a heavy coat, goatee-bearded under a baseball cap. He held a portable case cover under one arm, and walked with a brisk, nervous stride. She chopped that five seconds of footage, looped it, parcelled it, and shot it up to the cruiser, all while running out the main door and into the street outside. Some people were at the point of entering, and stood aside in surprise. She ignored them, scanning on full-spectrum.

"Ricey," she formulated, *"get this image out on the net, I reckon that's our guy."* It was a small street, no traffic, just a few wandering pedestrians. Streetlight shone wetly along the roadway.

"This guy?" came Vanessa's voice. *"Looks a bit like Ruben."*

Sandy nearly smiled. *"Yeah, that'd be a turn-up, huh?"* Exhaled hard, staring vainly up and down the street. From nearby above, an aircar's engines were throbbing in steady hover. *"So where d'you reckon he went? Public transport?"*

"Could be private . . . you're not getting any more traces?"

"Of what? He's not transmitting anything."

"Wait . . . there's a pair of aircars on emergency privilege another kilometre up the river, they're hovering. I read them as SIB. Looks like they might be on to something."

"Well, for now, that's as good as anything." She set off running down the street, boots pounding on the wet pavement.

"You don't want a lift?"

"No, you go ahead and ask them. Don't let on that I'm even here, they won't like it." The whine of hovering aircar engines shifted in pitch, cruising somewhere overhead and then away. *"One thing's for sure, with all this activity our boy will now know we're after him."*

"No doubt."

Sandy kept running, holding her speed within respectable parameters. A fast run, by unaugmented standards. Flying at sixty down the road would attract too much attention. She kept to the wet roadside under the dripping trees, ignoring the curious looks she got from people out walking. The district was mostly midlevel residential, with several-storey buildings, low apartments, a casual concentration of midsized living spaces amid the trees and taller apartment buildings. She glanced to her left as she ran, toward the river and the taller lines of buildings that were clustered there. The lights were brighter from the ground, and colourful displays flowed down the sides of buildings. Nightlife always clustered around the river, she'd noticed. Any river. The Shoban Delta had hundreds.

At that moment, her links found something strange. Surprising, because she hadn't been consciously aware she was uplinking . . . but that was typical enough. A single call along the basic cable net, voice audio and scrambled . . . nothing unusual about that, but this felt familiar. She locked onto it and began breaking it down. A split second's analysis showed that it would be difficult to decipher without further work . . . but the shielding was clearly familiar. She switched directions, crossing the street and heading down a side road, toward the riverfront and the gleaming light displays amid the apartment buildings.

"Ricey, I've got something. Over by the river . . . Keep an eye on my position, but don't let the damn SIB know anything."

"Damn right," Vanessa replied, *"they haven't told me anything. They recognise the callsign, evidently."*

Snowcat. Yes, she supposed they would. And they'd know that where there was Kresnov, there was Rice.

"What've you got?"

"I think he just made a call. Nothing specific, it's just a feeling . . . I might know roughly where he is." Running faster now, hurtling down the narrow, one-way street, walls on either side. Nudged past forty kph, and kept accelerating, jacket flying out behind her as her limbs pumped in powerful fast motion.

"You think?"

"Hunch, Ricey. Weird software."

"You're telling me."

The side street erupted into a busy nightlife zone, and Sandy skidded to a halt amid the busy pedestrian flow on the sidewalk. Up and down were restaurants, cafes and nightlife of every description. Low key, by some Tanushan standards, but busy, colourful and bustling enough. Groundcars cruised along the street in four lanes, tires hissing . . . She crossed at the first opportunity, knowing the grid sensors would probably bust her for "dangerous jaywalking," but that hardly mattered.

Up a garden alley between premises, past park benches where parents were attending to a noisy rabble of children with balloons and party hats—strange hour for a kids' party, Sandy couldn't help thinking as she jogged, at slower pace now, through the moderate numbers of people. Maybe their parents were taking them bar-hopping.

And out, then, onto the riverside walk. The water was dark and wide, shimmering with broken reflection. A curving walkway paved the bank, marked by decorative light posts. There was a public com-booth to the right, by some garden bushes. It was the right area, she thought . . . although the call had not been long enough nor precise enough to offer a clear location. But landlines were tougher to track than mobiles—landlines vanished into the mass of opti-cable-encrypted networks, airborne frequencies were more traceable and less directional. Unless they possessed quite her level of subharmonic technology, and she doubted that.

She started jogging to her right, along the broad walkway. There were many people walking up ahead, some strolling, some out jogging for the exercise. But the road hubs came closer to the river up this way, and she just had that hunch again—and could see, then, a figure walking up ahead, among the many figures. In a long, dark overcoat with something clutched under his arm. She kept jogging, vision zooming close, but unable to make out more than his back . . . A road joined the riverside up ahead, a cul-de-sac roundabout, cars parked to take in the view.

"*Ricey,*" she formulated sharply, "*I think I've got him . . .*" Transmitting details as she jogged.

"*Got that, don't scare him.*"

She scanned the cars at the roundabout, saw one set of windows darker than the others, and vision-switched . . . Saw someone watching in her direction. And caught the faint edges of a unidirectional transmission—the coated man abruptly turned around and stared. Sandy sprinted. The man sprinted. The car engine gunned to life.

"*Ricey, they're leaving!*" Abruptly her traffic-links disintegrated, and local-com went to hell . . . virus, she realised, weaving at increasing velocity past startled pedestrians as the coated man flung himself through an open car door, and the bright blue Ashanti sedan screeched away with no sign of speed buffers or central controls, and went howling out of sight up the street.

Sandy took a fifty kph shortcut across a grassy lawn, hurdled some bushes and the couple seated on the adjoining park bench, and went hurtling onto the cul-de-sac in time to hear an enormous screech of tires, and a loud, hammering crash from up ahead. Hit the road with boots skidding dangerously at velocities the basic human frame was not designed to cope with, muscles powering against the lack of traction. Shot past an oncoming car, rounded a mild bend and saw chaos up ahead—the blue Ashanti gracelessly entangled with another pair of cars, hoods and bodywork mangled, broken windows, smoke and wreckage fragments strewn across the road . . .

Doors were open from impact or escaping passengers—already two figures were off and running down the street, one limping . . . A third emerged stumbling, turned dazedly about as Sandy launched herself and slammed him over backward in a tangle of limbs, thudding into the side of another car. Sandy unwrapped him from her embrace . . . shielded from the worst of the impact but still unconscious. Checked pulse, pupils and breathing, and all were satisfactory. She'd made a dent in the side of the other car with her back, though.

All about were shouted voices and running footsteps . . . And above it all the clear shouts of "Clear the way! SIB!" She got up fast. A pair of plain-clothed women were racing up the street toward the gathering crowd about the auto wreck.

"CSA!" she yelled at them. "Two more went that way, you take care of this guy!"

"Snowcat!" one of the SIBs shouted back. "Is that Snowcat?!" Sandy ignored her and took off running. "Snowcat! You get back here right now! Stop or I'll shoot!"

She wouldn't dare, Sandy thought disgustedly, accelerating up the roadway, past milling, uncertain traffic as the network tried to make sense of both accident and virus, and adjust for both . . . And felt the tingling caress of a targeting sight brush the back of her skull.

"Snowcat!" came the more distant yell. Sandy ducked right and slid hip-first behind a dawdling car . . . Crack! And a shot went past, then up and sprinting through the sidewalk crowds amid panicking screams from frightened pedestrians. She ought, Sandy thought darkly as she ran, to turn and shoot the bitch—she was a public menace, and if some innocent bystander further up the road had taken that slug in the face, it would be no surprise. And she was shocked. The SIB were under instructions to shoot her, if they deemed necessary. Things were getting insane.

A commotion up ahead, cars stuck nose to bumper (a traffic jam in Tanusha!!), the limping escapee accosting some passing cyclist for his bike . . . Thud, as the angry cyclist decked him with an impressive right hook.

"CSA!" Sandy shouted as she ran up. "Keep him down and wait for help, good job!" And ran off, leaving a certain cyclist looking rather pleased with himself. The last runner took a left up ahead, back toward the river . . . It was the man with the coat, sprinting desperately, and Sandy closed the gap to the turn-off with effortless, powerful strides, shooting past the crawling traffic that was starting to block the road on the inbound lane.

Saw two figures running in from the right up ahead—plain-clothed, with weapons in hand, dodging past cars and onto the road . . . Sandy skidded left, lost traction entirely and leapt with the last of her footing, crashing headlong into the front bumper of a parked car as shots popped, a hard smacking of rounds into metal bodywork. Sandy rebounded, rolled and leapt, pistol abruptly in hand and firing four machine-rapid shots while airborne. Landed hard on her feet, spun and kept running, while the two new SIB agents fell, clutching their legs and shrieking. Shoved the pistol back into the shoulder harness and sprinted off down the laneway.

"Sandy!" came a terse, hard call in her ear. *"Cruiser coming your way, they're on to you. Central's nearly got that disruption virus down, we've got audio now, three minutes and every damn unit within twenty zones'll be coming down on your head."*

"Oh, fucking hell," Sandy retorted as she sprinted down the side road, "aren't they so fucking efficient all of a sudden." She could hear the engines keening nearby, drawing closer. "I just got shot at twice, they'll be using sniper cannon next."

"Not if I can help it."

Back onto the river walk then, pedestrians ahead ducking aside, shouted exclamations marking her target's passage. She accelerated again. The man was over a hundred metres ahead following her brief delay, but she could eat up that distance in no time . . .

Engines abruptly howled overhead, a large, dark cruiser swinging around the side of a tall building with running lights blazing, and a familiar, bulbous nose protrusion that meant electronics. It swung about sideways, slewing out over the river to the exclamation of many along the riverside. Some were now scattering, sensing trouble, the cruiser's side window winding ominously downward.

"Oh shit," Sandy complained, at full sprint and gaining fast. "I was just kidding about the sniper cannon, guys. This is silly." Her left hand itched for the pistol grip—a few quick shots at full sprint, targeting out the corner of her eye, would put a quick end to the attempted sniper now parallel with her and matching her pace along the riverfront. A weapon muzzle appeared. *"Ricey!"*

A second howling engine, cutting in from the right past the towers. It cut straight toward the SIB cruiser on an intersecting trajectory, forward lights blazing off nearby windows and water. The SIB cruiser hauled up and over like a stalling acrobat as Vanessa's car went howling past in front. Sandy resisted the temptation to stare—not having been aware that you could actually do that with a civilian aircar—but now her man ahead was turning in panic with a pistol in hand . . .

"Oh hell, don't do that . . ." She drew fast and shot it from his grip, closed the remaining distance before he could recover from the shock and pain, and nailed him with a shoulder tackle that might have only broken ribs, if he was lucky. About them, the remaining pedestrians either fell over screaming or ran at full speed somewhere else. She rolled on top of the man, who struggled, pinned beneath her effortless grip. Stared up at her with wide, frightened eyes, gasping for air.

"You're a complete idiot," she told him testily. "You do know that, don't you?" He blinked, too stunned to reply. A young guy, no more than twenty-five. European, no identifying marks. He didn't look like a terrorist. He looked like a college student. In the air about, engines were throbbing loudly. She looked, and saw the SIB cruiser coming back around. And looked the other way, to see Vanessa doing the same in a low, flat bank across the dark water at speed. She nearly laughed. War games with civilian toys. How absolutely absurd. "Just don't crash into the bastard, Ricey!"

Found the requisite frequency by reflex, and found SIB voices yelling in frantic protest as Vanessa's cruiser came screaming back at them . . . There were more engines from nearby, and a quick scan of restored traffic links showed many more marks on the way, CSA, police and SIB. Vanessa missed them by a couple of metres, and again the cruiser broke away, losing the rear end in an embarrassing airborne pirouette.

"Freeze!" yelled a nearby voice, and Sandy looked with unsurprised calm at a pair of uniformed police officers emerging from a nearby lane between buildings, weapons levelled.

"I'm CSA, you moron!" she called back, pistol out in one hand, just in case. Her cunning prisoner took advantage of her one-handed distraction to lash out and struggle—Sandy grabbed him more firmly with that one hand and smashed him back against the ground, hard. He stopped struggling. "Check your links!" She retuned to police frequency . . .

"... *callsign Snowcat!*" Vanessa was telling them, sounding utterly pissed off. "*Yes, that's right, you check it with central, you do that right now ...*"

Vanessa's cruiser was coming back low, decelerating as it headed toward them, and the SIB cruiser tried to manoeuvre around behind.

Vanessa's car remained conveniently in their way.

"Ricey," Sandy said plaintively, "I think they're trying to shoot me."

"*Jesus Christ, you idiot,*" came Vanessa's incredulous reply, "*you think this is FUNNY?! You utter maniac.*" Slipping the car about sideways as the SIB cruiser continued to move, seeking a clear angle and not getting it. Sandy found the universal, encrypted SIB frequency and broke in.

"Why are you trying to shoot me?" she asked them. "What'd I do?"

"*Who the hell ... ?*"

"*Who's on the frequency? Who's speaking ... ?*"

"*It's her, you idiots, she broke in ...*" And a mad scrambling of alternative subroutines and encoded adjustments ensued.

"I don't think they want to talk to me, Ricey," she said, back on her private channel.

"*I don't want to talk to you either, you're crazy.*"

"Oh, please?" Her prisoner, she realised, was staring up at her as she apparently talked to herself, not bothering to formulate. "You think I'm crazy too, don't you?" Blink. "What's your name?" Another blink. "You like blowing people up? You think it's funny?"

Nearby, the cops were walking over, weapons still drawn but no longer pointed. Satisfied, she guessed, that she was CSA, but confused as to everything else. For which she could hardly blame them. And her prisoner was now staring up at her with an entirely different expression. Absolute, unadulterated terror. Well, she supposed, the synthetic ferocity of her grip, at this range, could only be mistaken for basic augmentation for so long.

"Oh." She smiled pleasantly at him. "You just figured

out who I am, huh? That's flattering, really. I might just stay down like this for a while and let you shit yourself." In truth, she had no desire to stand up again while that be-damned SIB cruiser was still circling. Vanessa's engines were very loud now, as the cruiser came in for a landing alongside. The two cops arrived. One crouched beside her.

"Got a badge?" he asked, nonchalantly. Looking curiously at the young man pinned beneath her.

"Inside left pocket," Sandy told him.

He reached and removed it from her jacket. Looked at it, eyebrows raised.

"Well, Agent Cassidy," he said, "I reckon you can get up now."

"That cruiser's trying to kill me."

"Them? They're SIB."

"That's what I mean."

More footsteps were running up. Vanessa's engine was fading down, and more aircars could be heard in approaching hover from around about.

"Get out of the way!" shouted a new woman's voice. The cop stood up. "SIB! You! Put the gun to one side now, and get up slowly." Sandy looked up. It was one of the two SIB women from back at the car wreck. On the surrounding frequencies, clamorous queries were calling for information. Someone nearby was hovering low. She hoped they didn't collide. Unless it was with those bloody SIBs.

"This man just blew up the riverside back in Derry," she said mildly. "Don't you think you'd be better off pointing your gun at him instead of at a registered CSA agent?"

"Shut up and put the gun to one side! NOW!" The woman was joined by her partner. Both pistols trained on her face. They looked very serious. And very scared, she thought. And the absurdity was no longer quite so amusing.

There was a heavy clacking sound from the other direction. Both SIB women looked up. Sandy glanced carefully about.

"You've got five seconds to stop pointing those guns at

my partner," Vanessa said from the other end of a massive SWAT-issue assault rifle, "or I'll blow you both into very small pieces."

At this range, Sandy's links had a clear sense of the weapon's powered armscomp, ranging ominously. Both women stared at the lean, dark muzzle. At the mean, beautiful face of its wielder. Two male cops stood by in utter silence, and offered no comment.

"We can't just . . ." one of them blurted, and stopped as Vanessa raised the rifle to her shoulder and sighted manually down the barrel.

"One," she said.

Double-click, both pistol safeties went on, both pairs of hands were raised, and both women placed their pistols carefully on the ground.

"Don't *ever* fuck with SWAT," Vanessa told them. Her voice was nearly trembling. Sandy had never seen her so furious. "Ever. You got that?"

Two nods, slow and careful.

Sandy got up, amid the standing, unmoving SIBs, the cops, and the very slight, very angry and massively armed SWAT lieutenant. The air throbbed with hovering aircar engines, a mass of blinking running lights flared off the building sides and lit the dark river waters in a brilliant, multi-coloured display. She handed the stunned young man to the cops. Then scooped up both the SIBs' pistols. Lifted them casually to eye level, and broke the trigger mechanisms, one after another, with a hard compression of her thumb. Metal and plastics shrieked and popped, very loudly. Then Sandy handed them back to the two SIB agents, who took them with reluctant, trembling hands.

And she paused a moment longer, staring them curiously in the face. She saw the fear there. The pale faces, the dilated eyes. A shift to infrared showed blood pulsing very fast, hearts racing. She was between them and Vanessa's cannon. It wasn't Vanessa they were scared of. And she shook her head, with faint amazement.

"What d'you think I'm going to do?" she asked incredulously, over the whining racket of hovering air traffic echoing off the surrounding buildings and out over the water. "You think I'm going to hurt you?"

There was no reply. Just a couple of pale, staring faces, listening to her voice, but not hearing a thing. Sandy repressed a wince of disbelief.

"What's *wrong* with you people? Why do you just refuse to get it?"

"They'll never get it, Sandy," Vanessa said from behind, her voice hard. "Some people are just like that."

Sandy turned and looked at her, ignoring the two SIBs entirely. "*Someone* has to get it."

"I get it. That's enough."

Sandy gazed at her for a long moment. At the small, dark-haired lieutenant in the obligatory patch-and-pocket-lined ops jacket, hair tossed in a gusting breeze, rifle now lowering along her forearm grip. Flaring light from many aircars lit her face from many angles. Her dark eyes were smouldering. And honest, beyond the anger. Watching her.

"Yeah," Sandy murmured, beneath the echoing whine of many hovering aircars, shouts, running footsteps and approaching sirens. "I suppose it is."

The guard on duty outside Senate Chamber 5-C looked nervous as Sandy and Vanessa arrived from down the long, echoing hallway. For a brief moment, Sandy thought he was going to ask for their weapons. Or her weapons, more likely. A long, flat stare convinced him otherwise, and he opened the doors instead.

A broad waiting room, polished wooden floor, grand paintings and furniture. Filled with waiting agents, politicos, advisors and civil servants, most deep in discussion or engrossed in ongoing dialogue with their portable terminals. All fell silent as the new pair entered. Footsteps soft on the broad carpet, then squeaking on the wood before the door. The door handle clacked, deafening in the sudden silence. And drowned, abruptly, by the harsh exchange of voices from the room beyond.

Senate Chamber 5-C was like the Senate Hearing Chamber in miniature. Seven senators were seated behind a long, wood-panelled bench. Before the senators, seats for the accused. Although, Sandy thought as the adjutant closed the doors behind them, they probably didn't call them that. Half of the argument stopped as they came in. The other half lingered, in forceful self absorption. Sandy walked the aisle through the small seating gallery and stood before the accuseds' benches. Vanessa joined her. The last argument died a surprised, fading death. Senators, officials and agents stared at them. Sandy stood at ease, and felt decidedly unimpressed with the entire situation.

"Agent Kresnov," she announced flatly, "reporting as ordered."

"Ms. Kresnov." The head senator blinked. Reorienting his brain, evidently, away from the recent argument. Several senators regained their seats. Most were staring. To Sandy and Vanessa's right, Ulu N'Darie, CSA second-in-command, was scowling furiously. Another woman, tall and blonde, folded her arms and looked stonily unpleasant. Izerovski, Sandy remembered, with less than glee. The head of SIB, in her natural, political environment. Oh joy.

Then she spotted Naidu among the other agents scattered about and felt a little better.

"Ms. Kresnov," Izerovski said coldly, "where is your guard?" Sandy just looked at her. Waiting for that cryptic remark to be more fully explained. There was no hurry.

"I'm her guard," Vanessa said. And Sandy reconsidered the wisdom of letting Vanessa do the talking.

"You, Lieutenant Rice, are most certainly not a suitable guard. You are her partner. You have demonstrated yourself to be nearly the threat to peace and civil security tonight that she has. I have two good SIB agents in hospital, each with severe gunshot wounds to both legs, and the shooter is walking free about the corridors of power, fully armed by the look of her, and accompanied by her partner in crime. Senators, this is a disgraceful indication of the depths to which CSA policy regarding this particular individual have sunk—she is utterly out of control, and the CSA . . ."

"You grandstanding, two-faced fucking liar!" N'Darie exploded.

". . . And the CSA," Izerovski continued loudly, "are so completely lost and desperate in their present messed-up situation that they've just given her the keys to the castle, and this is the result . . ."

"Who caught the damn bomber, you lunatic?" N'Darie retorted. "SIB's only contribution is to open fire in a public space upon the one person genuinely attempting to apprehend the suspect . . . !"

"After she caused a major traffic accident in which three innocent civilians were needlessly injured, and refused to account for her activities when requested . . . !"

"So she needs to report her every movement for SIB's approval, even when the damn SIBs haven't a lucid clue what the hell's going on?"

"That's exactly right, Ms. N'Darie. By order of this here panel of senators, she does need to report her every movement to the SIB, and I've now got two good agents in hospital who will gladly tell you why!"

"You don't get it, do you?" N'Darie stood barely taller than Vanessa, small, black and compact. At that moment, she seemed much larger, as if swelling with rage. "Your agents owe their lives to this woman!" Pointing at Sandy with a trembling finger. "Any CSA agent under an unprovoked attack is fully authorised to kill in self defence. She *refrained*—does your tiny, manicured brain comprehend that much? She shot to wound, when she was perfectly entitled to blow their fucking heads off, and that's far more restraint than I've seen from your people whose only provocation was that she didn't tell them what she was doing, which they by all indications wouldn't have understood anyway, because all you goddamn SIBs are just too fucking STUPID!"

The room exploded, a yelling racket above the repeated hammerings of the chairman's gavel.

"Bit of bad blood here?" Sandy suggested, formulating internally.

Vanessa raised an eyebrow, as little perturbed by the racket as Sandy. *"No worse than one of my family reunions."*

Sandy smiled. *"Remind me never to meet your family."*

"You never do, you're always surfing."

Under repeated assault from the chairman's gavel, the noise began to recede. Another few whacks, and it died completely.

"Wish I was surfing now, actually," Sandy remarked.

"I wish you were surfing, too."

"People!" The chairman's dark face was angrily disapproving. "Remember where you are!"

"They do," Vanessa muttered, *"that's the damn problem."*

Sandy noticed an SIB agent's head turning in their direction, eyes curious, sensed a faint pulse of passive frequency scan . . . *"We're hawked, better keep the conversation verbal. You know the emergency freq."*

"Gotcha." Vanessa disconnected.

"Ms. Kresnov," said another senator. Kiet, his name panel read. Seated two chairs to her right, facing her—that side was Union, including the chairman. Except for the very end—he was Democrat, one of the minor Senate parties. Even worse. "Do you have anything to say for yourself?"

"I suppose that depends upon what I'm asked," Sandy said mildly. The woman alongside, Senator Zhu, was staring, greatly disconcerted. Well, Sandy supposed, this was most likely the first time any of these senators had seen her at this range. She wondered what Zhu found most disconcerting—her good looks, or her mere proximity.

"Why is she even armed?" the Democrats senator interrupted, as if reading her thoughts. Senator Rafael, Sandy read. Lean and darkly bearded, of uncertain ethnicity. He sounded alarmed. He *looked* alarmed, eyes wide and nervous lipped.

"I am a CSA agent, Senator," Sandy replied before Vanessa could muster some remark that might cost her a promotion.

"That, Ms. Kresnov, is a matter for serious debate," Senator Rafael retorted.

"This panel has no jurisdiction over internal CSA policy," N'Darie replied from the right, sounding somewhat more composed. "*Agent* Kresnov's present work is invaluable, and is recognised as such by all the relevant experts within the field . . ."

"At what cost, Ms. N'Darie?" erupted Rafael, with great agitation. "We have here a killer on the loose . . . Just look! Everywhere she goes, we have gunfire and explosions and people getting shot!"

"So stop shooting at her," Vanessa said coldly.

"Lieutenant Rice," Chairman Rasso said loudly, "I must warn you . . ."

"Of what? This woman is my friend, dammit. You've ordered the SIB to line her up in their target sights, and if she twitches, you open fire. The SIB are so incompetent at basic weaponry that this order effectively makes them a menace to civil society, which makes all of *you* a menace to civil society. We have legal advice looking into it right now, we'll be making a formal securities submission under Article 23 of the recently activated Security Act 91, and Judge Guderjaal will arrive at his recommendation in a day or two. At present, the odds look good that your present orders to the SIB are unconstitutional and unsafe. Keep at it long enough, and you'll be in jail. Ms. Izerovski included."

Five people started shouting at once. Izerovski overrode them all, her voice carrying most clearly above the racket—". . . have submitted our own recommendation with regards to Section Five Subsection A of Security Act 91, and have obtained a temporary suspension of duty upon this dangerous killer, taking her out of CSA active duty effective *immediately,* do you understand *that*, Lieutenant Rice?" Reaching for a paper upon a nearby senator's desk, and waving it before them.

Sandy looked at N'Darie, and saw dark frustration, but no surprise. So that was what they'd been arguing about earlier. Izerovski glared, with triumphant confidence.

"The suspension will continue for a period of one week, while the SIB continue our investigation into Ms. Kresnov and her place within the present CSA structure—and into the commands and instructions from her superiors that have placed her into this position of uncontrolled influence and roving power. This order has been signed by Justice Guderjaal himself. Ms. Kresnov, I require you now to hand over your sidearm and your badge, immediately."

A pair of SIB agents approached.

"You can't do this," Vanessa said harshly, stepping forward. "She was appointed to CSA under Security Act 91. You can't just override a special powers emergency!"

"Section Five, Subsection A, Lieutenant—as was explained to Ms. Kresnov just earlier today, after she had recklessly disabled a government vehicle with a League military attack barrier. Her continued legal status as a Callayan citizen is conditional upon her continued non-threatening good behaviour. If sufficient evidence is compiled that this condition has indeed been broken by Ms. Kresnov, the clause allows for a suspension—of a period to be determined by Justice Guderjaal himself—of that status, pending further investigation by the relevant authority, meaning the SIB. Such evidence is not now difficult to find."

The pair of SIB agents stood before Sandy. Both looked tense. The eyes of the man on the right flicked repeatedly in Vanessa's direction. Sandy ignored them both, studying the faces of the seven senators, watching from the safe, comforting distance of their bench. The varying expressions. The concern. The fear. A moment passed.

"So nice to see I'm going to get a fair, impartial hearing," Sandy said into that silence. There was no reply. In her peripheral vision, she could see N'Darie standing silently, dark and brooding.

"Ms. Kresnov," said the agent before her, "your weapon please." Extending a hand, intrusively near.

"That's *Agent* Kresnov to you, dickhead," Vanessa snarled, "and you keep the hell out of her face . . ."

"Ricey!" Sandy said sharply. Vanessa shut up, fuming.

Sandy reached into her jacket and drew the pistol from her holster. Checked the safety, and handed it to the agent, grip first. The badge followed, in the dark leather binder. And Sandy was surprised to feel the regret so strongly as the SIB agent checked both gun and badge and tucked them away for safekeeping.

The SIBs drew away, back to Izerovski's side. Sandy stood where she was, at military ease, eyeing the Senate Panel with expressionless distaste. On the right, a senator named Hamata alone looked displeased and guarded. Progress Party on that side of the bench. The others . . . just watched her. Tense, as if awaiting the explosion. And satisfied at her disarming.

"Ms. Kresnov," said Chairman Rasso carefully into the strained silence. Aware, perhaps, that senior CSA were present, and watching. Sandy could sense Naidu's eyes boring into the chairman's skull. His lips were pressed thin with disgust. N'Darie just fumed. "You will now inform this panel as to the precise events that led you to the riverfront at Lagosso this evening. Following that, you will inform this panel of precisely the events of earlier today when you launched your attack barrier assault upon the SIB cruiser."

"No," said Sandy. "I won't."

"I might remind you . . ." Izerovski began loudly, but Rasso cut her off.

"Ms. Izerovski, please, this is a Senate matter." Izerovski swallowed her tongue with difficulty. Rasso turned his flat African gaze back to Sandy. "Ms. Kresnov, I will remind you that you are, as of this moment, no longer technically a member of the CSA. Your benefits of Callayan citizenship are also under suspension. CSA internal operating codes can no longer protect you from this panel's questions, you are just another member of the public as far as this chamber is concerned. Now, you will answer the questions, or you will face legal consequences."

Sandy gazed at him.

"I have nothing to say to you. You are a security risk."

Rasso stared at her. "I beg your pardon?"

"Senator, whether I'm in the CSA or not, I remain a

CSA resource. I have an enormous quantity of classified knowledge. I think you'll find that the CSA charter has precedence here."

"Ms. Kresnov . . ."

"You're neither required nor permitted by the laws of the CSA charter to say anything to these clowns, Cassandra," N'Darie said calmly. She looked even a little pleased, in a furious, glowering sort of way. "I'm glad to see you've done your reading."

"Yessir." Calm and military. Whatever the discomfort it provoked on the Senate bench.

"Ms. N'Darie," Senator Rafael said with great exasperation, "I must say that I find the CSA's obstructive and undemocratic manner *extremely* disturbing. I believe that your conduct, in particular, here today has been disgraceful."

"As has yours, Senator," N'Darie retorted. "This entire panel is a disgrace, and we're going to take whatever legal action is required to put all of you back into your little box . . ."

"How DARE you speak in such a manner in here!" Rasso erupted, leaping to his feet. "How DARE you continue to . . ."

"The next time some fuckhead blows up half a Tanushan city block," N'Darie yelled at him, "we'll just let the bastard go, huh?! THAT's what you're proposing! Great God almighty, we have *terrorists* in this city blowing things up and killing people, and your only concern is to try and *kill* the one person who's in a decent position to stop them! Well, the next lunatic ideologue who comes along looking to blow things up, I hope to GOD he comes this way and gets this damn building first, because he'll be doing this entire forsaken planet an enormous favour!

"Agents. We're leaving." And with that she turned and stormed out, Naidu and the other CSA staff in tow.

"ASSISTANT DIRECTOR!" Rasso bellowed at their departing backs. "You come back here right this very moment, or I'll see you all held in contempt of this Senate!"

"There's not enough contempt in the WORLD, Mr. Rasso!" N'Darie yelled over her shoulder, and banged out the double doors. Sandy and Vanessa followed them out. As she left, Sandy caught one last sight of Izerovski, tall and blonde, arms imperiously folded in triumphant satisfaction at the departure of those unworthy heathens who ran before the might of her glorious, democratic institution.

Into the basement parking bay, through the shielded VIP corridor. Onto the reception apron, and the vehicle convoy was already waiting. Three black government cruisers with shielded windows, engines active.

"Kresnov, Rice," said N'Darie, "with me. We'll send someone to pick up your cruiser later." Short legs striding toward the centre vehicle, one escort heading for the front seat while the others dispersed to the support cruisers. The interior was large, with opposing seats. N'Darie took the rear and Naidu sat beside her, Sandy and Vanessa settling opposite. Doors whined closed and the engines powered up, transmission frequencies crackling with secure clearances, a steady flow of official code. Only when the convoy was airborne did N'Darie speak.

"That went badly." Flatly. Fixed Sandy with a sombre gaze. "But we weren't left with a choice. They want to fight, and we can't let them screw us, they've got no more legal authority than we do under present arrangements. We had to punch back."

"Yessir," Sandy said calmly. The Tanushan city lights were nearly as bright at 3:30 in the morning as they had been earlier that evening. Below and to the side, the Parliamentary complex fell away behind. A sprawling splendour of red arches and central domes. Congress House. The Senate building beyond the adjoining length of lawn, divided from Congress by the Mistal, a slim, meandering off-branch of the Shoban. Further beyond, and completing the central triangle, the Parliament building, with its multiple, flaring wings—including the rear wing, now famous for all the wrong reasons. The repairs, Sandy had heard, were still ongoing.

The three arms of power. One of them held the SIB's ear. The CSA, supposedly, answered straight to the top. Which raised the question . . .

"Sir . . . where is Chief Grey? I'd have thought he'd be present."

"It's just one attack, Cassandra," N'Darie replied. "He's busy."

Sandy glanced at Naidu. Naidu's lips pursed—non-committal. She didn't like it.

N'Darie reached into a pocket and withdrew a card. "Take this," she said, handing it over. "Security pass. Not as good as your old ID, but it'll get you in and out. In an unofficial capacity." Sandy looked at it. It certainly didn't look as good as her old leather-bound badge. Just a plastic tag to pin on her jacket.

"I'm still working with the CSA?" she asked.

"Of course you are. They can mess about with official titles as much as they like, they can't stop you working. And they can't stop us choosing to place our authority with whomever we like. That's internal policy, and that's none of their business."

But it *was* Benjamin Grey's business. And he'd been absent. As State Security Chief, the CSA was directly answerable to him, and he to the President. It was more official power than the SIB had. But the Senate, apparently, had so many political levers to pull with the President's Administration . . . Grey hadn't been there. The CSA and the SIB were having a screaming row that threatened to sever even cordial working relations, and Grey had something more important.

She spared another glance at Naidu. Naidu met her eyes briefly. And gave a faint, warning shake of his head.

"We're going to get this sorted out, Sandy," N'Darie said firmly, not seeing that gesture. Sandy blinked. It was the first time, to her memory, that N'Darie had used the nickname. "This is real lunatic stuff. Every damn politician is looking at the polling numbers and trying to figure how much noise to make about you. Those morons are getting real cocky right now, they're pushing real hard. We just have to ride it out."

"Yessir, I understand that. In fact, I was . . . kind of thinking." An old idea of hers, half-formed at best. One that she'd been meaning to bring up for a while now, but hadn't had the opportunity.

"Kind of thinking," repeated N'Darie. "Huh. What about?"

"What if I spoke to someone? Maybe some of the senators, or the congressors? The marginal ones?"

"Charm them, you mean?" Vanessa commented dryly. Sandy shrugged.

"What would you say?" N'Darie asked.

"I don't know. I just thought that . . . if they saw me, and saw who I really am . . ."

"And who are you?" N'Darie's stare was very direct, within a small, rounded face. In another life, N'Darie might have looked slightly comical. In this life, no one laughed unless invited. "I know who you are. Vanessa and Rajeev know. Director Ibrahim certainly does. We've spent time with you, we've seen what you've done and we know what you're like to work with.

"Sandy, politicians are different people. If you approach them, they'll assume it's political. Which it is. And not knowing you better, they won't know whether you're being genuine or whether you're just lying through your teeth. You can't have a nonpolitical conversation with a politician, not in this atmosphere, and certainly not coming from you. I'm sorry, it's a bad idea. It'd only cause more questions and more trouble."

"And I can't appeal to the public," Sandy said flatly.

"No way. Not unless you want to become a celebrity. We have a hard enough time managing media relations right now, Sandy. If you start attracting celebrity attention from this mob, it'll be a zoo, we'll get buried. Right now they're happily misdirected, and we're happy to let them be. If you make yourself the spotlight, *everyone* will want to target on you, and that's exactly what we don't want. Don't stick your head up in a crossfire, Sandy, you're a soldier, you ought to know that."

"They think I'm a killer."

"So we'll keep reminding them otherwise."

"How?" Fixing the Assistant-Chief with a firm, unblinking stare. "By reminding them of the Parliament Massacre? I killed twenty people there, it's not the advertisement I'm looking for."

"You killed twenty GIs, Sandy. That's different."

"GIs are people."

Silence in the aircar but for the muffled whine of engines. Passing tower light threw N'Darie's dark face into half-light, then angling back into darkness as they passed. She sighed.

"I'm sorry, I didn't mean it like that. But there's no easy answers here. We just have to try and survive, and do our jobs as best we can, in spite of those well meaning morons appointed to try and stop us. And we need to convince people that the SIBs have taken their eye way off the ball, and get them focused on what really matters. Until then, we can't do anything but keep our heads down and protect our turf with everything we've got."

Intel HQ remained as busy as ever, despite the hour. Screens flashed across the operations room. Holo-projection charts tracked movements, unit positions, traffic flows. Sandy sat in the side office above the main pit, where many eyes trained upon their screens, deciphering com-flows and encryption routines. Above and around them, on the higher walk, broader scale analysis was offered from surrounding offices. The pit was large and terminals numerous, many eyes bleary in the lingering hours of nightshift, with dawn approaching. Central operations was much larger. Intel Ops was merely a side branch, keeping tabs. Analysing, always analysing.

She sat on a desktop with a leg curled up for balance, an arm locked about, watching the screen—a young man behind a blank interview desk. Date and time scrolled by in the corner. She rubbed her eyes and took another sip of lukewarm coffee with her free hand.

The door opened and Naidu entered, a brief intrusion of Ops-pit noise. Silent again as the door closed.

"Girl, what on good Earth are you still doing here?" He walked to the side of the desk, looking at the screen.

"I dunno," Sandy said wearily, eyes not leaving the screen. "I just wanted to see the interview tape. Know what he's up to."

Naidu leaned a hand on the desk, the other thumb tucked characteristically into his belt below a moderate overhang of stomach.

"Jurgen Chavinski," he said heavily, "Human Reclamation Project. You know what the HRP are?"

"Lunatics," Sandy murmured. The young man on the screen appeared sullen, tired and disturbingly normal. His responses to questions were brief, at best. He remained determinedly uncooperative, and had been for the last hour.

"One of about fifty midrange lunatic groups in Tanusha, to be more precise. Farts, in Intel lingo."

Sandy spared him a brief, sideways glance.

"They just kind of float around," Naidu explained.

"Oh." Eyes back to the screen.

"Young Mr. Ruben had the HRP rather higher up on his alert list than I did, I must admit." He sighed, running a tired hand through longish, unruly hair. "I really should listen to Ari more often. As the name might suggest, they're virulently antibiotech, but, unlike Christian Vanguard, it's not for religious reasons."

"Where'd he get the bomb?"

"He won't say. We think he wrote the trigger code, and probably the sleeper Ari found. But there's any number of ways to make plastique with basic materials. The question is why, and what was he hoping to achieve. And the answer is that we don't know. His friends aren't any more communicative. All ex-university students, graduated or dropped out. All from Ricardo College, same year, obvious connection. Progressive Philosophy, all of them. Mr. Chavinski here graduated with honours. Stirling report card, you should read it. Said he was headed for big things."

Sandy made a face, and sipped her coffee. "They got that much right, I suppose."

"Nay, young lady, do not denigrate the grand designs of Tanushan higher education." Grandly, but the humour was forced through lack of sleep.

"And everyone on the boat was okay?"

"Very wet," Naidu said decidedly. "Very wet, very frightened, and complaining of eye and skin irritation through an overexposure to fire-retardant foam. No one badly hurt, except for a nesting parrot family in one of those riverside trees, the local environmentalists were quite upset. They're demanding we add cruelty to animals to the charges."

"Maybe the parrots were the target," Sandy murmured wryly.

"Ah yes, the right wing Anti-Parrot Alliance, I know them well." Sandy smiled. "Anyway, there were three business committees on the boat, Lexi Incorporated, Lantern Digital and Alitas Micro. All with plenty to talk about, of course, given how much business could change if Callay breaks away . . . There's the usual civil servants there, special invites, nothing serious. Lexi and Alitas are biotech." Of course, the obvious connection. "Both local."

Sandy blinked, and gave him a long, frowning look.

"Local? Not lemmings?"

"No . . ." Naidu rumbled, deep-throated consideration. "There are thousands of leads and possibilities, of course, so we're running the usual traces . . . but it could take a long time. Difficulties, you understand, are not from lack of leads in this game, they come from having too many. Most always there is something important directly under our noses, but to find it is like finding a teardrop in an ocean."

"Yeah." Sandy was coming to understand that only too well. And stared back at the screen.

"But you, young lady," said Naidu, "should go home and go to bed." He walked to the monitor, and turned it off. Sandy frowned. She'd been watching that. Unconcerned, Naidu stood before her, and put both hands on her shoulders. Looked hard into her eyes at that close range. "Are you all right?"

"All right?" She blinked. "Sure." Naidu looked at her for a long moment. She could see clearly the lines on his face, up this close. Worn wrinkles on dark brown skin. The pepper grey streaks through his light brown hair. His eyes were deep with accumulated years, and he held her gaze in a strange kind of paralysis.

"We do appreciate you here, you should know," he told her. And Sandy could think of nothing to say to that. "We appreciate what you've done, and who you are. The Boss and little Benny Grey might not always be able to stick up for you as much as they'd like, or we'd like, but never think we don't care. When the balloon goes up, young Sandy, you're one of us. Don't you forget it."

Sandy stared at him. Wondering exactly which balloon he was referring to, and why it should go up and not down. And wondering further if she ought to be insulted at being called "young Sandy." She was a combat veteran of many years' frontline experience. She was unaccustomed to condescension. Fear and loathing were far more familiar.

But Naidu was more than one hundred years old. Reputedly. He'd been in CSA Intel, the story went, before Tanusha was even built. An Old Earth native, from Bangalore, old India. Still the accent held, beyond the Tanushan-Indian tones. Like an artifact upon one of her apartment shelves, it held her attention, suggestive of things old and wise, and important.

"I won't forget it," she replied. "I know the politics aren't your fault."

Naidu gripped her shoulders more tightly. "And don't you worry about little Benny," he said, leaning forward for emphasis. Benjamin Grey, he meant. "No secret he doesn't like you, no secret at all. But he doesn't call the shots with the Boss, he just does the paperwork and stamps the forms."

"Why wasn't he at the Senate Chamber?" she asked.

"Because he's Administration. Neiland's Administration, you understand. Neiland's got her tits in a wringer on this, Sandy. Her own party don't like her position where you're concerned, and now the Senate's putting the wind up her. The last thing she can afford is to be caught up in a furball between CSA and SIB. That might force her to take sides, and that's the last thing she wants right now. So we're effectively on our own . . . and to be quite frank with you, I prefer it that way."

Sandy frowned at him. "But shouldn't Ibrahim have been there? He's the head, I'd have thought if we don't have Neiland entirely behind us, he'd at least put himself up there . . ."

"To defend you?" Naidu's eyes gleamed. "Definitely he would, over something like this. Never underestimate the old man, young Sandy. He sent the Beetle for a reason." The Beetle, Sandy had gathered, was N'Darie—small, black, round, and very hard-shelled. She wondered what the CSA Assistant Head thought of her nickname, assuming she knew about it.

"What reason? All she did was blow up and yell at people, I thought everyone knew she had a short fuse . . ." And stopped as it occurred to her. Blinked at Naidu.

"Ahhh." Smiling broadly. "Yes. Everyone does know. Never underestimate the old man, Sandy. The SIB thinks they won that round. Instead, they are only being manoeuvred into a more convenient position."

"Which is?"

"I have no earthly idea." Eyes gleaming with humour. "Trust the old man. He has more moves than a chess set." And he released her shoulders with a firm, departing whack on her arm. "Now get you to bed, and get some sleep before the next day's hard toil. It's more than I'll get myself, that is for certain."

When she arrived back at her apartment, it was to find that it had been searched. She dumped her day's kitbag upon the table, uplinking through the minder system to the security recorder, and watched the search progress, two hours beforehand, striding about the apartment as she did, checking for things missing, damaged or out of place.

The SIB—for clearly it was them—had gone through her things but moved or handled little. Doubtless they'd known they were being watched and that she'd review the security tape herself. And she saw, on the tape, the second gearbag removed from her closet, unzipped and searched through, and then shouldered.

She strode to the bedroom closet and opened it—the kitbag was gone, along with all her backup SWAT gear. Weapons included. And her specialised interface module. Dammit, she shouldn't have left it in there. It annoyed her no end. As did the documenter who had followed them about, taping the entire scene. At one point standing before her well-decorated living room walls and scanning over her accumulated artifacts, as if they could reveal some deep, dark secret of her malevolent psyche, to be decoded later by specially selected SIB "experts."

She strode back to the main room and scanned about, vision-shifting in search of suspicious traces. No bugs, they'd grown too wise for that. But doubtless she was being watched, even now. She uplinked a connection and the windows polarised to ninety percent black, though the gleaming view of lights faded only slightly from the inside. And she stood, in the centre of her room, and thought dark thoughts for a while. Wondering if she should call Vanessa. But that would only get her annoyed too, and disturb her sleep. There was nothing to be done about it, and no one to contact. Obviously, if she'd been officially suspended by a court order, the SIB would have received permission to enter her apartment and remove her remaining weapons and equipment. They were government issued, after all. As was the apartment, rent or no rent.

Well. She uplinked again to the door controls and wiped the original access codes. Transplanted her own. A temporary measure, she would do better later . . . but, for now, it would do. She accessed the room com and did the same there. A reasonable security measure, and if the SIB complained . . . well, if the SIB could get in, so could someone else.

She then removed her clothes, showered, stretched, and went to bed. And noticed, before she closed her eyes, that the wood carved Chinese dragon was slightly out of position beside the bedside comp. She turned it, so that its sharp, snarling fangs were facing directly toward her head upon the pillow, and its dark, wooden eyes gazed directly into her own. Then she turned over and went to sleep, content that her apartment was newly secured, and that the dragon by her bedside would watch over her, protectively, and guard her while she slept.

CHAPTER 5

She was awoken at 9:03 by Vanessa, ringing the call button. Sandy blinked her eyes awake, uplinked to check the outside corridor through the cameras there, and unlocked the door. Curled up again as Vanessa came in and shut it behind her.

She came through the bedroom doorway a few moments later, and took a running leap onto the bed, and onto Sandy in the process. Shouted, "Wake up!" into Sandy's ear, propped over her on all fours, as Sandy pretended to ignore her, liking bed better than the promise of the new day dawning. The sunlight was bright despite the polarised windows, but somehow the glow was missing, failing to warm her skin properly in the now not-so-early morning.

"Come on," Vanessa said, lying heavily on Sandy's side, "GIs aren't supposed to be lazy, you're setting a very bad precedent."

"Go away," Sandy complained, pulling the sheets more firmly about her.

"Hey, you due for your five-hundred-thousand-K check-up, or what?" Rapped her repeatedly on the head. "Did your elastic band break?" Sandy snorted, and made no effort to move. "Come on, Sandy, don't do this, this is a bad sci-fi plot—revolt of the machines, y'know? What if our toasters stopped working in the mornings, the hot water systems went on strike, the cars decided not to start? You can't go on strike in the middle of a techno-metropolis . . . the next thing you know, all the kitchen appliances will be demanding better hours and the refrigerators will refuse to turn on their little lights when you open the door, and then the entire city will go weak with hunger from not knowing what to eat . . ."

Sandy grabbed her into a fast headlock and stuffed the pillow over her head. Vanessa protested, with little effect beyond a muffled shouting, and ineffectual whacks from flailing limbs.

"Silence can be so relaxing," Sandy told the pillow. "Don't you think?" Removed the pillow. Vanessa stuck her tongue out defiantly. Sandy pushed her off the bed, and she landed with a thud.

"Ow."

Vanessa's head reappeared over the bedside, dark hair in disarray, grinning broadly.

"Pain," Sandy accused her, head back on her pillow, pulling her sheets back into some kind of order.

"You getting up? It's not like you're short on work, SWAT or no SWAT."

"Just a half hour longer." Burrowing back into her pillow.

Vanessa sat back on her heels, studying her with a smile.

"You're getting slack. This isn't the military spec ops officer I know and love. I mean, look at you, you're getting into fights with your superiors, your hair's getting long . . ." She messed Sandy's already dishevelled hair, Sandy swatting her away. ". . . your apartment's sprouting all kinds of unnecessary decorations, and now you're sleeping in late."

"I'm evolving," Sandy mumbled into her pillow.

"Into what?"

"Vanessa, the SIBs just searched my apartment and confiscated my gear," she said plaintively. "I'm feeling very pissed off. Have some sympathy."

"You're feeling sorry for yourself," Vanessa said with amazement as it dawned on her. "That's a first."

"I told you, I'm evolving."

"No, you're not, you're regressing. I can see your maturity and self control plummeting before my eyes."

"Good. I'm due a little self obsession, I've been serving other people's interests all my life and look what I've got from it."

"You've got me," Vanessa said reasonably.

"I've got a whole city whose President's butt I saved and whose security I restored after a mountain-sized breach, all of whom now hate me and want me dead. Why the fuck do I bother?"

No reply from Vanessa. She hadn't spoken loudly, or with great emotion, but now, somehow, a silence hung in the air. And she blinked her eyes open, realising exactly what she'd said. Where had that come from?

Vanessa sighed. Hauled herself to her feet, and sat on the bed beside her.

"Sandy . . . I think about two months before I met you, there was a big news story here because a senior businessman had been caught having sex with a high class prostitute. This guy was a bigshot, head of some political advisory committee or other, I forget. Anyway, he was found out because he and the girl he was screwing were getting real adventurous on the ninetieth-floor balcony—she was hanging onto the railings, he was giving it to her . . . and somehow she slipped and fell."

"Yeah, exactly," as she saw Sandy's wince. "She put a big hole in a passing car, made a real spectacle on the news. Just this pair of legs sticking up through the roof, high heels and all."

"Can see why the media liked it."

"Sure you can. And it's horrible, right? I mean this girl was a college student, she was just working so she could afford the tech-lessons that went with the fancy tape-teach she was getting, had a whole career plan laid out in front of her, a whole life and everything . . . and what a fucking stupid, undignified way to end it all in front of the whole planetary media—and then become a part of the circus sideshow of this guy's divorce and court proceedings . . . and the rearrangement of that whole advisory committee.

"And you know what? Within days, people were laughing themselves stupid about it." Sandy rolled her head on the pillow to meet Vanessa's meaningful gaze. "There were jokes on all the talk shows, traffic advisories on the aerial net warning airborne commuters to watch out for rapidly descending prostitutes below three hundred metres in the Ranarid District . . . Some people at the mardi gras the next month even had a car as a float, with a big pair of plastic legs mounted on top of the roof. A live street theatre group did this thing with hordes of desperate technogeeks wandering the streets of Ranarid staring skyward with great big fishing nets, hoping to catch beautiful naked women falling out of the sky . . ." Sandy finally lost control of the grin that had been building up, against her better judgment. Vanessa pointed at her in knowing triumph.

"You see, it's funny, right? And why's it funny?"

"It happened to someone else," said Sandy, sobering up immediately.

"Exactly. And this girl, she wasn't a person to them, or to anyone but her family and friends, she was just this . . . this joke . . . this prostitute who became a Tanushan urban legend. And, of course, it sums up what every cynical person ever thought about this city, that one day we'd all party or drug or booze or fuck ourselves to death. She was just a symbol, not a person, not someone's daughter, or someone's sister or best friend.

"So, now, what are you? To all the people out there? Who do they think you are?"

"Either death incarnate, or every lonely male technogeek's mastabatory fantasy."

"Well there, you see? You're already bringing happiness to thousands of lonely young men throughout the city . . ."

"If it made the general populace any happier," Sandy muttered, "I'd do the full spread, literally and figuratively."

"Sandy . . ." Vanessa gave an exasperated sigh,

". . . people don't have any opinion on you . . . because they don't know you. They have an opinion on murderous two-legged killing machines, but that's not you. That's just what some people are telling them is you, or what they're assuming is you. You're a symbol to them, an object of . . . of ideological perception, not a person. You're a news story, like that girl. People make comments and raise all kinds of fuss, but they're not talking about you, they're talking about what you represent to them. That's different. One day they'll learn the difference, and then . . ."

"You reckon?" Dryly.

"Yep, I damn well do. They're not going to have a choice. You're not about to vanish into obscurity, Sandy. If you stay here, you're going to be prominent, your skills alone make that clear enough. I mean, hell, you think you're going to stay in SWAT Four forever?"

Sandy just looked at her for a long moment. Put an arm under her head to keep the neck muscles from stiffening. "I hadn't thought that far."

"You've gotta give people around here some credit, Sandy, they're only ignorant where they think they can afford to be. I mean look at what's happened since Article 42 was introduced. Almost universal support, total revamp of local infonet protocols, even the most radical free-speechers barely whimpered. And excluding the SIB and esoteric academia," heavy sarcasm, "there's very wide support for the emergency powers . . . I mean, hell, you'd think in a place like this they'd be up in arms about the CSA getting extra authority, but most people support it. Some are even demanding we set up our own military rather than just contributing to the Fed Fleet. Which we'll probably do if we end up breaking away.

"All of that's a huge turnaround in popular opinion . . . If they can accept that, they can damn well accept you. And I think that whatever happens, they'll come to value you— you've got skills and knowledge they didn't value before, because they didn't think they needed them. Now things are all different, we're emerging independently into the big, bad world, and we'll need a big, bad guardian to hold our hand and help us through." Giving Sandy's leg a rough shake beneath the sheet.

"Great," Sandy murmured, "I can get a surgical upgrade for a dozen extra arms, work on my God complex." And she stretched, hugely, pushing down the bed from the wall behind her head. Something caught in her shoulder, then in several places down her back, and she pushed out harder, wriggling as she tried to get them to pop. Several did, but several more appeared . . . she shifted position again, reaching one-armed for the wall. Muscle contracted, like a rippling of cabled steel beneath the skin.

"You get it?" Vanessa asked with some concern.

"Nearly." Through gritted teeth. Pushed her right leg out to its fullest as the tension caught along the thigh and hamstring, and down into the calf. Something in her achilles and ankle not so much popped as cracked, almost audibly. "Ouch," she said redundantly.

"Jesus Christ," exclaimed Vanessa, watching the spread of rippling muscle across her shoulders and back as she rolled onto her stomach, swelling to multiples of their original size, writhing like snakes . . .

"If you find it unpleasant," Sandy said somewhat testily from face down on the mattress, "don't watch." Gave a final heave of tension, the bedsheet unfelt upon bulging shoulder and back muscles, and relaxed. Tension melted pleasantly away, sensation came prickling back into her skin, soft sheets and firm mattress in comfortable proportion.

"How are you doing, anyway?" Vanessa asked, a little warily. "I mean, considering . . . bullet holes and all." Meaning more than just bullet holes. Upon arrival in Tanusha she had suffered much, much worse.

"I'm okay." Rolling tiredly onto her back. "I'm tighter than usual, I get more kinks in weird places . . . small price for being in one piece." Vanessa's gaze trailed down her body beneath the sheet. Contemplatively. "What?" And realised that the thin sheet clung revealingly to her curves as she lay on her back.

"You're built like a hovertank," Vanessa observed.

"Damn sexy hovertank, though, huh?"

"Light recon model," Vanessa amended, "sleek, fast and high powered. Heavily armed and armoured for its size, though."

"I like that." Smiling. "I'm thinking a Ge-Vo 19. I worked with those a few times. Very sexy piece of hardware."

"Huh, I thought you'd given up all that macho hardware fascination for smelling flowers and appreciating classical music . . ."

"Macho?" Frowning. "*I'm* technology, Ricey, I'm not macho. Why assign masculine gender to universal concepts?"

"League argument!" Vanessa said triumphantly. "Recipe for butch chicks and effeminate men. How boring!"

"That's an interesting argument coming from a SWAT lieutenant. Tell me—you think if people in this city decided tomorrow that gravity was masculine that would mean all us women could suddenly fly around the room?"

"Your subtle point being?"

"That science is universal, technology is derived from science and therefore also universal, and that if women on this planet happen to believe that science is somehow less relevant to them, then they need their heads examined. I can't understand why you'd *want* to believe that . . . all the best jobs around are in technology, have been for hundreds of years. The things some women in the Federation pick out as being their grand ideal of femininity, you'd think they *wanted* to be the inferior gender . . . Say this much for the League, most League women find it as incredible as I do."

"Neatly argued and I totally agree, that being the point of my earlier sarcasm."

"Oh," said Sandy. Vanessa grinned.

"Come on, roll over, I'll get the rest of the kinks out."

"Okay, but no groping," Sandy warned, rolling face down as Vanessa shifted position to sit on the bed beside her waist.

"Just doing my bit for the Callayan military industrial establishment."

Come 9:45, and Vanessa really was late. "To hell with it," she sighed as she walked to the door, "this is what happens when they make me a babysitter. I'll just blame it on you." Sandy smiled, wincing as she flexed her shoulders and swung her arms, rejoicing at the relative lack of stiffness, for the moment. "You going to be okay?" Looking at her with what Sandy thought was genuine concern.

"Fine," she said. "You take care."

"I will. And you're going to stay happy all day? No moping aimlessly over your terrible predicament in life?"

Sandy grinned. Realising only too well why Vanessa had stayed so long and made herself late for morning pre-ops. She'd been cheering up her friend. Not that Command would necessarily disagree that keeping their friendly GI in a good mood was a good thing . . . but still, it was a commitment. "I'll be fine," she said.

"You better, I deal with pessimism very harshly, I'm warning you."

"Ricey?" Halting her as she turned to go.

"Hmm?" Sandy walked up and wrapped her into a big hug. Vanessa returned it with a happy grin. Unfazed, Sandy thought with mild amazement, at the potentially bone-crushing power of the arms that encircled her. But there was more to potential than mere technical ability. There was will, and intent. And she would much rather die than harm Vanessa. The most amazing thing was that Vanessa appeared to be aware of it. She released her, took her head in both hands, and planted a warm kiss firmly upon her forehead.

"You're the best," she told her, with great affection.

"I know," Vanessa replied, with a parting pat at her face. And grinned slyly, opening the door. "It's just a pity it's all wasted on you, huh?"

Sandy made herself a cup of Lebanese coffee, which, after much trial and error, Vanessa insisted to have discovered to be superior to any competing blend. The number of different brews amazed her, as so much civilian variety amazed her. It was a trivial irrelevance when one brew would comfortably have sufficed. It was the kind of trivial irrelevance that she enjoyed so much in civilian life, and she looked forward to sampling each variety for herself, to discern her own favourites.

The machine hummed and made aromatic gurgling noises as she cast her eyes along her decorated apartment wall, pausing briefly to take in the as-yet mostly empty bookshelf. The top two shelves, however, had been filled— her own request, when someone had suggested house-warming presents (another curious custom) upon her return from vacation three weeks ago. She'd requested books, preferring to shop for most other items herself, shopping being yet another much-loved addition to her tastes . . . but books were too numerous in number and title for her to possibly know where to start. She'd asked for any wellwishers to give her personal favourites of theirs, since she'd had only her own uneducated guesswork until now to direct her tastes.

Vanessa had presented her with a recent fictional work set during the French Revolution of the eighteenth century, which she'd already completed in several long nights of utter fascination when she should probably have been sleeping or working. Vanessa was half-French by ancestry herself (her preferred half, she claimed), which added to the intrigue. The rest she'd simply not had time to get to. From President Neiland came a beautifully bound hardcover copy of collected Chinese fables, stories and poems from the ages. From Rajeev Naidu, an historical romance set in old Mughal India—not surprising, she'd suspected Naidu of a romantic streak. Many of her SWAT teammates had provided various works of basic entertainment, thrillers and mysteries and the like. And from CSA Director Ibrahim, whom Sandy had expected to send her something of Afghan or Arabic ancestry, she had instead received a large, bound volume of collected works of a certain nineteenth-century

North American writer named Mark Twain. Ibrahim, she was gathering, was full of surprises.

The technogeeks (a term they embraced with gusto) of Intel had contributed their own works too . . . some science fiction, some technical, many with an historical bent for great periods of scientific evolution. One was a Federation perspective on the advent of GIs and GI-related technology in the League, and on the impact upon Federation politics—*Splitting Humanity*, it was called. Others were on great disasters in technological evolution. She hadn't gotten to any of them yet either, but her favourite title was *The Nanotech Calamity: When It Goes Nuts and Kills You*. And a second book on the same subject—*They Don't Always Do What They're Told*.

And Feddie lawmakers thought *she* was dangerous. Not all of the Federation's techno-cynics had become such without some pretty damn solid reason. Losing a few hundred million people in the twenty-fourth century because some genius hadn't realised a self-evolving artificial microorganism could just as easily become a human competitor as a human servant was just such a reason. You could program the little buggers to evolve. You could give them strict instructions on how to do so. You could even try to stop them from evolving at all. But somehow, the chaos gremlin in the numbers always twisted it to suit the gods-with-the-dice, and only *after* two hundred and thirty million deaths had the mathematicians found the kinks in the calculations that proved it. She'd seen T-shirt slogans dated to that time period that read, in various languages, "Don't Fuck with God." The mathematicians, despite quibbles about the terminology, agreed that the sentiment was in fact basically correct. Some universal laws refused to be controlled. Needed to be uncontrolled, many argued, for the universe to even exist. Random chaos was a naturally occurring artifact of nature, and woe betide the scientist who tried to fight it.

Nano had been very, *very* heavily regulated ever since, and the political repercussions had been the first stirrings of a technology-related split that had eventually led to the formation of the League, and then to the whole, messy war of containment. None of this stuff was *ever* simple. She'd been learning that since she'd first begun to read history.

Coffee poured, and relaxed in underwear and T-shirt, she settled into the chair before her workdesk, and activated the screen. A broad view of Santiello spanned to her right, darkened somewhat in the polarisation of the windows—she had no doubt those snooping SIB agents were out there still, monitoring from some comfortable vantage. Santiello—green trees, middle-density modern housing, parks—suburban comfort with tall towers rising sharply beyond, and spanning all around into the fading distance.

The screen bleeped at her—files received, she noted with a sip of her coffee, and a very large number indicating memory storage. She accessed, data-sift programs sorting for security threats and finding nothing. All but five messages were addressed to her from the CSA compound. She uploaded those and flashed visually through a mass of network security protocol programs, things she'd wanted checked or to get further information on . . . several had attached messages from CSA techs wanting further clarification on some point she'd made in earlier work. She shook her head in mild disbelief—Tanushan network infrastructure was incredibly advanced, but not with security in mind. The naivety of some of the designers amazed her.

Four of the remaining five messages were from government institutions. Three were from bureaucratic officials wanting clarification on some point of League military law or operating procedure. She knew far more about such matters than any resident CSA experts and generally received about twenty of them a week—for some reason some bureaucrats needed to know such things. She suspected most of them were financial modellers—famous for meticulous detail—and were trying to plot the effect of League economics on local circumstances . . . What her mostly military knowledge could tell them about League economics, she wasn't certain. Military expenditure levels, perhaps. The rest were probably just curious. The fourth message was from Mahudmita Rafasan, the President's senior legal advisor, advising her of the latest half dozen civil suits filed against her and the Neiland Administration by disgruntled residents demanding the rogue League GI be removed from official duties immediately. Well, she thought sourly, thanks to the SIB, we're halfway there.

The last message was neither from the CSA, Parliament or the bureaucracy. In fact, the location coding was alien to her, and had not been screened through CSA comsifters like most of her messages. She opened it, and found it addressed personally to her from a certain Ambassador Yao—the League Ambassador to Callay.

She stared at the heading for a long moment, coffee temporarily forgotten in her hand. She didn't like the fact that it hadn't been security sifted. There was no way that she knew of for anyone to reach her mailing address otherwise. But, of course, the League always had to do things the difficult, mysterious, clandestine way. She decided she wouldn't jump to conclusions until she'd at least read the message. It was seriously encrypted—League encryption, military grade, probably she was one of the few people in Tanusha capable of reading the content. Intentional, no doubt. She didn't like that either.

Dear Ms. Kresnov, the message read. *I sincerely hope that the following information may be of use to you. Please be aware that there are Federal Intelligence Agency personnel infiltrated through many of the visiting Earth delegations. Their intentions may be far from honourable.*

Tell me something I don't know, Sandy thought sourly. And since when were the FIA's intentions on anything honourable? To anyone but themselves, anyhow . . .

I have also recently received information through ongoing investigations currently being carried out by various apparatus appointed to the task by the new League Government. As you are aware, the recent FIA infiltration of Callay was supported by various clandestine agencies within the League. Our new government is attempting to root out these agencies, and determine the extent of their involvement.

Sandy didn't believe that for a second, having received some CSA intelligence of her own recently that, to her experienced eye, suggested otherwise. She read on, with an ever-firming stare.

It now appears that certain of these League agencies were in direct contact with Governor Dali prior to his appointment as Federal Governor to Callay four years ago. He visited Tokanagawa two years ago to attend an official function . . . and his Federation vessel returned a week late, having suffered "technical difficulties" at one of the jump points along the way. Intelligence now indicates the vessel had in fact been diverted one week off its course to a secret jump point meeting with these same League agencies. During this meeting he met with military personnel and intelligence personnel, including some from Dark Star. It now seems that the use of particular GI forces for the now infamous operations may have been discussed.

I understand that your duties will now compel you to share this information with your superiors—please do so with my blessing, as a sign of the new Administration's hopes for friendly relations in the future. I did, however, want this message to reach your eyes first, as a courtesy in consideration of your special relationship with some of those involved, and a token of respect in light of your many years of selfless service to the League . . . a debt that I do not believe the League will ever be sufficiently able to repay.

Your sincere admirer,

Gordon Yao

League Ambassador to Callay

It took her at least ten whole seconds to stop being furious. From that point on, she was merely mad. How dare he? How dare *anyone* from that mob of murderous lunatics attempt to gain her good will from something so trivial as . . .

She took a deep breath, and calmed herself further. Mahud. That was who he meant, regarding her "special relationship." Had Mahud been at this secret meeting in deep space? Had he met with Governor Dali? Perhaps Dali had needed assurance that the lead GI for the operation could be trusted.

Damn. She stared out the window, at the sunny,

pleasant vista of Tanushan suburbia beyond. Huge ramifications. Enormous. Previous speculation was that Dali was a puppet. That he hadn't known the precise scale or nature of what he was involved in. This meeting would prove otherwise—that he knew well in advance, and was personally involved in the planning process. And that he'd personally helped plan, or at least given his firsthand approval to a plan to kill the President and then use it as an excuse to assume power on Callay for himself. People had wondered to what extent he'd been an FIA man. This would indicate he was an FIA man all the way to the bone. Which in turn implied that the level of FIA interference in the operation of the Federation Grand Council was enormous. And if Dali was tried on Callay, under Callayan law, and was forced to admit such things before a horrified audience of Federation planetary representatives . . .

Another more personal thought occurred to her. Mahud had told her that he was not the only member of her old team to have survived. Pessivich, Rogers and Chu . . . Chu, her old friend. Pessivich and Rogers had been recent, she hadn't known them well. But Chu . . .

She accessed an uplink in a flash—an absent, background rush of sensory data—found the appropriate comcodings and relayed . . . Back came the reply—Ibrahim's office, Ibrahim's personal connection. Blink blink. She waited, watching it flash, a pulsing node in visual cyberspace. Blink blink. Connect, flare of lighted pathways, codings and encryption in place, a rushing, reflex awareness of lockdown security . . .

"*Hello, Cassandra.*" No warnings of "this better be important," Ibrahim didn't waste time with such threats. He assumed people already knew how serious matters had to be before contacting his personal connection.

"Sir, I need personal access to Governor Dali, with your permission. He and I need to have a chat."

Dali was reading a book when she entered, an empty teacup on the side table by his comfortable leather chair.

Sunlight gleamed through the broad windows of his "cell," here on the fifty-fifth storey of the government-owned Andara Tower in mid-western Tanusha. The view behind was typically spectacular, agleam with midmorning sunlight reflecting from tower glass. The heavy-security door clacked shut behind her, and she suffered a cold chill of remembrance, recalling just such a room in which she had been kept prisoner upon her first arrival on Callay.

Dali did not look up from his book. A raga was playing on the room audio system, a beautiful, ponderous meandering of minor-melody and tabla-rhythms. He sat with long legs crossed, the book resting upon one cross-braced knee, a posture made easier by loose kameez-pyjama pants beneath his collarless tunic top. It was common enough attire for senior Indian bureaucrats, a comfortable, middling formality. *Birth of the Pan-African Union*, the book was entitled, although the author's name was Indian. She wondered if it had occurred to him that an African author might also have something interesting to say on the matter. And reckoned that no, considering Dali's background and reputation, it probably hadn't.

She stopped before the opposing chair. Dali made her wait for a full ten seconds. She was just about to take her seat anyway, when he looked up.

"Ms. Kresnov." With a blandness verging on disinterest. Dali had a long face, large nose and deep, dark eyes with drooping eyelids. It seemed to Sandy a face designed with disdainful expressions in mind. Although, perhaps Dali had merely had more practice than most. "Please have a seat. Would you like me to request a cup of tea for you? The staff here are most obliging."

"No, thank you, Mr. Dali."

"I believe the correct form of address is Governor Dali, my child," the Governor said mildly as she sat. "I have not been deprived of that position, whatever my present circumstance."

"Merely a matter of time, Governor."

Dali gave a long, deliberate shrug. "Perhaps. The

wheels of administration do turn, even out here in the colonies."

It might have been bitterness. Or perhaps merely defiance, belittling the system that currently held him prisoner. It mattered little to Sandy either way.

"I know about your meeting with League officials out at Point Chavez," she said without preamble. Dali blinked at her in astonishment. "You were aboard the Federation transport vessel *Mongolia*, on your way back from Tokanagawa two years and four standard months ago. You sidetracked to Point Chavez and called it "technical difficulties" afterward. *Mongolia's* logs were mysteriously damaged in transit, which prevented jump time dilation from showing the extra, unscheduled jumps—I checked. During your meeting at Point Chavez, certain League officials discussed with you their plans for the infiltration mission that has landed you in this detention. I want to know who those people were and who was with them, and what you discussed."

Dali continued to stare at her for several long moments. Then he pursed his lips deliberately, carefully folded his book, and placed it on the small side table beside his empty teacup.

"Ms. Kresnov," he said with careful deliberation, "it is clear that your frontline infantry training has given you precious little preparation for the subtleties of politics and interviewing protocols. Even if such a fanciful tale were true, why on Earth should I ever choose to answer such incriminating accusations? This entire room is bugged by CSA operatives who hang upon my every word. I am hardly obliged by my role as Governor to say anything under such circumstances."

"What you say in here," Sandy said calmly, "is not permissible in a court of law. Only official statements taken by appointed legal officers are deemed admissible, anything else could be considered duress. I have sources, Governor Dali. League sources. Intelligence sources. Things that may reach my ears, you understand, that are not available to my CSA colleagues. The new government on Ryssa is trying to clean up the old mess. They're discovering many *very* interesting things regarding operations carried out by the old League for the infiltration of illegal biotech data into Federation corporations. Particularly in relation to clandestine cooperation with the FIA. Whom I believe you know very well indeed, Governor Dali."

No reply from Dali. No disdainful dismissals of her interviewing techniques, certainly. Strategy was her strong point. Seeing all the angles. She'd been good at politics even from the removed distance of Dark Star spec ops missions. Where covert strategies were concerned, the likes of Dali did not trouble her. She could handle him.

"The League are interested in Callay, Governor," she continued. "Especially considering our potential breakaway. Your little secrets are no longer safe with them."

"Young lady," Dali said with commendable firmness, "you would seriously believe what the League tells you? Surely you, of all people, would not be so foolish as to believe that the war has actually *ended*? Dear girl, it has merely been postponed to a more convenient date. The entire thirty year conflict that gave birth to you was nothing more than an opening skirmish. The League do not give up on their precious ideals so easily, they have no intention of remaining beholden to the interests of the Federation. They see in the present environment nothing more than an opportunity, a chance to split the Federation. They will lie and fabricate and obfuscate to their hearts' content to achieve their goals."

"A chance to split the Federation," Sandy echoed, "that you gave to them on a plate."

"I?" Blinking repeatedly, large eyes wide in feigned disbelief. Like an owl, Sandy recalled one of Vanessa's descriptions. "Ms. Kresnov, I am but a humble servant of the Federation. I serve at the wishes of my masters."

"I know." Her stare flat and entirely level. "That's just the problem."

The stare appeared to be having an effect. Dali swallowed, eyes darting briefly away, fidgeting at his collar.

About his brow had appeared the faintest hint of perspiration, clearly visible with a simple spectrum shift. It happened with people who knew what she was. And feared it.

"You are wasting your time," he said shortly, recrossing his legs and shifting uncomfortably. "I am under no obligation to respond to such blatant lies and incriminatory accusations. I have nothing more to say to you. Good day, Ms. Kresnov." He picked up his book and made to recommence reading where he'd left off.

"The deaths you've caused don't bother you, do they?"

"People die, Ms. Kresnov, in all forms of conflict."

"The good guys aren't supposed to kill their own side."

"Good *day,* Ms. Kresnov."

"Do you know what the CSA's had me doing during much of my time here? I've been rechecking over this city's security protocols, particularly on network systems . . . but also for physical defences." Dali stared determinedly at the pages of his book. "Physical defences such as these." She gestured about at the pleasant, spacious apartment. "Defending this place, this entire floor. They aren't very adequate, you know. You might imagine how much experience I've had breaking through defensive security considerably more imposing than this. I'm quite sure the FIA's better covert operations teams could break these defences if they chose.

"I wonder how badly they'd wish to stop you from testifying? It would be interesting to know, wouldn't it? You could do them a lot of damage if you did. And they've shown an alarming willingness to kill whoever gets in their way."

"You do not scare me, Ms. Kresnov." Not "young lady" now, Sandy noted with some satisfaction. "The Grand Council will allow no harm to come to me."

"The Grand Council control the FIA?" Sandy asked mildly. Dali blinked. "How interesting. Did the Grand Council then order the President assassinated?"

"Of *course* not . . . !"

"Then the Grand Council *don't* control the FIA? Equally upsetting news, renegade Intelligence operatives running about killing people without the supervision or knowledge of the proper democratically elected authorities. And bad news for your own security, Governor, since the Grand Council evidently cannot protect you from these rampaging assassins. I *could* order these security mechanisms that protect you upgraded, you realise, if I were sufficiently persuaded of their inadequacy." A considered pause. "And if I were given sufficient reason to care."

"You would *blackmail* me?" With incredulous indignation, his book now forgotten in his lap. "With fear of my own life?"

"They're your people, Governor," Sandy said mildly. "You made your bed with them, you did their bidding, and now they give you cause to fear for your life. How is this my responsibility?"

Dali glared at her. Too proud a man, Sandy reckoned with cool calculation, to collapse in a heap and beg for mercy. So proud, in fact, that he felt obliged to defend, with great indignation, every perceived verbal slight to his dignity. It made him a very easy target.

"And what, pray tell," he said coldly, "shall be the trade-off in this dishonourable game of quid pro quo?"

"Your meeting at Chavez Point. Who did you meet with, and what did you discuss?"

"I admit to nothing of the kind," Dali said shortly. "I was frequently briefed by FIA operatives, because in my role as Governor I am frequently in need of input from Federal Intelligence. I heard speak of many covert League activities." His eyes narrowed. "It was a friend of yours who plotted the raid to kill the President, was it not? And now you suspect I had something to do with the planning of the operation that set him upon his course?

"I assure you that I did not. I did hear speak, however, of others. The League did not kill off all its inconveniently high-designation GIs, you surely realise. There were more besides your friend Mahud who survived the calamity of your Dark Star team that sent you fleeing to the Federation, Ms. Kresnov. Perhaps your contacts within the League Embassy here have determined to make use of your emotional connection, Ms. Kresnov, to gain your good favour, and perhaps to make you an unwitting accomplice to their bidding. Perhaps you should consider such possibilities more closely before running off to meetings with the Federal Governor because dear Mr. Yao of the Embassy sent you a friendly, helpful message."

She did not particularly admire Dali in any way. She certainly didn't like him. But for all that, she knew she couldn't accuse him of stupidity.

"And I assure you, Governor Dali," she said coolly, "that the very *last* thing that I'm emotionally vulnerable to is appeals to past loyalties from the League, new Administration or otherwise."

"So you say, Ms. Kresnov, so you say. And yet you came all this way, and took time from your doubtless very busy CSA schedule, to question me about meetings that involve persons to whom you had a close emotional attachment?"

He had not, she realised, heard of her suspension from CSA operations by the SIB—the "cell" was comfortable, yet very secure all the same. She had no wish to volunteer the information to him.

"No, Governor," she told him, "I did not come here merely for personal reasons. I came here to blackmail you, as you put it, with the knowledge of threats to your safety. The fact that elements within the League sent me that message at all demonstrates that your secrets are no longer safe with them. What I can find out, Federation member world governments will also find out—when I tell them. Momentum will be created through these revelations for your trial to take place here on Callay. The closer that day comes, the more alarmed your friends in the FIA will become. They will attempt to prevent you from testifying, one way or another. You know it, and I know it."

"You let them kill me," Dali said with great, trembling intensity, "and you shall never learn the answers to the questions you seek."

"Oh, I think we may, Mr. Dali. If our League contacts continue to prove cooperative, and momentum among Federation worlds and within the bureaucracy, and among Grand Council reps, continues to swing our way, I think we may. Only, it will take a little longer . . . and you will be dead. An inconvenience, but not an unmanageable one. Except for you, of course."

"You *cannot* threaten me in this way!" Dali smacked his book upon the side table, hard down upon the saucer rim, catapulting the teacup across the room to shatter upon the floor. Risen to his feet in the same movement, he towered over her, trembling with dark, quivering rage. "This is intolerable! This is against all conventions of civilised Federation law! People shall hear of this outrage!"

"That the FIA is prepared to kill you to silence you?" Sandy blinked up at him in mild surprise. "Surely that would only confirm all the member worlds' greatest fears? Are these ruthless assassinations a part of the civilised conventions of Federation law of which you speak? The people of Callay wish to be free from such civilised conventions, Mr. Dali. They tire of them.

"I am not the one threatening you, Mr. Dali. I am offering to protect you. It's your own people who are the present danger to your life. Your loyalty to them is admirable. But please tell me, how much loyalty does one owe to people who would kill you once you become inconvenient? I was faced with just such a decision once. I made what I believe was a civilised choice in the face of barbarity. I do not believe you can defend civilised notions through acts of barbarism. Evidently elements of the League and Federation security apparatuses disagree with me. As a man who professes to value the concept of civilisation in all its moral dimensions, I would ask you to think upon this, and reconsider your position."

"I will not," Dali hissed, "stand here and be lectured to on morality and humanity by a . . . a . . . a *machine*!"

Sandy was on her feet so fast she was in Dali's face before he'd even registered her movement.

"I'm trying to be *nice* to you, you little piece of shit," she said in the deadly, frozen calm that followed. Dali's eyes were wide, fear stark and plain upon his face, his breath frozen, pupils dilated. "I could kill you so fast you'd be in little pieces scattered about this room before you realised what was happening. There's a part of me that wants to. But I won't do it. I choose not to, for my own reasons, despite all that you and your sordid little plans have done to me and people I love. Organic biology doesn't give you a monopoly on humanity *or* morality, you bigoted lunatic. I'm *better* than you. I don't believe any cause is worth murderous criminality to perpetuate. Your time is *over.* The only question is whether you're going to come out of it alive, and on the winning side—or dead. Your choice. What's it going to be?"

She didn't get much further. But it was enough to impress the security personnel monitoring the "cell," though. They told her on her way out that it was more than any interviewer had gotten from Dali in the last week at least. Plus they had just enjoyed seeing him sweat, she could tell.

She took the main lift down. It was security-coded and off-limits to nonofficial passengers. She'd barely stepped into the broad underground tower carpark when an incoming transmission registered in her inner ear.

"*So how'd the meeting with Dali go?*" Ari asked her as she accessed the signal. It only surprised her a little—Ibrahim was evidently keeping Ari up to date, or at least giving Ari the resources to let him keep himself up to date. Her unscheduled meeting had evidently attracted attention.

"You're hopping frequencies again," she said evasively, heading off along lines of sleek groundcars toward the motorcycle park, "this isn't the same encryption as last time."

"*Just um . . . fiddling. Habit of mine . . . anyway, you let me take you to lunch, and we'll discuss the latest machinations of these dastardly League folk.*" Typically abrupt, in that increasingly familiar Ari Ruben style—and not taking evasion for an answer.

"What . . . now?" She'd been thinking it wiser to head

back home to Santiello, considering the very obvious SIB vehicle that had tracked her all the way over.

"*Sure, if you insist.*"

"Ari . . ." she sighed, not bothering with silent formulation as the carpark was empty this far down, ". . . well, for one thing, I'm kind of busy, there's this thing called planetary security that's been on my mind lately, and . . ."

"*Oh that . . . look, it's a big galaxy, what's one more planet . . .*"

". . . and, secondly, the SIB has me locked down pretty solid right now. I don't know if I can get out without shooting, and that doesn't seem a good idea at the moment."

"*Now that's . . . that's a big pity, because I was thinking maybe tandoori prawns with fetta cheese, maybe a makani fruit shake and apricot ice cream . . . homemade fresh, not that synth stuff . . .*"

"Who the hell . . . ? Who's been telling you my favourites?" And then, because there was only one logical answer . . . "Bloody Vanessa. How much did that weasel charge you?"

"*No, I can't tell you that . . . just, well, there may have been the promise of sexual favours, but I can't . . .*"

"Hers or yours?"

"*I don't know whether to feel pleased or insulted . . . look, you're hungry, right? Of course you are, you've been working hard all morning, I mean getting shot at must really work up an appetite, so I think you really ought to . . .*"

"You have absolutely no respect for SIB surveillance, do you?"

"*Surveillance? No, you're wrong, I have equally as much respect for SIB surveillance as I do for the rest of the SIB's wonderful abilities . . . punctuation is their strong point, you know, I find their punctuation abilities highly admirable. I was considering taking a course in it myself, Nothing makes modern law enforcement work in this city like punctuation. You know that's how Izerovski got to where she is today? Her inverted commas are just . . . pure genius, you read one of her reports . . . her use of the*" *semicolon also, I find, has a certain post-romanticised colour about it . . ."*

Sandy lost control of a grin, shaking her head in disbelief. "If I keep saying no often enough, is there any chance you'll shut up and leave me alone?"

"Um . . . oh, I guess there's a very small chance, I mean, if you had another spare hour to waste in conversation you might get lucky. You know though, really, Cassandra, I hear from your SWAT team that you're not the type to play hard to get, so I'd actually thought my chances weren't all that . . ."

"Thank you, Ari," Sandy interrupted dryly. "Do you have a location in mind, and do you have any simple, non-violent suggestions for beating an SIB tail?"

"Well, sometimes I find that if you produce a small, red rubber ball, and you throw it to them so that it bounces around, it holds them so mesmerised that you'll be able to sneak around without . . ."

"I can feel my vaunted GI's patience slipping, Ari . . ." And broke off as something arrived on an adjoining frequency . . . seriously encrypted, bound up in the main body of Ari's code. She received, check-scanned, and opened it. SIB transmission defensive barrier, she recognised it immediately, the kind that . . . oh.

"I haven't just sent that to you. If asked, you made it yourself."

"I'm a network genius, I have this stuff just lying around you know."

"Of course you do. Here's the address . . ." More code followed, easily decipherable. *"Try not to get lost, please be on time, and for godsake, wear something appropriate or they won't let you in, okay?"*

"I'm wearing what I've got on, Ari . . ."

"What have you got on? Describe it to me, if you please, in long and lingering detail . . ."

"Goodbye, Ari, I'll see you there."

The Prabati SE-12 was the CSA's one concession to a somewhat liberal interpretation of Tanusha's finance and tax laws. It had not been cheap, Tanushan technology rarely was. But motorbikes generally came with hefty taxation duties that put them nearly in price range as lower model aircars. CSA employees, however, received exemptions for transport. Getting her listed as an official, tax-privileged CSA employee had been "exercise in creative legality number one."

Number two had been the loan the CSA had taken out in the name of April Cassidy. Number three had been using the technically illegitimate credit she'd brought with her from Rita Prime as collateral against the loan in their own internal books . . . which would be reviewed, at some point, by independent auditors.

Whose eyebrows, Sandy thought as she climbed onto the smoothly humming, angular machine, would be raised very high indeed. It wasn't like the credit was hot. She'd earned it on Rita Prime as a software engineer, her employment for Boushun Information in Guangban was a matter of basic record that anyone could check. But that identity had been fake, as had her entire existence as a Federation citizen, which rendered the money . . . well, that was the question CSA lawyers were pondering over right now. Legally earned by an illegal entity, now given legal sanctuary under emergency privilege by the separate laws of a second world within the Federation . . .

Great fun for lawyers. They were bound to set at least five new precedents that she knew of. She pulled on her helmet—a brief display of control graphics across the visor—and gave the throttle a thunderous twist. In the meantime, the bike was great fun. And most importantly, it operated outside the central Tanushan traffic control. Which today was going to come in very handy.

She cruised to the express up-ramp, a long, winding rotation of ferrocrete incline—and a long way up for motorbikes. Traffic planners insisted on reserving all the convenient parking spaces for "civilised" transport, meaning anything that had four wheels and locked permanently into the central traffic control system. The exit gate deducted an automatic fee as she cruised up the final off-ramp and into bright sunshine and busy streets. Traffic

Central showed approaching cars from both directions, possible opening windows, and course projections, counting down the seconds. Motorbikes made the automated systems nervous, if that was possible, with regulatory overkill the inevitable result. She uplinked into the system and scanned the surrounding network as the traffic passed. Cut through several layers of obscuring code traffic . . . and found the SIB tracer program rather quickly.

Traffic broke and she cruised out onto the main road, smoothly accelerating up to seventy kph, at which point the buffers immediately cut the throttle. Watched an external picture of the regional traffic grid, tracing her own position at seventy along the road. Sure enough, there was another vehicle following almost immediately—with none-too-subtle timing—barely a block behind. She isolated the SIB trace code as she cruised, and began analysing. Two minutes and another district later, she decided that she really didn't need Ari's little piece of code after all. There were things that League military code-workers knew that SIB code-workers had evidently yet to suspect.

At the next set of traffic lights, she drew up alongside the car ahead, ignoring protests from central. A simple hack-and-rearrange transferred what the SIB's code had recognised as her bike onto the car alongside. The lights went green and she let the car pull ahead before following for three blocks. A bend took her momentarily out of view from the car behind . . . she indicated, and turned a quick left across oncoming traffic—central squawked, but then the traffic was intervening, and the SIB car went past down the road, unaware as it trailed the wrong signature. Another ten seconds would doubtless reveal their mistake, and send everyone scrambling back to the main central control map to refind her location—ludicrous that they should keep their tracer program separate from central codings. It was a crude security measure at best, and it rendered that system entirely vulnerable to this kind of simple manipulation, if one had the key to get in.

But a search of central would reveal her position once more in short order . . . and so, at the next crossstreet, she indicated right, and pulled the bike up onto the sidewalk instead. Street sensors immediately lost contact with the bike's CPU, and both she and the Prabati abruptly vanished from the central grid. She cruised slowly along the sidewalk, wary of unsuspecting pedestrians, and musing that it could really be so easy. Info-addicts, they never thought of non-data-related solutions. No fancy code in existence was any use against a well-placed bullet, bomb, or axe. Or a motorcycle rider with the temerity to dare ride her bike along the footpath for a block or two.

She uplinked mentally to CSA Central while she was at it, and asked for an operational cover. Those codes were something the SIB had not yet found a way to legally confiscate, and ten seconds later her bike was registered as a four-wheeled family sedan. Basic procedure for any CSA operative, disguising your presence on the main traffic network. Impossible to do while being watched, but a brief moment out of view . . . She ducked out between a pair of leafy suburban trees, bumped down onto the road, turned a corner and accelerated once more along the straight, past a school crossing and pleasant neighbourhood storefronts. She'd have to watch her movements now—any behaviour not in keeping with her new identity, meaning any deviation from central control, could be noted by SIB monitors as suspicious, and suggestive of a car that was not in fact a car. But that aside, she was entirely, laughably, in the clear. For today.

Ari's eating spot was in Zaiko District, forty kilometres eastward from Santiello, toward the ocean. A broad bend in the river stretched away to her left as Sandy climbed the last in the flight of broad stone steps beneath one of Zaiko's numerous office towers. Too many, she thought, gazing over the wide span of water as she walked, listening to the busy noise of tourists and markets along the riverfront below. River cruisers lined the near bend of shore, stretching up to the bridge that spanned the river behind. Beyond this right-angled elbow in the river's flow, the water ran directly away, its full length awash with pleasure cruisers and smaller craft until it vanished around another bend perhaps a kilometre further along.

The walk was crowded here above the riverfront, yet not so crowded as the milling hordes that spilled about the stalls, shops, ticket sellers and varied entertainers along the riverbank walk below, and the many cruisers bobbing against their restraints in the water beyond. She held to the left along the railing, with a good view over those below, and soon spotted the many outdoor tables in a cordoned area ahead, set apart from the walkway pedestrians by pot plants and leafy fronds.

Ari pulled his roguish dark glasses down his nose to look her up and down as she pulled out a chair and sat.

"Hello." With a genuine smile. "You're looking well." Sandy restrained a smile, thankful that cargo pants passed for loosely casual in Tanusha—the pockets were a convenience, and she was too much the soldier to avoid convenience for style. The T-shirt and jacket, though, were NOT Tanushan-feminine, nor the running shoes. She only hoped her drab, practical self did not prove too much of a giveaway among the saris, dresses, suits and varied artistic fusions passing here along the walkway, or the riverfront below.

"I apologise for the absence of cleavage. I'll do better next time."

"You look fantastic, I've had girlfriends who'd be jealous that it takes you so little effort."

"I don't make an effort, that'd be unfair on the competition, considering my advantage."

"Which advantage?"

"Custom design, as opposed to mostly random genetics." Resting chin on hands, elbows on the table to contemplate the view of choppy water and passing boats. Bright sunlight glinted in a million refractions. Cooking smells wafted up from below on the breeze—a barbecue at a tourist food stall. Perfume from the neighbouring flower box. Boat engines thrummed above a wash of churning water, dulled beneath the surrounding echo of traffic, particularly heavy here in one of Tanusha's most built-up commercial districts. "Nice view, you come here a lot?"

"This cafe? Never been here before in my life. Tanusha's like that, seems silly to eat at the same place twice when there's so much around that's yet to be sampled."

Sandy gave him a long, considering look. He looked quite flash, she thought, by her own neophyte fashion reckoning. A dark, casual shirt with just a few buttons at the collar, a heavier jacket shouldered upon the back of his chair. Bare arms lithe, with an athletic quantity of muscle that hinted at a similar build beneath, a sealed synthetic bandage about the lower half of his left forearm—apparently healing as fast as medical engineering had led her to expect it would. The sunglasses were hardly regulation.

"You hungry? I've taken the, um, liberty of ordering for both of us—there's a bit of a rush. I hope you like tandoori chicken and salad, they had the prawns but it was going to take too long."

"Chicken's wonderful. What's the rush?"

"Aha." He held up a portending finger. "I've got you a present." And dug into the jacket draped over the back of his chair. Sandy glanced carefully about . . . about half the neighbouring tables were filled. In this section of seating and the ones alongside, the air was filled with conversation and clinking cutlery. Still really too early for lunch, but some of these business types had probably missed breakfast. It would no doubt get totally crowded in another hour.

Ari placed a leather-bound binder on the table beside the plant-frond arrangement. It looked familiar. Sandy frowned and picked it up. It flicked open to reveal her CSA badge—shield, ID signature, photo, everything. She read the seal with her own auto-scan . . . it uplinked and came back clean from CSA HQ itself. It was genuine.

"Happy Holi, Christmas, Ramadan or whatever's closest," Ari offered.

"Devali, I think."

"That too. I'll give you the other item later." Her gun, he meant. She turned her frown upon him.

"Where did you get this?"

"Admin, where does anyone get ID from?" Popped a complimentary fruit piece into his mouth.

"Who authorised it?" With forced patience.

Ari shrugged. "I did," he said around the mouthful. "I need you. It's just for show, you understand, you're technically suspended . . . It's just that overriding imperatives have led me to exercise my discretionary powers to more fully utilise your abilities . . ." With a sardonic smile at his own use of bureaucratic jargon. ". . . in which case you'll need the badge to get you places and operate in the field, obviously." Sandy stared at him, utterly unblinking. Ari stopped chewing. "What?"

"What if the SIB find out?"

"Better that they don't."

"What if *anyone* finds out? What if someone traces back my ID, checks my status with CSA oper . . ."

"Can't." He smiled, lazy as a cat on a sunlit windowsill. "Emergency legislation, no one checks our operational files, not even the SIB. Full operational security, full nondisclosure. Why'd you think the SIBs are so pissed? You're a CSA agent because we say you are, and there's no evidence to contradict us."

"Because you won't let them have it."

"Exactly." And took another piece of fruit.

"This is how things work in a civilian democratic system?"

"Sandy . . ." He leaned forward, with some deliberation, "the system isn't like the military. You take what it gives you, and what you can get away with when you need it. That's what Ibrahim's brought us the last six years he's been in charge—we're concerned with results, the SIBs are concerned with procedure. Now, like I said, I need you, and Ibrahim agrees, so . . ."

"Ibrahim approved this?"

"Sandy, nothing that happens to you within the CSA

happens without Ibrahim's approval, trust me." She continued staring. Not knowing whether to be relieved or wary. It felt nice to have her badge back. What she was being asked to do in return . . . that was another question. "You realise you haven't blinked in the last sixty seconds? Isn't that uncomfortable?"

"It's a reflex I get when something requires my very full attention." Holding his gaze without a millimetre's deviation. "Or when I think someone's determined to get me into trouble."

"Sandy, we're all in trouble. That's our job."

"I'm noticing. So why do you need me?"

At that moment lunch arrived, and they waited while a pair of plates were placed before them, with extra salad, bread and dip. Interesting Indian-Italian combination, she pondered, tandoori spices plus green salad, olive oils, bread . . . The only thing missing was the wine, Ari had ordered fruit juice instead. A pity . . . she liked wine, and, of course, it had absolutely no effect on her mental function at all.

"I need you," said Ari when the waiter had left, cutting into his lasagna as a breeze gusted in from the river, cool in the bright sun, "because I think you might be useful finding the person I'm looking for." Took a rich, cheese-smothered mouthful.

"Who?" Taking a mouthful of tandoori chicken. Delicious, as it always was.

"Name's Sai Va. Vietnamese name, I don't know if he is or not. He's a big-time hacker, worked for a long time in illegal VR, arranged all kinds of data transfers and copies, tape-teach, memory enhancement, the whole underground range. The guy's a dataform wizard, he's got more translation codes accumulated than most law enforcement databases."

"What'd he do?" Washing down the chicken with a bite of salad and a sip of drink.

"He broke into Lexi Incorporated, stole a big chunk of mainframe data. Itineraries included, travel plans, meetings, that kind of thing."

Sandy blinked, considering that. Lexi Incorporated? They'd been on the boat last night when Jurgen Chavinski and the Human Reclamation Project had tried to blow them out of the water. And she made the next obvious connection.

"You think Sai Va gave the HRP the schedule for Lexi's boating cruise?"

"It definitely looks that way."

"Why?"

"I'm not sure. Word is Sai Va's latest employer was the Hornsvaag Four—they're GGs, goodtime gangs, mafia by any other name—there's six leaders, don't know where they got the 'Four' from. Good thing about Tanusha, you can make the most money by doing things legally, so the cream of the genius tends to avoid the mafia." He shrugged theatrically. "Anyhow, as you know, GGs are a big part of the League infiltration network in Tanusha, they'll take anyone's business for enough money. You heard about the new lemmings at Gordon Airport last night? The ones who took so long to get through?"

"Sure." Frowning as she swallowed her next mouthful. "They were still stuck out there just before the bomb went off, after that I wasn't watching. Who were they?"

"League delegation." The cup froze halfway to Sandy's lips, her eyes locked hard onto Ari's. Ari's return gaze was calmly thoughtful, even curious. The cup continued to her lips, and she took a long, considered sip. "Big one," Ari added. "Word is there were GIs in the group arriving. Officially registered, full documentation." Sandy nearly swore. "Apparently it's not illegal, there's nothing in the regulations prohibiting the League from appointing GIs as official security under the relevant diplomatic articles that govern these things. So long as they stay at the Embassy, it's all covered by diplomatic immunity. That's what the hold-up was about, some immigration officials made a fuss but got overruled."

And just *now* Neiland wanted to talk to her about likely positions the League would take regarding Dali's impending testimony? She took a deep breath to cover the surge of frustration. Neiland was under no obligation to share such information with her. Neiland would have been breaching protocols to tell her precisely *why* now, of all times, she needed a League-side opinion of League-side attitudes toward the present crisis. What would the new League Administration think? What would they want? Damn sure it mattered now, the new Administration just sent a delegation to Tanusha, doubtless to partake in . . . whatever they thought worth partaking in. She was no expert on what the new Administration would want. It all seemed like chaos over there right now.

It certainly made more sense of the timing of Ambassador Yao's message to her—he had just received the information himself, because it had just arrived on those League ships with the new delegation. So were the League here to talk, or to listen? Or worse, to make "constructive headway"? And then she thought back, with an unpleasantly cold feeling in her gut, to Ari's initial point.

"So what does this have to do with Sai Va and hacking into Lexi Incorporated? And why would any mafia group want to help get Lexi blown up, anyway?"

"Exactly—they don't. It's bad for business. They get quite a lot of work from minor biotech people, tracking down various black market tech for study. Everyone knows the corporations are the biggest buyers on the black market, why attack your own best client?" Ari stabbed a piece of salad with his fork, and pointed it at her with emphasis. "The thing is that Sai Va's a dedicated anarchist in the truest of underground traditions, he'd only take the Lexi job to cause trouble. The GGs were stupid to hire him, but then that's GGs—too many stim implants, too few functioning brain cells left in the cerebral cortex. And, of course, it's not the GGs' idea, it's just that some fool comes along from their old League contacts and offers them a huge pile of credit to arrange it, and their beady little eyes light up like Holi decorations and they go searching for the most qualified person they can find with that money, without giving a second thought to whether he's reliable or not . . ."

"The League paid this mafia gang to employ Sai Va to hack Lexi?" With some incredulity, realising how silly it sounded all compressed into one sentence. Ari nodded, eyebrows raised somewhat glumly. Ate the salad piece off his fork, and went to work on the lasagna again. "What did the League want with Lexi?"

"Who knows?" Shovelling another forkful into his mouth. "Lexi's big, they're one of the most influential corporates on Callay, biotech or otherwise. Their opinion gets listened to in the corridors of power, they lobby like a six hundred kilo krais dragon with a toothache, and they know *everyone* . . . and their bank account details. So if the League could get their info, find out who they're talking to, find out all kinds of things about where the whole corporate scene's at regarding Article 42, and therefore where the League's best plays lie . . . And where the vulnerable angles are. Who knows, maybe there's still some unfinished business there from the whole thing you were involved in. Maybe the League still has contacts there."

"Old League, you mean? Not the new Administration?"

Ari gazed at her. "There's a difference?"

"Isn't there?"

Ari shrugged. "New bottle, old wine. Or maybe not. We just don't know yet what their foreign policy will be."

"Self-interested self interest," Sandy muttered.

"Sure. But implemented how? The old regime did things the nasty, sneaky way, tying up with their worst enemies in the FIA when it suited them. These new guys might look at a breakaway Callay as a potential new ally. Wouldn't surprise me if they start acting real nice and cooperative all of a sudden."

"That'd put them at odds with their old FIA contacts," Sandy pointed out. "With the whole old League Intel network here, like the people who instructed Sai Va to hack Lexi. If it's really changed, we could be looking at a local

League civil war between old regime and new regime operatives here."

Ari smiled at her, pleasantly surprised. "That's amazing, you're a natural at this stuff."

"I'm a natural cynic, if that's a compliment. I always count on League dark ops trying to screw everything up."

"They've certainly been trying," Ari agreed.

"Only Sai Va's an anarchist lunatic who doesn't care which big organisation he screws," she ventured, "and so a few buddies in the fellow lunatic scene ask him if he knows anyone big they could try and blow up, and he offers them Lexi."

Ari nodded, chewing contentedly. As if further pleased she was doing so well.

"It's certainly the only way that bunch of amateurs could draw a bead on Lexi," he agreed. "So now the GGs have put two and two together . . . and made five, incidentally . . . and they're after Sai Va." Sandy raised her eyebrows. "His main hideout's been ransacked, I was just there this morning, and the GGs might just have enough favours to call in from enough people to put him in real hot water, because, of course, *they* don't want to get the blame for blowing up Lexi . . . So Sai Va's gone to ground before they can extract revenge one toe at a time."

"And now the League's here," Sandy added. Ari nodded, speechless for a moment with a mouthful. "And you just *know* they're going to want to clean up their mess . . ." She didn't feel at all happy about it. Ari nodded again, reluctantly conceding. ". . . with GIs."

He smiled, finally swallowing. "And that's why I invited you along. Even up the odds a bit."

Sandy gave him a very flat, dark look.

"Gee, Ari, you really know how to make an invitation to lunch into such a romantic occasion."

Ari shrugged. "What can I say? I'm just a romantic, dashing, handsome kind of guy."

CHAPTER 6

Ari hadn't chosen Zaiko just for the view. Clustered, busy urbanity crowded thick and close to the river bend. Ari led Sandy along a roadway busy with midday traffic holding to centrally governed speeds. The pedestrian traffic was mostly office workers, clustered into cafes and restaurants along the stretch, crowding streetside tables beneath rows of towering neon signage. And beneath gleaming towers soaring higher still against the clear blue sky.

They crossed at a ped-crossing, into the mouth of a huge, open mall flanked by holographic displays, the awning-style ceiling stretching over them many storeys overhead. Everything in this place, Sandy noted as they walked, was tech. Other regions of Tanusha had many stores with traditional clothes, ethnic restaurants, chic fashion, books, ornaments, traditional medicines and others. Downtown Zaiko, it seemed, was all rad-tech fashion. Clothes stores sported displays of wild hair, neon colours and body piercings. Tech stores abounded—display sets, interlink modules, vehicular upgrades, net intel appliances, plus all manner and range of gizmos and generally useless yet trendy junk . . . which accounted for a good half of the Federation consumer tech market, she recalled hearing one economist saying on TV. A particularly plush-looking shopfront advertised an upstairs surgery with "the latest advances in sensory enhancement technology." And another announced a special package deal to "get a visual and audio upgrade, we'll upgrade your net interface to a VX-1800 for free!"

"Sounds real quality," Sandy suggested dryly, nodding at the frontage as they passed.

"Oh no," Ari said unconcerned, "they're not too bad. Everyone here's registered, licensed and legal. They're just low-class establishments for people who can't afford better. You wouldn't catch a professional there, legal or otherwise."

"Where do the pros go?"

"Well, of course, legal pros get it paid for by their employer . . . in my case, now, the CSA. That's a full hospital job . . . though, of course, if you're rich enough you can afford that too, so long as it's legal. Of course, CSA has access to a whole range of stuff that's not available to the general public."

She knew that well enough, Vanessa had capabilities that would have gotten a public citizen arrested. But she also knew that not all public citizens abided by those restrictions. She had no doubt that the man walking beside her had numbered among them, before his CSA days. Maybe that was part of the attraction of joining? For his comrade Kazuma, in particular, she could well guess.

"And where do the illegals go?" she asked him.

"I'll show you."

He led her into a nondescript corridor off the main mall between two Chinese restaurants, and past a few small shops beyond. The corridor turned left at a decorated Chinese-style gateway, and an even more nondescript flight of stairs headed underground on the right. Ari led her down with the confident stride of someone who knew precisely where he was going, dark boots rattling a quick descent. A passageway opened to the right of the stairs, past the stairway's faded wooden railings. Sandy stared about in astonishment as they reached the passage and kept walking.

The passageway was gloomy, the lighting a poor industrial fluorescent, shadowy in patches. The floor was a worn and untended ferrocrete, the walls little more than the ferrocrete base of the buildings above. Torn posters adorned the walls, new plastered over old, pictures advertising what might have been music, parties or other gatherings . . . it was hard to tell, the writing was mostly a combination of Chinese characters, Hindi, and something that she vaguely recognised as stylised Sanskrit. Her memory implants allowed her to read just about any language ever written, although slowly, but this stylised, jargon-dense, colloquial stuff was difficult. There were no doors along the immediate stretch ahead, just posters, the occasional graffiti and some exposed plumbing that looked suspiciously jerry-rigged through rough holes drilled in the ceiling and floor.

"Wow," she said, keeping a brisk pace at Ari's shoulder, "this is the first genuine dump I've seen since I've been in Tanusha."

"You haven't seen anything yet, this is just the first level." Ari's long strides ate up the distance quickly—GI or not, her shorter legs had to hurry to keep up. "The planners weren't as omnipotent as they like to pretend. There were lots of sites like this underground, intended for storage, parking, underground manufacturing, whatever. As the city grew it became apparent that some of them weren't viable for their original designation. No one wanted them, the official real estate agencies wouldn't touch them with bio-sanitation gloves. They got bought up and renovated by whatever groups could find a use for them. And being underground, they're not made accountable to the style and culture police."

"What's wrong with the style regulations?" Shifting to local network scan, and finding an immediate, god-awful mass of heavily shielded local systems. "They certainly keep the city beautiful."

"They're *mandatory*," Ari said with emphatic humour. "Can't have it, you see. Some people don't like anything mandatory."

Sandy gave him a sideways glance. "Friends of yours?"

Ari shrugged. "Maybe. On my bad days." And he reached into his right pants pocket, withdrew the pistol Sandy had spotted long before, and handed it to her. She took it wordlessly, withdrew it briefly from the tight holster, and gave it the usual once-over. Once finished she tucked the holster into a thigh pocket, checked the safety a final time and pushed the pistol into her shoulder holster beneath the jacket.

The passageway ended at an open doorway to the right, blocked only by a curtain of dangling beads. Ari brushed through it first, Sandy following to find herself on a walkway a level above the broad, open floor of what looked like a restaurant. More decorative than she'd have guessed from the passageway. Suspended lights and decorations along the ceiling above a floor filled with tables. A large, open bar along the far side, the wall behind stacked with a profusion of drinks.

A stairway led down to the floor. Sandy eyed the lights and holography rigging along the ceiling corners, rotating reflective panels . . . the place would come alive at night. Now it was empty and echoing, table surfaces bare but for standing menus and glasses. A man polished glasses and arranged drinks behind the bar, and a robot server stalked on backward, bird-like legs among the tables, polishing and preening.

She kept an eye on the robot as they made the floor. It was not a common sight in Tanusha, most restaurateurs preferring human service to automated. And the rapidly accumulating security map on her uplinks showed her enough nonstandard barriers and access points to make her suspicious of all kinds of unsuspected internal setups. Robots of any kind could integrate into that, there was no telling what a few technical wizards could implant into its CPU-integrated software.

"Ari!" called the broad, jovial man behind the bar. "What brings you down here at such an ungodly hour?"

"Hi, Ahmed," said Ari, walking over to lean upon the bar. It was cut into a wave shape, stools along the bends.

Sandy remained behind by one of the tables, fully uplinked and watching the long-toed, stalking gait of the server-bot that wound its way among the tables like a tame, headless heron. The aircon whirr was particularly loud ... they were under a tower/retail complex, two levels down, and a reflexive hack into the publicly available building schematics showed her the relevant blueprints. The air venting wasn't even connected to the main system above, it was all separate, as was the powergrid. And, of course, the comnet. Highly inefficient. Unless someone was paranoid enough to want to limit all points of access. Which explained the complicated barrier functions at limited access nodes in the comnet, restricting all unauthorised use.

And there was a certain, unnatural sweet smell in the air that caught her attention ... purifier, from the aircon, self-recycling. She knew that smell very well, from space stations and other self-contained facilities, usually military. And now this limited entry, a single passageway leading down to a restaurant ... manned by a single sentry plus robot while all the others who lived and worked down this way would no doubt be fast asleep from a long night's activity. She was beginning to form an idea of exactly what kind of place this was.

"I'm looking for Arnoud," Ari said to the broad, Arabic man behind the bar, "is he around?"

"Oh, gee, I dunno," said Ahmed with theatrical ignorance. "Lotta people looking for Arnoud lately, you know? Lotta people ... but I could check ..." And got a better look at Sandy as she took slow steps out from behind Ari, keeping the stalking server-bot in view, and getting a better reception of room-mounted scanners. She'd detected four so far, all heavily shielded. "Oh baby! Ari, who's your new partner, huh? My faith in you is restored, my man, much better taste than that other little slanty eyed bitch . .." Leaned forward heavily on the bar, the open top buttons of his shirt revealing copious amounts of black, curly hair across his bulging, muscular chest. Grinning unpleasantly. "Hey, baby! What's your name, honey?"

"You don't want to do that," Ari told him, smiling broadly.

"Why not? She frigid or something?"

"Just trust me. You *don't* want to do that."

Sandy ignored them, having found a vulnerable gap through one of the remote security nodes that linked the monitors from this room to a central system . . . she acquired the signal, probed and received a reply. Reconfigured that coding's barrier elements into her own mutation—basic League-configured military applications, it all ran pretty much automatically through the internal visuals in her head. The mutation confirmed itself complete a micro-second later and she sent it . . . the security node accepted it as one of its own coding family, and then she was in, and the local network opened up before her. It wasn't very big, geographically, just this little underground area, one large city block coming within a hundred metres of the river. But it contained . . . she did a fast count, and came to 296 separate, self-contained, heavily barricaded networks. A living warren of independent network identities. A hacker haven.

"Arnoud's not in," said Ahmed, continuing to watch Sandy as she strolled, his eyes trailing up and down appreciatively. "He's moved, didn't say where . . . guess he wanted a change of scene."

"Okay, that's what he paid you to say," Ari said pleasantly enough. "Why don't you quit screwing me around and tell me before I get angry and hurt you?"

"Ari Ari Ari . . ." Ahmed turned to him, much aggrieved, hands wide and imploring. "I do no such thing, I tell you he's gone, that's all he tells anyone, he doesn't exactly advertise, you know?"

"Arnoud," Ari had briefed Sandy in the remainder of their lunch, "was a close associate of Sai Va's. He lived down here with his own little tribe of friends, fellow netsters all, amassing considerable fortunes through legal work and paying taxes like any regular citizen . . . which provided an effective cover for all his other favourite activities.

"Ahmed," Ari said with measured calm, "if he'd left, I'd have heard. I haven't heard."

"Hey, you know, even you can't keep up with everything, Ari," Ahmed said reasonably.

"Don't bet on it. Now if I just walk in there, I'll trip his security systems and there'll be trouble . . . I'll make sure you get blamed for it, Ahmed, believe me . . ."

"They've been branched," Sandy announced the instant her netsearch found it. Ari and Ahmed both stared at her. "Someone's spliced the intranet triggers. I can see it clearly, it's a League format program, doesn't show up real well on Federation systems." Racing along internal visual schematics, a quick scan of relevant corridors and elevator shafts . . . "There's at least another four ways into here. I think someone's inside, I can't pin where, that security's a different format entirely."

Ari pulled the pistol from the back of his waistband and levelled it at Ahmed's chest with the cool expression of a man about to pull the trigger with no remorse at all. "I see the League XO-grid barriers you got from the Verdrahn GGs doesn't seem to be working today, Ahmed . . . I just *know* you can read that stuff when it tries to break in."

"How big's the leak?" Sandy asked, calmly pulling her own weapon, accessing as much from the local grid as she could without causing alarm to any tripwires the intruders would surely have placed alongside the usual security mess. Ahmed stood frozen, eyes wide and previously expressive mouth firmly shut.

"Could be real big," said Ari, "not many people use League infiltration software around here, narrows down the options. Ahmed, talk."

"'Bout what?"

Sandy strode over, grabbed his arm and yanked him flying over the bar counter. He hit the ground with an awkward flail of limbs, face down as Sandy twisted the arm up behind him. Too startled to even yell.

"As you probably just figured," she told him, "I'm a GI. Talk or I'll rip your arm off. Who's in there and what are they after?"

"GGs," Ahmed gasped, recovering from the stunning impact, "they want Arnoud, they think he helped Sai Va. Revenge, you know? Not real happy boys, don't like to be screwed around . . ."

"Let's go," said Ari, moving out from behind the bar, headed across to the pair of doors in the far restaurant wall . . . Sandy saw the left-side doorway move from the corner of her eye, snapped her right arm out and levelled a rapid burst, sending the emerging gunman flying backward, heavy rifle flailing away . . . tumbling slowly in the dazed slow motion of abrupt combat reflex. She registered the model. The falling body. The long cloak and jacket. The wild hair. The TS-4 assault sweeper, military grade and hardly befitting even Tanushan mafia. And she guessed what was coming.

"Get down!" she yelled at Ari, whose pistol was only now coming up to meet the falling threat. Sprinted across the table-strewn floor, across the doorways as weapons fire erupted, destruction shredding tables, chairs and walls in a deafening roar as she reached the side wall at full acceleration. Sprang up and ran three paces across the vertical surface, gathered before falling, and leapt full power back across at the doors, firing in midair trajectory. Rounds struck the splintering doorway, already shredded from the other side, then she hit the wall in hard collision ten metres from her springboard, then hit the floor.

The man she'd first shot exploded back through the door, apparently unharmed, his weapon swinging down onto her . . . She scythed his legs from under him with an explosive twist, grabbed a shoulder in mid-fall to smash his head to the floor—noting the hardened thud of body armour even as she disarmed him—and smacked through the still-swinging doorway. Bludgeoned the big man beyond with the rifle and was amazed when he caught it and swung back with his meaty left . . . which she caught, leapt an explosive knee into his midriff, hammered an airborne right foot into the corridor wall for the leverage to smash him into the opposite wall as he doubled over, crunched and rebounded as violently as the physics of a confined space would allow.

The corridor beyond was clear, the doorway she'd just come through was a nuisance, so she kicked it off its hinges in an explosion of wood fragments, broken hinges taking pieces of old wall with them. Spun one-armed back around the corner in time to find Ari already going through the second doorway . . . damn. Uplinks raced ahead through surrounding schematics—barrier functions locking down potential threats, isolating access points, colonising transmission nodes . . . it triggered counter alarms and traps but she didn't care, an activated trap could not surprise, she hated surprises. She covered Ari's doorway, noting the scene of ruin in the restaurant, Ahmed scrambling terrified back behind the bar for cover, miraculously untouched amid the shattered kindling of chairs and tables, a huge swathe of devastation that included a vicious line of holes through decorations and paintings along the far wall. The server-bot stalked gingerly through the ruin, long-fingered arms reaching to remove bits of wreckage and place them on its body tray for transport, seeking the previous orderliness. Not so smart after all.

Ari's doorway was missing a big central hole where the gunman had opened fire with something very heavy from the other side . . . her own rounds had gone through that hole, she knew she'd hit something. But the body armour. She'd never heard of Tanushan mafia being so well armed. Or trained—remembering the big man catching her first blow. Seriously augmented reflexes to match her like that. Fast, augmented, heavily armed and seemingly ruthless. Not GGs. Which meant . . .

"This guy's gone," came Ari's voice on uplink. *"You hit him, there's no bullet holes . . . must be body armour, hallway's clean, you clear?"*

"Clear. I got two . . . and a better weapon . . ." Crouching as she formulated, searching the fallen man's coat for magazines, her weapon still covering Ari's door and her own corridor simultaneously. *"Who are they?"*

"*More anarchist types . . . call them assassins, we've got a few, don't advertise them much, GGs hire them for big jobs . . . I'm going after Arnoud, take the other corridor, you'll get there faster . . .*"

"*No way, you stay there and wait for me . . .*" The spare mags locked together on electro-lock, snapped in turn to the loaded mag, and she spun back to collect the big man's weapon where he'd fallen. "*You go in there uncovered against this lot, you'll get killed . . .*"

"*Sandy, I can't wait, you follow the corridor to this point . . .*" An encrypted attachment came through in a rush of adjoining data that unfolded across her internal schematic . . . "*Get there fast and . . .*"

"*Ari, I'm ranking combat ops here, I'm giving you an order! Ari!*" Grabbing up the second weapon and mags, and wondering again at the lunacy of working in an organisation that only issued her with popguns on field ops against military-spec assault rifles and body armour . . . "*Ari, you fucking lunatic!*" And . . . "shit" to herself, audibly.

Couldn't operate with two heavy weapons out of a suit, she needed a free arm for leverage . . . Placed one weapon's muzzle to the floor and kicked down on it, breaking it explosively inwards, and moved off at a light, springing jog down the dark corridor, reluctant to leave ammo behind but not dressed to carry it. Anyway, with aim like hers, fire volume wasn't an imperative.

The local grid was a mess, it was difficult to get a clear look—individual barrier functions were activated, isolating and attacking her own probing seeker functions and disrupting her reception . . . she winced as the schematic overlay flickered and buzzed, figuring the possible points of entry for the infiltrators as she ran, cross-referencing that with the location Ari had fed to her. The corridor ended in a T-junction, a broad ferrocrete hallway lit by flickering neon . . . the schematic showed her stairs, doorways, adjoining rooms. Darted a quick look each way, found it empty and ran right.

Macro-scan graphic had now pieced together enough

glimpses of the entire layout to give her a general overview
of the place—it flashed to life across her internal vision, a
big, three-levelled rectangle of right-angled corridors, each
lined with separate rooms. A few common rooms on the
lowest level, a generator function that routed power from
god-knew where, but mostly just accommodation, like a
big, dull ferrocrete hotel. With corridor ambience like this,
she reckoned it should have been damn cheap. But
somehow she doubted it was.

Locked doorways along the sides as she ran, residents
typically asleep at this hour, she guessed. If they weren't
asleep, they certainly wouldn't be coming out now. And
heard popping fire echoing from where Ari could have been
. . . she couldn't reach him, had neither com nor scan reception in this much local shielding and fragmentation. But
basic tactical awareness told her where he ought to be . . .

She took a hard left down a dingy narrow corridor,
edging sideways past big protruding sewerage pipes,
booted feet scuffing echoes off the walls . . . the air smelt
different, and that told her something of the ventilation
too. Paused at the opening to the next, larger hallway . . .
it stood empty and shadowed with industrial fluorescent.
Heavy doors lined the walls with irregularity, security key-
pads prominent by each. Sounds of muted footsteps echoed
on maximum enhancement, voices, something high
pitched that could have been a whimper . . . plus the ever-
present hum of ventilation, the tick of improvised water
pipes, a rustling that might have been a small rodent.
Super-enhanced hearing was not always useful, it was difficult to prioritise. Next corridor down, the schematic
showed her. This was main residential. People lived here,
isolated, cut off from the teeming masses of the city above.
Gloomy existence, she registered vaguely beyond the over-
poweringly sharpened combat reflex.

She darted a quick left, ran along several doorways,
spotted the stairwell doorway, grasped the handle and
yanked, flattening herself to the wall alongside . . . the
door-trap exploded, door, debris and dust erupting vio-

lently across the hallway. Sandy ducked straight into it and rattled down the stairs beyond, figuring the device was a recent plant, again military grade and antipersonnel, probably a five-gram nitro-charge with laser trigger on the doorframe. It had been planted low on the opening side, standard operational boobytrap to cover an exposed flank. The lower stairwell door had one too, this time on her side of the door . . . She took aim from the stairwell bend and fired. Everything vanished in a flash of blinding debris through which she ran and dived, rolling out into the hallway beyond.

Shot the gunman ten metres away who was still flinching from the blast, then snap-rolled up into a spinning sidekick on the poor unfortunate who'd been sheltering beside the doorframe—he flew four metres through the air, bounced diagonally off the wall, tumbled and bounced away in a spinning flail of limbs. Rearranged her shoulder holster back into place as she resumed her fast jog . . . The man she'd kicked was still alive, thanks to the body armour, and her kindly impulse to limit his flight to a mere four metres—when the far end of the corridor would not have been beyond her. Ditto the man she'd shot—one round low to the left abdomen where the vest would absorb enough power to keep the wound shallow. She'd seen blood, but heatscan showed the continual pulse of warmth through his jugular, he'd only lost consciousness. Shaved head but for a central strip of hair tied back into a long ponytail. Dark shades askew. Black trench coat, rings and a few tattoos. Self-appointed renegades, getting their jollies on some techno-warrior fantasy—serious enhancements, military-grade weapons, pay cheques from mafia in need of jobs performed . . . a great life for the anti-socially inclined. Utterly disconnected from the grander scheme of reality and consequences. This guy probably never reckoned on the real world ever leaping up and biting him on his tattooed, unsuspecting, pathetic, ignorant arse.

"Think again," she murmured to herself, the corridor ahead a mass of colour-swathed blues and greys, and red footprints of recent heat. And further distant sounds that echoed the corridors on frequencies the unaided human ear could not hear. Two rounds fired so far . . . probably ammo wouldn't be a problem after all. Flank penetrated, it would probably take the remainder another few seconds to respond . . .

A rifle appeared around a corner ahead, scanning remotely . . . Sandy shot it from the wielder's hands, and accelerated explosively as a grenade followed—standard timer-fuse, she had time to note as it flew. Someone had panicked and forgotten to count off. She was past it and diving across the adjoining corridor before it exploded, firing low on semi-automatic as she flew half-propelled by the blast, cutting the gunman's legs from under him. Came back around the corner as fast as she could recover her momentum, spared a brief check of the downed man as he sprawled screaming and convulsing—there was a lot of blood, but she guessed his micro-augmentations would shut off the blood flow before it got dangerous, and probably knock him out cold too for safety.

Further progress was blocked by a heavy metal grill-door across the corridor, with full security precautions. She smashed it off its hinges with a front kick—not caring about the alarms it doubtless triggered through the complex—and proceeded around the twisted, sparking gate, noting the trailing wires and guessing their function. Crouched low, with rifle levelled at the heavy security doorway ahead that terminated the corridor. A bubble-recess in a wall alongside for full-spectrum scanners was the most obvious of the sur-veillance measures, and the door itself was heavy inset metal, chip marks around the frame where it appeared to have been jerry-rigged into a standard doorframe. She guessed it was locked tight like a bank vault.

She put a round through the bubble, which exploded in scattering fragments, and another into a less conspicuous indentation alongside the door from which she could sense active scan emissions . . . they'd know she was here, sub-tlety was pointless now. And tried a fast override-and-hack of the door systems with her most capable attack barrier on the network . . . it broke through one barrier, was blind-sided by another, and then the whole visual picture in her mind's eye began to disintegrate as hidden counter-func-tions materialised from the network in swirling snarls of electronic mayhem. Secondary barrier elements recon-structed themselves behind the first, impeding further progress. Damn underground netsters, she should have guessed they'd have better defensive software against League attack barriers than the government did . . .

And she wound up her best sidekick, executed with full and proper technique from the close-combat manual . . . WHAM! The impact reverberated through the narrow ferrocrete corridor like a pile driver concussion, billowing dust erupting from about the doorframe as ferrocrete shat-tered from the force, and the whole heavy door framework rocked backward several centimetres. A second kick, this time not connecting quite properly as a hip-flexor protested unexpectedly—she rammed herself backward several metres, flew through the air, hit and rolled back-ward to her feet, suppressing a curse. Overhead an exposed water mains broke, hissing water spraying the walls and floor. Damn muscles weren't allowing her to execute with proper technique. She only weighed sixty kilos, smashing something with a force of several thousand kilos pressure per square centimetre would throw her ten metres back down the hall if she didn't execute properly. The Chinese had figured the mechanical basics out over a thousand years ago . . . now she just had to convince her less-than-optimum body to perform it properly. Though if she'd had another firm wall to put her back against, she could have just levered it open like a hydraulic jack.

She walked back amid the drenching spray of water, feeling the slightly awkward, rolling gait brought on by the hard contraction of steely leg muscles. The door looked like it had bent away from the frame just a little at the top right corner . . . she visualised the physics of it, the weak-ness and the required point of impact, tensioning and rippling the required torso, leg and shoulder muscles for the motion to come. Acquired the proper tension, a hard, bulging pressure beneath her skin, and leapt. Full shoulder rotation, the hips came about and slammed the right foot heel-first through the door at blistering velocity, sending the impact straight back up her leg and thigh . . . The door exploded off its reinforced hinges and rammed edge-first into the wall beyond, exposed circuits crackling smoke beneath the water spray as she completed the full spin and sprang through the twisted doorframe . . . and found that someone had beaten her in.

A broad living room spread to the left of the narrow entrance hall across which the main door was now impaled, sliced into the opposite wall. A huge hole gaped in the living room's ceiling, a pile of dusty, crumbling ferrocrete scattered upon the stone-paved floor . . . she recognised the signature of an explosive charge immediately. Shaped for maximum downward force, it made a precise, clean hole through concussion-vulnerable materials like ferrocrete, bending the support struts like so . . . She edged forward, rifle slowly pivoting, examining the hole through one side of her peripheral vision, noting the telltales.

The partition to the second half of the room was low, the interior space spanning a broad floor paved with more dark stone. Low, dark, modern furnishings and dim, moody lighting. A big wall-vision unit on the left above the dining table, the sleek gloom cut brightly open by a large, brightly lit fish tank in the far wall, colourful fish floating dreamily in an oasis of light. But for the explosive entry, there was very little damage, and the heavy-security residence retained its intended darkly sophisticated feel of moody atmosphere. Underground tech-heads liked it, she guessed, edging past the main partition into the broad living space, noting the full VR headsets and immersion hookups trailing wires about the thick leather sofa set, and the broad bank of display units surrounding the twin chairs in the far corner by the fish tank. The floor beneath those units, she saw with little surprise, was soaked with blood.

She rounded the side of the display setup, and found a body sprawled, machine-pistol limply in hand, a single round drilled neatly through the centre of his forehead, a similar hole in the wall behind where he would have been sitting when the intruders had blasted their way in through the ceiling. A light weapon, for it not to have taken his head off. Short range, light, mobile, good for close-in fighting. Professionals.

The display screens were off, connecting cables ripped clear. The body pulled far enough aside to allow one or two people to sit or stand, access the terminals, get what they'd come for and leave the way they'd come, up through the ceiling. She took a deep breath, rifle unerringly sighted upon the darkened room that to combat-vision looked alive and gleaming with bright and complicated detail. She knew exactly what this op was, she'd done them herself. She could have been revisiting the scene of her own past history. Only she'd have hoped to put a hole through this half-competent techie's shoulder, not his head. No need for it, normally. Someone was on very strict orders.

She did a fast search of the apartment's other rooms, finding only empty, if moderately flashy, residential quarters, bedrooms and a bathroom—all recently occupied and occasionally littered with empty cans or bottles, display readers or technical manuals of varying description. Finished her search in time to hear a scuffing of sound beyond the outside hiss of water from the broken pipe, then coming through the door . . . just the right sound and pace to be Ari, she guessed. He wasn't bothering to slow down, evidently having guessed who'd caused the carnage outside. He came in somewhat less wet than she, paused briefly to consider the scene in the living room, then came striding over to where she was reexamining the body by the terminal centre. He was breathing hard but by no means exhausted. His right hand grasped an identical TS-4 to her own, its muzzle glowing red hot to her heat sensitive vision, though whether that had been from his own firing, or that of its previous owner, she had no way of telling.

"This wasn't any bunch of amateur assassins," she told him without preamble, "this was professional combat ops. The only professional combat ops in Tanusha who aren't working for us just arrived in the League Embassy."

"GIs?" He looked surprised, but only a little. Paused at her side to consider the sprawled body on the floor, and the precision of the bullet hole. Exhaled with a hard grimace. "Yeah, I'll buy that. How'd they get in and blow a hole without triggering alarms?"

"Same way the League always does it," Sandy replied, moving to a covering position in the centre of the room as Ari stepped over the body and began examining the monitors and equipment around the workstation. "I think that's what I picked up before, it wasn't the GGs' thugs at all, it was the GIs. The GGs must have put people to cover their flanks, then discovered they'd been beaten here, I'd guess they've gone off to look for them."

"Yeah, well, they better hope they don't find them." Peering behind one terminal unit to examine the damage. "This is all fucked, no prints or anything . . . any more bodies?"

"Nothing. If there was anyone here, the GIs took them with . . . this guy's probably only dead because he resisted and the mission brief didn't include carrying injured targets."

"Um . . . I reckon instead they got out early, maybe someone tipped them off." Ari straightened up, glancing about, biting absently at his bottom lip. Halfway between boyish indecision and cool, measured consideration. Dark-browed eyes narrowed with a certain intelligent intensity. "There's no point in hostages, the data's in the mainframe, you get that and get out. Hostages just get in the way."

Sandy nodded, it was logical. "What data?" she asked. "Sai Va's contacts? Locations?"

Ari gave her a sceptical sideways look.

"Dammit, if they got just a quarter of what these guys are involved with, it'll be a lot more than just Sai Va." Pointed at the corpse at his feet. "That's Lu Fayao, the SIB has been trying to get enough evidence to bust him for the last three years. He's got access formulations to parts of the network even Ibrahim's not allowed to have. Assuming this was League GIs, who's it likely to be and how many?"

Sandy took a deep breath, vision fixed upon the precise, person-wide hole in the ceiling. Visualising the broader regional schematic, the number of troops required to infiltrate, cover, execute and fade . . .

"I'd reckon a single tac-section, five GIs, probably mid-20s." Pause. "Maybe higher." A wary look from Ari. She didn't blame him. She didn't like the idea much herself. "They'll be decked out for black ops, real silent stuff, nothing dramatic. Their intel will be excellent, to get in like this without detection."

"Yeah, well, we got a lot of League contacts after the big blowup—but we were never going to get all of them . . ." He performed a brief recheck of his new weapon, handling it with an easy familiarity that raised Sandy's suspicions of Ari's previous associations even further. ". . . let's go, we might still get something if we move fast."

"This job's a half hour old, Ari," Sandy replied as he strode past, "they'll have gotten out within five minutes the way these guys operate . . ."

"Uh-uh." Ari shook his head, pausing beside the pile of ferrocrete rubble beneath the ceiling hole, eyeing the ragged rim cautiously. "These guys have at least two other contacts down here in the warren, if they got in this quietly they'll have searched those places too . . ." Gave her a quick, distracted look. "You coming?" And leapt—with the easy grace of athletic augmentation—caught a handful of rim one-handed and hauled himself quickly up and out of sight.

Sandy stared. And followed, restraining her frustration with an effort. Leapt, caught and yanked herself through with a fast vault, and found herself in an upper apartment room with similar furnishings and lived-in appearance . . . no sign of the occupants, possibly tied up in an adjoining room. She had no time to check, and Ari was already headed out the front door, which was closed but unlocked, evidently hacked the quiet way.

"*Ari!*" she snapped on the private connection, and he paused to let her edge past and sneak first look into the main hallway. When she didn't draw fire, Ari moved to go past . . . Sandy grabbed him by the jacket collar, pivoted smoothly and thumped him back against the wall of the entrance corridor. He blinked at her in dazed alarm as she fixed him with a hard, point-blank stare.

"You didn't say anything about other sites," she whispered harshly . . . uplinked communication was probably smarter in the hallways, but she needed to make a point. "What else haven't you told me?"

"Sandy . . . look, this is very important . . ."

"D'you know why they never assigned me with a direct commanding officer for field ops in Dark Star? Because they knew damn well I'd shoot him if he fucked around with the lives of my team, and they knew it was damned unlikely he'd know better than me what to do. Do you think *you* know better?"

Ari blinked again, somewhat stunned. Not your sexy, cuddly pet GI now, huh? She kept her stare dangerously direct. He took a hurried breath.

"Sandy, this isn't a Dark Star op, there are civilian concerns here and you don't know all the angles . . ."

"Because you don't fucking tell me anything. Who are these other people and why didn't you tell me about them before?"

"Sandy . . . they're just more contacts of Sai Va's, I didn't think it'd be that important . . ."

"Jesus Christ, Ari, when you put me into a firefight, you tell me *everything*! When it comes to survival I'm not negotiable, you got me?" A brief, wary nod. Not frightened, she doubted she could ever bluff him into thinking she might actually hurt him. Just wary. And about bloody time, too. "Now where are these people, and how can we get there?"

Again the uplink connected to hers, she accessed and

the picture drew itself clearly across her internal schematic, two rooms at differing points of the underground complex.

"You take the north one," Ari suggested, unperturbed by the forearm pressure that pinned him to the wall. "I'll get the other . . . these GIs, could they access your com-links?"

League software, Dark Star formalities . . . she made a face. "It's possible." Released him with a dark, warning look. Ari tugged his shirt back into place as if nothing had happened. "We'll keep it silent . . . I'll meet you at yours, I move faster. Ari, if you get in their way, surrender—they'll know we're here now, they'll know it's you, and they're not going to want to kill CSA operatives. You *can't* shoot your way out, it's just not possible. Agreed?"

His eyes flashed with an unexpected, crooked smile. "I'm learning." And he left at a jog, giving her a flamboyant whack on the backside as he passed. Sandy took a brief moment to shake her head in disbelief before running after him.

Their paths diverged at the first cross-corridor, his headed left while she sprang lightly on ahead, vision-scanning for any signs of telltale movement or recent heat-imprints. The schematic unfolded before her—the new site Ari had assigned her was over on the north side of the warren . . . surprising in its isolation, no nearby escape routes. Possibly a good thing, given that routes out were also routes in.

She duck-scanned at the next T-junction, finding only another empty length of dingy corridor . . . sounds echoed, soft footsteps and voices from several hallways down, doubtless some of the locals had awoken to the commotion and braved the outside. She resolved to factor unarmed civilians into her firing equations, pushed off left and kept running. Another right—wide doorways in the scarred ferrocrete on her left, open space littered with empty crates and boxes—warehouse space she guessed, ignoring the darting run of a long-bodied rodent across the corridor before her. The air smelt stale, more fluoros were out, plunging sections of echoing hallway into shadow. Another cross-corridor ahead, the air smelling different as the ventilation currents changed, and a big, ragged hole in the left wall dripped leaking water and condensation from cracks somewhere higher in the structure . . .

She stopped, her back to the right-side wall at the T-junction. Something wasn't right. Her target apartment was just several more corners away through the increasingly dank and crumbling corridors. She visualised it on her schematic, a broad view showing her present relation to the tower retail complex above, and the flanking streets and entry points, ventilation and com-grids . . . she was out from under the overhead complex now, a side street was several storeys directly overhead. Dirt between here and the surface, which explained the damp—being built on a frequently rain-soaked river delta, Tanusha was wet. The soil gathered a lot of moisture and care was taken in building plans to avoid too much underground construction as it would displace the sponge-like qualities and cause the rivers to overflow and flood.

She reopened several adjoining links in a darting flash of electronic intent, connected into adjoining systems and saw that Ari's target apartment was directly under the main overhead tower complex, and barely ten metres from an elevator shaft. The elevator shaft had a security override to prevent it from descending down this far, and the shaft itself registered as blocked—all this lower part was "unofficial infrastructure," doubtless the owners of the overhead complex didn't advertise the nature of the residencies that existed below. She vision flashed across the registrar notice of tenant companies, scrolling rapidly until she hit . . . Tetsu Incorporated, Administration and Marketing Division.

She recalled the raid she and SWAT Four had led on Tetsu nearly a month previous, in the midst of the FIA-infiltration crisis that unfolded following the Parliament Massacre and the attempt upon President Neiland's life. Up to their necks in it, Tetsu had been. Federal Intelligence Agency plants in middle management feeding illegal biotech data to equally illegal FIA anti-GI researchers. And separate League plants accepting the illegal knowledge that the League were willingly feeding them in an attempt to undermine the biotech restriction regime that remained strenuously enforced throughout the entire Federation. Ari had known the League delegation was newly arrived in town, GIs and all. He hadn't been surprised to find those GIs apparently involved in this present mess. And he'd sent her off in this direction, while he himself headed toward the most obvious entry point for a League infiltration—any League team would be likely still to possess Tetsu access codes, and possibly still have contacts inside, and could come down on the tower landing pads . . .

Dammit, Ari, was her first and immediate thought, what don't you want me to find out?

She ran, fast, internal schematic showing her the quickest shortcut to reach Ari's intended destination, trusting that superior reflexes alone should be adequate to deal with any non-GI threat between here and there. Empty corridors echoed, and she kept her footsteps light and springy, bouncing on her toes with the reflex of long operational practice.

Found the apartment quickly enough—no security barrier this time, the door had been smashed open, contents strewn about the inside, but thankfully no more bodies. She darted back out and on down the adjoining corridor, the open elevator shaft upon her left, doors also forced wide, residual heat from footprints fading quickly on the scuffed ferrocrete outside. She glanced cautiously inside and upwards, weapon ready . . . the shaft zoomed high and empty but for the central cables. There was no physical obstruction blocking the way, whatever the schematic said—a false reading then, placed there to confuse intruders. Probably certain persons who knew the codes simply used the elevator to ride in and out of the warren.

Another hack-and-scan on the schematic showed that an adjoining elevator further up—one that did not descend down this far—was already on call from the ground floor

. . . and the ground floor door to this shaft, which she could see just two levels above her present position, had been hacked. Ari, she guessed. On his way up to the Tetsu level. She shouldered the rifle strap, took a moment to tense the leg muscles in correct proportions, and leapt . . . a calculated release of energy that shot her two levels up the elevator shaft . . . and grasped the central cable at the apex with a steely grip. Had barely begun an override and hack of the opposing elevator door when one of the remote seeker functions she had implanted on the local network abruptly activated another portion of internal schematic. Codes and visual locations flashed across her vision, and she immediately recognised military-grade encryption. Not just military. League. Dark Star.

She threw out a trace seeker immediately. A brief pause as it replicated itself across a series of regional network sources . . . At that moment the elevator cable to which she clung descended abruptly with an activating whine. She switched fast to the opposite cable and caught a ride up, twisted a leg to get some awkward leverage and jumped off as she passed the second floor door. Caught and balanced precariously on the narrow ledge, hacking a second path to this elevator door . . . building security intervened this time, wise now to old tricks . . .

From above her a whistling presence was coming down fast. She didn't need a glance to know how swiftly the car was approaching, and there wasn't enough space for her and it. Hit the door system with her least subtle attack barrier and the electronics simply fried. She smacked an elbow into one door edge to make a dent, got her fingers into the resultant gap and pulled . . . with a grating crunch of protesting mechanisms the doors opened. Into an open hallway on the tower's lower levels, people in suits passing—abrupt shock of alternative locations, the surroundings suddenly bright and gleamingly corporate. She unshouldered the rifle and tossed it back into the elevator shaft, then set off running with a loose, casual gait . . . building security flared red alarm across her internal schematic, registering the infiltration in the elevator shaft. Surely security guards would be on their way.

And then the trace seeker came back to her with what it figured was a reasonable fix on a mobile source on the main road outside the building, moving away at foot speed toward the river . . . Security rounded the corner up ahead, a pair of blue suits with tasers. Sandy produced her badge from a back pocket as she ran, paused long enough for one of them to scan-verify the seal (even security squibs had that basic enhancement in Tanusha), and ignored the following questions, dodging past several more suits as the hallway curved left. The right wall was all transparent, overlooking the road. Glass doors opened onto an open-air cafe overlooking the street below . . . she darted through, skipping quickly between tables and startled diners toward the far right corner of the balcony. Grasped the railings and looked out toward the river.

A four-lane road, traffic banked at the lights of an intersection. Crowded sidewalks, pedestrians walking in the bright sunshine . . . a typically busy downtown Zaiko scene. Another block beyond, the street ended in greenery and a walkway skirting the broad, blue expanse of the river. She overlaid the location her seeker trace had shown on the internal schematic . . . a brief disorientation of distorted vision, graphical lines matching up reference points and measuring distances . . . then came clear, a single, coloured spot flashing clearly upon the right-hand sidewalk amid the passing crowds. Another moment's calculation, adjusting for movement at time of detection, speed and time elapsed . . . the circle vanished and reappeared further on toward the river, moving at walking speed. She frowned, vision-zooming upon the people within the circle, knowing all too well it was an imprecise guess, her target could have changed directions, crossed the street, stopped or started running . . . but there, in the middle of the visually imposed circle, was a man with a heavy jacket, zippers on the shoulders and pocketed cargo pants. Like her own. Black skin, dark sunglasses, hands in pockets and apparently unworried by the heat on this sunny Tanushan day. Cocky bastard. If she'd picked that last transmission, no doubt others would have too. Certain mafia types, especially, having access to League codes that League operatives had been stupid enough to lend them . . .

"Excuse me, ma'am," came a waiter's voice at her elbow, no doubt concerned at the consternation of the other patrons at this rude arrival, "can I help you with something?"

"How 'bout a rope?" Sandy asked. And hurdled the railing before the waiter could consider what the hell she was talking about. Yells of desperate alarm from behind as she fell . . . The broad transparent awning covering the tower's entrance spread directly below at a forty-five-degree downslope. She hit it feet-and-backside first, slid to the rim and leapt off with an extra shove, aiming for an empty space of sidewalk she'd spotted on the way down, hit, rolled with a hand to her side to keep the pistol in place—and set off running as pedestrians around leapt or stopped in double-take startlement at this woman who fell from the sky and into their midst.

She ran comfortably fast, weaving between pedestrians and certain their numbers would block her from view at this distance . . . Ahead the lights on the crossstreet were changing and she put on an extra burst of speed, edging onto the road to avoid collisions and leaping onto the far pavement just as the lights changed . . . her uplinks registered the traffic-net's disapproval, her image caught on visual and no doubt analysed for fines and warnings at Traffic Central, but no big deal, the CSA would pay for it.

She caught a glimpse of the man up ahead as he neared the crossstreet before the riverside park, strolling apparently unawares . . . A groundcar leapt the grass-verged curb opposite with a squeal of tires, men leaping out. Her target vanished with explosive speed into the doorway of the corner building, the five men from the groundcar pouring after him, obviously armed beneath their expensive jackets. She was already sprinting, edging once more onto the road to gain a clear path, uplinks registering a mess of active scans, attack barriers and encoded IDs. Nothing official, nothing CSA, mostly very illegal. She reckoned she'd just found the Tanushan mafia in person, this time without their violent and well-armed mercenaries. And the man they were after was a damn fool for transmitting that signal from the street . . . which could easily mean he was an amateur. Or new in town.

Bashed through the wooden doorway, through the entrance foyer and found two employees sprawled unconscious upon a broad, open nightclub floor . . . uplinks informed her with a rush of three-dimensional data that the building was five storeys of "entertainment complex," nightclub, VR gaming, backroom gambling and backroom sex, all equally expensive . . . and now the local network barriers were making a total mess of her attempts to lock onto local sources.

"CSA!" she yelled at the three startled-looking employees working on the dance floor lighting and sound system in a sea of assorted cables and switches. "Which way'd they go?" A stunned silence, shattered by three tough, tattooed gentlemen who rushed from a side doorway and blocked her path . . .

"You get!" one yelled. "This private property! CSA not allowed, you get!" Very menacingly. She registered the sprawl of tattoos across thick-muscled arms, connected that with the mass of encrypted barriers clogging the network premises, and realised to her extreme displeasure that this too was a GGs establishment. And these guys looked like Yakuza, an ancient phenomenon she'd heard of but never thought to encounter directly . . . bloody Tanushan antiquities, how many of these damn gangs were there, anyway?

Gunfire erupted from back rooms above, heads snapped around and she moved—one grabbed at her and she hit him in the stomach. Snap-kicked the second across the shoulder and threw the third halfway across the dance floor, then raced through the side door and up the next stairway before the three groaning bodies had barely hit the floor.

Got a sudden connection as she reached the second floor and ripped the pistol from her shoulder holster, her systems breaking through the infiltrated chaos on the networks and the complexity hit her in a rush . . . her floor, her level, her present location and the layout around her. Other people's locations, too, and the obscuring mass of static where some new infiltrator was attempting to cover his location and systems . . . More gunfire ahead. Corridor walls and doorways fled past her as she took the corners bouncing off the suavely deep green and decoration-trimmed walls, and once off a staff member. She could hear only too well that some of that fire was rapid-auto, and from the local men's positions on the links, she guessed it wasn't them. Whoever it was, they were coming up a stairwell down the next corridor . . . it loomed ahead, and she slid feet-first along the shiny surface . . . saw the dark figure appearing at the top of the stairwell and yelled, "CSA!," smacking the side of the corridor with her feet and bracing.

Covering gunfire erupted as the gunman ducked back, Sandy ignoring the ill-aimed fire that smacked the walls and ceiling about. Unloaded a rapid ten shots into the stairwell banisters and railings, knowing she hit nothing even as the wood splintered and kicked fragments, but hoping to scare him back down those stairs . . . and remembering vaguely that she wasn't supposed to kill him anyway, even if he shot at her.

Something dark lobbed over the stairwell as she lay braced on one side . . . she tensed a leg and kicked off in barely a split second, hurling herself back down the corridor into a rolling ball, uncoiling once more for a second spring with that momentum as the grenade exploded behind her with a thump that rattled the walls and sent plaster and wood fragments showering about her. She knew the footsteps would be coming even before she heard them, rolled quickly to a crouch by the wall in barely enough time for a black figure to dash blindingly fast by the corridor mouth . . . she snapped fire, one-handed reflex, knowing even then that she'd scored multiple hits. The lack of impact holes in the far wall confirmed it. Scampered forward through the billowing dust of the explosion, pressed her back to the left wall and leaned right . . . even without seeing, she knew there was no body lying there, having heard the footsteps continue onward at frantic pace. Body armour, perhaps . . . but she'd aimed for the legs.

Damn he was fast. And well armed. It gave her a bad, bad feeling.

Yells and footsteps from back down the stairwell. Pursuers climbing . . . she set off in fast pursuit herself, not wanting regular security to try tackling this particular gunman, even if they were only mafia. She skidded to a halt at the next corridor, snapped a fast look around . . .

"Freeze!" yelled a voice from back at the stairwell, obscured through the drifting dust.

"I'm CSA!" she yelled back. "Stay back and I'll get him!"

"CSA, my fuckin' arse!" came the reply, and Sandy spun about the corner in time to avoid a volley of shots that splintered the plastered walls. Buggered, she thought calmly, if she was going to tolerate that crap behind her . . . she had enough to worry about in front.

She snapped a quick look around the corner, pistol out left-handed and fired two fast shots into the murky dust . . . multiple screams and yells of "my fuckin' arm!" and "my leg, my leg!" and she moved off at speed, content that pursuit would now pause for a long moment.

The gunman was not hard to follow, even if her uplinks into the local establishment security failed to grasp the location . . . the lingering effects of whatever virus this guy was using to cover himself, she thought, sliding up against a doorway that should have been locked but instead hung partly off its hinges, bashed open with great force. A quick scan of the layout showed the most likely escape, and she sprinted beyond the doorway, ducked through a bathroom to the frightened yells of several sheltering in the toilet stalls, crashed foot-first through the far door, bounced hard right off the wall, skidded for acceleration, smacked off the right wall to fly sideways into the next upward stairwell, leapt four metres vertically onto the adjoining flight to save time, sprang through that doorway, shoved off hard left and leapt for a flying kick at the end doorway. It exploded off its hinges, as she flew foot first and dropping, pistol out and searching . . . The blow hit her unexpectedly in midair from the side, and she snapped a right fist back into hard contact, losing balance to thump the ground shoulder first and tumbled before coming back fast to her feet.

A moment's fast register, time-lapsed—motion and sound like treacle, blurred and slow. A storeroom. Boxes and junk surrounding. A man waiting for her by the doorway. She'd lost weapon. He'd been thumped in the head, hard. He was still alive. Which meant he was a GI. Like she'd thought. Get him before he recovers.

Her tackle smashed him over backward, locking his gun arm and fighting for leverage even as they somersaulted, him regripping to counter, abandoning the gun, which clattered free as they ceased rolling . . . and suddenly he found a hold, twisted and kicked with force that flung her hard into the nearby wall—her grip on his jacket held and spun him hard about to a crouch. Sandy came off the wall and spun for a full-power kick that smashed him flying eight metres sideways through the air, hammering awkwardly off the wall with force enough to fracture stylish brickwork, and fell out of sight behind some boxes.

She grabbed up his fallen automatic . . . and saw it was a palm-reader, not operable without a personalised operator's signature. Got a good grip and broke it with a brief burst of applied power, a shriek and crack as the handle bent, looking about for her own weapon, full heat scan . . . no reds from hot muzzles, only blues, and the reddish tinge of recent footsteps, and the cracked imprint where the other GI had hit the wall . . .

"Looking for this?" came a voice from behind those boxes. The man was standing, if a little awkwardly, holding her pistol in his hand. Grinned at her as she stared, the muzzle centred with effortless precision upon the centre of her chest. CSA weapons were not palm-readers, securitied only by uplink verification, which was of course vulnerable to rearrangement with the kinds of interface systems a GI had available. Now, staring down the barrel of her own pistol, she wondered why that should be so.

The GI had the appearance of an African man. Whatever that meant, for a GI. Shorter than average, as usual. Not especially muscular or broad, also as usual. Handsome, strong, jet-black features, military-inspired jacket and pants, with many pockets. He stepped around the boxes, and stood before her, not four metres distant. Limping slightly. So she had hit him . . . she eyed several small holes in his pant legs, about the thighs. Sweet fuck-all good it'd do against a GI, with that little civilian pea-shooter. Especially in the thighs. Best to go for a knee or an elbow . . . you could always get lucky. Or the throat or an eye, for a half-chance killshot. Headshots with low-calibre weapons were just an annoyance.

"Cassandra Kresnov, I presume," the GI said. Smiling broadly, in a very handsome way. More than amused. Like he was genuinely pleased to see her.

"Who the fuck are you?" she asked, in no mood for pleasantries with someone pointing a gun at her. Past the deadly combat calm, she suffered a cold tingle up the spine. A GI, one who knew her name. It narrowed the possibilities alarmingly. The man shook his head in amazement.

"I have heard *so* much about you." The cold tingle got worse. He seemed very pleased, for someone she'd just put bullets into and smashed full-force into a wall. "This is amazing. I had expected we would meet, but not so soon. Fate, perhaps."

On the net, there was commotion, people moving and shouting. New arrivals—police and incoming CSA. Somewhere downstairs, a directing shout.

"Who are you?"

He sighed. "Patience. I must go. Don't look for terrorists, Cassandra, they aren't important. The game is elsewhere." Footsteps from somewhere down the corridors. He backed away, headed for the rear window across the storeroom, which was she could see on her schematic within leaping distance of the rear laneway, and escape—for a GI. Sandy regathered herself . . . as soon as he was out that window, she was going after him, gun or no gun. From the last look he gave her, she realised with dismay that he knew it.

"I apologise," he said—and shot her twice in the stomach.

The blows kicked her backward, doubling over with painful force . . . the window shattered, the GI tossed the pistol away, sprang onto the windowsill and leapt into empty space. Several long seconds later, a light thump, then nothing. Sandy made to move for her weapon . . . and realised that it bloody hurt. Gasping, she fell to one knee, holding her middle. Bastard. Utter, fucking bastard. A downward glance showed two small holes in her shirt, and a light, creeping red wetness. Her stomach muscles refused to untense, cramped tight and painful. The cramp spread into her back, and down through her hips and thighs . . . and she recalled certain long ago lessons in GI anatomy, and how stomach muscles connected into nearly everything else, and which loosening exercises needed to be employed to prevent various strains and immobilities . . .

"Oh shit," she muttered to empty air as the pain got worse, "I'm going to get you, you little prick. I'm *really* going to get you . . ."

More voices, getting closer, and she staggered back to her feet, desperately ignoring the pain as she staggered toward her pistol, lying on the floor amid stacks of crates and boxes. He evidently knew something about the CSA, too, in abandoning the weapon—no physical ID locks, but they *did* come with inbuilt trackers that could only be activated by an uplink signal from the wearer or their partner, and thank God for the latter provision in light of the SIB . . .

She squatted, wincing in pain, picked up the pistol, checked and safetied it by reflex, in case the GI had subtly broken or bent some important mechanism. Discovered otherwise, everything appeared to work. Every movement hurt. Stabs of pain shot through her stomach . . . combat reflex was wearing off, and when that happened, the pain came back.

"CSA!" she yelled, as footsteps rushed the doorway, training her weapon on the opening. The footsteps stopped prudently short, perhaps recalling the last time she'd announced those three letters. "If I see any weapons, I'll shoot first this time!"

"This is our fucking premises, you bitch!" came the harsh reply. "Private property. Do you snake morons even know what that means?" Snake . . . derogatory street slang for CSA, she remembered. It was the first time she'd heard it directed at herself.

"Civil emergency!" she retorted, loudly enough to carry well beyond the immediate corridor. "Do you know what that means? It means you point a gun at me, I'll blow your fucking head off!"

Rushdial . . . click—"*Ari, I got a stand-off here, I hope you've been following what's going on . . .*"

"How d'we know you're even CSA? Where'd the guy go, huh? How d'we know your e-ID's not fake? You could be working with him!"

"*Ten seconds, Sandy, I'm nearly there.*" He sounded out of breath—impossible he hadn't realised he'd gone the wrong way, if the GGs had detected that transmission burst, then surely Ari had. He'd probably reversed the elevator and come straight back down on override express.

On the surrounding net, police and CSA active barriers probed the electronic premises, erecting security barriers. Closing transmissions told of approaching vehicles, ground and airborne. Chatter asked for identification, situation . . . Ari's codes, then, responding calmly, covering for her . . . Pause from the corridor. Sounds echoed on full hearing enhancement, heavy breathing, feet shuffling, the electronic code of interlinked transmission and soft, muffled conversation . . . the guys who'd leapt from the car were either from this particular gang, she realised, or from another gang with ties to this Yakuza bunch. She knew such ties existed, gangs here were about profit more than anything, mutual beneficial business relationships were the norm. They'd been cruising, seen their target fortuitously strolling toward friendly premises, and sprung an improvised trap to drive him inside. Bad move, as it turned out. Probably they hadn't known precisely what he was. They should have figured, considering his League codes . . . and she remembered Ari saying the GGs weren't known for their criminal genius . . .

"*Sandy, can you get out the rear window?*"

"Yes." A faint stab of midriff pain through the combat calm. "*Why?*"

"*SIB on the way, among others, if we leave now we can claim hot pursuit . . . he did go out the rear window, didn't he?*"

"Yes." Ari had very good links indeed if he could track that. "*I'll meet you out back. What about these guys?*"

"*I think I just convinced them. This place is as good as surrounded, they're not going anywhere.*"

Zaiko, the next thought occurred to her. Hotbed of activity. Underground and mafia groups in close proximity. A techno haven. No doubt such proximity had been useful in the past, all such underground activity thrived on access to illegal technologies—the GGs for profit, Ari's underground friends for reasons of ideology and lifestyle. Now relations between the two groups seemed a case of familiarity breeding contempt. Another thing Ari hadn't precisely laid out for her.

She walked backward to the window, pistol not wavering from the doorway. Eased herself up onto the ledge, one-handed. Stomach muscles refused to cooperate, shot uncontrollable pain and cramp through her back and legs. She hissed, softly, grabbed the overhead sill with her free hand, pistol still levelled, and glanced under her arm and down. A short space of backyard/garden, high-walled and green. A driving lane beyond that, with a heavy-locked gate for people access. Five storeys, straight down. Shit. This was going to hurt. The garden grass looked a little softer, so she got her feet on the ledge beneath her, and jumped gently outward.

Fell, turning as she went, extending her legs and tensing for impact. Her body not cooperating—that didn't feel right. The drop lasted a long time.

The impact smashed her knees up into her chest, which wasn't supposed to happen, the stunning shock ripped right through her body. Curled up on her knees, she fell slowly onto her side, gasping, in shock more than pain.

"Sandy!" Footsteps running from nearby, and a hand grabbed her arm . . . dangerous, in her present state, but she withheld a reflex shove with effort. "Jesus, are you . . . damn, you're shot. How . . . ?"

"I'm okay." Hoarsely, struggling upright with his assistance. Her legs nearly failed to cooperate, she felt weak and trembling all over. Pressed her free hand to her stomach . . . there wasn't much in the way of capillaries between the hard stomach muscle and surface dermal layer, and GIs required very little blood compared to humans, but losing large quantities was still not a good idea. The shirt felt very wet beneath her hand, and she knew the jump hadn't helped. "Where's the car?"

"It's coming, I called it as soon as I got that transmission . . ." Leading her by the arm, pausing briefly as his linkup codes overrode the rear gate, and swung it open. ". . . what happened? Lucky shot?"

"No." Ari, it seemed, had a very high opinion of her martial capabilities. She wondered vaguely if he were disappointed. "GI." Out into the laneway—high-walled to the sides and a long walk to either exit. Ari leaned her against the side wall, his own hand pressed over her own. She breathed deeply, pain returning as the combat reflex diminished, trying to loosen her diaphragm as breathing became awkward. "Smart one. Damn smart."

"How smart?" Thoughts racing at lightning speed through his dark eyes, a thick eyebrow furrowing. "Better than . . . than what, a 35?"

"Ari, I have no idea." Breathlessly, half doubled over, backside to the wall, his hand steadying on her shoulder. "But he sure wasn't any reg. I think that whole job downstairs

wasn't a five person team at all, I think it was just him."
Remembering the speed, the dark shape flying down the corridor. Not as good as her, that was sure. But good enough.

"Damn League special delivery," Ari muttered, eyes even more intent. Thinking fast. That wasn't good. But she was too dazed to probe further. Sirens from the street out front, local cops first on the scene. "How bad is it?" Attention switching abruptly back to her, looking very concerned. "I mean, it didn't penetrate, did it?"

"No. Muscles stop anything low-calibre. But it beats the shit out of them." She tried straightening, and found that she could, barely. "I'm okay. Didn't realise those damn CSA toys packed such a punch. He'll be limping too, at least."

"You hit him?"

"Yeah, about three times in the thighs. Won't bother him so much, thigh muscles are isolated."

Ari stared. "Hang on . . . if he's a GI . . ." gesticulating with one puzzled hand, ". . . and he got enough time to hit you twice in the stomach . . . he wasn't trying to kill you?"

"No."

"Then what . . . ?" He was interrupted by a low, sleek vehicle that turned into the far end of the laneway, accelerating to zoom quickly toward them—police cruiser, blue with flashing lights. And she caught a sense of Ari's brief burst-transmission in that direction.

"Tell you later," she said, straightening a bit more to avoid unwanted questions from the police, zipping her jacket to hide the blood. The police car pulled up quickly beside them, two blue-uniformed officers climbing quickly out.

"You two all right?" one asked.

"Fine," said Ari, "you better get in there, we've got a lead on the guy that got away, we're going after him."

"You need backup?"

"No. Careful with those fools in there. They were expecting guests, they're armed but they seem willing to reason with emergency legislation . . . but be fucking careful, and don't put your guns away for anything. Got it?"

"Got it." A can-do nod from both police as another two cruisers appeared up the end of the lane, closing fast. Then Ari's car, driving on auto.

"Come on." With a surreptitious hand on Sandy's shoulder, Ari led the way past the two police cars as they pulled up behind the first, then his own car pulled up, doors opening, and they climbed inside. Ari did a fast uplink to the navcomp and the car backed out the way it had come. Sandy half-collapsed in the chair, pressing hard with her hand and wincing in acute discomfort.

"What's up with those guys, anyway?" she asked, to deflect further questions as he glanced worriedly across at her.

"The thugs?"

"Yeah." With a hiss, shifting position carefully.

"Umm . . ." He shrugged. ". . . just crims. Like crims anywhere, I suppose."

"They're allowed to carry guns around like that?" Incredulously. "Why don't you arrest them? I thought firearm possession was mostly illegal?"

The car reached the end of the lane and pulled out into a gap in the traffic, several more police cruisers waiting for them at the end, lights flashing. And accelerated away. Ari shrugged again.

"They work there. You'll never find weapons there normally, they always get tip-offs and hide them, and there's too much red tape in getting search warrants. Law gets sick of trying eventually and tries to bust them for something else." Damn infotech society, Sandy thought sourly. Everyone seemed to know what everyone else was doing. "Besides, they have their uses, we overlook the odd bit of black-marketeering in exchange for information on the big boys or bad crims. We have inside sources, keep the small stuff contained and nail the big stuff to the wall. Priorities, you know."

Sandy gave him a dubious sideways glance.

"That works?"

Ari glanced back. "You're really going to have to get

more precise with this vague terminology, Sandy . . . I mean, um, *works*, for example, has multiple possible translations available within the, um, broader law enforcement lexicon." Sandy just gazed at him, unblinkingly. Ari coughed. "We keep the small stuff contained, generally, and nail the big stuff. Generally."

"I'm pleased to hear that. Generally." The car paused at a traffic light. It seemed a pointless inconvenience, in the circumstances. She wished Ari had an aircar.

"So what do you make of this GI?" A little tentatively, Sandy thought.

"The prick shot me." She was not, she felt, in the right mood to discuss it presently. "I'm not happy about it."

Ari blinked. "Well, logically, I'd imagine that might follow. What'd he look like?"

"Black. Where are we going?"

"Oh, um, I figured we didn't want a hospital since the SIB might track that . . . and they probably couldn't help much, anyway . . . so I thought a friend's place, just to patch you up. So . . . African-black? Or Indian-black?"

"African . . . Fucking Norwegian-black, I don't know. Which friend's place?"

"You wouldn't recognise the name."

Jesus. She was losing her temper now. That rarely happened. Being shot with her own weapon infuriated her. The way it had happened doubly infuriated her. The fools with their guns who hadn't believed she was CSA infuriated her. The fact that there were GIs in Tanusha again, breaking into places and stealing their databases . . . oh, that was it, she could feel the anger surging, at that single thought.

"Fucking GIs," she muttered into Ari's continuing silence, as the lights went green and the car accelerated once more. "I hate fucking GIs."

Ari gave her another, tentative sideways look. "Surely you don't mean that?"

Sandy stared out the windows, and fumed. Silence was her only answer.

CHAPTER 7

She awoke. Lay for a moment, in the darkened room, listening. Distant air traffic. Bustling city sound, faint and dreamy. Omnipresent. Like the sigh of a gentle breeze through forest leaves. A lazy, reflex hearing-shift, to finer detail. The whine of a maglev line. An aircar, a gentle throbbing pulse on some nearby skylane. Nearer sound . . . music, and drums. From somewhere outside, neither close nor distant. The suggestion of laughter, and cheering voices, rising in faint waves above the city's gentle murmur.

She blinked her eyes open more fully. She was lying on her back in a darkened room, gazing at the ceiling. That was distinctly strange. How did she get here?

Faint snatches of memory swam to her recall. Ari. Ari had brought her here. Remembered being assisted up some steps. Remembered pain. Some people, strangers, in their house. Nothing more.

House. She was in a house. She blinked lazy, uncooperative vision into some kind of focus, shading into UV in the dim glow of street light that fell through broad, nearby windows. Turned her head, over toward the windows. It was a broad, open floor, of tiles or . . . slate, she guessed dreamily. Plastered walls. An arched brickwork doorway. The broad windows led out onto a balcony, with many plants and decorative railings.

Aestheticisms. One could not go anywhere, in Tanusha, without running into aestheticisms. This one was European, perhaps Mediterranean. Stone, brick, plaster, glazed patterns and trimming, plants and paintings . . . God, she shut her eyes tightly, feeling her head spinning, a slow and unpleasant disorientation. She was not sure where she was. It seemed a fitting predicament, here in Tanusha, among old cultures and old things that should not have held meaning for her, but somehow evoked . . . whatever they evoked, she was not sure. Music, drifting faintly through the room. She listened for a long moment, with dazed curiosity.

A door opened across the room, artificial light spilling briefly through the doorway. Sandy glanced, and saw a man. Instinctively, she knew he was no threat, and she lay still, naked beneath the bed covers, as the man approached across the hard slate floor with light, careful steps. Listening to the music drifting from down the street.

"Hello, Cassandra." A tall man, lightly wringing his hands. A blue turban and a handsome, trimmed beard. "The machine told me you were awake." She blinked at him for a moment. Then looked left, at the portable monitoring equipment there, on top of a wooden bedside table. And realised the connector plug was attached to the insert socket at the back of her head.

"How are you feeling?"

"Where am I?" Her voice was clear and strong, if a little dazed. That relieved her. Another time, she vaguely remembered, she'd awoken much the same as this to find it hardly working at all.

"You're at my house in Nagpur, Cassandra." A mild, congenial voice. Comfortingly so. "I'm a friend of Ari's, my name is Amitraj Singh, I'm a doctor. He brought you here for my assistance. You were shot."

Shot. Yes, she definitely remembered that. Strangely, the memories did not impact on her in a rush. She felt calm in the agreeably cool, mild atmosphere of this darkened, pleasant room.

"I remember." The memories helped. They triggered others. Events slipped back into place and she felt her waking rationality smoothly returning. "You'll be a biotech surgeon, then?"

"Yes." With a smile in the darkness. "I'm an old friend of Ari's." Ari, it was increasingly apparent, had a lot of old friends. She did not bring it up.

"How badly was I hurt?" More badly than she'd thought, evidently.

"You were suffering from the effects of what I've heard referred to as "impact concussion." Of course I've only read about it secondhand from League information, and I've never experienced it directly . . . you're familiar with the condition yourself, I imagine?"

"Sure." She felt with a hand over her stomach beneath the sheets. Felt bandaging, applying pressure. Large bandages, with cold, lumpy objects beneath. Coldpacks, for muscular reconsolidation. The doctor had read the right reports.

"Impact concussion" referred to the shockwave that ripped through a GI's body following projectile strikes. Synth-alloy myomer tensed from human-density tissue to armour-density in micro-seconds under compression, the rate of compression determined by the force of the strike. Which triggered sympathetic reactions in adjoining muscle groups, which in turn conducted the force of the strike right through the GI's body at far greater power than for a regular human's, where the kinetic energy would dissipate amid the soft tissue. A leg shot could do more damage to a GI's spinal cord than to the leg itself, as impact force was transmitted up the ferrous-enamel bone of the skeletal structure.

"I didn't think it'd hurt that bad," she murmured, rubbing her cold bulges beneath the bandages. Cold temperatures allowed myomer muscle to contract, tighten, and reconsolidate. The coldpacks would help her badly bruised, compacted and wrenched stomach muscles recover their normal state.

"Ari said you'd been shot before, within the last month." Ah, she realised. Of course. "GI muscles take time to recover, Cassandra, just like human muscles. Your stomach muscles, and probably your entire torso region, does not appear to have fully reconsolidated from that incident, and so was not able to withstand the concussion as normal. And you've been very busy lately . . . have you been managing to stretch regularly?"

Sandy put aside any lingering concerns of the "doctor's" legitimacy—obviously he was a real doctor . . . not a GI himself yet already he was lecturing her, the genuine article, on the proper care and good health of her artificial body.

"Half hour a day," she replied, stretching slightly beneath the covers. She felt stiff. Achingly, immobilisingly stiff. But surprisingly free of pain, and increasingly clearheaded as whatever drugs he'd given her to relax the muscles and take the slugs out began to wear off. "My best friend gives good massages, too."

"Hmm. I had heard it can take three months or more for a full recovery . . . it's a question of structural engineering more than actual health. Your previous, um, clean incisions, were a relatively simple matter, damage inflicted at predictable, healable locations. This is far more widespread and invasive, if less immediately traumatic. You've been . . . um, rather active, I take it, since you arrived here?"

Sandy smiled faintly. "Could say."

"And how are you feeling now?"

"Better. Stiff, but no real pain." A brief, diverted scan showed her the time—6:50. Just after sunset. "Where's Ari?"

"I'm afraid he didn't say." With mild amusement. "That being rather the way with Ari. You might have noticed."

"Yeah." She sighed. "No message for me?"

"No." Regretfully. "I'm afraid not."

It was very predictable. It meant something. She needed some space, just for a moment. Or more than a moment. She needed space to figure out what was going on, and what she was going to do.

"Okay. Thanks for your help. If you could just wait outside, I'll be out in a minute." A rapid blink.

"Um . . . Cassandra . . . I don't think I would advise you getting out of bed right now, much less going out once again into that . . . that chaos out there." Things had been happening, evidently, while she slept. "I really think you should have at least one night's quiet rest . . . I'm not entirely clear on the effects of repeated impact concussion such as this, but I do think the risks that you'll reinjure yourself, or somehow make the damage worse, are rather high."

"Thank you for your advice—I take it on board—and I appreciate everything you've done to help. But could you please wait outside?" Another blink. Not about to argue, she guessed, when she put it like that. She held his attention with an effortless, unblinking gaze.

"Well . . . if you insist. But I'll tell Ari I warned you against it . . . I have to go out, I'm needed at work, but my friends outside will take care of you. Your . . . um, clothes are on the chair over there."

"Thank you," she repeated, as he reluctantly left the room, closing the door behind him. She flopped back onto the pillows, gazing at the ceiling. Damn. Damn that bloody GI. She doubted he'd meant his shots to be this debilitating. Which did her little good now. Of all the stupid inconveniences. Ari hadn't dragged her away from effective house arrest in the expectation that she'd fall at the first hurdle. Some help she'd proved to be. And now he'd left her, gone off on his own wild chase. With Ari, she thought, the trail could lead him anywhere . . . Out there, somewhere in the dark, dangerous night. So beautiful, in the glow of light through the windows, and the gentle murmur of sound. And so deceptive.

Ari. Speaking of deceptive. Bringing her along to track down this mysterious Sai Va, yet as soon as the trail led to League GIs on League business, he'd sent her off in the wrong direction while he set off in solitary pursuit . . . an irony that it'd meant she was closer than he was to the source of that transmission signal when she heard it, and thus faster to respond. But Ari hadn't been shocked to hear that the GI in question was higher designation, nor at her assessment that he'd most likely done the whole raid on Sai Va's friends solo. And Ari himself had volunteered the information about the newly arrived League delegation, and their accompanying party of GIs.

Maybe . . . maybe Ari hadn't wanted her to catch up with that particular GI. Maybe he'd known who he was, and what he was. Smart. High-designation. She herself was the only truly human-level GI yet created, mentally speaking. All high-designation GIs had resided in Dark Star, the League's most lethal special operations combat unit. She'd had the run of Dark Star most of her life, she knew all the ins and outs. She knew all the high-des GIs personally, many of them had been in her own combat team, the one her superiors had ordered eliminated when they became politically inconvenient. Keeping high-des GIs in Dark Star was a matter of covert policy . . . not technically allowed. To this day most League politicians remained unaware of the existence of quite so many unauthorised high-des GIs—her own existence in particular—especially since the embarrassment of her escape and abandonment of Dark Star and the League entirely.

But those high-des GIs that Parliament were aware of, and did authorise, were all assigned to Dark Star as a matter of top-level policy. This GI was smart. Very smart, very capable, and she'd never seen nor heard of him before in her life. So where was he from? And was that what Ari hadn't wanted her to know? How would Ari have known? How on Earth could his intelligence on such things be superior to hers? She'd been passing on a great deal of classified information about League operational matters to CSA Intel for the last month since the emergency legislation and Article 42 . . . they simply didn't know that much, not even Ari. No, that couldn't be it. Could it?

Damn civilians. She closed her eyes, breathing deeply to stop her head from spinning. The Senate banned her, Ari appropriated her on his business and then lied to her, and now she'd run headlong into something she was certain many people in officialdom had much rather she hadn't—a smart League GI who knew her name, and possessed an inexplicable quantity of charm, a rare quality among combat GIs, to say the least. Doubtless they would worry about her loyalties. Even after the bastard had shot her.

It was enough to make her claustrophobic. Too many restrictions did that to her. Too many commands. The world of possibilities was vast, and she needed to find her own way, and her own answers to these and others of her most pressing problems. Like she always had.

She'd been blinkered, she realised now. Hemmed in. Tanusha was civilian, and foreign, and Federation . . . and she was military, and League, and a GI, most of all. And she had been feeling overwhelmed by recent events, the trauma of her first arrival here, the discovery and loss of her old friend Mahud, and the feelings of guilt, loss and personal responsibility that went with it all. And having Vanessa for a friend had been such a big change, as had everyday operations with the CSA, and she had allowed herself the unaccustomed comfort of being led, and sometimes pampered, and having other people thinking for her—because it was all so different, and she was taking a long time to recover her personal confidence in matters operational.

And being led was dangerous. She was not regular CSA, she was far more sensitive politically. Her place within the institution was tenuous at best, whatever badge she held in the familiar leather binder. She could not afford the luxury of believing that she was safe in letting others do her thinking for her. She had always been independent, even within Dark Star command, back in the League. Different from all her comrades. Separated from most of her straight human command and support. Free to formulate operational tactics as she saw fit, and to include or ignore advice on such matters however she wished. She had been without that independence for too long now. She needed it back.

All this she thought while lying alone in the comfortable, darkened silence, listening to the gentle sounds of the city. And to the rhythmic drumming and melody that reminded her of everything she had left her military life in hope of discovering—which she had discovered, and more besides. Now it was time to stop being frightened of it.

She got up, carefully, unwrapped the outer bandages, and dressed. The stiffness hurt, and she was careful not to strain her midriff, but the inconvenience was manageable. Her shoulder holster was also upon the chair, slung across the back, pistol and all. She gave the weapon a brief check, and the magazines in her jacket pocket, and called Vanessa's uplink. Got back an engaged signal . . . which meant she was operational, and not available to casual callers.

Stretched her hamstrings for a moment, dialling through the needed links to CSA Central. The display gave the usual chaotic mess of meetings, functions and sensitive security spots . . . and a disturbing number of active-security "reds," designating currently running hotspots. A deeper scan revealed that one was a hostage drama, which had been running in Junshi for some time . . . just several kilometres away from her and Vanessa's apartments. Several were post-active shootings, sweepers collecting data and corpses. Most appeared to be gang-related. Fighting over the black market spoils, no doubt, in a fluid environment of rapidly changing power structures—determined by who held what information, and who had been talking to which visiting delegation, and which way the rumour winds were blowing . . . God. She wasn't even going to get into that. It gave her a headache just thinking about it.

At least the politicians were safely at home for the day, the debating over. Officially, anyway . . . doubtless it all continued, after hours, in private, debugged, security-perimetered rooms with various delegates and interest groups. She hoped Parliamentary security wasn't being stretched too thin in the confusion. With the stockmarket crashed more than twenty percent (an unheard-of calamity in Tanusha), some of the would-be assassins could easily be bank and fund managers in three-piece suits. Tanusha, the happy city, was today no longer quite so happy.

Dinner was basic Indian, a tandoori chicken with rice, and she shovelled it down with relish. Something about getting shot at that made her famished. Company sat about on the lounge chairs, and tried not to stare as she ate. Five of them, excluding the recently departed Doctor Singh. Ari's friends. Hackers, jackers, netsters, technogeeks, link-jockeys . . . the "underground," by any multitude of names. Monitoring equipment trailed cables and hookups across the floor like a crazed North Synian climbing vine, devouring furniture, rugs and open floorboards. Racks of control boxes piled against one wall by the stereo system. Custom-rigged tech, all of it, and mostly cutting edge despite the haphazard appearance. "Watching the furball," the man named Carlo had called it. Transmission tracking on the network. The underground were busy all right. There was a lot to watch.

"Do you need to eat very much?"

Sandy glanced up at the questioner—Anita, a small Indian woman with a shaved head and butterfly tattoos on her eyelids that fluttered when she blinked. Holographic job. Weird, Sandy thought as she chewed, savouring the delicious flavour. But then, they wouldn't be underground if they weren't weird. It came with the territory.

"Three times a day," she managed around that mouthful, ignoring the awe-struck stares focused on her from all sides. Watching her eat. She hoped the fascination did not extend to other bodily functions. "Balanced metabolism, it's not so different."

Grins and giggles from the group. Evidently they found that amusing.

"You know," called Carlo from the kitchen as he came strolling over, beer bottles in hand, "I . . . I really thought you'd be taller." Tossed a beer to Tariq, who caught and opened. "I mean, you're . . . you're what, one-sixty-seven/sixty-eight? I heard this guy Stommel saying you were, like, seven foot tall or something . . ." Half-crazed-grin. ". . . so I'm like . . ."

"Yeah, but you know Stommel," Pushpa, the second Indian woman, complained with exasperation, "he's just an alpha2 addict, never gets off the stupid thing . . ."

"Fuzz-freak," Tojo added, to more laughter and comments, seated on the floor with his back to the sofa, playing with his baby son, who looked barely a year old. And the only one of them, Sandy thought, who didn't speak in technogeek lingo. Poor kid. His first words would probably be jargon. She kept eating, watching the stubby-limbed little guy bouncing up and down in his father's broad hands, looking incredulously bewildered as only small children could. And she wondered what he was thinking.

"So . . . so why didn't they make you taller?" Carlo again. She glanced up, shovelling another forkload into her mouth. Besides being famished, she loved tandoori, and wouldn't stop in midmeal for anything less than a house fire.

"Harder to hit," she responded glibly, muffled past her mouthful. Carlo grinned, maniacally. A strange-looking guy, a drawn and angular face with close-curled hair, big teeth and bulging eyes. Like a skull, she reckoned. Obviously, she'd guessed from previous conversation, a total, unmitigated genius with infotech. And very weird.

"No," she corrected herself when she'd swallowed, "it's more just efficiency. Combat-myomer doesn't handle well in large volumes; if I were thirty centimetres taller I'd suffer chronic tension, it's bad enough now at this size."

"So how strong are you?"

A shrug, and another mouthful. "Hard to say." Muffled. "A lot of it's leverage. Strength's tough to measure objectively, ask a physicist."

"But, like, I mean, you could damage anyone here, right?" Again the crazy grin, with suggestive anticipation.

"Carlo!" Anita protested, "don't say it like that, that's rude! You sound like one of the damn Rainbow Coalition!"

"Human skull strength is actually a *really* objective measure, for hand power," Carlo continued unperturbed, "because the curvature of the skull combined with . . ."

"Carlo!"

Sandy kept eating, enjoying the distraction, which allowed more attention to her food. And these guys interrupted and jumped all over each other at a moment's notice, launching off into all kinds of curious, odd and sometimes apparently irrelevant strings of associated thought, much of it technical and some of it not . . .

"No, what she's saying," the older, Arabic man named Tariq was now saying, "is really very true from a standpoint of pure physics. I mean she may well be strong enough, hypothetically, to lift your average Telosian rhino up by the tail and swing it about her head . . ."

"Painful," suggested Pushpa.

"And extremely messy for the poor bloody rhino when its tail rips off," Carlo retorted, "speaking of physics."

". . . but without the proper leverage," Tariq continued with forced patience, "her own relatively low mass would not allow . . ."

Etc, etc. Tojo's little son was going for a walk, on short, uncertain little legs. She watched as he pottered several steps, wavered, then fell on his arse. His dad lay on his stomach behind him, watching, hands ready to assist. A big, shave-headed African man with tattoos and piercings. He was the only adult in the room not totally fixated upon her. The toddler tried again, and Sandy lost track of the conversation, watching with intrigue as she ate.

"His mother is Chinese?" she asked Tojo after a moment. Tojo looked up at her, surprised.

"Um . . . Chinese, Vietnamese, and a *little* touch of Thai." He had the nice, deep voice of many Africans, but the manner was different. Sensitive and expressive. If she hadn't known he had a wife, she'd have guessed he might be gay. Most civilian hetero men his size seemed to like the "macho thing" . . . "She's a bitsa—bitsa this, bitsa that. I'm second generation Botswanan, parents straight off the ship from Africa two years before I was born. And Mac . . . he's a little mongrel, aren't cha'? Aren't cha' a little mongrel?" Affectionately patting his son on the backside.

The kid stopped pottering, and stared about wide-eyed, chewing a finger with indecision. Sandy smiled. The conversation had stopped, her fascination matched by theirs with her. She ignored them.

"I'd ask if I could hold him," Sandy said around her final mouthful, "but I'd understand if you said no. I mean, considering."

Tojo blinked. "Oh no, no," he protested, getting to his feet, "don't be silly, we all know what you are, we're not thick." Lifted his son quickly under the armpits, and handed him to Sandy. Sandy smiled broadly, with real pleasure, and placed her empty plate aside on the table. Took the dangling child out of Tojo's broad hands, giving Tojo a thankful smile. He crouched alongside.

"Who's that?" In hushed baby talk, as the toddler stared at this new adult person into whose charge he had been unexpectedly deposited. "I wonder who that is? Who's this pretty blonde woman? Who is it?"

Not a clue, Sandy thought, smiling at the little boy, holding him upright in her lap. He was the only person in the room who didn't know. And therefore probably the only person from whom she could expect a totally straight response. Up to and including piddling on her leg. Mac. Short for Macintosh . . . apparently significant, among underground computer-philes, for reasons she didn't understand. She thought it a terrible waste, though, and an inappropriate name for a person with such an interesting ethnic background. But a lot of techno types were like that. Certainly the League was full of them. Had built an entire collective ideology upon them, disregarding old concepts of ethnicity, gender and other "increasingly meaningless" cultural affectations. Some of these guys were League sympathisers, no question. She certainly guessed Tojo was. It explained why he trusted her with his son, where others would turn pale, sweaty and fidgety at the mere suggestion.

"Hi, bubs," she said to him. "You know, I've got a friend who used to be as big as you." In a fair approximation of baby talk, she thought. "In fact, everyone used to be as big as you, once. Except me."

Playing for the audience, she chided herself. All about her, faces were staring, smiling or grinning. There was supposed to be some kind of huge, emotional, revelatory moment, she guessed, when a person of artificial construction held a child for one of the rare times in her life, and realised with great, dramatic force the true difference between herself and every other straight, biological human. But she felt nothing like that. It didn't even feel strange.

Mac nearly smiled, then stared again. Sandy imitated his smile, exaggeratedly. Mac stared in astonishment, pulling at gums with a gooey forefinger. Then grinned delightedly, and gurgled. About the room, everyone laughed. As if that reaction were somehow significant. Sandy pulled a face. He gurgled again, and bounced with excitement, arms flapping.

She supposed it was just that she knew what she was, and was at peace with it. She couldn't really think of a time when she hadn't been. It was the other "GI cliche," she supposed—a desperate yearning for humanity. Which was pathetic, and aroused her deepest indignation. It supposed that humanity was somehow lacking in the first place. Humanity had nothing to do with what she was made of. It was who she was, and what she did. Bouncing a baby boy upon her knee, she felt affection, and intrigue, and . . . and something else, indefinable and warm and pleasant. She didn't need some team of damn shrinks or academic philosophers to put names to what she felt, or how she felt it, or why . . . she didn't care. And they could call her whatever they liked—GI, artificial human, android (though that grated, as Motherworld residents had been known to steam at the tag of "Earthling") . . . none of that mattered either, in the end. Human, by any other name. The details didn't matter. She was Sandy. That was enough.

Though if some fat newspaper prick editorialised her

as a "robot" one more time, she was going to take a stroll to his big, high-rise office, up to the eightieth floor, where all such media importances surely resided, and lob him gently out the window.

And she handed Mac back to his father, not wanting to stretch that generosity too far . . . the kid flailed wantingly at her in the process, and Tojo decided that he liked her blonde hair. Held him close enough to grab a few handfuls, which Sandy tolerated with a grin until he began dribbling on her jacket. Then she heaved herself reluctantly to her feet.

"Okay . . . I gotta ask a favour. I badly need a massage before I stiffen up like a plank. Who's got strong hands?"

"Not me, I'm afraid," Tariq replied, hands warding, "my darling wife would kill me."

"No she would not," Pushpa corrected, "she would inflict great pain and suffering, but leave you horribly alive and dripping gruesomely at the end." Pushpa was apparently calm and mostly sensible by comparison to the rest of them.

"How badly?" Carlo asked, predictably. "What'll happen if you don't get one?"

"I told you, I'll stiffen up like a plank."

"For God's sake," said Anita, "don't let him do it, he hasn't set hands on a woman as attractive as you in his life, he'll barely be able to reach you past the enormous erection."

"Thank you, Madam," Carlo said with a madly grinning bow in his seat, "for the compliment."

"You've just spoiled my dinner," Tariq complained.

"No, that's your fourth beer," Pushpa told him.

Sandy stood in the middle of the rapid exchange and blinked from side to side. Beginning, she realised, to enjoy these weird, misfit, super-intelligent people, and their utterly un-hip, uncool, un-fad-ish ways. Ari came from here, she realised. This was his society. His home. His politics. God . . . he was an escapee, a misfit among the misfits. Handsome, athletic, broad-minded . . . he'd run away to the CSA, to officialdom, to operational expense accounts, cool wardrobes and non-regulation sunglasses. To politics. To bureaucracy.

The ultimate sin among the anti-officialdom—he'd taken a side. And she wished, suddenly, that she had longer to stay and question these people, and learn more of Ari's politics, and theirs, and where they saw it all going in the near future. Well, there was still the massage . . .

"Come on," she said as she pulled off her jacket and lay face down on the floor before the sofa, "I don't care who, just someone screw up some courage and volunteer." Carlo leapt forward, but Anita beat him to it. Stuck her tongue out at him, and Carlo retreated, grinning, to his seat. Carlo seemed to grin at everything. A compulsive grinner. Weird, weird, weird.

"So someone tell me about Ari," she said, as Anita knelt alongside and grabbed firmly at her tight shoulders, kneading deep. "Who is he, where did he come from, and what's the guy's problem?"

"Bloody hell," Tariq retorted, with the tired exasperation of an older man who had seen and done it all before, "how many years do you have to spare?"

"You sure I can't drop you there directly?" Pushpa asked her, with the anxiousness of someone very keen to assist. The car rolled into the drive-through stop off, a slow pace in the queue as cars arrived and departed further up amid a flow of commuters.

"The fewer people who know my exact movements, the safer I feel," Sandy replied.

"You . . . you really think they could trace you from *that*?" Anita gasped from the backseat. Anita and Pushpa were a team, friends since school, they said. And unpossessed, at that time, of the standard obsessions for youthful Indian girls in Tanusha, like parties and dancing, and like clothes, jewellery, and the money to buy them. Tech-science majors, they now made more money from their network consultancy than most of their high school class combined—but still dressed like struggling artists or philosophy majors. Or in Anita's case, a fringe-cult punk. Weird again. Sandy liked them.

"I've no idea," she told Anita. "It just makes me happier. No point taking risks."

"Hey look, security," Pushpa said, nodding toward the maglev station entrance. Sandy looked at the four uniforms on standby before the doors, and the van parked nearby. And remembered a security procedural tidbit she remembered reading from her review file.

"In the event of terrorist threat or perceived threat to vital public infrastructure . . ." she trailed off . . . probably shouldn't recite the entire passage and verse before these two.

"Wow," said Anita, leaning forward between the two front seats, "they must really be running low on manpower, there's only four, it should be eight of them for a maglev."

Maglevs, of course, being "A Grade" infrastructure . . . Sandy frowned, and turned to look at Anita.

"How do you know that?"

Anita pouted. "Know what? I didn't say anything, you must be hearing voices."

Sandy sighed, and leaned back in her seat. Hackers. If there was information, they got it, somewhere, somehow.

"So what do we tell Ari if he calls?" Pushpa wanted to know.

"You have to tell him anything?" Sandy replied. "He's not taking my calls, serves him right."

"You sure you shouldn't wait for him?" the other persisted.

"He's got his leads," Sandy said. "I've got mine." The car pulled up at the next designated mark, and the doors whirred open automatically. "Hey, nice to meet you both, I'm sure I'll be seeing more of you in the future."

"Oh, I hope so!" Anita said, enthusiastically shaking her hand.

"Don't work too hard," said Pushpa, in her turn.

Sandy smiled. "I'll try not to. Take care." And left the car to Anita's final call of, "And for godsake, don't trust the CSA!"

Which made her grin as she joined the flow of pedestrians headed for the maglev entrance, and the car lane bumped haltingly along behind. Paranoid to the last, these hackers. And maybe with good cause. But she was flattered that Anita would automatically include her as "us" in the "us and them" equation. Unconditional love was a strange response to be facing, particularly from such intelligent people . . . but any Tanushan League-sympathetic technophile would just *die* to meet a real GI in person, let alone the famous, super-advanced *friendly* GI the Neiland Administration had befriended. She didn't trust it. But it beat the hell out of the alternative.

She tried Ari's connection again on the maglev. She was seated by the window at the very rear of the open tube, with a good, long, winding view of the people-filled interior. No response, not even an engaged signal to acknowledge the call. Busy, Ari? More secrets to pursue? Contacts to meet? She wondered. Mostly she wondered just how much she didn't know, and how much Ari hadn't told her.

CSA uplinks showed it was pointless to try Vanessa again—she'd been rotated onto standby at the hostage crisis, and her heart sank when she saw it. Please God, no shooting. Vanessa would be fine, she was sure, but civilians, targets and high-power firearms did not mix, and such unpleasant combinations could stain the memory for the rest of a person's life. Please no shooting. But she could only hope.

Another connection . . . and a temporary hold, then an auto-recognition . . . fuzzy static pause, then click . . .

"*Cassandra?*" came Director Ibrahim's voice. "*Where are you?*" The auto-rec rechecking her freqs and racing through a positioning analysis . . . she didn't mind, there were two people in Tanusha whose systems she trusted implicitly—one was Vanessa, and the other was Ibrahim. Ari, she thought a little darkly, was a long way from qualifying. Especially after tonight. "*Ari said you'd been shot?*"

"I had, but I'm fine now. Where is he, do you know?"

"*He's busy . . . Cassandra, I tried to contact you earlier but you were apparently unconscious. I have spent much of today warding off queries and accusations from the SIB. Cassandra, apparently Ms. Izerovski was most upset after her agents 'lost' you on your motorcycle this morning."*

"*Have they placed me at Cloud Nine?*" As the possibility suddenly occurred to her—Cloud Nine was the name of the premises the GI had been chased into. The CSA were doing the follow-up investigations now, taking various mafia types into custody for questioning. Not that anyone expected them to be helpful.

"*No . . . field investigation is not an SIB strong point, Cassandra, particularly not in fluid, chaotic realtime scenarios . . . although I do not discount the possibility that they may place you there eventually.*" He sounded calm, as was Ibrahim's habit. The slight edge to his voice may have been adrenaline. Other people functioned worse in a crisis. Some functioned better in direct proportion to the seriousness of the situation. Ibrahim was one of the latter. And she wondered if it could be his Sunni-Afghan ancestry, perhaps, that made such a positive out of adversity. Or predisposed him to love a good fight. "*I'm afraid the situation is actually much worse than that.*"

"*Of course it is,*" she formulated, dryly.

"*Cassandra, Izerovsky has informed the Senate Security Panel of your 'escape from Senate-mandated surveillance,' to use her words.*" Among the many passengers on the train, Sandy refrained from swearing, or placing her head in her hands. "*The Security Panel have been demanding an interview with me personally. I have declined. They have accused me of orchestrating the whole thing, and have formally placed a deposition with the Parliament, requesting my resignation effective immediately.*"

Incredible. It took her breath away, the sheer, bloody-minded, single-focused stupidity. Demand the CSA Director's resignation over that small matter, in the middle of a Federation-wide crisis? Those were their priorities?

"*You're not going to accept it, I hope?*"

"*Only if Allah should command it, Cassandra.*" With a dry, deadpan, implacable resolve. "*To the best of my knowl-*

edge, Allah cares little for the workings of the Senate Security Panel, and has no seat at the table."

Nor did Allah have a place in the Neiland Administration, Sandy thought. Which meant Ibrahim was not intending to step down for any politician. Not now. The very prospect of changing horses in mid-stream was horrifying in its implications for planetary security. That anyone senior should possibly suggest such a thing, over any matter, was completely incomprehensible to her.

"News of this has spread through the major political parties, Cassandra. They cannot leak to the press without breaching security guidelines, but I cannot guarantee that the unofficial rumour mill will not carry this further." No, he certainly could not. She'd discovered just today, with Ari's friends, how far and wide the rumour mill spread. *"However, the President herself is of the opinion that this could prove sufficient distraction in tomorrow's debating session to effectively derail the day's proceedings. Some Members have threatened to withdraw from the process indefinitely until the Neiland Administration makes its position clear on this matter."*

"What do you want me to do?" She could feel him building up to it. She didn't like the implications. The whole damn thing had been his idea, after all . . .

"Cassandra, the President and I feel it would help matters considerably if you could make an appearance before a full sitting of the Parliament tomorrow morning." She blinked. Should have seen that one coming too. "The President and I . . ." Bloody Katia Neiland and her wild improvisations on the run. It had her smell about it, the whole thing. *"You have been making some progress on your review of Tanushan security systems with regard to the threat of military-style infiltration. The President and I feel that a formal presentation from you on your findings so far would enable the Members to see for themselves the value of your presence here, and thus take the SIB's legs out from under them on this issue, so to speak."*

To Sandy's vision, the interior of the maglev appeared to darken somewhat, the combat redness descending. Sounds came thickly, slurred and broken into individual vibrations . . . she'd been blind-sided again by officialdom. It was becoming a habit. Of course, she was supposed to leap at this opportunity, a chance to prove herself before the elected representatives of the Callayan Parliament . . . she wondered if Ibrahim had planned this too, predicting the SIB's reaction when he authorised Ari to go walkabout with her. Or if the whole thing had been Neiland's idea from the beginning. Once again, she was the pawn, and she didn't like it one bit.

"*Sir . . . my review is very preliminary to this point, I have no detailed analysis prepared, and in fact I should remind you that the whole thing is so far beyond my regular experience and qualifications that it was little more than an experiment in the first place.*"

"*I am aware of that, Cassandra. The sitting will not expect a detailed presentation, only a broad overview. Your preliminary opinions, not analytical conclusions. That is all that is required of you. In the meantime, I suggest you get some rest, and perhaps make some preparations, if possible. If you give me your location I'll send someone to accompany you—the President requires it, to give her credible denial of SIB claims that you have been left improperly supervised, you understand.*"

"*I do understand. I'm afraid that will have to wait, I'm busy.*" Pause.

"*Cassandra, I do not feel that now is the time for you to be 'busy.' Political events have taken a turn, and whether you like it or not . . .*"

"*With respect, sir,*" Sandy formulated, in her coldest replicated tones, "*you began this. I know Ari's your boy. You put him onto this lead, and then he put me onto it, and now I'm going to finish it. If you want someone to supervise me, put me in contact with Ari and I'll tell him where to meet me.*"

"*Ari is indisposed, Cassandra.*" Ibrahim knew *exactly* where Ari was, Sandy was sure. "*Cassandra, I am under rather direct instruction from the highest civilian authority on this planet. As you might understand, such instructions are not to be taken lightly.*"

"*So I suppose you know everything about League operations in this city?" Sandy replied. No response from Ibrahim. *"There is a delegation here. Which of course no one would ever dare have informed me of in advance, me being ex-League and all, lest my sympathies suddenly change direction. There's a delegation here, and I don't doubt they're in discussion with all relevant parties regarding the current direction of Article 42. Now obviously, if you're so eager for me to go home and sleep, you'll be fully informed as to the League delegation's present operations, their numbers, their personnel, and GIs in particular, the people they're meeting with, etc, etc. Because the GI at Cloud Nine was very pleased to see me, before he shot me, and called me by name. I had this strange, crazy idea they might talk to me, where they would not to someone else. Perhaps I could learn something. But, of course, if that particular information is of no real use to you, I could just go home and sleep, as per your recommendation."*

Still there was no reply. The maglev whined in deceleration, a station stop approaching, and some passengers got to their feet. The night-time city slowed its gleaming rush past the windows, a thick line of traffic passing below, hemmed by explosive thickets of holographic neon and sidewalk traffic.

Then, *"Stay out of trouble, Agent Kresnov. Talk to them, if possible, no more. If they don't want to see you, don't push your luck, you've been shot once already today and you do not want to make that a habit in this city. I'll expect a full report at the earliest."*

"Sir, I shall exercise the utmost circumspection, cognisance and diligence, I assure you." An influence of Indian bureaucratic English, she had discovered, that led to the usual proliferation of pointless vocabulary through the back corridors of CSA officialdom. Vanessa hated it. Sandy found it amusing.

"I'm very sure. Oh-nine-hundred tomorrow, Agent Kresnov. The Parliament shall be waiting." Damn right they would be. She'd bet her life on it. *"And Cassandra? Please bear in mind the possibility that your old comrade Chu may no longer be alive."*

The maglev began accelerating once more. Sandy gazed at the whizzing platform, lights and people in a gathering blur, then at the buildings and roads below, lines of moving, lighted traffic.

So Ibrahim was aware of her other motivation. Even if she had not yet fully admitted it to herself, Ibrahim was aware. She had not wanted to think about it so openly. Finding Mahud, only to lose him once more, had been a pain almost beyond her capacity to bear. Hoping for news of Chu was almost too painful, especially when it came this close, somewhere within the League Embassy compound. But whatever her need for useful delusions, Ibrahim had no such luxury.

"*I'll bear that in mind, sir.*" Quietly.

"*I know you will. And I wish you luck.*"

The maglev got her halfway across town. The adjoining subway got her to Zaiko, and she walked the rest of the way. Barely an hour from leaving the house, and she was there—Tanushan mass-transit was a marvel, and nearly military-like in its precision. If only, she mused, the city's people were as orderly as their machines. But then, on reflection, that would not work either. People chaos was the energy that drove the seamless technological systems, as surely as hydrogen combustion powered her motorcycle. You could cut the combustion, but doing so would cost you power.

Her bike awaited her in the cycle-park a short stroll from the riverside where she and Ari had enjoyed lunch earlier that day—it seemed eons away. People still strolled the sidewalk beneath the trees along the riverside walk, although the outdoor cafes were largely shut, tables packed away for the night as 9:00 PM approached . . . Zaiko was a tourist and business spot, mostly, only in the more residential regions did the cafes and restaurants stay open till the wee hours. She climbed onto the bike, unhooking the helmet from the rear lock, and pondering further if her "people-chaos theory" applied equally to Old Earth too. Of course it did. The proof could be found in the colourful confusion emanating from a broad apartment balcony across the road—an Indian wedding of one ethnic division or another. Colourful dress, flashing fabrics and jewellery, thunderingly rhythmic music and many people dancing on the balcony that overlooked the river . . . no doubt some illegal fireworks would follow, they usually did at such occasions, to the police's continual dismay.

Back on Earth, China was a great power, but India ruled overall. Or would do, if they ever figured out who was really in charge. The self-professed most chaotic nation on Earth, its technological prowess was nearly as legendary as its people's love of parties, theatrics, and political crises. The Chinese had never fully abandoned their fear of chaos. The Indians embraced it. And so the Chinese remained perpetually frustrated by the fact that despite their immense collective power, Indians continually outnumbered them in most truly revolutionary fields by two-to-one or more. China continued to hold itself separate from the world, as a national and ethnic entity. Indians diverged, spread, travelled and multiplied. And so when FTL truly arrived, the Indians went first, and the Chinese followed for fear of being left behind . . . or in many cases to escape the conservative, Earth-bound mindset in search of alternative ideologies. The League was full of Chinese. Chinese and LEUs—for Los Estados Unidos, as ex–United States of America residents were widely known in the League—the latter group endeavouring to confirm its cultural heritage, in search of a new great frontier, and the former group wishing to escape and start anew. The Federation held many of all cultural groups, but the Indians, equally comfortable in both the old world and the new, were particularly prominent. "Going League" implied the agreement with a particular "progressive" philosophy, and the majority of Indians felt uncomfortable in surroundings that offered no arguments, ideological battles or mad political catfights. Those that had "gone League" were derided as fanatics, extremists, or Pakistanis upset with the reunification, and looking for a new Kashmir.

Apolitical city my arse, Sandy thought, as she gunned the bike into life. Tanushans were only apolitical because their carefully constructed environment gave them no cause to be otherwise, even on the biggest issues of all, and there had been nothing overtly traumatic to argue about. Well, now they had cause, and the old cultural instincts were leaping back to life, and dragging most other ethnicities with them.

India, she recalled, was also called the most ideological country on Earth . . . that and chaos, apparently, went hand in hand. It had condemned them to what in hindsight was unbelievable poverty for a full half-century after nationhood, many centuries ago, when the rest of the world was developing fast. Then the ideology had switched to capitalism—a supposedly "Western" concept, it had then been thought—which the Indians in conjunction with the Chinese had absorbed and "Indianised" as thoroughly as they'd absorbed and Indianised the genteel English sport of cricket, or cups of tea, or the English language itself. And by 2050, she recalled from her historical readings, the great "Western" capitalist powers were complaining bitterly about the Indianisation of global economics, and the threatened trade sanctions against European nations who failed to fight against the encroaching "cultural sterility" of the modern economy . . . a Western phenomenon that Indians, East Asians, and Africans recoiled from in horror to this day. Cultural ideology, the Western powers complained, had no place in economics. To which the Indians had responded that cultural ideology was about what was good for the soul, and if Western economics had nothing to say on this matter, then who needed it? And so the entire apparatus of the global economy had never been the same since . . . and, Sandy couldn't help but think, thank God for it. Thank God for culture, and thank God for the perspective it brought upon the dry, rational worlds of science and finance.

Here, and now, the ideology was yet to be decided. Biotech. GIs. The value of organic, human life. The nature of humanity itself. The deciding issues that separated League from Federation. With her in the middle, trying to help them make up their minds.

She flicked on the headlight, helmet in place, and cruised smoothly out along the road. Colourful party-pops lit the streetside behind her, a cascading fall of blue, green and saffron light, and the angular office-front windows bloomed in spectacular reflection as she passed.

The League Embassy did not appear on any map. Not in those words, anyhow. From her pagoda view atop the temple, Sandy had a good view of the grounds across the avenue, though somewhat obscured by leafy trees before and within the grounds. Behind the high, wrought-iron fence lay an estate in miniature—a wide grassy lawn with a U-turn driveway that swept in front of the columns of the patio before the main entrance. The building itself was two-storey, rectangular and whitewashed end to end. Building and grounds together reminded her of the images she'd viewed of old British colonial properties in India, dating from the time of the occupying Raj. Only the scale was smaller—squeezed between a pair of modest, low-key office buildings. A casual passerby might dismiss such a building as another of Tanusha's many pieces of historical nostalgia, and not spare it a second thought. And not notice that the gates were locked, the physical and network security intense, and there was no sign or advertisement to announce the building's purpose to the street. A light, civilian-level query of the net-presence came back to her as "government building," with no more information provided.

There were a lot of those, of course, and high security was hardly rare among them. Of course, discovering which was the League Embassy was easy enough, if you knew who to ask. Previously, it had not been an issue. Now, she watched on full-zoom/infrared, and counted the soldiers on the roof, laid flat behind the lining flowerbeds with rifles at ready. There were eight visible, and doubtless more inside and about the grounds. They'd been receiving a lot of "interested queries" lately, she guessed. And that being League property in there, they were allowed to provide their own firepower as insurance to keep the natives at arm's length.

Her preliminary scanning done, she descended the stone staircase and into the temple proper, leaving the pagoda's several other occupants to enjoy the night air alone. Candles and coloured lamps lit the main floor, red light misty with the fumes of burning incense amid the many rows of ceiling pillars that held up the roof. Many people moved between, barefoot and leisurely, and queued before various iconic statues or alcoves, to pray or make offerings, or light more incense. Red and saffron flower petals littered the stone floor, alternately rough and smooth underfoot. A sadhu in robes, with a long beard, swept the floor clear amid the throng, immersed in his endless task.

She ducked a hanging flower banner, and avoided a random clump of devotees praying before a two metre, many-armed icon, adorned with many garlands of coloured flowers. Her route took her past an adjoining decoratively styled doorway, through which she viewed a broad room, and perhaps a hundred people seated cross-legged upon an enormous carpet. On a low platform in front sat a yogi, robed and tangle-bearded, leading a meditation. Hands outstretched and palms out, murmuring incantations through his beard, an assistant seated to one side, a small gong before her crossed ankles. Sandy had only a very vague idea of what that was all about. But it looked peaceful, in the still of that broad, stone-walled room, surrounded on all sides by tapestries, flower decorations and icons, with only the light, unearthly chime of the gong to break the silence, and the yogi's unceasing murmurs. A light wind blew incense, sent tapestries drifting sideways, a light scattering of flower petals across the stone floor.

Sandy held that image with her as she descended the stone-wrought staircase, keeping in the downward stream as more people ascended the stairs upon the opposite side. She was still pondering the mass, silent meditation and murmured chants as she retrieved her boots from the simple wooden rack, and inserted a basic credit deposit into the temple's one concession to technology—a visitor's card-scanner, for upkeep donations. Wondering if, one day, she could join such a session herself, just for curiosity. One day, perhaps, when circumstances would allow her to do as she should have done tonight, in all honesty, and leave her gun with a holy man at the door. And with her boots refastened, she departed into the street, through the gathering throng at the entry gate, and the cries of the mystic doomsayer upon his box, largely ignored by the mostly (but not entirely) Indian patrons, who gathered and chattered with friends and family—temples were common enough gathering spots for the socially inclined.

"The decadence of Tanusha has angered the Gods!" the holy man yelled above the voices and occasional traffic, in clear Tanushan English. A young man, with scarcely a beard nor a blemish upon his face, and dressed only in a pile of old robes. European, Sandy noted with interest. His tone seemed suspiciously Christian-sermonising. Probably a convert, getting his delivery styles confused, raving like a missionary. Most Tanushan Hindus disdained them. "Rama is displeased, yes, hear me, displeased and angry at our politicians and their conniving ways! His emissary shall descend upon us, and that emissary will be the Goddess Kali, and she shall descend upon us all with the very wrath of Heaven, and smite the wickedness of all ungodly folk—the followers of Mohammed, Christ and the Buddha too, yes, no one shall be saved from their descent into base greed and consumerism, and the vile lust for credit, and for wicked twists of mortal shape beyond our natural means! All that is living and ungodly shall be punished, and shall suffer eternal condemnation for all incarnations ever onward!"

His cries rolled on, over the heads of the unheeding masses, as the only person who was perhaps truly listening, and pondering the content of his words, strolled unhurriedly away up the sidewalk. A pistol in her side-holster and determination upon her mind, on her way to meet the devil.

The "backdoor" was easy enough to find for someone with intimate knowledge of League network security formulations. The electronic trail led her to a small office building nearby, and the floor of Denzler Securities, which registered as a small, niche-specialty network security business. A few words with the polite lady on reception there, and a brief mention of the name "Cassandra Kresnov," saw her hurried to a big, black street-cruiser with tint-out windows and armoured bodywork, and driven into the Embassy grounds through the main gate. Uplinked and sensitive to adjoining link codes, Sandy had a clear sense of the massive security integration as the car hummed up the driveway —the multiple overlaying network scans, the grounds surveillance, the interlocking fields of fire of many well-placed marksmen . . . The car continued past the front entrance and onto the less official rear driveway that curled around the side.

It stopped at the rear, which was even more impressive, with a broad, bannistered verandah overlooking lush, green lawns and a thick covering of trees. Sandy paused for a moment as she climbed from the open door and surveyed the grounds on a multiple-spectrum sweep—a high wall surrounded the Embassy to the sides and rear, and thick tree-cover blocked a clear view from higher office windows. Besides which, the entire, picturesque grounds were a cross-grid of trigger sensors. Puzzlingly, several peacocks wandered the maze with impunity . . . intelligent sensors, perhaps, with a preference for peacocks. She gazed more closely at a pair of the birds as she was escorted by two guards up the path to the verandah steps, marvelling at the male's gorgeous plumage . . . very easy to see why females could not resist. If she hadn't known the birds were real Earth natives (no doubt imported under some special enviro-friendly protections), she would have thought them a fanciful, customised concoction from some bio-lab. League-side, of course, as such things were likewise illegal in the Federation, much to the black market's delight.

Peacocks. She pondered that puzzle as she was led (or, more correctly, escorted) into an exquisite corridor of polished floorboards and eighteenth century paintings and decorations . . . historical nostalgia, as only Federation worlds knew how. British-occupied India, she thought, surveying a framed photograph, in black and white, of an Indian family in European-styled clothing, gathered for a leisurely day in the sun. A curious point in history to be so painstakingly remembered, given the evident Tanushan-Indian pride in their traditional, indigenous heritage.

A turn through a broad sitting room, with large windows overlooking the rear lawns, and more gorgeous furnishings, and then a dining room beyond with several uniformed staff setting the table with gleaming china and crystal. Then another hallway, and voices beyond, muffled by shut doors, and more staff intent on business . . . she was not, Sandy guessed, the only visitor present in the Embassy right now. In fact, judging by the degree of informal transmission traffic flying about on the local circuit, she was clearly intruding on a never-ending circle of talkfests. Thus the many harried staff, and the many closed doors, and the back-way route chosen by her escort.

Several more backdoors later, she arrived at another, plain wooden door. A guard opened it, briefly surveyed the interior, then turned to face Sandy.

"If you could wait in here, Ms. Kresnov," he said, in an inflectionless tone, "the Ambassador himself will be with you shortly."

An IR shift showed fairly cool blue hues across visible portions of the guard's body. And no visible pulse from a jugular, the most obvious giveaway. She herself looked much the same in an IR scan.

"What designation are you?" she asked the guard curiously.

"Please await the Ambassador in this room, Ms. Kresnov," the GI replied, stony-faced. "I assure you it is secure and unbugged."

She sighed. "As fun as upgrade surgery, you must be a reg." Looked him fully in the face, with careful scrutiny. Thinking it had been a long time since she'd had such face-to-face contact with any member of the artificial League soldiery who hadn't been trying to kill her at the time. "Do you know who I am?"

Patient silence from both guards. She gave up, and entered the room. Doubtless they'd find out soon enough. The door shut firmly behind her, and footsteps departed.

The room was difficult to put a name to. A study, perhaps? There were bookshelves, and a desk before the drawn curtains of the window . . . she reckoned it must look out over the front lawns, and the street beyond the wrought-iron fence. Best leave the curtains closed. A portrait on the wall, a white-bearded man in a plumed orange turban, his moustache intriguingly pointed as if in satirical protest at the stern glare on his face.

She strolled to the bookcase, stretching and flexing her shoulders within her jacket. Old titles. Old-style binding. Such books, she knew, were popular in Tanusha as much for their decorative value upon the bookshelf as their contents. The same information on disk could be had for a fraction of the cost. The kind of impracticality that so many in the League found exasperating, but which remained so firmly entrenched here in the Federation. And she wondered again at this choice of premises for the League Embassy. Technically League property, but all Tanushan land was planned and accounted for in advance . . . no doubt it was a lease, the terms of which stated occupancy and care of all pre-existing assets.

Tanushan humour, she guessed, with growing amusement. Federation humour, at the anti-nostalgia, anti-history League. And more, an Indian embrace of an aspect of their history many Indians preferred to forget, the ignobility of a time when others had ruled their destiny. But they remembered regardless, and recalled it in the greatest detail, in the belief that in the act of recalling where they'd been, they would more accurately come to understand where they were, and who they were. The League condemned such notions as restrictive and tiresome. And this . . . this building, and this choice of site for the Embassy, was the administration of Callay and Tanusha laughing at them.

Several browsed books and standing stretches later, the door opened, and Ambassador Gordon Yao entered. Or Yao

Gordon, she reflected, if one were in keeping with Chinese formalities. Closed the door behind him, and turned to face her. He wore a slick, wide-at-the-middle black tuxedo, a lot of gleaming hair spray, and a broad, welcoming smile.

"Cassandra." Beaming at her in a manner that was almost fatherly. And sighed, happily. "Cassandra. It is *so* good to finally meet you, I can't tell you how excited I was when they told me you had finally shown up. I would have extended you an invitation for dinner long ago, but there was never a quiet moment for either of us since your arrival, and . . . well, it did not seem entirely appropriate."

Sandy carefully replaced the book she had been browsing on its shelf, folded her arms and looked him over. A somewhat portly Chinese gentleman, with broad, friendly features . . . a quick flash-retrieve to a memory file, several matching ID images, age, height, previous assignments, the full CSA file, one of numerous she'd taken on since they'd taken her on board. Yao seemed harmless enough, a career diplomat, no military service or shady dealings, just a civil servant bureaucrat fluent in nineteen languages and with a taste for travel. Nineteen . . . she blinked in astonishment. Tape-teach made it easier, but it still required some talent.

"Hello, Ambassador," she said quietly. "Lovely place you have here."

"Oh it is, it is," Yao agreed, with surprising enthusiasm, strolling several paces into the room. "You know, it was originally intended as the Indian Trade Representative's building, but then some Indian media found out the design and protested that it didn't send the right *message*." With great amusement, his broad face jovial. "As if Delhi should worry that Tanushans were in danger of forgetting their true heritage, such typical Earth-bound ignorance of the outer worlds. And so some Tanushan planning bureaucrat, no doubt in a fit of hysteria, decided that this should become the League Embassy. You do get the joke, of course?"

"I do." Sandy discovered, to her own partial surprise,

that she was disappointed. She hadn't wanted Yao to be likable. Nor even interesting. Unfortunately, he had so far appeared both.

"I have been told that about you," Yao said, nodding curiously. Watching her with great intrigue. And, apparently, absolutely no fear at all. Quite the contrary, in fact. "You always took an interest in old heritage. Books and music. Your supervisors were most surprised, I gather."

"You are aware, of course, that I did not come here to reminisce."

Yao smiled broadly. "Of course, I understand. You are working for the CSA now. And how have the CSA been treating you? Are you finding civilian life agreeable?"

"Most agreeable."

"And you did receive my message, I trust?"

"I did. I called on Governor Dali personally."

"Did you? And was he . . . forthcoming?"

"No."

"I am keeping a most senior delegation of bankers and finance officials waiting," Yao continued, covering her laconic silences with nimble skill. He indicated back toward the door. "I told them I had an important call . . . would you please mind waiting another fifteen minutes? We were just concluding."

"Of course." And because Ibrahim's curiosity meant that she really ought to ask . . . "What do banks and finance companies want with the League?"

"Money," said Yao, with a grateful wink as he departed once more. "I'll be back shortly . . . Cassandra, it's just *wonderful* to meet you, I'll send someone for you very soon."

The door shut. Sandy gazed at it for a moment. Wondering, now, at the wisdom of coming here at all. Memories crowded, old, jittery reflexes, well remembered claustrophobia and fears. Worries over her supervision. Frustration at the caution of those she had contact with. The paranoia of her direct superiors. The unscheduled "check-ups" for psyche evaluation, which had long since ceased to yield meaningful results, so easily had she learned to manipulate the questions. It felt surreal to be back here again, among these people.

And she remembered, unbidden, Vanessa recounting with great humour one of her worst recurring nightmares—that she found herself still a teenager, and back in school, unprepared with major exams looming. The horror, Vanessa had opined with typically enthusiastic wit, had come not so much from school, but from the realisation that her entire life since, and all her newfound maturity and self-assurance, was all a lie, a transparent film that lay fragile and flimsy across the mass of childhood insecurities that was her true self.

Sandy had never known childhood. Had never been to school, nor shared those experiences. But that was what this felt like, only ten times worse. Back again, where she'd never, ever wanted to be, ever again. And Yao was friendly, and treated her as if she were one of his own. Damned if she was. It made her mad just to think of it. And being what she was, Sandy disliked being mad. Mad had never been a good idea. Unlike most people, she could not afford to lose her temper.

She felt tense, all over. Anita had good fingers, but already the tightness was returning, a slow, inexorable creeping that bled through her muscles and joints. The one and perhaps only thing she would willingly trade with a straight—a body that didn't cramp itself into knots every twenty hours without rigorous persuasion to do otherwise. Getting shot surely hadn't helped.

Well, there was enough space on the floor, and so she lay down on her back, put her arms above her head and stretched. She could only reach a little before her stomach pulled tight with a painful jab, sympathetic pains chasing and tingling their way through hips, back and hamstrings . . . she winced, relaxing that. Her tightening shoulders informed her they needed more work. Which her stomach would prevent. Damn. She tried wriggling sideways. Grabbed one wrist overhead and pulled over. It caught an as-yet undiscovered spot at the rear of her shoulder joint, which unwound with a nearly audible pop! A whole knot of muscle tightness went with it. She relaxed again, still wriggling, trying to find the next lot of vulnerable tight spots. Little good it'd do her. Impact concussion had thrown everything out of whack, she was tightening fast. Invulnerable killing machine, my arse . . .

The door handle turned and she froze in midreach for her weapon . . . a slow entry was no way to assault a GI in a closed room, all her instincts remained green. Voices from somewhere down the corridor outside . . . probably a visiting delegation member exploring, or lost on the way to the toilet. A little girl stuck her head around the corner, peering cautiously. Paused in amazement, seeing Sandy sprawled upon the floor, flat on her back. Sandy waved with her free hand.

"Hi." The girl took it for an invitation, ducked quickly inside the room and shut the door. Turned back to Sandy.

"What are you doing on the floor?" Chinese, with more than a passing resemblance to Mr. Yao, she reckoned. Short hair attractively arranged about a decorative blue hairband. She wore a matching blue dress of a denim-like fabric, neat and tidy. Polished brown leather shoes. She looked, Sandy thought, like a child who had been dressed for an occasion by her parents. A late occasion, at nearly 11:00 PM.

"I'm stretching. I'm very stiff, I've had a busy day." Propped herself up on her elbows, watching the girl curiously. The number of genuine conversations she'd had with children could be counted on one hand. Or maybe two. Several of those had been under circumstances she'd rather forget. To be approached, out of the blue, was very rare.

"Why do it in here?" the girl asked, somewhat dubiously. "You know there's a gym in the outer wing?" She looked about twelve, Sandy guessed. Young enough for innocence, old enough for basic maturity. She'd gathered. Although different children matured at different rates. Tape-teach and alternative learning methods could lead to discrepancies. And parents counted for a lot. Her curiosity deepened.

"I'm a guest, I don't know my way around. I got told to wait in here." Pulled herself properly upright and crossed her legs. "Are you Ambassador Yao's daughter?" A nod. Which explained the late hour—surely an Ambassador's twelve-year-old would be used to it by now. "Do you live here? At the Embassy?"

"No, we all got pulled in here by *security*." With disdainful emphasis. "They say it's too *dangerous* at home. So we've gotta live here now, until everything calms down." She sounded utterly annoyed with the whole scenario. Sandy empathised. "I haven't been off the grounds for the last week, not even with an escort." She strolled briskly to the chair by the table before the window, pulled it out and thumped herself down there. "I'm so *bored* I can't stand it." Sandy smiled faintly to herself, straightening her back and arching. It was an interesting perspective. She liked interesting perspectives.

"There are worse things in life than being bored, you know," she said.

"No there's *not*," said the girl sullenly, kicking her heels. Looked at Sandy. "What are you here for, anyway? I bet you're not with this stupid finance committee, you're dressed better. They all dress like narks."

"You like the way I'm dressed?"

"Yeah, I like casual. Leather's great. Dad won't let me wear casual in public." She made a face. "Says we've got appearances to keep up. Fat lot of good that does."

Mature kid, Sandy reckoned, to voice so many opinions so clearly, and with a complete stranger. Confident. And totally naive of the dangers.

"Your dad's an important man," she replied. Being a noncontroversial devil's advocate. "He's got a lot of responsibilities, you can't blame him for that. He's just good at his job."

"So people keep telling me. So what *are* you?" With growing impatience, and curiosity. Sandy reckoned telling anything but the truth could be problematic. Possibly dangerous.

"I'm a GI."

"Get *out*, you are not." With derisive irritation at so stupid a comment. As if she thought she was being made fun of. "GIs are narks. They're all *yessir* and *no sir*, they couldn't have a conversation to save their lives. Not the muscle-headed peabrains in this place, anyway."

"No, I am a GI. I work for the CSA. You watch the news at all?" The girl stared at her for a moment. Then it dawned on her. Excitedly.

"Oh no *way*!" With amazement. "That's you?" Sandy reached into her jacket, pulled out Ari's newly issued CSA badge and tossed it to her. The girl caught, opened and stared at it. "Oh wow! April Cassidy . . . so that's your name! Dad said some stuff about you earlier, I think . . . oh wow, he must be excited to see you, huh?"

A Federation child, Sandy reflected, might have reacted with terror. Or at least nervous apprehension. This girl was League bred, through and through. As the Ambassador's daughter, GIs were just a normal part of life, guarding the doorways, patrolling the perimeter, keeping an eye on things. Totally unexpectedly, the thought gave her a twinge of regret. All the children out there in Tanusha right now, doubtless terrified into nightmares and bed wetting by their parents' tales of the evil machine-people that lurk on the other side of the invisible Federation-League border. League children, by contrast, associated GIs with safety, guardianship and unconditional trust. Neither was correct, but the League kids had it closer to the mark. In her opinion.

"Why would he be so excited to see me?" Curious. Ambassador Yao had been very enthusiastic. Surprisingly so.

"You're such big news, everyone's heard of you! Dad was saying you left the League because of all the corruption in the ISO."

"Did he now?" It was a good enough explanation to a kid. Though "corrupt" wasn't quite the word she'd have used for the Internal Security Organisation.

"Yeah, he said the ISO's gotten much better now that

the new government's in power, they shook everything up, lots of people got sacked. That's why he wanted to see you, he thought maybe you'd like to come back to the League."

The simplicity took her breath away. For a moment, she couldn't think of anything to say. Where to begin? Why *couldn't* she return? There were so many reasons. But how to explain it? She wasn't sure that she could.

"It's not just the ISO . . ." she said finally, ". . . what's your name, by the way?"

"Ying."

"Ying. It's far more than the ISO, Ying. It's the whole system. It's no place for a person like me. For a GI like me. I just don't like it there, and I don't think they'd want me back anyway."

"Why not? I mean, if they've fixed everything?"

Sandy sighed. Restrained a smile.

"They didn't fix anything, Ying. Not really. I've read the CSA reports, I know what's been happening since I left. They sacked the most visible people, the ones who were embarrassing the politicians. The ones the media could pick on. Problem is, the people who ran the whole special operations section that I was part of weren't very visible. They never got punished, they just disappeared from sight for a while. They'll reappear eventually, they always do."

"Recruitment" was the monster department of League wartime administration. With barely half a billion people in the League, versus roughly twenty-seven billion in the Federation, the League relied upon Recruitment to even up the odds through the production of GIs. Recruitment was so full of secrets and broken rules that no League politician even liked to admit the extent of its powers—namely, that if it didn't exist, the League's war-fighting capability would be naught. Sandy had no wish to rush back into its embrace.

"But wouldn't you like to go somewhere where people don't hate you?" Ying asked. She looked puzzled.

"Not all people here hate me." With more confidence than she felt. "It's just a few. They make a lot of noise, that's all."

"You'd get treated better in the League," Ying replied, with great certainty. "You fought in the war for them, they'd be really grateful."

"Maybe." She'd be dead real fast if she went back, new administration or not. She knew far too much. She was taking a risk even being here. She questioned her sanity even now. More so when the door opened at that moment, and the GI who'd shot her not so many hours earlier walked into the room.

"Mustafa!" Ying said brightly. "You'll never guess who this is!"

The handsome African-featured man looked at Sandy. He wore a casual jacket, the kind beneath which weapons could comfortably be concealed, with many convenient pockets. Likewise comfortable pants and shoes. Dark, intelligent eyes, gleaming with familiar recognition. Sandy was not surprised. She'd been expecting him.

"I'd guess . . ." the GI named Mustafa said, making a show of hard thought, chin in hand, ". . . she's a GI. A really special GI. Am I right?"

"You knew!" Ying was annoyed. "How did you know?"

"We can tell, Ms. Yao," he said, with mysterious knowing. "We GIs, we automatically know each other, it's like a special psychic bond that we all share."

Ying stared, wide-eyed. And stared at Sandy.

"He's talking crap," Sandy advised the girl, calmly, still seated cross-legged, stretching her back. "On a busy street I wouldn't know him from the next person. We met before."

"You met?" Ying was amazed. "How could you have met, Mustafa's only been here a day?"

"Like I said," repeated Mustafa, "it's a special psychic connection." His eyes remained locked on Sandy's, lively and penetrating. Sandy's return stare was inexpressive. "We both just happened to end up at the same place, at the same time, looking for the same thing." He shrugged. "A little coincidence, a little romance, a little exchange of fire . . . I found the encounter most invigorating."

Sandy sat quietly. Feeling cold. She'd suspected this, the moment she'd first confronted him. Had always suspected it, really, on one level or another. Even though she lacked all evidence, and had searched frequently, she still suspected. And now, it seemed, the proof confronted her.

"What's your designation?" she asked him, quietly. No way was this man a reg. Nor even a mod. She'd known mods. Her entire team had consisted of them.

"GI-5182-IT." With a calm, almost amused look. He knew what that meant to her. He knew the shock at hearing those numbers. Most evidently, he knew a hell of a lot more about her than she did about him. "You thought you were the only one." A flat statement. Already knowing the answer.

"Obviously." She'd seen it coming. She hadn't wanted to be shaken. But she was. So much of her life had been lived in the supposed knowledge that she was unique. The only one. The sole GI to possess this particular level of mental sophistication, by design. It shouldn't have mattered. But it did. And she didn't have a clue what that meant. 5182 . . . higher than her. Not that that meant anything. And . . . IT? Intel? She'd never heard of that. Of GIs designated with anything other than frontline combat in mind. Her own designation was HK, for Hunter/Killer. She didn't know whether that meant he should be scared of her, or vice versa.

"Was that why you came here?" he asked. "To find out more?"

Sandy refocused more fully upon his face, with sudden intensity. More about you? Don't flatter yourself.

"I work for the CSA," she replied flatly. "You were observed committing criminal acts at a crime scene. I'm here because the League is sticking its nose in where it doesn't belong. I want the details."

"You observed no such thing," Mustafa said with amusement. "I was merely strolling down a street to take what I had intended to be a very pleasant walk along the river when a gang of hoodlums accosted me and forced me into a chase through a building to escape. How you happened to be there too I have no idea."

"You might want to try explaining to the CSA the death of one Lu Fayao in premises nearby, they'll be most interested."

"Ah yes," said Mustafa, nodding with exaggerated realisation. "The CSA. That glorious, upstanding Tanushan institution. Federation institution, I should say. How are they treating you? Defenders of the liberal political idealism that they are? Doubtless you've made countless friends, and everyone's welcomed you with open arms?" With palpable, humoured sarcasm.

Sandy thought of the dark looks, the bitching, the wafts of undercurrents, things said behind her back, complaints lodged by various senior officials and department heads, alarmed meetings in Ibrahim's office after hours . . . and she thought of Vanessa. A warm, pleasant thought, right there. And the technogeeks in Intel, clustering enthusiastically about, wanting to please. Ibrahim's measured confidence. N'Darie red-faced and yelling before the Senate Security Council, defending her.

"I have friends," she told Mustafa, with quiet certainty. "I have friends the likes of whom I've never known before."

Mustafa snorted. And settled himself comfortably on the floor opposite, a leg stretched out before him, somewhat gingerly. Stretched, carefully. It caught Sandy off guard, just for a moment. Triggered old memories . . . GIs so often conversed in such settings, seated or lying flat, stretching out. An idle moment was a moment to stretch. GIs always stretched during informal conversation, particularly with each other. She hadn't realised she'd missed it until that very moment.

"I don't doubt you have individual friends . . . but do you really think that the system is ever going to accept you?" Incredulously. "Just look at where you are now . . . there are interest groups on all sides against you, particularly the religions, the Senate is mostly against you, the media is mostly against you . . . Cassandra, if it were just the fringe, that would be one thing, but it's the *mainstream* here. This is the major dividing ideology that separates League from Federation, this isn't just going to go away overnight."

"Mustafa." Flatly. Not liking this lecture from any League jackboot, let alone a GI. Not to mention someone who'd just recently plugged her with two rounds from point-blank range. She was rational. She didn't take it personally. But she had her limits. "What's your full name?"

"Major Mustafa Ramoja, at your service." Leaning gingerly forward to clasp his ankle with both hands. Very tender in the thighs, she noted. Well, they were even. Kind of.

"Mustafa's a Turkish name. You look African. You know why that works?"

"Not a clue." Still stretching, eyeing her curiously.

"African Renaissance, late twenty-first century. Africa finally caught up with the rest of the world, lots of manoeuvring for trade blocks, counters to the India/China split . . . the Middle East's the natural sphere of African influence. Arabs and Africans became close, Islam became dominant in Africa. Cairo became the capital of the Arab/African alliance. Lots of cross-cultural moves, some Turkish or other Middle Eastern names became popular among Islamic Africans. Lots of GIs have cross-cultural names. Me, for example. I've often wondered why."

"Does it matter?" With quizzical regard. Sandy restrained her disbelief.

"Only fools and League ask that question. You can't understand the Federation without knowing why that matters. You can't understand Callay or Tanusha without knowing why it matters. Biotech ideology didn't just materialise, it was created by a whole host of cultural, religious and historical factors. This whole Article 42 debate is governed entirely by those factors. And in you come, the bloody know-it-all League, with your supposed tech-edge and your damn superior, self-inflicted ignorance, and think you can fix it all. Running into sensitive sites, stealing information with all guns blazing, telling me I don't know what *I'm* doing trying to make a home here . . . what the hell are *you* doing here, anyway? Hasn't Ryssa had enough of their little covert adventures? Haven't they figured what damage it causes, for them and everyone else?"

Her voice was raised beyond what she'd intended. She was losing her cool. It'd been happening with disturbing frequency lately. Ramoja's gaze showed that he'd noticed.

"*Are* you trying to make a home here?" he asked.

She wriggled her spine, creating tension ripples that flexed through her shoulders.

"I'm sure as hell not going back with you." With firm intensity. "Not after I've been here. The claustrophobia would be stifling."

"Claustrophobia?" Frowning.

"You don't have a clue, do you?" His return gaze was calmly uncomprehending. She shook her head faintly. "Forget it. Life's too short."

"We should take a walk. I have questions."

"Yeah. Me too. I'll have the CSA make your life real difficult if you don't answer them satisfactorily, believe me."

"My questions for yours." Patiently. "Quid pro quo."

"That's Latin," she jabbed, in determined pursuit. "You know what it means, literally?"

"No, what?"

"I've no idea. But it's the difference between the two of us. You don't care. I do."

"Why?" he asked calmly, eyebrows raised.

"You tell me," she replied, her stare burning. "I'm the product of League intentions and League designs. League wanted me this way. Capable of seeing the broader strategic implications. Know thy enemy. I'm good at that. I was so damn good at that, I realised my enemy wasn't who I thought it was. There's a lesson in there for all of you. Until you figure it out, I'll never go back. Ever."

Ambassador Yao entered the room before Ramoja could reply. Blinked in surprise, seeing Ying seated on the chair opposite, listening with bewildered fascination. Did a fast double-take, then frowned and said something force-fully in Mandarin . . . something about illicit wanderings, homework and little girls who should learn to do what their parents told them . . . Mandarin was Sandy's best non-English language, she'd heard enough of it in the League. Ying scowled and got to her feet.

"I gotta go." In vaguely accented English—Ryssa accent, Sandy reckoned, though it'd been a while since she'd heard it. "Are you gonna come back and visit some-time?"

Sandy managed a lopsided smile. "It's possible." She held out her hand. Ying walked over and took it, and they shook. "Nice to meet you, Ying. Don't grow up to be a fool like your elders, huh?"

"What're my chances?" Ying retorted as she left. Passed her father, who held the door open for her. Sandy's gaze rested on the Ambassador.

"That depends," she said.

"The one thing I have never understood about straights," Ramoja was saying as they walked slowly across the gravel drive at the back of the house, "is why they overprotect their children." Stones crunched beneath their feet. Sandy recognised the car that had brought her in, among the others. Several guards stood nearby, rifles in hand. Standard defensive format, the positions and angles translated reflex-ively in her head. "Young Ms. Yao seems a very intelligent child. She was learning of important issues that will shape her life in years ahead. Yet the Ambassador removed her, and was displeased."

Ambassador Yao had left them to their discussion, feeling that perhaps his presence would have been intruding. And perhaps it would.

"Most civilians in modern societies place a value upon childhood innocence, Major," Sandy replied. Scanning the garden as she walked. Trees and landscaped flowerbeds. A pond and artificial stream spanned by a footbridge. Light from the house spilled golden across the broad lawns, and trees cast long shadows that fled toward the rear wall, crossed and overlapping as the night reasserted itself. "Life is so chaotic, there are so many hard truths and reasons to be cynical. People think childhood should be sacrosanct. A refuge of innocence."

"Amazing." Ramoja smiled faintly to himself. "Such a broad universe, and so much to learn. I often wonder why people don't take more pride in themselves and their capabilities. At being able to cope with the universe, and understand it properly. Yet they call it cynicism, and shield their children from it, thus creating unrealistic expectations and adding to the weight of disillusionment when it does finally arrive with adulthood." They left the gravel, feet suddenly soft on springy grass. "So much modern civilisation in the Federation seems built on regret and self-doubt. Regret that they ever achieved modernity in the first place, and self-doubt at failing to live up to the standards lauded in the common mythology of premodernity, glorifying some bygone era that never truly existed in the first place."

Inexplicably, Sandy found herself fighting back a smile, and turned her head to make sure Ramoja didn't see it. Fancy a GI making such ruminations. It was also unsettling. She had no idea why it suddenly struck her as funny. Perhaps she was thinking of her team, back in Dark Star, and the blank stares they'd given her when she'd indulged in similar ponderings herself.

"I can feel a League diatribe coming on," she volunteered dryly, cycling through spectrums to see the patterned distortion caused by a local laser-grid detection system hidden nearby, laid flat barely millimetres above the grass between trees. Easy to spot, if you knew what to look for . . . with super-enhanced vision, of course.

"It *is* a League advantage," Ramoja said, unperturbed. His methodical approach was all GI, and all military. His voice was melodious, and often thoughtful. His manner was always calm. A more bookish, studious version of herself, she guessed. That was unsettling too. "Less of the old, mythological baggage means a fresher, more realistic view of the universe, and of humans generally. The Federation is always being bound up in cultural mores that are increasingly meaningless in a modern society, whether it's engagement with the Talee or other nearby alien civilisations, or the pursuit of synthetic replication biotech, or the labyrinth of mostly conflicting legislation surrounding the protection of genetic coding data . . . the whole Birthfile accreditation system is a bureaucratic nightmare and a security sieve. The Federation will never catch up with the League as long as these kinds of basic progress continue to be held back."

"Who won the war?" Sandy reminded him.

"Size is no indication of moral righteousness."

"Yes it is. It indicates that the vast majority of humanity are not yet ready for the kinds of advances that the League espouses. That's democracy."

"The League is no part of Federation democracy, what right does the Federation have to impose its will on the League?"

"Every right, since the League always claims to be acting in the best interests of the species. With a hand on their heart and the anthem playing in the background, a tear of patriotic humanism spilling down each rosy cheek."

"I can't believe," Ramoja said, fixing her with a hard sideways look, "that you could possibly find yourself identifying with a set of philosophies that actively deny your right to even exist."

Sandy snorted, running a hand through loose, more-than-regulation-length hair. Beside Ramoja and his African shave-cut, she felt smugly *unregulation*. She liked it. She felt *herself*.

"What do I have to do with it? If a policy's wrong, it's wrong. Where I happen to fit into the equation is irrelevant."

"You really went Federation?" Eyes narrowed, some of his bookish, distant intellectualism lost for the moment. A military GI once again, blunt and dangerous. "You really switched? Or are you just angry, looking for vengeance?"

"You think you'd be alive if I were?" Not bothering to look at him and dignify that remark. The flowerbeds beneath the spreading trees to their left held concealed scanners, ankle-level tripwires that deactivated with measured stagger as they approached.

"I do." With typical military confidence. "You're no better than me. Today proved that."

"If you're so sure, Major, you've got a problem. Yes, I went Federation. I'd been leaning that way for a long time. It took drastic circumstances to make me realise it."

For a moment, Ramoja didn't say anything. The murmur of night traffic was louder, from ground traffic on the front road to the repetitive, drifting whine of aircars overhead, small spots of light moving across the darkened sky, the occasional brighter, faster flash of a lower altitude lane.

"I know what happened to your team. It was inexcusable, those responsible have been punished." Yeah, right. She was surprised at her own level of cool on the matter. She was not, she knew, over it. She was just in no mood to blow her stack about it. Ramoja would believe what he believed, she knew better than to think a fit of temper could change that where logic had failed. "You have my sympathies."

"I don't understand," she replied coolly, "how someone who knows what his own side is responsible for, and how little respect they truly have for the artificial lives they've created, could continue to serve so unswervingly."

"No bureaucratic system is perfect, Captain," Ramoja replied, with cool, effortless efficiency. "As a temporarily assigned recruit of the CSA, you can obviously understand that."

"The CSA makes honest mistakes, Major. They're caused by too many checks and balances, too much bureaucratic supervision, the usual civilian red tape. It prevents excess. It irritated me at first. But then I realised what it prevents. Far better to have a morally centred gridlock than seamlessly efficient fucking fascist murder."

Temper again. Where had that come from? Ramoja

looked at her, eyes narrowed in direct consideration. She shoved her hands into her jacket pockets, and surveyed the still-distant rear garden wall.

"You've changed, Captain." With grim, contemplative certainty. Smug prick, Sandy thought. "You are not as your duty reports illustrated. You have less control, certainly for a GI brought up on development tape and instinctive discipline. You are emotional. It clouds your judgment."

Sandy repressed a smirk. "You're just a walking 'android cliché,' aren't you?" Shot him a sideways look, and got only blank incomprehension in return. Shook her head in faint disbelief. "It's amazing. You'd scare the shit out of people here. That's the problem with all the bullshit they believe about GIs, all the clichés their bad TV shows and VR games have taught them, they're all frighteningly close to reality. But a lot of clichés are. How d'you know so much about me, anyway? You read up before you came here?"

"I read my share. Your case is not unknown among League hierarchy, Captain."

No, she bet it wasn't. Ramoja had a knack for understatement, it seemed.

"You're ISO, aren't you?" It suddenly fit. She stopped as they reached the decorative little stream that cut through the springily even lawn, bubbling over strategically placed rocks and miniature rapids. No frogs, though. Built across a broad river delta, Tanusha was full of frogs. But she couldn't hear them croaking. Maybe all the electronic security scared them away. "This whole thing's ISO. That's why I never knew you existed. That's why you're qualified to do data-raids on civilian targets."

Ramoja smiled, an ironic twisting of handsome, full lips. "I'm surprised you didn't realise that earlier."

"Yeah, well, ISO aren't known to trust GIs in ops all too much. Fancy them having their own pet GI, and high-des too. They commission you?"

Ramoja turned to face her fully, arms folded, frowning at her like he was trying to figure her out.

"They *requested* me. Really, Captain, I find your evident

distaste for the processes of your own creation quite surprising."

"League Internal Security Organisation requests a high-designation GI for their own specific purposes, and you don't find that just a little alarming?"

"Based on your model, Captain, and the remarkable success that you attained."

Sandy stared at him. Shit. She really wished he hadn't said that.

"You suggest we're related or something, I'll kick your arse."

Ramoja smiled. Abruptly charming, in a most handsome, broad-featured manner.

"After a sense, Captain, we're all related. I know the ISO quite intimately. I was brought up there, if you like. It is an honourable organisation, with the best interests of the League at heart. They've treated me as nothing less than an equal for all my waking memory."

Bet they did, Sandy thought, watching his face with expressionless intensity. Taller than her, a clipped, lean shadow in the dark. Dark Star had left her to fend for herself, mostly. She had her team to socialise with, and various straight humans about, whether ship or station-board, or planetside between tours.

But the ISO didn't work in combat teams. Individual-oriented organisation, like all Intel. With their own advanced GI. No other GIs to socialise with, just straights. One of the gang. Of course they treated him well . . . operationally, if they wanted him to be any use, they didn't have a choice. In Dark Star, she'd tolerated the inevitable few non-GI officers and assorted supervisors who hadn't welcomed her company—she could ignore them if she wished, and go elsewhere. Ramoja hadn't had that option. She could just imagine the instructions before his first days on the job . . . "Be nice to the GI, or else." Or else he'll get mad and kill you. Or become increasingly disillusioned with the entire League ideology, and defect to the Federation.

Only she'd managed that without excessive ill-treatment, for the most part. So where'd it come from? Why was she here, on this side, and Ramoja, the opposite? What was wrong with him? Or, come to that, with her?

"The Zaiko Warren," she said, firmly stepping on the turmoil in her brain. "What were you doing there?"

"You are mistaken, Captain, I was not there."

"A GI killed a man by the name of Lu Fayao in the Zaiko Warren," Sandy continued impassively. "Lu Fayao was a member of a shadowy Tanushan underground group who indulge in all kinds of illicit information-crime-related activities. This group is connected to a hacker named Sai Va, who just happens to be a dedicated anarchist—a common affliction among the underground. Sai Va used League-issue attack codes to infiltrate Lexi Incorporated. Sai Va then passed on the scheduling information from this infiltration to a bunch of radical ideologues called the Human Reclamation Project. They used it to plan and execute an attack upon top Lexi executives. You do understand, Mr. Ramoja, that whichever League agency or operative who allowed Sai Va access to those League-issue attack codes is therefore directly responsible for whatever purposes that information was put to after it was stolen?"

A calm, expectant look from Ramoja, waiting for her to come to her final point.

"The League retains many operational activities in Tanusha that the CSA finds greatly concerning," Sandy continued. "Your ties to Tanushan mafia groups and their black-market trade in illegal biotech and other information foremost among them. On behalf of the CSA, I'm here to formally request you sever all such ties and contacts, and ask all such groups acting on your behalf or upon the understanding of your future support to cease, and cease immediately—before we have any more explosions or mafia-funded goons running around public areas firing military-grade weapons at anyone who comes into sight."

"And the League is to blame for the existence of Tanushan mafia?" Ramoja asked mildly. "For the presence of self-styled assassins, who dress and operate in the manner of drug-crazed civilians who play too much combat-VR and watch too much television?"

"Not for their presence, Mr. Ramoja." Coldly. "For their employment."

"I assure you, Captain, League operatives would never seek to employ such erratic and unreliable individuals on any matter."

"Friends of yours did."

"No friends of *mine*, Captain. I am a recent arrival here. I did not initiate any activities. I am here to put things right. League operating policy has been less than perfect in the past, I'll warrant. Thus my presence."

"*You're* their fix?" Vision locked onto him with deadly intensity. "You're their idea of a problem solver? Jesus . . . you transmitted League encryption on an open street near active and operational net-monitoring software. How do you think the GGs found you so fast? How do you think I was tracking you? You don't even understand the basics of a civilian infotech network infrastructure, this is an entirely alien operating environment for you . . ."

"Oh, I knew you would track me." Smiling calmly. "Your patterns were very obvious on the network. I wanted you to catch up." Sandy's gaze remained unwavering and unresponsive. "The mafia—the GGs, as you call them— were a possible nuisance, but I thought it worth the risk to meet you, Cassandra. Well worth the risk indeed."

She could feel her stomach tightening. Memory of the bullet strikes of that meeting . . . but also the cold, hollow feeling that not everything was as it had previously seemed. Ambassador Yao, so delighted to meet her. His daughter Ying, telling of her father's hopes for the possible return of their runaway GI . . . Obviously it had been on the Ambassador's mind a lot, if he had even confided in his daughter about it. The new GI contingent arrived with the new League delegation, sent by a new League administration in power after the new elections that had crushed the old hardliners in a massive landslide. So much new. So much changed since she'd been a soldier of the League armed forces. New hopes and new priorities for a new administration. Loose ends to tie up. Lost sheep to gather back into the flock.

"I'm never going back," she said softly. "Never."

"ISO would welcome you, Cassandra," said Ramoja. A soft, comforting note to his voice. "You appear to have shown a real flair for intelligence of late. You need not return to your old post at Dark Star . . . special ops alone does appear something of a waste for a creative intellect of your credentials."

"You put me back in Intel," she said, just as softly, "I'll go through Recruitment back offices with an assault rifle, I guarantee it. Clean out all the human waste your shiny new government didn't have the guts to axe."

"They are no longer a factor, Cassandra." Eyes narrowing somewhat, despite the conciliatory tone. "Every administration has its factions. Just look at the Callayan Parliament."

"The Callayan Parliament never murdered my friends."

"Many of them would like to murder you, given the chance."

"And my friends here would try and stop them. I have people here who value me for who I am rather than what I am. In the League everyone associated with me has some kind of vested interest or position to protect. No one in the Federation shares responsibility for my existence. In some ways I'm less politicised here than back there. I'm certainly much safer. I don't think you can realise just how many powerful people would want to silence me if I returned unless you've actually served in the frontlines during the war, and know just how much there is to cover up . . ."

"So I've heard speculated before." Ramoja cut her off, his brow furrowed. "I think you'd be surprised at the extent of ISO resources within all branches of the military . . ."

"And what d'you reckon happened to Torres Station? What do your reports tell you?"

"An unfortunate accident." His frown deepening. "Federation warships blew their own station rather than let us have it, they weren't aware of the civilians still on board."

"I *took* that damn station, me and another team under my command. I bet you didn't know that either." No, the look on his face said as much. "I took it with minimal loss on either side. We got the command centre and shut down the guard stations which let the ships in. It was a damn pirate raid for the Fourth Fleet, we stole their supplies, then loaded their civvies onto transports for deposit elsewhere while they blew the station. Feddie cruisers were using it for home base from which to raid our shipping through the Batik Corridor. They *said* they'd get all the civvies off before they blew it, but I thought the cargo manifests didn't add up with the extra supplies they were taking on board—I checked it and they were a full seven thousand people short of what I already knew were on that station. Seven thousand. Just like the Feddie newscasts said, seven thousand civilian deaths. They had the choice between cargo or saving those seven thousand . . . they chose the cargo, sealed the exits with all those people still aboard, backed off and blew it just as the Feddie reinforcements came in from jump . . . Jump approach is autofire, the Fed captains themselves could never be certain in the reassessment that some of their rounds hadn't mistracked in the confusion immediately after jump. They could never rule out the possibility that they *had* blown their own station by mistake—that was the Fourth's intention. And, of course, the civvies they had taken on board were no wiser. They couldn't see what was happening, all they knew was they'd come under attack after the undock, the last transport hadn't been able to dock and the station had been hit by Federation fire."

"Then how do *you* know?" His dark stare was intense. "You hadn't access to bridge data either, you wouldn't have seen what was going on."

"I asked the Captain." Meeting his gaze with expressionless certainty. "Carlotta Teig, Captain of *Firebird*, common ride of mine in the Fourth—fast assault carrier, perfect for Dark Star ops, I'm sure you know it. Ask her when you get back. Tell her I sent you. She won't be surprised. She's a tough, cynical old thing, always told me I was wasted in the military—one more thing she was right on. Sure as hell she wasn't surprised when I went AWOL. You ask her, privately and off the record. She'll tell you what happened at Torres Station. She nearly resigned herself after that one. She bitched so hard they would have removed her but they didn't want a mutiny on *Firebird*, she was that popular."

Ramoja's frown remained. Intent. Troubled. A light breeze shifted the branches about the broad, grassy yard, gentle whispers in the dark. Water bubbled in the landscaped stream, splashing over carefully laid pebbles beneath the ornate, arching footbridge. Something in Ramoja's gaze unsettled her. As if he himself was unsettled. She hadn't expected that at all.

"What?" she asked him.

A pause from Ramoja before replying. Then . . .

"Captain Carlotta Teig is dead. Suicide. A few months ago. She overdosed on neuro-enhancement prescription pills, left a suicide note telling of the lack of purpose in her life after the new Expenditures Review Committee announced the decommissioning of *Firebird*."

Sandy stared at the pretty little footbridge for a long moment, nestled among the drooping native willows that swayed in the nighttime breeze. Took a deep, slow breath.

"I'm very sorry," Ramoja said with quiet sincerity. "I know from your review files that the two of you got along. She invited you for dinner and backgammon on occasion." He had done his homework on her if he knew that much. "She wrote in her diary that she thought you yourself were one of the most hopeful, positive things to come from the entire war. She said that you were a clear demonstration of the 'ultimate futility of violence.' It seemed to me a curious sentiment from one of the League's most accomplished naval captains. I wondered what she meant."

"She believed in her politics," Sandy said quietly, gazing

at the little bridge, peaceful and calm. It helped against the growing pain in her throat. "Not in violence. She always hated the necessity." Another deep breath. She wiped at her eyes. Ramoja watched in sombre curiosity. "She meant that the best weapon is intelligence. Intelligence with which to kill the enemy. But my intelligence made me wonder if I should be befriending them instead. She thought that was wonderful. Said it gave her hope for the universe."

Long-suppressed memories came rushing to the surface. Late-shift meals in Teig's quarters, a glass of whisky for the Captain, tea for herself—whisky did nothing for her. "My condolences," Teig had said upon hearing that, and meant it. Ship smells, metal and synthetics, dull-smelling air from the purifiers. The comfortable, familiar rustle of jumpsuit fatigues. Sparse furnishings, a complete lack of clutter, all loose items locked away in case of sudden manoeuvrings. The clank and whine of cylinder rotation, the gravity that kept them seated.

Discussions of politics. Economics. The bread and butter of what the fighting was all about. Teig was committed passionately to the League cause, whatever her distaste for some of the methods. Sandy herself, the Captain had told her, was reason enough to believe the League position on artificial humanity was sound—far from the old fears of artificial intelligences turning on their creators, Sandy's greater intelligence increased her degree of emotional attachment and commitment. The irony, Teig had said, was that in their search to create a more lethal killing machine, League bioengineers had made her less dangerous, not more so. A machine could kill innocents and feel no remorse. A greater, more developed intellect would agonise about whether to pull the trigger—morality was nothing if not a higher intellectual function. Sandy herself hadn't been all too sure of the rationale behind the argument, having read a great deal about certain highly intelligent tyrants in past human history, but she was willing to concede the Captain's basic point, if only to make herself feel better.

What had happened to Sandy's team must have hit Teig hard also, when she heard. She'd never had a chance to talk to her before leaving. Leaving had been a fast decision, a spur-of-the-moment thing. Just a fake ID with some fancy hack-work to get her a spot on an outgoing freighter from G-4 station in Argonis orbit. By the time the over-stretched, undermanned staff at that chaotic base station realised she was missing, the freighter had already jumped, and there was no way of telling if she'd actually been on it, so many freighters had been coming and going in those last, desperate, chaotic months before the final election, and the peace treaty that had immediately followed the old administration's overthrow. The battered military infra-structure had been struggling under impossible resource demands, plummeting budgets, horrendous periphery casualties due to the newly aggressive Federation assault squadrons having perfected decimating system strikes that left League shipping and system infrastructural facilities smashed and defenceless. There was no hope in hell that anyone was going to be able to trace the whereabouts of one maybe-AWOL GI who was awfully good at forging elec-tronic credentials for whatever purpose she required. And who had technical skills that made her an automatic selec-tion for any merchant's crew in need of an extra specialist or two . . . and in those times, that meant everyone, per-sonnel were abandoning posts to see to their families in the crisis and there weren't enough hands to go around. She'd just vanished. And of those she'd left behind . . . several might possibly have taken it hard. Teig had been one.

But hard enough to suicide? No chance. Teig had a family she'd been greatly looking forward to seeing again. Teig had wanted to go to a rock concert again—live, loud, and sweaty—she'd talked about it often. Teig would have been happy for her, getting out and off on her own while the whole marvellous, glorious League system imploded like a collapsing neutron star behind her. Teig knew damn well she'd head to the Federation. But she doubted greatly that that explained Teig's death. No. Far more likely it was

Torres Station and a few other such incidents, and threats of review before newly appointed investigatory committees established under the new administration. Certain folks in the old administration would have felt mighty threatened by such a prospect. Dear God. Now . . . *now*, of all times, she wanted to kill someone. She had a pretty fair idea she knew who.

"If she was going to kill herself," Sandy said quietly, "she'd have blown her brains out. Pills were not her style." And turned a damp-eyed, burning stare at Ramoja. "Neither was suicide. There's no fucking way, Ramoja. No fucking way. You know that, don't you?"

"It was mentioned as a possibility," Ramoja replied sombrely. "Things in the last year have been crazy. Everything's changed, from the economy to the administration. It's been chaos, and many investigations have been launched. Intelligence and law enforcement resources have been severely stretched. Not all investigations begun have yet been completed."

"If you need anything. *Anything.* You come ask me. I'll give you anything you need to get the fuckers who killed her. Or any other similar matter you have on file. You say the ISO's improved . . . you do this, you damn well prove it to me, nail these scum to the wall. Hard."

"Madam," Ramoja said with all seriousness, "it would be my great pleasure." Their stares locked. He seemed sincere, Sandy reckoned. Greatly so. "Cassandra, the war has ended. It allowed much to develop within the bureaucracies that was not desirable, most of it kept from public view by wartime security restrictions. But there is a new administration in power now. Things are not perfect, it will be a long time until they are, if ever. But the steps are being taken, and the ISO is stepping alongside. On the civilian, democratic side. You must believe me on that."

"Surely you didn't come all this way just for me. What did you expect to find when you arrived here? What was your mission?"

"To help put things right." Sandy just looked at him,

unimpressed by such cryptic utterances. He took a breath. "I certainly hoped not to find that unauthorised parties had been allowed access to classified League attack codes. We are in the process of tracing the parties involved. The leak will be plugged, I assure you."

That was the raid. Sai Va's accomplices. Tracking him, and tracking who'd given him those codes. She brushed loose hair from her brow as a light gust caught at it, her gaze unwavering.

"Lu Fayao was a Tanushan citizen," she said. "A criminal, perhaps, but not a convicted one. His death qualifies as murder. Surely you realise that."

"Prove that I was there," Ramoja replied—a certain, quiet challenge. "Prove that it wasn't self defence. Prove that the perpetrator wasn't under orders. Prove that in the grand scheme of events currently under way in this city, one minor criminal's death really matters. Shutting down such dangerous leaks will save lives. The choice is obvious. And diplomatic immunity still applies, as it does for all the other hundreds of official representatives from various other Federation worlds and administrations who are currently engaged in bilateral or multilateral negotiations that could easily result in far more deaths than one single disruptive underworld influence."

It was as good as an admission. Probably he knew that any recordings she made would be of little legal use in a court, given her presently dubious legal status with the CSA. And diplomatic immunity meant it wouldn't get to court even if she was right.

And the message was clear and straightforward enough—League resources had been used in an attempt to kill people on that boat. The League resented being implicated for something it had never condoned. The League meant to demonstrate to various wayward Tanushan groups how dangerous it was to make them angry. If only, Sandy thought sourly, they hadn't established so many dubious connections with so many of these dubious groups in the first place as an article of League foreign policy.

Former foreign policy, Ramoja insisted. Did that mean that the entire events of last month were not approved by the current League administration? The temporary removal of the Callayan President from office following the attempt upon her life? She wasn't willing to bet on it. Biotech infiltration into the Federation private sector was one of those peripheral activities that no League government liked to associate itself with directly. But that did not mean they didn't know it was going on . . . just that they'd failed to take steps to stop it, or moderate the implementation. Individual League field agency commanders, usually ideological extremists, had the final say. And the glimpses of potential profits involved in the new technologies now drove Tanushan BT corporations to press for independence from the Federation, and freedom from those restrictive, profit-squeezing anti-BT regulations. Potential profit determined political ideology. Ideological determinism. League foreign policy at work.

That it had necessitated cutting her open on an operating table while she'd been awake and screaming . . . a small price to pay for the future progress and ideological stability of the human species. The needs of the many, the line went, outweighed the needs of the few.

It had taken many years for Sandy to learn to distrust such logic. The many *were* the few, after all, only multiplied. And if a civilisation could not even guarantee the rights of the few, the rights of the many were surely beyond their grasp.

A familiar sound interrupted her next question. A sharp, distant echo. Again, and once more . . . the same sound, deflected off multiple highrises. Thump. And another . . . Explosion. Perhaps fifteen kilometres off, maybe more. She and Ramoja stared at each other for a moment, with knowing recognition . . . Sandy uplinked at rapid speed, and found . . . Junshi. She hadn't realised it'd been that close. The hostage drama. Vanessa. Shit.

"Offensive," said Ramoja, his eyes distant. Concentrating. "Penetration explosive. Probably they took out a wall."

Several walls, ceilings, and probably floors too, with Vanessa in charge. She didn't do things by halves.

"I've gotta go." Quietly. "I'll speak with you later."

"Captain . . ." Ramoja frowned in surprise. ". . . we have much to talk about yet, I was hoping to ask you about . . ."

"Plenty of time later," Sandy replied, turning and striding back toward the brightly lit rear verandah, and the guards on ready standby about the railings and parked cars at the rear. Ramoja accompanied her, matching her pace. She felt suddenly tight, tense and claustrophobic. Scared. She had to get over there. "Please don't venture outside of these premises more than necessary, for everyone's benefit."

"It rarely proves necessary." Still frowning, with evident puzzlement. "You are leaving because of the hostage drama? They were always going to attack, Cassandra, and most likely at night. The hijackers are a most disagreeable sect, something religious, I forget the name. Probably your CSA has put their best SWAT commander onto the job. From what I've heard of local SWAT, he should be perfectly adequate. I don't understand why you must leave now."

"No," Sandy muttered, striding faster toward the verandah. The tightness in her stomach pulled on recent wounds, a painful cramping. "No, I don't imagine you would." And realised something in a sudden shock, and turned on him forcefully . . .

"Chu! Is Chu still alive? Do you know where she is?"

Ramoja looked totally blank for a moment. Then recalling . . .

"Rhian Chu, your old Dark Star comrade?"

"Yes!" With agonised impatience, heart beating hard against her ribcage . . .

"I'm sorry, Cassandra . . . I don't know." Helplessly, alarmed at her evident distress. "Honestly, I don't . . . those elements that took in the survivors of your unit were among the first to technically "disappear" when everything started collapsing in those final days . . . I just don't know. She might be alive, but I've no way of telling."

A new sound reached her maximised hearing, a faint, drifting reverberation on the cool breeze . . . weapons fire, light and percussive. Lots of it. She turned and ran.

CHAPTER 8

The eastern border road along Junshi Park was a mass of cluttered emergency vehicles, tracer-lights and clustered, sheltered personnel. Sandy halted her Prabati before the roadblock and flashed her ID at the policewoman ... got a somewhat dubious look from the cop, then a signal to pull the barrier aside. Simple metal barriers, Sandy noted, as used in road construction—the police were unused to this sort of thing, and had no more specialised equipment. She repocketed her ID and nudged the throttle, the Prabati accelerating smoothly away and up the main, six-lane road toward the chaos ahead.

Firetrucks, police cars, equipment vans and control vehicles blocked the road several hundred metres further on, the odd civilian cruiser dispersed among the ground vehicles. Toward the perimeter of those sat several aircars, sleek lines with bulbous nose and rear field-gens, and a single hulking, broad-shouldered flyer, thrusters angled down at the road surface. She sped down the empty stretch of open lanes with the forethought of someone who knew the precise meaning of "field of fire" firsthand. Applied brakes as she hit two hundred kph, coming to a sharp, nose-standing halt by the flyer's broad, armoured side. Stood the bike, deactivated the engine and racked the helmet, sparing a skyward glance at the humming, whining reverberations that hovered about the site overhead . . . several aircars that her Ops-site active uplink tagged as CSA surveillance, and a circling flyer in orbit several kilometres out—SWAT backup, Team Six—running lights off and barely visible on normal light. Traffic Central had rerouted all civilian air traffic out to a kilometre. There were now many grounded vehicles within the exclusion perimeter that had been stuck there for half the day . . . doubtless their drivers weren't happy about it.

She stretched briefly, arms overhead, trying to loosen her shoulders and back, irritated at how fast she was stiffening up. Her stomach hurt when she tensed.

Beyond the wrought-iron fence around Junshi Park on the right, IR vision caught emergency personnel moving in the dark through the greenery, sweeping to keep it clear. CSA uplink showed the whole park was off limits . . . big place to cordon off, she'd walked through Junshi Park, it was broad and beautiful, only a half hour's run from home.

Gave arms and legs a final shake to get the remaining kinks out, and ran quickly to the first firetruck, then on through the vehicles beyond, up onto the road verge to give waiting vehicles a wide berth—along with the various uniformed and plainclothed officers, agents and public services officials crouched and waiting behind their cars. All lights off, she was pleased to see . . . there'd been a worrying habit of leaving emergency lights flashing at such occurrences, for reasons she knew not, all it did was interfere with surveillance gear and draw fire. But there were far too many people here, she reckoned, dodging along the verge for some room—too many spectators, too many officials come to survey the action, too many pointless suits taking notes and sipping tea.

Then the building came into view past the nearside obstruction, and she ducked left and halted behind a police car bonnet, crouched more to remain inconspicuous than for protection. They were not sure about the nearer building, she'd gathered, and the regular cops had volunteered to sweep it floor by floor . . . not strictly their job, but there simply was not the personnel to do it full kit. Thus the blockade stretching far down Park Street, beyond the bend, although the affected address, number 214, was out of view. There had been numerous shots fired at police in the opening stages, writing off several vehicles, and no one was taking chances. No one had been hit, though. It told her something about the calibre of terrorist they were dealing with, and their weapons.

Number 214 was billowing smoke along the front half of its top storey, where the Roads and Safety Branch of the Department of Central Services was located. Why the Human Salvation Jihad had targeted Roads and Safety was anyone's guess. Probably because they were so inoffensive no one would ever have suspected them a target, and security was lax. She scanned full-spectrum through the smoke and darkness . . . plenty of broken windows on the top two levels, lots of smoke but no fire. Evidently the fire systems were still working. OSA uplink showed the SWAT team inserted, from floor and ceiling simultaneously, large chunks of which were now missing . . . yeah, she thought, reckoning over the graphical construct she saw in her mind, that was a Vanessa pattern, wreckage everywhere. Extreme violence, efficiently applied. Ricey would have made an excellent spec ops, on either side of the war. Though she was glad she wasn't.

The problem now was the bedamned Tanushan architecture. It was one of the first axioms she'd learned upon being assigned to SWAT—Tanushan architects are a pain in the arse for active insertions. Not content with designing a building with square back and sides, manic aestheticism had driven some Tanushan design genius to make 214 Park Street into a "curvaceous rectangular prism," like a box but tapered upward, curved at the corners and rounded here toward the front where it looked out onto the road, and Junshi Park beyond. Lovely view, nice architecture, it had doubtless made the planners happy. The problem was the natural skylights, multiple-storey central atriums and the adjoining rear connection to 221—

the building behind, which was office space blending to a retail/food hall square blending to shopping stretch . . . everything blended. Again, pretty and aesthetic. For an armoured assault against well-secured, trigger-happy defenders, a bloody nightmare. Her present access to the tac-net showed her enough for a very educated guess at the cause of the present hold-up. But not confirmation. She needed to talk to someone.

And that would be . . . she glanced quickly across and noted the biggest truck with the biggest aerial antennae, several importances in uniforms and suits gathered at the rear. Too damn easy to spot. Lucky the terrorists had nothing heavier than rifles . . . Damn, it'd be easier if she could just talk to Vanessa direct, but Vanessa was locked into the command circuit and that was tight security, she didn't want to break that and cause alarms, that would be just plain reckless.

Vanessa had command, SWAT Six supervised from the circling flyer, and from there the relay went back to CSA HQ, and down to this ground station. CSA HQ was always monitored by associated services, they doled out information to whoever they felt needed to know—Parliament, SIB, even news services on rare occasions, though not on this occasion, thank God. If she called HQ, the SIB would monitor it, and that wouldn't be good. She doubted they'd ever suspect she'd be calling from the on-site ground station. And, of course, there were no SIBs actually here. On a field op crawling with sweaty cops and SWAT grunts, heaven forbid.

She moved, crouched low and weaving past the sides of cars, and behind several police snipers, heavy-mag laser rifles plugged into portable recharge—good for snipers, lasers avoided the need for deflection shots. She just hoped they knew the difficulties with reflective glass and smoke penetration. She personally preferred slugs, nothing argued with velocity. Pulled up at the rear of the control van and straightened, stomach hurting, and shouldered her way between several suited men who could have been insurance salesmen for all she knew . . .

"Who's in charge?" And was nearly surprised at how people jumped, heads snapping about. Had it been that long since she'd used her best command voice? The van's side was open, graphical screen displays alight inside, more personnel in chairs or standing behind . . .

"Who the hell are you?" one man shot back at her, incredulously, with the frayed air of someone who'd had to deal with wandering bureaucrats too many times now. Sandy pulled her badge and tossed it to him, jumped up to the van's sideboard as he caught it and another protested . . . She caught sight of a policeman with Commander rank on his shoulders, consulting with several others further down, and shouldered toward him past men a head taller than her.

"Commander, you in charge?"

He glanced up, frowning, face lit up in the wash from multiple screens and the hushed, working atmosphere of tense voices and speaker-com.

"Who are you?" his second snapped, displeased at the interruption. Another man. Jesus, it was over eighty percent men, she guessed, and at least half of them Indian . . . she'd heard they dominated the more specialised segments of basic policing, anything involving guns and potential violence. Had heard grumblings about the Old Boy Raj at police HQ.

"I'm Ibrahim's secret weapon, I want a duty uplink, I can help."

"Says she's CSA," came a voice behind her, recent arrival from outside. "April Cassidy, Intelligence." Sarcastically. Sandy uplinked to police files, fast, and broke about twenty security procedures with a flurry of attack overrides through the security barriers . . .

"We don't need Intel here, thank you," the colonel said dryly. "Please step outside, you're not wanted here." She found the files she wanted, cracked them open with no regard for subtlety, unleashed a flood of information that racketed past at speed . . .

"Commander Azim, right?" Pressing the side wall as

someone edged past in the enclosed space. "Nikil Azim, age fifty-three, fifteen years in special security, four commendations, one for active service. You're not in charge here, Commander, you're just supervising. Command rests with SWAT Four Commander Rice, I want to speak to her. I'm on temporary assignment to Intel, I'm technically SWAT Four, she's my CO." Frowns all round at that.

"Don't you know *anything*?" said the second, incredulously. A lieutenant, Sandy saw. "Go through CSA HQ. Don't bother us, follow procedure and stay the fuck out of our faces."

A hand grabbed her shoulder from behind. Civilian men always tried to solve command disputes with aggression. Especially civilian men in positions of power. They thought it made them more effective. Sandy wondered briefly how such twisted logic had ever crawled from under a rock and seen the light of day. It limited her options severely.

"Come on, blondie, let's go," said the man behind her, pulling at her shoulder. The lieutenant returned to his discussion slate, shaking his head and muttering something about bloody pathetic females . . . She took the man's hand off her shoulder, and squeezed. He turned white. A twist, and his knees hit the floor. She grabbed a handful of belt and a handful of shirt collar, lifted, carried him back to the open van door, and threw him out. He crash-landed five metres away and tumbled.

"Don't call me blondie," she called after him. Hit the door close mechanism, and the side of the van came whining shut behind as she squeezed back up the narrow aisle to where the Commander and his lieutenant were standing stunned. The lieutenant panicked and tried to reach for his gun. Sandy grabbed his arm and yanked him forward, then dumped him back up against the reinforced side wall, and pinned him there with a straight arm to the upper chest.

"Commander," she said calmly, "if you'd bothered to read CSA priority reports to all police personnel of your rank and security clearance, you'd know exactly who April Cassidy is, particularly the April Cassidy connected to SWAT Four under Lieutenant Rice. That you haven't read such reports is alarming. It suggests to me there's something fundamentally unsound with the present relationship between the CSA and Tanushan police. Worse, it's put us at this unfortunate impasse. What do you think we can do to rectify this unseemly situation?"

The Commander stared, eyes wide beneath his blue baseball cap. Too collected to react further, when any reaction would be fear or shock. A man lunged at her from back along the aisle. She kicked him in the stomach. He hit the floor behind the row of seats and curled into a gasping, wheezing ball.

"Sir," the lieutenant managed, in a small voice past the pressure on his chest, "I think she's the GI." The Commander stared at him. The lieutenant nodded, knowingly.

"I am so pleased," said the Commander, "to be surrounded by such *genius* intellects." The lieutenant winced. The Commander turned to Sandy. "Agent Cassidy, perhaps you'd like to speak to Lieutenant Rice?"

"I'd be delighted." Released the lieutenant as the Commander reached around for a headset. The lieutenant stood where she'd pinned him, unwilling to move. A full head taller than her and much broader, frozen as if confronted by a poisonous snake ready to strike. She smiled and patted him on the cheek. He winced at that, too. The Commander gave her the headset and she fixed it on, fixed the mobile source to where her belt would be if she'd worn one, squeezed past an end chair and swung herself up to seat her backside on a vacant console panel by the command chair. It gave her a good view of the van interior. A row of faces, all staring at her in the dim, artificial working light.

"Get back to work," she admonished them, "we're just discussing duty protocols." Some nervous glances back and forth at that. "What's the matter, haven't you seen a pretty girl before?" That got a response, a few nervous titters from the largely male ops crew.

"Come on, people," announced the Commander, clapping his hands, "back at it. She's just our friendly neighbourhood GI, we mistook her for someone else, our fault. Come on, there's three of those bastards still alive in there. There's lives at stake, let's pay some attention!"

It got them going again, with a few remaining nervous sideways glances. Someone was helping the man she'd kicked back to his feet, helping him get his breath back.

"Leaping on a GI bare-handed, Senior Constable," Sandy called, "you itching for a promotion or just looking to get your name in the paper?" Dialling up her connection, waiting for the security net to confirm it.

"How 'bout a raise?" someone quipped.

"He okay?" Sandy pressed.

An acknowledging hand raised from the man himself, bent over and recovering, a hand to his middle.

"I'm okay."

"Next time try using a cannon," she advised. He spared her a wary sideways look. She returned a crooked smile. And was nearly surprised at the return smile, slight as it was. But not greatly surprised. She'd commanded forces most of her life. GIs were different from straights, but some things remained in common. Like compliments only carrying as much weight as the person who delivered them. From her to these guys . . . she'd just made the Senior Constable a hero. All power, she recalled, came from the barrel of a gun—or something like that—surely it applied to violence generally . . . Now who'd said that? Someone she'd read, she couldn't remember. Violent species. But that wasn't her fault, she was what she was. The trick was applying it properly. Irrational macho impulses sure didn't help.

Her call connected. It would flash as an insignificant suggestion light somewhere on Vanessa's visor display, nothing distracting. Vanessa would get to it when she felt ready. Sandy was somewhat surprised when the link clicked active almost immediately.

"*Hey, babe.*" Vanessa's voice, hard-edged but cool. "*Was wondering how long you'd take.*"

"Ricey, what's happened?"

"*Three point insertion, points four and five to cover the lower bridgeway. Got five of the original eight almost immediately but couldn't find the last three, they were inside somewhere . . .*" Pause for a hard breath, talking at a calm, steady volume, ". . . *bloody architecture, there's no human way to cover all the routes. They're in a lower crossover between Ceta five-nine-A and nine-nine-C . . .*" Flash of three-dimensional graphic on the OSA, a red-light spot near the base of the second central atrium. ". . . *and they've got a kid for a hostage.*"

"You're joking."

"*I wish. It happened in the morning, I think someone'd brought him to work first before school. Six years old. You want active?*"

"Yes, please." An associated link opened up. She accessed and data rushed in, full realtime schematic, comp-sim of all available data from all active units inside the building and out, shot back to HQ then out again. You couldn't trust all of it, some was guesswork, but once you knew the software parameters, you could figure which guesses were more accurate than others.

Vanessa and all SWAT Four had them surrounded, spread on several levels in typical crossfire pattern. Unable to fire because of the kid. Stand-off. Someone was trying to bring in a negotiator but there didn't seem much to negotiate. Negotiations, from what she'd seen of case files, were fraught with difficulties . . . fine for distraught, suicidal civvies and isolated lunatics whose lives had taken a turn for the worse—if they weren't susceptible to persuasion, they usually wouldn't have gone nuts in the first place. These guys didn't seem particularly persuadable. And having just seen five of their comrades killed, they weren't likely to buy any line about how "we don't want anyone to get hurt."

And they'd killed a hostage, she noted. Point-blank shot to the head, and dumped the body, when they figured they were being stalled. That'd been the trigger for Secretary Grey to order the assault. Even so, motivation remained an elusive variable . . .

"Sandy, hold on a second, I've got to check on something . . ."
And the connection blanked out, temporary hold.
Crouched in her armour somewhere in that building,
Vanessa no doubt had many other things to think about.
Sandy pulled the headset speaker from her mouth, and gestured to the lieutenant . . . the Commander was busy
again, talking on another connection, possibly about her,
she didn't care. The lieutenant approached, a little gingerly. Probably he reckoned she was picking on him.

"What's Human Salvation Jihad and what have they
asked for?" He took a deep, nervous breath . . . not a bad-
looking guy, she considered vaguely. European, square-
jawed and hunky. Seated up on her console, she could just
about look him in the eye.

"Um, well they're Islamic extremists . . ."

"Yeah, I got that." Dryly.

He swallowed again. "The Muslim League's denounced
them, of course. Says they're an affront to all Muslims and
pretty much urged us to kill 'em all . . ."

"That's pretty much how I'm thinking." She'd read
reports suggesting that martyrdom needed a critical mass
of popular support in order to flourish in Islamic society. It
didn't get that in Tanusha, where the concept of religious
war was very passé. What they had here was another nos-
talgic lunatic fringe cult harking back to days long gone.
She reckoned most Tanushans, and Muslims in particular
to judge from those she'd met, would want to keep it that
way—in the past. The first step to doing so was to make
this kind of murderous lunacy non-survivable. She got the
impression most Tanushans were still somewhat ignorant
of just how good their top law enforcement was (meaning
SWAT) at the application of lethal force . . . prior to recent
times the SIB had gotten all the press, all legalistic and
"civilised," doubtless some fools in the present mess
thought they'd get a prison cell and a media platform from
which to continue their "grand movement." The fact that
crazy civvies with rifles were just target practice for
Tanushan SWAT was not yet widely appreciated. The

sooner they got the message, the better. Martyrdom as a possible outcome could be romantic. As a one hundred percent guaranteed death sentence, it became less so. Tanushans enjoyed life too much to volunteer for an execution, whatever their political beliefs. And ninety-nine-point-nine percent of Tanushans, and Tanushan Muslims in particular, would have precisely zero sympathy for people who murdered innocents and threatened small children in the name of their enlightened, merciful religion. "What do they want?"

"So far they've demanded that Callay stay within the Federation, that President Neiland renounce all possible moves toward liberalising the biotech regime, that you yourself be put on trial for crimes against humanity, the standard ultra-Federation stance."

Her uplink showed her a fast scrawl of personal detail . . . several confirmed names, a couple of university degrees, some odd jobs, a few faces . . . nothing remarkable, just ordinary Tanushans. Four men and four women, which she wouldn't have expected from extreme Islamic conservatives—maybe they hadn't read up on the full program in their history books. Running conversation on the audio . . . *Bird Two has no visual on Ceta-five-nine . . . Hector Three, can you get a laser track on Ceta-five-nine windows? . . . Hector One has field of fire across Ceta, good visual, no obstructions . . . SWAT Four, further confirm, frequency secure, access AZ three nineteen . . . This is SWAT Four, confirm frequency clearance . . .*

That last was Hiraki, Vanessa's second. He listened to more of the chatter than Vanessa did, filtered for her . . . click, and the headphones came back to life.

"*Hey, Sandy, I just changed position here, I got a nice view across the atrium from level three . . . Let's see, I can't gas 'cause they've got masks, can't neuralise 'cause the walls are resistant, can't charge 'cause of the kid . . . I reckon a basic sneak-and-shoot would solve it, but I'm figuring a thirty percent chance the kid will get hit in the process. He deserves better odds if we can get 'em for him. I'll take any advice you've got right now.*"

"They said anything lately?"

"Uh . . . *'Death to fascist unbelievers,'* I think was the last one."

"So you can't see any happy reconciliation happening here?"

"Sandy, if they were scared of dying, they'd be screaming for mercy about now, it got real graphic on the top floor. It's not like they don't realise the consequences. Wu from Intel tells me he thinks they're drugged up, judging from the voice patterns." She remembered Wu, another bookish type, specialist in psycho-interface and mind-altering effects. She'd been impressed by him. *"Why you asking, you think you wanna talk to them personally?"*

"No. Can't let them know it's hopeless, they might just kill themselves and the kid too." Down the van's length, faces were turned her way. The Commander among them, watching intently. Listening on Vanessa's channel. "I've got a solution. I can't guarantee it. If you want to wait and look for something softer, that's fine, you're in charge, it's your call. But if they want to be martyrs and they've been tape-psyching themselves, they might not value that hostage very much at all. What's your call?"

The power was down in the building, but it didn't trouble her vision any. Up several flights of the near stairwell, then along the level three corridor, newly acquired boots squeaking on the shiny floor. The boots weren't all that she'd newly acquired. Light armour encased her torso, basic arm and leg guards, power-neutral, for protection only. A bare helmet, no faceguard. She needed neither the breather nor the visor, just the armscomp interface and the single external sight before her left eye. A gloved hand gripped a Sanda 40 light-assault weapon—an electro-mag shooter, on full V it could put holes in armourplate. She'd used bigger. For now, against unarmoured civilians, it felt like overkill. The whole situation was overkill. All the commotion, the hovering aircraft and crowds of official onlookers. For a handful of brain-tranqued civvies with self-inflicted delusions of Godly virtue.

She wasn't sure at all about this whole God business. But she reckoned she knew enough to make a few basic judgments. God was no politician. God took no sides, and played no favourites. God stopped no bullets. If God worried over his flock, it was because his flock's behaviour gave him good reason to. She wondered how he'd explain it all to these three fools, when they met him in several minutes' time.

Bloody waste. She didn't feel good at all. Her stomach was tense, and hurt to the point of cramping. The tension gripped all over. But it was more than the injury. She was scared. And revolted. Imagining such lives, in happy Tanusha, and all the other things one could have chosen to do with them. Family, friends, arts, travel, adventure. Instead of religiously inspired murder and a violent death. And if Allah *was* up there, waiting for them . . . man, was he going to be pissed. She remembered, with the fleeting dance of a stress-filled mind, a recent case in Tanushan courts where a major theological movement had sued a bunch of radical extremists for tarnishing God's reputation . . . But God, for better or worse, was no lawyer either. She couldn't remember who'd won.

She followed the tac-grid layout of the building, accurate to the nearest millimetre, past open doors and planned office space. Cups of tea and personal gear left lying on desktops where they had been left when the chaos broke out and emergency evacuation had sent everyone racing for the exits. She met Vanessa at the corridor end that looked out over the atrium. She knew it was Vanessa because she recognised the armour suit, supple-flexed ceramic over corded myomer. Crouched by the corner with a rifle to her shoulder that looked big enough to bring down small aircraft. The smaller antipersonnel gun fixed to the back of her shoulder . . . she'd thought ahead to the heavy stuff. Probably she'd seen this coming.

She peered over Vanessa's shoulder. Open atrium, a hole that descended through all floors from the skylight high above. An aircar passed over, running lights out, a dark shadow against the invisible stars. A static crackle on her inner ear, not the headset . . . she accessed, private frequency, away from prying ears.

"*What's the plan, hotshot?*" Her and Vanessa's secret encryption, her own League issue. In all her memory, she couldn't recall having shared it with anyone outside Dark Star before. "*Something cunning and subtle, no doubt?*"

"No," she sighed. Leaned her back against the wall and squatted. Rested there for a moment, gazing sightlessly at the opposite wall. "*Not even particularly clever. Definitely not subtle.*"

"*Then why haven't I thought of it?*"

"*If you possessed my capabilities, you would have. Good commanders only think within their capabilities.*"

Silence from Vanessa. To Sandy's side, the armoured firing posture never altered. The faceless armoured visor glared emotionlessly down the extended muzzle of the rifle.

"*What's the problem then?*" Vanessa missed little. Even on active ops.

"*I don't want to do this.*" Helplessly. The Sanda braced effortlessly across her knees. Rested the helmet against the wall. It felt strange. She had more hair now, and it sat differently than she remembered.

"*Why not? You seriously thought you could serve here with the CSA and SWAT without having to take lives again at some point?*"

It was a less comforting response than she'd hoped for. But then, it was stupid to have wanted comforting. She never had before. What was wrong with her? She snorted distastefully and moved to regather herself. Vanessa grabbed her arm, a hard, cool, armoured grip. Dangerous with any unarmoured person but her.

"*Sorry. Didn't mean that. I just saw the guy they shot up there, I'm not feeling real remorseful right now.*"

"*Me neither. Not like that. It just feels like . . . murder.*"

"*You'll feel worse if they kill the kid while we delay. You're that sure it's going to work?*" Sandy sighed, and pulled herself painfully to her feet.

"*It's me, Ricey. They're already dead.*"

The three targets were in the level two corridor opposite the atrium. The corridor ran tangentially away from the curved atrium wall—typical geometrically inspired design by a bunch of architects who worked in terror of straight lines and right angles. It was a silly place to get trapped, considering the ballistic possibilities it offered . . . one thin, curving wall between half the corridor's length and Vanessa's cannon. With just three people, they lacked the numbers to cover more than the one corridor, or break out with any covering fire. They were stuck, taking periodic potshots blind around the corners from either end.

Sandy stood directly above the corridor, on level three. She could see Vanessa opposite, across the cylindrical hole that pierced all floors from the ceiling down. The railing was a simple metal and glass circle around the perimeter. Several other SWAT troops covered from other floors, and other corridor corners.

Sandy uplinked, and locked into the building's receptor network. League-issue attack software got her fast into the main controls . . . augmented troops were stupid to conduct ops in a network-wired environment with civilian-issue uplinks, the naivety amazed her. If you could talk to the network, the network could talk to you. And they'd been talking . . . CSA procedure 'til now had been simply to block them, lacking further applications, but analysis of those outgoing calls had been enough to tell her the type, model and general capabilities of the terrorists' hardware.

She selected a specific program, made a few mental adjustments on internal visual, and applied it to the correct central controls . . . several moments of activation, then the building's receptor hardware sent out a basic contact code, with modulations. Searching for connections, as with any incoming call to a building occupant, but this time with more specific focus, according to the parameters she'd fed it. It found the three occupants of the corridor below her, and activated a response sub-freq. Standard call-and-reply. Civilian units did that. Within milliseconds, her software package in central control had read and triangulated the response, and transmitted those locations into her tac-grid picture. She passed it on to Vanessa. The three transmitter locations, precise to the millimetre, in the corridor below. As good as jump up and yell "I'm here!" If you don't shield your com or interface, someone will hack it and use the response for target practice. Amateurs.

"The middle guy will be holding the hostage," Vanessa said. All in a line. It *was* murder.

"Two rounds in the first interval on my hack," she said, holding up two fingers to Vanessa. Across the open atrium space, Vanessa held up two fingers in reply, then braced the cannon more firmly. It looked about as tall as herself. Without the suit, she'd have barely been able to hold it steady. *"Three, two, one, hack."*

Vanessa fired, twice. Explosions ripped the air beneath, and Sandy leapt the balcony, hand gripped on the railing as she fell, swinging her back in. Released and landed amid erupting smoke from Vanessa's concussion rounds, which had ripped through the side of the corridor and detonated in all kinds of smoke and fury. Zero visibility, but her rifle's therma-sensor penetrated easily enough . . . she fired three times in quick succession, walked into the blinding smoke, grabbed the limp bundle sprawled upon the floor, grasped him firmly under one arm and walked out backward, just in case. Feeling foolish, because they were dead, but procedures were procedures . . . or in her case, perhaps, habits.

Smoke cleared at the atrium opening, and a pair of Vanessa's guys were there to take the kid off her and rush him to the exit. Several others rushed into the corridor from both ends to make certain, and suddenly there was confusion on the network, green lights given and people rushing for all the entrances . . . shit, she suddenly felt an urge to be elsewhere, before the whole place became a seething mass of note-taking officialdom, and stunned further because she'd just killed three people and she was totally, utterly horrified at how fucking easy it was, and how calmly she could do such things and immediately start worrying about the bureaucratic aftermath . . .

"Sandy." Muffled voice to her side. "You okay?" Stared

into the fearsome artificial visage of Hitoru Hiraki, eyes peering past the shielded lenses with evident concern. She realised she was standing dead still amid the drifting smoke from the corridor entrance, rifle limp in one hand . . . she checked the safety, and found she'd already applied it, although she couldn't remember doing so. Habits again.

"I'm fine," she said. Her own voice sounded strange to her ears. Tired. Hiraki unhooked his visor with a hiss of disconnecting seals. Sandy undid her helmet strap and stowed the whole thing from the rear collar connection. Then Vanessa was approaching . . . it could only be her— the smallest size of suit armour available—lugging the massive weapon over her shoulder which stuck up and threatened to catch on low doorways. That and the "Have a nice day" emblazoned above a smiley face upon her helmet's forehead.

She undid her visor as she walked closer, then unhooked the connections and did the whole helmet, pulled loose and dangling in one hand. Stopped before her. Eyeing her with a reluctant half-twist to her lips, as if in apology. And raised an eyebrow, questioningly. Amazing, Sandy couldn't help thinking, in that dazed, helpless instant, to have someone who knew exactly how she felt. She'd never had that before. Vanessa just *knew*.

"Too easy," she murmured tiredly. Took a deep breath, and ran a gloved hand through her tousled hair. In the corridors beyond, back toward the main entrance, she could hear people running, the first of the outside commotion headed inward. "Just . . . too easy." Her voice nearly broke, although whether from tiredness or something else, she couldn't tell.

"I know," Vanessa said. "But no one else could have done it."

She knew that. Three targets at different ranges— tracked only through the weapons armscomp—and zero visibility . . . a standard human nervous system, even severely augmented, did not possess the degree of interface required to have acquired absolute target certainty in the split second available, with a hostage in the middle. They'd been such simple targets. She couldn't possibly have missed. But a straight human would have seen only confused shadows, and would have been unable to translate what armscomp was telling them into reliable targeting information . . . she just saw. She was designed for it. It was no effort at all.

"How's the kid?" she asked, abruptly realising. "I didn't have time to look . . ."

"Bruised," said Hiraki. "Sharma thinks they might have drugged him, he should be okay." Put a firm, armoured hand on the back of Sandy's neck, and gave her an affirmative shake. "Good job, Sandy. *Good* job. You saved a life today." And strode off with thudding, armoured steps to see to the clean up.

"For once, he means," Sandy muttered.

"He meant what he said," Vanessa said firmly. Behind her, armed police were running in, taking up positions. Investigators followed, and paramedics rushing stretchers, just in case. If they'd known it was her doing the shooting, they might not have bothered.

"Should have shot to wound," Sandy muttered, watching the circus come swarming in, lugging forensics and sim-scans. "Didn't need to kill them."

Vanessa rolled her eyes. "Jesus, Sandy, cut out the bullshit . . . if you'd shot to wound, I'd have to kick you out of the force."

And she was right. Sandy knew that, everyone knew that. It was illegal to shoot to wound in a hostage situation. The lives of hostages were paramount, any actions lessening the hostages' chances of survival were impermissible, including leaving the hostage-takers alive. The other letters Vanessa had emblazoned across an armoured shoulder spelled out the word KISS—Keep It Simple, Stupid. Unnecessary complications increased the chances of failure. That meant killing. But Sandy was feeling sorry for herself.

Dropped her head with a sigh, slumped back against the side wall as the first suits and paras came rushing past, loaded with equipment. Still exasperated, Vanessa took her head with both hands, and planted a firm kiss on her forehead.

"Quit moping, if you hadn't done it I'd have had to." Dropped her hands onto both armoured shoulders, staring her hard in the face. "I already got two myself upstairs. D'you see me crying about it? No. And d'you know why?"

"You're an obsessive, hyperactive morality freak," Sandy murmured, but her heart wasn't in it. Vanessa ignored her.

"Because I'm not such a naive little girl that I've managed to convince myself that these things won't be necessary any longer. I know you got out of the League expecting that everything would be better elsewhere . . . I've got news for you, Sandy, it's not. There's bad shit that happens in all corners of the universe, and if you happen to have skills particularly suited to dealing with bad shit, and are employed to use those skills, you can expect to continue seeing your share."

"I'm not a naive little girl." Quietly, as a group trundled a pair of stretchers between them and the atrium railing. "I'm a highly decorated special ops combat veteran."

"You're an ignorant, idealistic, wide-eyed army-bumpkin, Sandy." With ferocious affection, dark eyes intense and narrow. "It's what makes you so irresistibly gorgeous. Now, as your effective CO, I'm ordering you to get your cute little blonde head together and snap to some kind of orderly, soldierly attitude of common sense and efficiency or I'll kick your butt so hard you'll hit the ceiling. You hearing me?"

Sandy raised her gaze to meet her eyes directly. It hurt, being knocked down several pegs by the best friend she'd ever had. But Vanessa, she knew from experience, was usually right about these things. It wasn't a skill she'd seen very much of, in the League military. Personal skills. But Vanessa had them in as ample a quantity as she had martial skills, and SWAT Four was all the more effective for it. So why had Vanessa's marriage ended up in such a mess?

Civilians. God . . . she stretched hard, and ran both hands through her hair. Her stomach hurt, as did a dozen other places, jolted for the worse by her rapid descent and landing. It was all too confusing. But that, she supposed reluctantly, was Vanessa's point. Sandy the bumpkin. Always confused, always staring about at the civilian world with wide-eyed fascination or bewilderment. Of course Vanessa was right. She felt lost.

"Help," she said in a small voice. Vanessa reached a hand, brushed it through Sandy's hair and rested it there, just gazing, with a wry, affectionate, exasperated smile . . .

"Lieutenant Rice." A recently familiar voice, coming closer. They glanced and saw Commander Azim striding toward them, eyeing the smoke-strewn corridor behind with sharp consideration. Glanced at Sandy, then at Vanessa, stopping before them, his lieutenant in tow. Vanessa reluctantly dropped her hand from Sandy's hair.

"Commander. Can you handle it from here? We're getting out, we've got a flyer down on the roof in five minutes."

"I'll want an . . . um . . ." Another glance at the paramedics moving amid the dissipating smoke. ". . . the full report for admin, if you'll arrange the protocol . . . how long d'you think that will take?"

"Fucked if I know," Vanessa told him flatly. He repressed a grimace, evidently reckoning the obvious truth in that, amidst this chaos. Glanced again at Sandy.

"Your idea, Agent Cassidy?" With another glance at the apparent carnage within the corridor.

"My orders," Vanessa replied. The Commander nodded, regarding them warily. And, realising he wasn't going to get any further response, nodded his respect and edged past, headed to inspect the damage. The broad lieutenant paused, as did the two men with him.

"Bloody good job," he told Sandy, and passed with a whack at her shoulder armour. The other two voiced similar praise.

"I'm becoming an underground success in this city," Sandy muttered as they departed in the other direction.

"Funny, considering this is exactly the kind of thing that terrifies so many people about me."

"Bah." Vanessa made a disgusted face, ushering Sandy along with a hand to her armoured back. "They're all hypocrites, they don't mind you being dangerous, Sandy, just so long as you kill the right people."

They were halfway through armour lockdown back at the Doghouse when her right hip totally seized, taking the thigh and most of her lower back with it. Half-armoured only from the waist down, Sandy hit the ground between stowage lockers with a hard thud and rolled for space, contorted with pain and desperately fighting the cramp that wrenched up her back and snapped her leg out as straight as a metal beam amid alarmed shouts from those around.

"Back!" she shouted, half seated and straining past gritted teeth to grab her elusive toes as her calf began to go, pulling the heel back and pointing her foot away from her. Vanessa burst around a couple of startled SWAT troops and gave a startled yelp, moved to dash forward . . .

"Get the fuck back!" Sandy yelled at her, and Vanessa stumbled to an uncertain halt before her. "I'll put a fucking hole in you, keep back!" Someone grabbed Vanessa's shoulders and roughly jerked her back several metres.

The tension gripped Sandy's right shoulder blade with ferocious power, pulling hard along her spine. She thumped back against the floor, grabbing her right wrist and pulling the arm up hard above her, trying to counter the pressure.

"Sandy!" Vanessa's voice, with incredulous alarm. "What's wrong, Sandy?"

"Looks like cramp," Devakul observed more calmly.

"Bloody hell," someone exclaimed, incredulously.

"Yeah, no shit," Sandy snarled past the tension, stretched tight and rigid on the floor between armour lockers. "Bloody stupid, I should have known this would happen." It hurt . . . God, she'd forgotten how much it hurt. It had only happened a few times before to her

memory, all after injuries, all when her schedule had prevented her from using as much caution as she'd ought to.

"What can we do?"

"Wait."

Eventually the tightness began to fade, first from the hip
and lower back, then from the extremities. Her right knee
began to bend, and she pulled it up. It came reluctantly, like
a stuck door hinge. Grabbed her shin with both hands and
pulled, drawing the knee up against her chest, armoured
thigh-guard heavy against her bare singlet, bare arms
straining to keep the knee from springing back out again.
The resistance slowly faded, as did the worst of the pain.

"Okay now?" Vanessa asked. Sandy looked up at her. A
crowd had gathered, half of SWAT Four, some half-
armoured, others like Vanessa sweaty and crumpled in
their undershirts and tangled biosensors.

"Yeah." Released her leg and got her elbows under her as
Vanessa came scampering around to her side. "Jesus, if you
see that happen again, don't come rushing in. I could get a
convulsion or a sudden unlock, it'd take your head off."

"Can you move?" Zago was at her other side, the two
of them working on her armour buckles, clacking open the
connections.

"What brought that on?" Vanessa, she thought, looked
quite shocked. She didn't like that. She sometimes suspected that Vanessa hadn't necessarily accepted what she
really was, but had rather chosen to overlook it . . .

"I'm okay," she said with some irritation, choosing not
to assist them with her armour for now. "I'm just over-
worked, I haven't been stretching properly . . ."

"Shit, you mean this is going to happen a lot?" Vanessa
retorted with alarm.

"No, just after I get shot and keep working like
nothing's happened . . ."

"You got shot!" Incredulously. "When! Where?"

"LT," Zago said calmly, working to get Sandy's boot
ties unhooked, "it couldn't have been in our furball, none
of them fired a shot."

"Why didn't you tell me?" Accusingly. "Jesus, you can't just keep running around after you get shot, Sandy, what the fuck were you thinking! I'd never have let you take point if I'd known . . ."

"Exactly why I didn't tell you," Sandy retorted, "you're not qualified to know what difference it makes, Ricey, I am."

"Qualified? I'm your damn CO, that's all the qualification I need . . ."

"Vanessa, just . . ." Sandy winced, holding up a forestalling right hand, ". . . just stay a little calm, huh? I'm a GI, you seem to keep forgetting . . ."

"Forgetting! Christ, how can I forget? You get shot and you're off running around like an action hero . . . where'd you get shot? How?"

"As soon as you've calmed down a little, I'll tell you everything."

"She's right, LT," said Singh, squatting nearby with observant interest. "You're getting hysterical." Vanessa glared at him.

"You shut the fuck up."

CHAPTER 9

The Doghouse was as chaotic as she'd seen it. Med ward was filled with minor cases, exhausted SWAT grunts treating various sprains, strains and armour stresses. All found time to watch with interest as she was found a table and duly set upon by several enthusiastic medics, who were joined in short time by the resident augment-surgeon, then two assistants, then a biotech specialist who appeared out of breath, having evidently run down from Intel to "assist" . . . while she lay almost naked on the exam bench and tried not to feel ridiculous amid the crush.

Treatments and technical possibilities were offered, and questions asked . . . when directed at her, she mostly just shrugged helplessly and reminded them tiredly that she was a grunt, not a doctor. Previous midriff bandaging was cut away, wounds inspected, recleaned—provoking argument over correct disinfectant, with added earnestness due to the enhanced GI vulnerability to microorganisms—and then basic electro-stim applied. Someone found a sonic-scanner and wheeled it over, and then began mapping with the handset to compile a three-dimensional picture. After a search someone found the benex supply they'd ordered from labs especially for her—a myomer relaxant, they called it benex for short. Sandy knew little beyond that, except that it'd always been used for short term relief from extreme stresses. More discussion over dosage and location of hypo-shots, about which she was more useful, having had plenty back League-side.

Basic stress relief achieved, then came the full physical . . . blood pressure, pulse rate, nervous feedback, blood chemistry—the basics were very human-ish, and provoked further intrigue from surrounding meds, and no few of the present, aching SWATs. Yes, she replied to one curious question, her chin rested on folded hands upon the bench, GIs did get sick, especially if they didn't exercise, eat well, or suffered vitamin deficiencies. Yes, she'd several times had flu, or something close to it. GI immune systems were heavily engineered and required frequent boosts, artificial micros simply didn't handle virus and organic micros as well as straight human systems. Yes, she'd once known a GI to drop dead from a particularly nasty measles strain. Yes, straights serving with GIs for long periods required extra boosters for the GIs' safety more than their own. No, that wasn't likely to be a problem with her, she was one of the lucky fifty percent of GIs with few quirks in their immune systems. But the odd extra shot for those she most frequently came into contact with in the CSA definitely would not hurt her feelings.

The rest was just physical recovery, several benex shots into major muscle groups, and a lot of electro-stim and massage. With little more to be done, excess medical personnel drifted reluctantly away to more pressing concerns. Freed of the crowd, she lay mostly on her stomach, a polite towel across her buttocks, and took the time to chat with the other SWATs. All were from other teams, and all had been busy—personnel were alternating between rapid reaction, fixed security and mobile patrols, and sometimes, particularly in the evenings—when the delegations were all most actively engaged—patrols in pairs or fours, just to make sure there were trained shooters on scene quickly if something went wrong. The police were doing an okay job, but . . . well—eyes were rolled—you wouldn't want them leading the charge when the shots started flying. And they'd been flying all too frequently of late. Qualified, combat-capable personnel were suddenly in very short supply across Tanusha with its fifty-seven million inhabitants. All the grunts looked tired, and some of the men didn't look like they'd shaved in days. Several were troubled by various augments acting up under the strain of too much time in armour—supplemented arm and leg ligaments, tendon sheaths, muscle attachments, all the key points. And she found room to be glad that whatever her problems, at least she didn't have to put up with *that*—mutually opposing systems, organic and artificial. She was all one system. And that, of course, was the GI performance advantage.

Some thoughtful tech actually brought her clothes up, having somehow finagled access to her locker, and she got dressed to the protests of several grunts that no one ever did that for them . . . the embarrassed tech (male, of course) retreated before things got ugly. Then out into the unseasonal traffic in the med halls, walking loose limbed and flexing within her casual duty pants and jacket, readjusting her stride for the unpredictable looseness of muscles brought on by the benex shots. Several passing whitecoats recognised her and offered greetings, which she returned—she'd gotten to know these halls well enough in past weeks, recovering from previous, more serious injuries.

The adjoining wing took her back to Doghouse proper, bypassing the chaotic duty rooms that Medical had been so thoughtfully situated next to. Corridor windows gave her an overview as she left Med, the broad landing pad crowded with armoured flyers in a blaze of floodlights . . . maintenance and flight crews were making standby walkarounds, with no time for more intensive checks. The open flight-bay beyond was lit yellow by the work lights, awash with the scuttling activity of three times the usual operational load of flyers and other vehicles. She could see small groups consulting out on the pads, arms waving over the whine of thrusters, fingers being pointed in many different directions. Even as she watched a new team was disembarking, a line of armoured figures doing a quick jog toward a waiting flyer, running lights blinking in readiness. SWAT Nine, she saw with a quick zoom . . . and they were twelve-strong, four short of full strength. Injuries and maintenance breakdowns . . . the schedule was starting to take its toll.

Nine SWAT teams to cover fifty-seven million people and several tens of thousands of senior foreign delegates . . . not enough. Not even close. But the cops weren't trained for lethal force on the required scale, and the SIBs were discovering that legal edicts and SCIPS had their limits against determined political subversion of whatever ilk or motivation. Who the hell else was there? In this usually peaceful city? Investigations was huge, a great sprawl of compound across the whole West Block, and had many personnel in various departments capable of basic weapons, but they'd been overstretched from even before the whole constitutional crisis, let alone now that the floodgates had opened and all the crazies were pouring out of the woodwork . . .

She puzzled over it all the way to debrief, over on the west side of the Doghouse, facing Central. Too far a walk, was the other thought that came to mind. Too much admin in SWAT . . . it wasn't a large operation, really, just nine SWAT teams . . . in Dark Star they'd managed three times the strikepower with half the admin, at least. She'd yet to figure what half the SWAT admin people did. Worse, she didn't think admin itself was entirely sure.

Debrief had already started when she got there . . . it was a lot to get through, most of which had happened at 214 Park Street well before she had gotten there. The crowd of Intel attending was nearly as large as the assembled SWAT Four, seated or standing about the front and sides of the class-sized room, watching the main display, full tac-graphic unfolding across the front display. The team lounged in more comfortable deep cushions, some sprawled with feet up, others seated against the back wall with legs out and jackets unzipped, hair wet and dishevelled from recent showers, cold packs and strapping held to troublesome augments or plain muscle strains. All paused to look when she entered.

"Hey, babe, you okay?" Vanessa was seated up front in a thick reclining chair—commander's seat, boots up on the rim of the long, central table. A long, concerned look from weary dark eyes under untidy, curling dark hair.

"No worse than the rest of you lot," Sandy replied.

"That bad, huh?" Vanessa held out a hand. Sandy went over and took it, a brief, public handclasp, and a pat at her backside as she went to the back of the room. More hands extended from reclining, exhausted grunts, and more pats as she passed . . . and with some, even a brief, approving contact of eyes. It felt good. She messed Singh's hair as she passed, knocked knuckles with Kuntoro, and headed straight for Bjornssen and Hiraki, seated against the rear wall by the corner against the windows. There was no room, but Bjornssen got the idea and spread his long legs. Sandy dumped herself unceremoniously between and leaned back against him—Bjornssen was a big man, a head taller and far broader than her, and it seemed a waste of chest space when the wall was all taken. He surprised her by wrapping arms around her tightly, and giving her a brief, affectionate shake . . . not always the most light-hearted man, Bjornssen—dour and matter-of-fact at most times. Viking heritage, he liked to call it. Ethnic heritage was the most chic of fashion accessories in Tanusha, Sandy reckoned. Something real. Something you couldn't buy. There weren't many of those left, these days.

"These guys have a clue?" she asked Hiraki in a low voice as the debrief continued and multigraphical displays swung and glowed across the huge forward screen. Hiraki scanned the row of watching, note-consulting Intels across the front of the room with narrowed, thoughtful eyes. And gave a faint shrug.

"They function." Sandy rolled her head against Bjornssen's broad shoulder and gave him a flat look.

"All Intel functions," she retorted softly. The scene at Park Street had been a mess, and she wasn't at all sure there'd been a need for it. Someone should have exercised a command prerogative. It was a CSA operation, it should have been a CSA call.

Hiraki shrugged again. "We are still alive."

"Thank Vanessa for that."

"True. But nonetheless." The assistance hadn't gotten them killed, he meant. Bad assistance could do that. Hiraki seemed aware of it.

"You smell nice," Bjornssen remarked in her ear.

"GI pheromones." She rolled her head back, rested against the big Scandinavian's jaw. "Potent and highly addictive."

"Soap."

She smiled. "That too." And she took a moment to enjoy the close male proximity, as up the front the debrief continued, and grunts pretended to pay attention. It was for Intel's benefit, not theirs—they'd been there, they didn't need someone else to tell them what had happened. Vanessa, to her credit, fielded most of the questions, and let her team rest. With Bjornssen's warmth against her back, his breath in her ear and arms loosely about her, Sandy realised something with great abruptness.

"Oh God, I desperately need a fuck." Bjornssen managed to keep his laughter below audible volume. "Oh, what?" Still quietly, but with some indignation. "It's easy for you, I can't find anyone who's not terrified of me or isn't some totally obsessive Intel geek."

"I think Rupa wins the pool," Hiraki murmured with amusement.

Sandy rolled her head back and frowned at him. "What?"

"Some people made bets on how long you'd take to ask someone. There is much amazement you've lasted so long."

Sandy snorted. "Vanessa's rumours, I bet, no respect for my self-control."

"Pity you're not gay," Bjornssen said in her ear.

"God, I've heard that *sooo* many times lately." Pause. And she realised why he'd said it. And, in a further flash of insight, what else they must have talked about, behind her back. "Look, it's just as well I'm not, it wouldn't be real smart for Vanessa to fall in love with me. Don't worry about her, she'll be fine. She's hot for that techie girl down in Ops-mech, anyway. Lopez."

"No, no, no," Bjornssen said with quiet amusement. "She just wants a woman again after so long. She was very good for a very long time. We were all amazed. But she likes girls. It was very hard for her. Lopez is the first target, that's all."

Sandy thought about that for a moment. Gazed out the windows to the right, at the multistorey, blazing lights of the Central compound, the major offices of admin and Intel. All awake with endless activity, despite the increasingly late hour.

"And," added Bjornssen, "it has been extra frustrating for her having you around."

"Frustrating?" She didn't like the sound of that. "Why?"

"Because you are exactly her type, Sandy." Brushed some loose, damp hair back from her ear. "Exactly. But she knows she cannot have you, and so she goes hunting for others."

"Why am I her type?" Suspiciously. SWAT grunts who played psycho-analyst. She didn't trust it, this newly discovered side to Bjornssen. Some overconfident types reckoned they knew everything. Bjornssen was certainly confident.

"Pretty. Strong. Dangerous."

"Unattainable," Hiraki added with nodding certainty from alongside.

Sandy gave him a long look. "I think you're underestimating her."

Hiraki shrugged again . . . a controlled, precise gesture on him. Relaxed.

"We have known her much longer. You are new here."

Sandy shook her head. "You're forgetting I'm a GI.

You saw her just now when I cramped, she nearly panicked. And she never panics. No way has she come to terms with what I am yet. No way. She's intrigued, sure, but she's *not* attracted."

"Now it is you underestimating her," Bjornssen replied, "our LT is not so easily put off, believe me . . ."

"Would *you* fuck me?" A moment's consternation from Bjornssen. "Oh, come on, you're Scandinavian, you like blondes with nice arses, I heard you say so—that's me."

Hiraki was looking at *him* now, mildly curious. Bjornssen gave an exasperated sigh.

"Well . . . I mean, Sandy, you're very pretty . . ." Mildly patronising, Sandy thought dryly, tolerating another light shake, ". . . and you smell very nice . . . but no. No, I do not think I could." A light shrug against her back. "I'm very sorry. I don't mean any offence, but I'm . . . I'm just not attracted to GIs."

"Now there's a wild generalisation," Sandy retorted quietly. "If no one had told you, you wouldn't even realise . . ."

"But I am not the LT," he continued, ignoring her. "She is extremely stubborn and she is not scared of anything . . ."

"Bullshit, everyone's scared of something."

"You," Hiraki said. Looking at her, calm intent in dark, slanted eyes. "What are you scared of?" Sandy met his gaze, firmly. And decided she would *not* be drawn into such personal revelations at this time.

"Of going more than a month without sex. It's *bad* for me. I'll wear out my fingers." There was a pause in the room, other conversation halted. Bjornssen put a hand on her face and turned her head toward the front of the room. Senior Intels were looking at her. Several of the team turned to look, too. Someone had asked her a question. Ooops. "What?"

She managed to say it with incredulous innocence, and several grunts sneezed laughter.

"Agent," said the head Intel . . . Richter, Sandy

recalled her name was . . . "I appreciate that you've had a long and hard day, but we're on rather a tight schedule and we'd like to be done here as soon as possible, so could you *please* pay attention?"

It was all Sandy could do to keep from smiling. She had *never*, in all her memory, been caught not paying attention in a briefing. Probably because she always had been paying attention. There had been an undercurrent of contempt, back in Dark Star, for civilian ill-discipline. Strange now to find herself becoming one of those unruly, undisciplined few. Strange, but not unwelcome.

"But, Marlie," someone protested, "you're so damn boring." Tired, repressed laughter around the room. A few of the Intels hid smiles with difficulty. Richter waited impatiently for it to finish.

"I'm sorry," Sandy said, with a diplomatic smile. "What was the question?"

She was directed into Ibrahim's office by a weary staffer, who murmured something about her being expected . . . further down the waiting foyer, the main Ops hall was buzzing, screens alive and displaying to all surrounding alcoves and offices. A warren of early morning activity at three in the morning. Like a Chinese ghost story, someone had said to her recently—things only get really nasty when the sun goes down. She pushed through the main doors, the inner corridor all deserted, as were the meeting rooms and adjoining offices behind glass walls. Ibrahim's office was the one you couldn't see into, a plain door with "Director" on it. Real flashy. It suited the man entirely.

She knocked, and thought to do up her old duty jacket properly, at least, and close the zippers on the shoulder pockets—her old military reflexes remained very much intact, she thought wryly, reaching further to zip her thigh pockets too. The realisation failed to bother her. She was what she was. No reply, and she knocked again. Uplinked to the local security grid—an old reflex—and found everything very much in order, and totally impenetrable.

Glanced about the corridor again . . . everyone was either out consulting, working or resting. She grasped the door handle and found it unlocked.

The office was dark. Her vision switched accordingly, and she walked in, unneeding of the light. A dark bundle lay on the floor along the right-hand wall . . . a person, wrapped in a blanket, on cushions borrowed from the room's one sofa. She closed the door behind her, blocking out the light from the corridor, but with vision tuned to IR that made it easier to see. Only the compound lights gleamed brightly through the windows, casting faint, multi-directional shadows across the floor.

"Sir." No response. His breathing was deep and steady beneath the blankets. "Sir." She padded softly over, not wanting to startle him. Knelt on the floor beside the improvised bed of cushions, and shook gently at his shoulder. "Mr. Ibrahim." He caught a breath. "Sir, it's Cassandra Kresnov. You wished to see me."

"Hmmm." A low, waking groan. "Cassandra." Another deep breath. "Just a moment."

"Can I get you a glass of water? Or there was a drinks dispenser in the corridor, I think?"

"No . . . no, I shouldn't want to wake more than necessary." He pulled himself half upright, wincing and rubbing at his eyes. His dark hair was shaven too short for disarray . . . shorter than she'd remembered. She decided he must have had it done recently, to avoid precisely that appearance in days when he had so little time for grooming. Practical solutions from perhaps the most practical person she'd ever met. And one of the most complex.

She remained kneeling, to avoid him having to stand. Ibrahim leaned himself back against the wall, collar open and shirt rumpled. Looking, to Sandy's curious interest, suddenly a man. Flesh and bone, dishevelled, tired and newly woken from sleep, instead of the formal, implacable figure of authority to which she'd become accustomed. He leaned his head back and fixed her with a heavy-lidded gaze, an arm hooked about an upraised knee for support.

"What compelled you to join the mission in Junshi?" he asked, direct and to the point, as always.

Sitting on her heels was uncomfortable, and pulled at recently sore muscles she did not want pulled. She shifted to sit on her backside, arms about drawn up knees, mirroring her boss.

"I don't know." Ibrahim evidently didn't believe that. She sighed, lightly. "Vanessa. The whole team. I was nearby, I wanted to see that they were okay, or if I could help. As it turned out, I could."

She half expected a reprimand. A warning against breaking procedure, or upsetting the local cops.

"It was well done," he said instead. Not elaborate praise. But coming from Ibrahim, it was better than a medal. And she was surprised at how pleased she was to hear it. "What did you think of the operation in total?"

"Fortuitously successful," she replied, analysis reflexes kicking in, knowing well what Ibrahim expected from her. "Highly chaotic, far too disorganised, far too little chain of command. It worked this time because the opposition were poorly trained and equipped, all they had on their side was motivation. Against more formidable opposition I feel the operation would more likely have failed than succeeded, with losses suffered and the objective not completed."

"Hmmm." Ibrahim nodded, lips pursed. Appearing hardly surprised at the assessment. Thoughtful. "Suggestions?"

"Streamline," she said automatically. "Individual Tanushan departments appear generally competent. The CSA is mostly so, and SWAT in particular. SWAT Four is as good a strike team as I've seen, among straights—that's my unbiased military opinion. The police function well enough, and all the in-betweens do their jobs effectively. There's just too many of those in-betweens. Cut the numbers by a half to two-thirds and you'll have a force that functions with the absolute minimum of wasted energy, and the maximum possible focus upon the mission at hand. Right now, everyone's just getting in each other's way."

Ibrahim said nothing for a moment. It was a moment longer before she realised he was smiling. To her astonishment, the smile grew broader. He restrained it with difficulty, and put hand-to-mouth, like a man with a troublesome cough. Sighed, heavily, and fixed her with a look of as pure and genuine amusement as she'd ever seen from him, head back against the wall.

"If only you could help me run this agency," he explained. "I have this argument constantly with my political superiors. I am frequently informed . . ." with heavier sarcasm than she'd ever heard him use, ". . . that my views on the operational brief of the CSA, and thus its structural requirements, are out of step with the current political trends." Sandy blinked. His eyes fixed on her with tired bemusement. "Less muscle, more analysis. In this information age, I am told, the emphasis should be upon prevention. I attempt to convince them that human beings cannot be *prevented* from anything. *That*, most of all, is a legacy of their information age—people will do what people will do, in all their varied, wonderful and not-so-wonderful extremes, and no amount of prevention, short of dictatorship, can stop them. But this is what happens in a society run by technocrats and utopian idealists. They fear the chaos, but the chaos is life." A shrug. "A city must be allowed to live. A people must. And I fear most of all that the present alarmist climate may precipitate far more prevention than is warranted. As a student of history yourself, Cassandra, you would know the dangers of too much prevention."

Sandy repressed a smile. "I've only read a little, sir. I haven't been alive long enough to read more. But I've seen the beginnings of a League autocracy at work in a system that always lauded democracy even more strongly than the Federation. I know what you're saying."

"Indeed." Ibrahim nodded, amusement lingering in his lidded gaze. "All bureaucracies intend to create order, Cassandra. That is their nature. Too little order is to be feared. Too much order, even more so. Alternative possibilities are necessary, but too many of the wrong kind can be dangerous. The balance is delicate. And so I distrust my own professional nature. It haunts my sleep."

Such confessions to her from Ibrahim were not unknown. She sometimes wondered if he were testing her moral judgment. Searching for her agreement or otherwise. Or merely seeking her comprehension. Comprehension of what, she was not sure. Of moral dimensions, perhaps. Of complexities. Perhaps he worried, as did many members of the Senate and Congress, that she did not fully appreciate the human delicacies of the Callayan democratic system. Or maybe he felt that he understood better than most the pressures that she was under from the workings of that system, and sought only her understanding. And, perhaps, her forgiveness.

"Good that I woke you then," she said lightly, "if your sleep was so troubled."

Ibrahim smiled, and ran a hand over tired, angular features, rubbing his eyes and stifling a yawn. Afghani features, from the hawk nose and prominent cheekbones to the cut of his trimmed beard.

"Did you meet Ambassador Yao?" he asked.

"I did." And in the expectant silence that followed, "He seems civil enough. Pleasant, actually. He appeared very pleased to see me."

"What did you discuss?"

"Very little, actually. He was busy with meetings—financiers and bankers, he said." She paused. "Most of my time was spent in discussion with a high-designation League GI. The same GI whom I tracked from the Zaiko Warren to the Cloud Nine establishment, the one who shot me." A moment's sombre consideration from Ibrahim. No great surprise. Doubtless Ari had already briefed him on the salient points. And probably a great deal more besides. More, certainly, than Ari had chosen to share with her.

"How high a designation?" Little to her surprise—the man rarely missed a thing.

She took a deep breath. "GI-5182-IT. He said." More sombre consideration. "Attached to the Internal Security

Organisation, League version of the FIA. That's why I never knew he existed, I never had full access to ISO files. It never occurred to me that the military was not the only department drawing resources from Recruitment."

"Do you think there may be more GIs in the League intelligence circles? High designation or otherwise?"

Sandy let out a small sigh. "I suppose it's possible. Ramoja wasn't forthcoming on that. Or rather I didn't have time to ask him, the Junshi situation cut our time short." And to Ibrahim's querying look, "That's his name, Mustafa Ramoja. Rank of Major. He said."

Ibrahim's lips moved slightly, as if replaying the name in his mind. A slight concentration, as if in some mild bemusement, eyes momentarily distant.

"Does the name mean something to you, sir?" she ventured.

"No. No, I merely wonder at the apparently random selection of GI names . . . he is a man of African appearance, then?" More of Ari's briefing.

She nodded. "West African, yes." Handsome bastard, too . . . but most GIs were. "The implied cultural affiliations don't appear to hold much significance for him, however. As with most GIs. I'd been hoping for more enlightenment from an Intel GI, though, outside the intellectual vacuum of Dark Star."

"As you yourself are enlightened?"

"I don't consider myself European, sir." A faint smile. "And as for my name, my verbal Russian begins and ends with 'Nyet.'"

"In Russia itself, of course, you would be Kresnova. Being female." The musing surprised her. Ibrahim did not muse often. Though, he was bleary-eyed with sleep, propped seated against the wall on the cushions that made up his temporary mattress . . . it appeared to have taken an edge off his usual, authoritative formality. He smiled at her. "Do you know that there are some in Parliament who bear President Neiland ill-feeling for appointing me as CSA director, mostly because of my Pashtun heritage?"

"Really?"

"Of course, there is little racism on Callay . . . but ethnic grudges apparently do not qualify for classification. My people have long been warriors—when motivated to put down their ploughs and spinning wheels. Frequently bloody, self-destructive, misguided warriors at that. This heritage continues to be celebrated in the old country today, I hear. It makes the local pacifists nervous. Perhaps they fear I will declare a Jihad on them all, declare sharia law and begin issuing fatwas against my most vocal critics."

"Will you?" With amusement.

"I had considered it, in my darker moments." A faint smile. "I value my heritage, Cassandra. It is a part of me, and I by no means claim the stereotypes entirely misguided. As a GI yourself, I think perhaps you understand how I feel. It is no sin to be a warrior, Cassandra. It merely depends on the cause."

"Some warriors will invent causes," Sandy said quietly, "in the absence of obvious ones. Perhaps humans are a race of warriors at heart, always searching for something to fight for."

"Perhaps." Ibrahim's smile faded slightly. "Most people's greatest strengths are also their greatest failings, after all."

"I once read a writer's opinion that humans impose narrative upon everything, and conflict is the base substance of all narrative. Thus we cannot help but find conflict wherever we go."

"I disagree." The smile fully returned. "Narrative *is* everywhere. And we are its subject." And switched the subject before she could puzzle over *that* one . . . "How smart do you reckon this man Ramoja to be?"

"Man," Sandy noted. Not "GI." Politeness, she reckoned. And more, a clear statement of respectful nondiscrimination. She welcomed it.

"He's a clever GI, no question. Illegally clever, by League laws. Like me."

"As clever as you?" With eyebrows raised. Sandy restrained a smile, and glanced briefly at the floor.

"As clever as me," she repeated, with mild irony. Halfway embarrassed at the praise. She didn't get embarrassed often. "I don't know, sir. How clever am I?" Meeting his gaze questioningly.

"Far more clever than any of those who would hate you, I have no doubt. That covers a good portion of the supposedly brightest minds on Callay." And Sandy found time to be glad that it was a physical impossibility for a GI to blush. "Cassandra. Did Ramoja attempt to recruit you back to the League?"

Sandy sighed. No sir, Ibrahim never missed much at all.

"Yessir." Shifted her posture, hooking an arm about her opposite leg as the tension strain began to ache once more. "Generally speaking. He attempted to convince me that the new government has changed things. That I could serve in the ISO instead of Dark Star, where things are supposedly better." Pause. "That people would always hate me in the Federation, and I should give up on ever trying to be accepted here."

"And what did you tell him?"

Sandy spared him a moment's consideration, eyes narrowed in thought. Worried, Mr. Ibrahim? Or just obliged by higher powers to keep checking my loyalty for your reports?

"Sir, Vanessa loves me." Quietly, in the subdued hush of the darkened office. Light drifted slowly beyond the windows, a flyer arriving at a nearby pad, running lights blinking. "SWAT Four mostly likes me. A lot of others in SWAT do too, I think. There are people in CSA Intel whom I genuinely believe I can call friends, or could, given some more time to get to know each other. The President likes me, whatever her more ruthless political tendencies. Some of her staff do. You yourself, and the Assistant Director, have shown me nothing but support and respect. And just today I met some ordinary Tanushans . . . if that isn't a total oxymoron . . . who were utterly delighted to make my acquaintance and pledged to help me out in any way they knew how, if necessary.

"Sir, that's a hell of a lot more friends than I *ever* had back in the League. In some respects the . . . the emotional intensity was greater with my old Dark Star team. But less, too, because there was so little of my other life that they could even understand if I tried to talk to them about it. And the straights more or less kept to themselves.

"I . . . I don't know if I can honestly say I'm emotionally committed to the Parliament, or the laws, or whatever. But to the people . . . or at least to those people, and the aspects of the society that made them who they are . . . that's something I'd love to belong to, sir. I'm committed to that. Entirely so."

"There are people here who would kill you, Cassandra, if they could." Sombrely, his lidded, dark eyes effortlessly penetrating with something that felt like . . . wisdom, she supposed. The calm, effortless application of knowledge and reason. It held her utterly unmoving. "There are religious radicals, some of them from my own faith, who regard your very creation as a blasphemous act before Allah. There are technophobes who simply cannot comprehend that a person of inorganic construction could ever be worthy of the basic concepts of humanity we hold so dear. There are politicians with votes to be won by fanning the flames of ignorant hysteria. There are academics with reputations to be made by criticising the precedent your presence sets for Callay and the Federation more broadly. And there are a great many ordinary Callayans who know only what they're told, or what they see on the broadband news and entertainments, and simply find the concept of what you are frightening, for any number of reasons, some of them reasonable, many of them not. You know all of this. Do you tell me now that you were never, and will never be, tempted by his offer?"

At another time, and another moment, she might have taken a long, agonised pause for consideration before replying. Now, she found herself smiling. A subtle, dangerous little smile, amusement in her eyes.

"I like the chaos," she said softly. "Chaos suits me. It

helps me think. Makes me feel alive. People have crazy ideas. And wonderful ones too. I think it's connected, you can't have one without the other." The smile grew a little broader. "So I can't really complain that people hate me. They also love me, or find me fascinating, or confusing, or terrifying . . ." She gave a light shrug. "I'll cope. I'll be fine. In a fluid society, people can always change their minds."

"Precisely what the League hopes," Ibrahim returned. She shrugged again.

"Sure, maybe I'm doing the League a favour . . . if I could get Callayans to like me at least a little. Change their attitude toward biotech. But I don't care either way. People will be people. And I'd much rather be here than locked into some League institution, watching from afar. At least people here know how to have fun."

Ibrahim was very amused. His eyes gleamed in the dark, lips smiling broadly. She couldn't remember having seen him so amused before. Lately, there hadn't been much to be amused about.

"*Is* Callay going to break away from the Federation, sir?" she asked directly. It seemed the right time to venture the question. Ibrahim smiled faintly.

"Cassandra, I could not tell you if I knew. But it is impossible to know regardless, there are so many talks proceeding between so many different power factions with unpredictable interests and hidden agendas." He thought for a moment. "Many are hung up on the question of Governor Dali. I feel he is the key. If he would testify as to the extent of the FIA's crimes, and the Grand Council's complicity, it would certainly swing the present negotiating position of President Neiland and all the Federation member worlds in their arguments with the Federalists."

Sandy frowned. "If Dali told what he knew, and what he was involved in . . . surely that would strengthen the breakaway vote? If Dali's testimony proved that the entire Federation system is implicated in the FIA's crimes, wouldn't that create the two-thirds majority here that Neiland needs for Callay to break from the Federation?"

"Or," said Ibrahim, nodding slowly, "create enough of a scandal back on Earth itself to force the Grand Council to a major review of itself. Possibly a review of the entire Federation system. It wasn't meant to be like this, Cassandra, Earth was not meant to have as much power as it presently has within the Grand Council and the Federation bureaucracy in general. The war put all the extremists in charge, just like in the League, and centralised all power around the Earth bureaucracy. The war has ended, but, on both sides, the damage continues."

Sandy thought of Captain Teig. And all the people killed at last month's Parliament Massacre, and other accompanying bloodbaths. And of the contracting calamity that was the League economy right now, as the restructuring swept through the old wartime centralisation like a wrecking ball—the travel-delayed news reports of mass layoffs, bureaucratic collapse, criminal gangs and even food riots, on some of the unluckier worlds. And she remembered certain Old Earth sayings about chickens coming home to roost . . .

"So reform of the Federation is possible, too?" she asked, still frowning. "As opposed to breaking away?"

Ibrahim gave a gentle shrug against the wall at his back.

"Breaking away is difficult. Politicians look for compromise. It certainly seems possible." No idle comment that, Sandy was sure. She stared at him closely for several long seconds. "But Dali is the key. And he has not been at all cooperative, he merely waits for the injunction to end so that the Earth delegation here can take him back to Earth, and Federal jurisdiction. He needs to say nothing to us, and he knows it."

"Can the injunction become permanent? Can we actually win and keep him here?"

"It's possible." He didn't sound very optimistic. "Callayan law versus Federal law. Federal law usually triumphs. But these are extraordinary times, setting extraordinary precedents. In law, precedents are everything."

Damn it was tiring, trying to hold all these factors, these possible outcomes in her head. Had civilian societies always worked like this? It amazed her that they didn't all collapse in disaster more frequently. It seemed like any person trying to keep things running would soon become like a juggler tossing too many balls—eventually one would slip, the rhythm would break and the whole lot come crashing down.

"Did Ramoja know anything about Chu?" Ibrahim asked quietly. Catching her off guard yet once more. She took a deep breath.

"I nearly forgot, there was so much else. I had to leave abruptly when Park Street went off, I only got in a quick question. He said he didn't know." A silent pause. Somewhere beyond the drawn blinds at the window, blinking lights from an approaching flyer flashed in colour. "He said the group that picked up the survivors of my team had vanished when the collapse set in after the election. No way of knowing where they are."

"It's better than knowing she's dead, Cassandra. Now you have hope."

Sandy gazed at the faint impression of lights through the blinds, watching them descend.

"A little hope," she said softly, "can be a painful thing."

Sleep meant mattresses upon an empty office floor, desks and integrated workspaces pushed to one side to make room for rows of SWAT grunts who couldn't find anywhere else in the chaotic, never-ending buzz of activity where they could lie down in peace. About half of them were already asleep by the time Vanessa made it up from final debrief, bureaucracy, armour maintenance and scheduling reviews. Hiraki followed in tow, equally exhausted, having arguably more responsibilities as second-in-command than even his CO.

"Great," Sandy heard Vanessa say quietly from across the darkened room, surveying the floor strewn with bedrolls full of sleeping bodies among the rearranged desks, "all my babies are sleeping while we're slaving away. Makes me so happy."

"Quit bitching, LT," came Singh's whisper from somewhere amid the dark mass of bedrolls. "You wanted the promotion, you get more pay, you take the chores."

Hiraki kicked one of the bedrolls as he stepped among them.

"Ow!" said Singh.

"Respect your superior," said Hiraki, continuing over to the clear space that had been left for him, Vanessa and Sandy. As always with Hiraki, it was difficult to know how seriously to take it.

"That's a good strategy," Vanessa approved, stepping her own light way over toward Sandy's seat against the far wall. "I might try that."

"Aiming for the head is more effective," Hiraki added, sitting to stretch, legs in a wide V before him, "but ultimately counterproductive."

"No chance of damage with Arvid," someone added helpfully.

"Oh right, so it's pick on Arvid time," Singh muttered, rolling over and rubbing at his backside.

There wasn't much chance of the conversation waking anyone—those asleep were dead to the world, and the talking took place at what would have been inaudible volumes were it not for security-level hearing enhancements. They tended to fade while unconscious, and keep from waking people up. Vanessa stopped behind Sandy's chair, where she sat with her feet up on the workdesk, reading off the broad, activated screen that lit the darkened gloom with a faint, artificial light.

"What's this?" Vanessa knelt behind her, putting a chin on her shoulder to read. Her cheek was warm against Sandy's ear, her short hair tickling. Sandy smiled. She'd never had such an intimate connection with any non-GI before. The relationships with her Dark Star team had been paternal, a brooding mother caring for her flock, protecting them from a world she understood far better than they. Here, with Vanessa, she was uncertain if that paternalism had not in fact been reversed. It was a very warm, very pleasant feeling, and totally new to her. She rested her own head against Vanessa's, and sighed.

"Just work. Network security, other stuff I've been working on."

Vanessa's dark, tired eyes scanned the mass of data-technicalities across the screen, visual three-dimensional representations, adjoining text/data adjuncts, multiple visual layers to be blinked up at need. Simple format.

"You can read this crap?" Vanessa sounded amazed. Sandy shrugged gently beneath the weight of Vanessa's chin.

"Just data. Data's . . ."

". . . Easy, yeah, I remember, you told me." Put an arm around her for balance, sagged tiredly against the back of the chair. "Studying for the Parliament appearance?"

"Yeah. Wouldn't mind making a good impression."

"This won't do it." With a nod at the screen.

Sandy frowned. "How d'you mean?"

"Sandy, no one doubts your abilities. They *expect* you to have amazing skills. And comprehensive knowledge from all your military experience. They need to be convinced that you'll use it to their advantage, and to Callay's advantage . . . and that politicians like them won't get the blame for you screwing them over."

Sandy let out a long breath. "Well I'm not sure if there's going to be a personality exam prepared. I'd like to just convince them I'm useful."

"Oh, they know you're useful. They just need to be convinced you're not dangerous."

"I am dangerous."

"Not to them."

"Yes I am. If I turn out useful and trustworthy, that's a master stroke to the President. Makes her look like a genius, helps all her allies, makes her opponents and all the people who opposed me look like misguided bigots . . ."

"That'd make half the Callayan population misguided bigots with them . . ."

"Sure, but who's going to remember that afterward? The public's always right, Vanessa, even when they're being total morons—that's the main thing I've learned about democracies. People are fickle, they change their minds and leave politicians who've committed fully one way or the other stranded. If politicians perform backflips, or look two-faced, it's because the public forces them to be."

"Wow." With weary amazement against her shoulder. "You've been here less than two months and you're already turning into a total political cynic."

"No I'm not. I like that the public can change their mind. It means politicians have to be flexible, and take all public mood-swings into account. Nothing's more dangerous than a narrow-focused leadership with a closed mind. Look at the League."

"True," Vanessa conceded. "They'll love you for that bit of rationale, it clears them of any blame for being slippery worms."

"Maybe I'll try it on them. Anyway, I'm expecting to be attacked by people who desperately want me to be the bad guy, because it serves their purposes. There's your cynicism."

"Sure, the media do that all the time. They get great ratings mileage by demonising you. Then as soon as the public mood swings, they'll go after great ratings by lauding you as a hero instead." Wrapped both arms more firmly about Sandy and the chair with a sigh, weariness gathering. "So, you've had a busy day, huh? Two firefights, catching up with your old buddies at the Embassy, flirting with Ari . . ."

"No, I don't flirt with Ari, Ari flirts with me."

"Ah, that's right, you don't think it qualifies as flirting unless there's penetration . . ."

"You're not accusing me of being unsubtle, are you?"

Vanessa grinned. "Never. You ready to desert back to the League yet?"

Vanessa's flippancy still surprised her. But only a little this time.

"Has that worried you?" Sandy retorted.

"Just a little, yeah." Sandy frowned. Vanessa didn't sound anywhere near as flippant there. "I mean you've hardly been warmly received. Pea-brained morons in admin, conservative politicians, religious leaders, alarmist media . . ."

"I don't spend my time with them," Sandy cut her off. "I spend my time with you and your guys and Intel, mostly."

"It doesn't hurt? Being tiraded against in public? Burned in effigy?"

"Maybe. But I'm used to it. I think I'm coming to understand the politics of it, how ordinary people think, how they receive and construct their information, their view on the universe. I see hope. Truthfully, I'm far more of a political hot potato back in the League. Recruitment there has never admitted to creating a GI like me. I don't know if the public's found out by now but there'll be hell to pay when they do, I'd have to live in isolation from all the furore that would start. I'm far freer here than I would be there."

"That's true."

Sandy felt the weight increasing against the back of her chair, as if Vanessa was slowly falling asleep. She reached and put a hand to the back of Vanessa's head, a gentle, improvised embrace.

"I wouldn't leave you," she murmured. "I've never had a friend like you."

"I've never had a friend like me either." Dazedly tired.

Sandy ruffled her hair, and planted a long kiss on her cheek. "Go to bed."

"Bed. That's a good idea." Rested her forehead against Sandy's for a long moment first. A simple gesture. It made Sandy feel warm all over. This was what love felt like. She'd felt it before, with GIs of her old team. But somehow it'd never been quite like this. They'd loved her as a reflex, their squad leader being the central figure in their universe, holding them all in awe with her capabilities. It'd been impossible for them to feel otherwise. She'd loved them back, affection for affection.

Vanessa, though, had a choice. Vanessa was her own person, and was under no obligations over where to place her affections. And Vanessa was amazing. She'd studied business, but ended up hating the corporate world for its moral sterility. She was smart enough to be very rich if she'd wanted. Pretty enough to have spent a life accumulating adoring menfolk (and the occasional woman) in a salivating pile at her feet. Personable enough to have hobnobbed and brown-nosed her way up the corporate and social ladders to the very top.

And instead, she'd gone against all the social norms for pretty, intelligent, sophisticated young women who preferred books to VR-sims and knew the French Revolution for an historical event beyond the famous Parisian nightclub on Ramprakash Road. She'd joined the CSA, become a SWAT grunt and gone on to become SWAT's most celebrated team leader, for which she received a moderate government salary, public anonymity and, lately, a reasonable chance at violent death or injury. She saw the universe in big-picture, and wanted what she did in life to matter. Lately, it had mattered—a great, great deal, in fact. It was the kind of imaginative, morally centred, dedicated passion Sandy had always suspected of existing in the civilian world, and particularly in the Federation, free from dogma, military discipline and a narrow-focused view of the universe. Not everyone had it. But Vanessa did. Vanessa, to Sandy's eyes, was amazingly, incredibly special.

And of all the people Vanessa had chosen to love as a close friend, she'd chosen *her.* It blew her away.

Vanessa got up on weary legs and swaggered slowly over occupied bedrolls in the dark to her empty bedroll beside where Hiraki was still stretching, bent low and grasping one extended ankle, forehead to shin.

"You sure you'll be able to sleep without your bed of nails?" someone nearby teased him in a low voice. Hiraki fancied himself as something of a modern day samurai, and led a very disciplined, frugal lifestyle by any standards, let alone Tanushan standards.

"Sleep, vile scum," was Hiraki's reply. Everyone liked Hiraki. But they were glad Vanessa was squad CO.

Vanessa pulled off her tracksuit and stretched, a sinuous rippling of slim, wiry, muscular limbs. Someone wolf-whistled while she was bent to touch her toes, clad only in underpants and small, cut-off undershirt that left her flat stomach bare.

"Children," came Zago's deep, murmured reprimand from across the room. "I'm surrounded by immature children, one sleep-out and everyone thinks they're back in school camp." Zago was in his fifties, married with five children, and enjoyed his role as squad "senior." Someone farted. All those still awake collapsed with laughter. An enhanced vision-shift through the dark showed Sandy that even Hiraki was smiling. Vanessa just sat on the floor, head in hand, shaking uncontrollably. It was a release of tension. Sandy had seen it even among supposedly tension-resistant GIs. Straights required far more, she'd discovered.

"Do GIs fart?" someone thought to ask.

"I refuse to answer," Sandy replied, "on the grounds that any statement may be self-incriminating."

"Children," repeated Zago. Vanessa resumed stretching upon her bedroll.

"Do that bending-over stretch again, LT," came Singh's voice. "I was enjoying that."

"You won't enjoy me breaking your kneecaps," retorted Rupa Sharma, SWAT Four's only other woman besides Sandy and their beloved CO.

"You could do it instead, Rupa, I don't mind either way." Some laughter and poking went on across where Sharma was lying. A smacking sound of Sharma swatting someone away.

"I knew it had to be a mistake trying to sleep in a room full of this many men," she muttered.

"Where's your sense of adventure, Rupa? This is your chance to be a sexual legend! A shot at the record books!"

"I'd rather sleep in a farm yard."

"Whatever gets you going, I guess."

"Well," said Vanessa, finishing her stretching and climbing tiredly into her sleeping bag, "you guys can do what you want over there, but I warn you, any attempt to penetrate the CO will be met with stern disapproval and extra duty."

"Arvid," Sandy added over the muffled giggles from around the room, "I'll have you know I *own* those record books."

"I'll believe that," Singh said agreeably. "Good night everybody, sleep well, and try not to think of the LT's tight little arse and shapely thighs . . ."

"There's nothing further from my mind, I assure you," said Kuntoro, who was gay.

"Seriously," Sharma complained, "someone take him out in the corridor and shoot him."

"Can't," said the usually laconic Tsing, "Requisition Order 32b, non-operations-related ammunition requested for the purposes of disposing of irritating squadmates must first be signed for against the authorisation of . . ."

And was cut off by exhausted, uncontrolled laughter—even Sandy found herself grinning. And reflected that most of her old Dark Star team would probably have been asleep by now . . . except maybe Tran and Mahud, who alone of her team might have stayed awake talking while the others followed procedure and went to sleep. Again, civilians did things differently. Perhaps, she thought, whatever the situation's difficulties, a few minutes' extra sleep were not as important as the emotional comfort of knowing one was not alone. In Dark Star, they had fought because fighting was the act that defined their existence. In SWAT Four, they fought for their homeworld against those who wished to harm it. It was a cause they all shared, even the macho types like Johnson, whose primary reason for joining was "tough-guy" self image. Even through their casual banter, they reminded each other of the togetherness, and sense of community, that drove them in their task. The togetherness was what they were fighting for. A place, a people and a cause.

Sandy smiled to herself in the dark, feet up on the table and reading from her screen as the conversation continued in hushed, laughing tones . . . feeling that something very significant had slipped profoundly into place. This was what it felt like to belong to something. To be willing to fight, and even to die for it. And for the first time in her life, she knew what she was fighting for—it was messy, it was complicated, it was often exasperating and downright infuriating. But it was something worth protecting, and something that was in evident need of her protection. And after so many years of uncertainty, regret and doubt, this sudden, delightful onset of clarity felt like . . . liberation.

CHAPTER 10

The Grand Congressional Hearings Chamber was as impressive to sit in as the name suggested it ought. Located on the fifth floor of the massive nine-storey Parliament complex, the ceiling extended all the way up to the roof in a grand, arching dome, patterned with tiles and inlays of Islamic inspiration. The lighting setup reminded Sandy of mosques she had ventured into, a circular arrangement of long, suspended lamps that formed a clear circle above the middle of the huge room between ceiling and floor. The lamps themselves were more in the style of European chandeliers, though, as were the wall panelling, and the enormous, wooden altarlike benches at the front of the room.

Sandy sat at the centre of the long table before the elevated, arching semicircle of benches with their carved panelling and plush chairs, her laptop set before her as she waited for the huge, noisy crowd in the chamber seats behind to arrange itself into some kind of orderliness. She estimated seating for perhaps six hundred. Some, she'd been informed by Rani Bannerjee, the President's new senior advisor, were being filled by congressors or senators not presently occupied with other matters. Most were taken by yet more lemmings, members of one or another off-world delegation, along with the many interested Callayan onlookers. Visitors' passes to the Parliament were rare these days, and most journalists had been banned from the room for this occasion, but still, milling behind her this jostling, unsettled crowd . . . she caught snatches of conversation, some of it technical, but much of it, as she'd feared, specifically about her.

". . . wish she'd turn around . . ." was the gist of many conversations, as eager, curious, wary civilians strained for a look at this most significant of curiosities to descend upon their world of late. She had no intention of turning around. She'd gotten here early, straight from the small VIP flyer pad at the side of the complex, and sat in her required seat specifically in order to get here ahead of the gallery crowd and sit like this with her back to them as they entered. Not that she cared if they saw her face or not—the closed-circuit TV could, and would transmit these proceedings all through the corridors of power. Closed-circuit transmissions ran on fancy embedded encryption that erased themselves at any attempt to copy and disseminate, and did so in ways that could also melt the utilised equipment. She'd studied the software herself, briefly, and had been satisfied. This broadcast would only be seen once, and that only in select offices of power.

"Nervous?" asked Mahudmita Rafasan from alongside. The President's senior legal advisor was dressed rather conservatively today, in a dark outfit that looked almost as much dress as sari, with silvery trimmings and only a patterned orange shoulder-sash for the obligatory flash of colour. Earrings, bangles and other jewellery were untypically sparse and modest, and her gleaming black hair was bound conveniently short at the back.

"Wishing I'd sat in on the security checks," was Sandy's only comment, uplinked to the room's security systems, for what little she could access past the impenetrable barriers that enclosed all the Parliament complex's systems.

"The, um, detectors and searches in the corridors are quite thorough," Rafasan reassured her, with a familiar nervous fidget at the bangles upon her left wrist. There was a ring there too, on the fourth finger, where a wedding ring might be upon a European. This ring, Rafasan had told her some time before, was a mark of graduation from her law school, some fifty years before . . . Rafasan was seventy-five years old, though it was impossible to tell to look at her. She could have been a young thirty, and a very attractive one at that. Not all biotech advances, Sandy reflected, were disdained in Tanusha. It was the kind of hypocrisy in the Federation's antibiotech stance that the League never failed to point out at every opportunity.

"Even so," Sandy replied, running her eyes across the lower front bench before her, "I'm never comfortable with so many people at my back." The congressors were all in place and seated, some examining notes, some taking in the scene before them. The second, upper bench held fifteen, the lower one eleven. Elected representatives, seated here in numbers reflecting the numbers of the lower house—seventeen for Union Party, and nine for Progress Party. A two-party system in the lower house, with their preference system and elimination ballots. Only in the proportional representation of the Senate, housed in the second point of the Callayan governmental triangle but a kilometre from here, did the minor parties run amok.

Security stood at various strategic points about the room, armed and alert. Most were facing the crowd . . . white-shirted uniforms with gold badges upon their chests. All members of the gallery were VIPs of a sort, security cleared, sifted, and further checked in the outside hall before entry . . . standard procedure these days with or without the presence of controversial, ex–Dark Star GIs. In truth, Sandy reflected, she was less concerned at the possibility of rogue terrorists in the gallery than at the presence of several leading Tanushan journalists of whose presence Rani Bannerjee had also informed her. There might be no legal means to broadcast her image or voice, but there was nothing to stop print or broadcast media from transmitting her words second-hand when she spoke in a public setting.

Do not, Bannerjee had further counselled her just minutes before, under any circumstances, say anything controversial. Be dull, boring and listless if necessary.

Exactly what constituted a controversy, Sandy remained unsure. She suspected it rather depended upon who was listening. And on a world like Callay, surely the only way to avoid offending anyone was to say nothing at all. It was all Neiland's problem now. She was surprised at exactly how cool she was about it. She only wished there'd been some way of keeping her gun . . . but, of course, she remained technically suspended due to the SIB's investigation, and it would not do to be seen wielding a weapon in direct defiance of that suspension in the Parliament complex itself. Her weapon remained with an Agent Odano, a junior recruit from Investigations who'd been assigned to run this errand, and was presently seated in the gallery some short distance behind. He also had her badge. "Don't throw them to me if there's trouble," Sandy had told him on the flyer ride in. "I'll get to you first, believe me." He'd believed her.

A bell rang, a clear, rapid chiming. How anachronistic, Sandy thought, watching with interest as the sound emanated from a small, silver bell in front of the chairman. He was seated in the centre of the front row, a man of Arabic appearance, clad in the white robe permissible in Tanushan politics for those politicians who liked to display their cultural heritage instead of settling for the universal blandness of suits and ties. He wore a thick, black beard, which gave Sandy some indication as to his political leanings. Although, she'd been learning in Tanusha not to take anything for granted.

"The records shall note that the time is ten thirty-five on Central Time Monday the fifteenth of March, 2543."

League time, it occurred to Sandy in idle thought, was tri-month-and-twelve when converted to the universal League calendar—decimals and averages—the general average of League-world years made convenient for the time-dilation of travelling starships and peoples a long, long way from Earth's rotational schedules. It made more sense than Callay's system of cramming a 325-day year into the same twelve Earth months, with months running to twenty-six or twenty-seven days to compensate. But none of the League's months were named after great Roman emperors who had lived more than two thousand years before, and were thus, in Sandy's estimation, rendered quite dull by comparison. Long live inefficiency and point-less complexity. She was certain that the reminder of past eras and histories was far more valuable than any gain in basic numerical efficiency.

"I," the chairman continued, "Khaled Hassan, declare this special Congressional Hearing open, and the speaker today is one . . . Ms. April Cassidy." With emphasis that Sandy thought might be wry sarcasm. A murmur echoed from the clustered gallery behind. Some muted laughter. Tittering, nervous excitement. Rafasan spared her a nervous glance. Sandy sighed. "Ms. Cassidy . . . just a pro-cedural thing, could you please make sure you speak directly into the microphone so everyone can hear?"

"Yes, sir."

Another tittering murmur from the gallery. She won-dered if maybe she'd said the wrong thing, reminding people of her military past . . . well, she couldn't help that, calling people in positions of authority "sir" was as unshakeable a habit as breathing. She determined to keep her tone polite and deferential, free from the drill instructor formality that would surely intimidate a crowd such as this, however formal the occasion. She'd never been keen on drill anyhow.

"Now, Ms. Cassidy . . . I understand you have a presen-tation for us, on behest of the President herself . . . in order to demonstrate to us all, I gather, the nature and . . . well, *importance* of your more recent work here on Callay . . ." in the slow, pausing, long-winded manner of a professional bureaucrat, ". . . but first, if you would allow, of course, I would like to ask the freedom as chairman to ask you a few questions . . . on behalf of my colleagues here, who will of course have their turn, as per the standing orders of this hearing chamber, to ask of you their own questions upon your completion of this . . . presentation of yours. Is this sequence of events . . . acceptable to you?"

"Yes, sir, perfectly acceptable."

More murmuring. And it occurred to her in a flash . . . it was her voice. A good voice, to be sure, firm and strong. But high, clear, and unmistakably female. Wow. It amazed her that they were amazed. Just her luck to end up on one of the few worlds left in all human space where the idea of women as fighters still raised some eyebrows. They damn well knew the rest of human space had largely moved on, they simply didn't care, and women themselves were among the loudest objectors. And now this . . . not only a GI, but a *female* one. And blonde. In Tanusha, when a teenage Indian, Arabic or Chinese girl wanted to upset her father, she dyed her hair blonde and wore European-style skirts several sizes too short. Blonde women were the sexually exotic, or, as Vanessa would say with a snort, the archetypal decadent, cultureless European morality vacuum. Not that anyone had noticed any shortage of libidinous activity among the Tanushan population in general of late, but some ethnic stereotypes died harder than others. It didn't seem something that most European Tanushans were trying very hard to fling off. Sandy empathised.

"Very well, then, Ms. Cassidy . . ." Hassan paused for a moment, reading from the screen before him, stroking absently at his ample beard. ". . . first of all, could I perhaps inquire if 'April Cassidy' is in fact your real name? There was some conjecture earlier, among my colleagues . . . some said it was only a CSA-given pseudonym."

Sandy smiled. "April Cassidy is a pseudonym, Mr. Hassan." Her voice echoed clearly through the chamber, projected from invisible speakers with great clarity. "My real name remains protected for now, as do my other personal details."

"I see." Another beard stroke, watching her with curiosity. He seemed, Sandy reckoned, a rather mild sort of man. Union Party Leftist, Bannerjee had briefed her. Muslim, of course, but in the measured, secular way of most mainstream Callayan politicians where religious affiliations were concerned. "And how did you come about this . . . rather curious pseudonym, if I may ask?"

"Of course." Repressing a broader smile. "I chose it myself. From a couple of public figures back League-side. Something I didn't think anyone would automatically associate with me."

"Which pair of public figures?"

"If you must know, Mr. Hassan, from a pair of holovid porn stars."

Utter, disbelieving silence for a moment. Then a surge of laughter, building to general commotion. Fading just as quickly as people remembered they weren't supposed to make any noise. To her left, Sandy saw that Rafasan was staring at her with a somewhat stricken expression . . . poor woman, she'd been hoping her administration's tame GI would make this session easy on her, what with her usual chaotic schedule now including the injunction proceedings against Governor Dali's extradition as well. Sandy managed with difficulty to stop her smile turning into a grin.

"I remembered one male soldier under my command in Dark Star," she continued with unfazed amusement, "once made the observation to me that this one particular porn star looked rather like myself . . . it was a long, boring period with nothing much to do, you understand, and they were looking for various entertainments to pass the time." More amusement from the gallery. "Anyhow, this lady's name, I believe, was something-or-other Cassidy. Her partner's name was April." Outright guffaws from directly behind her. Rafasan was just staring, in utter disbelief. "I put the two together. I thought it catchy."

And she sat for a long moment, and surveyed the carnage she had wrought upon the sombre, orderly proceedings in just a few short moments, with laughter and hubbub from the gallery, and numerous congressors exchanging disbelieving looks, and sometimes laughter, in their utter surprise.

"Well," said a woman on the Progress Party side of the benches, "this hearing has started absolutely *nothing* like I'd expected." Which provoked even more laughter, a continuing release of built-up tension. On the Union side of the benches, the mirth was considerably more subdued. Although suspicious of Progress Party motives in general, she was certainly happy to have them there. They were the ones, generally speaking, who were not scared of her. Some were using her to attack Neiland and Union in general, but attacks on herself were comparatively rare from Progress.

"You realise that you'll never live this down?" asked another Progress rep with a broad smile.

"Sir," Sandy replied, "right now, that's the least of my problems."

From there it was details and procedure. She was fine with that—she'd done her share of briefings before this, before panels of very senior League military officers, and occasionally League Government bureaucrats or elected representatives. This, of course, was entirely different, both in surroundings and content. But concentration had always been a strong point of hers, and she simply focused on the information upon the laptop screen before her, and shut out the rest of the room.

She started with the Plexus Grid. Built by Plexus Corporation to make the Callayan system navigable to the frequent traffic of freighters and passenger liners that plied the lanes, it had undergone numerous upgrades in the two hundred years since Callay had been first settled. The most extensive upgrades, of course, had occurred between seventy-five and fifty Callayan years ago, when the newly founded technology-based centre of Tanusha had been first commissioned upon the Shoban River Delta, just south of the coastal fringe of the Tuez Range, on the eastern coast of Taj, the second largest of the northern continental landmasses. No one had quite predicted just how successful an experiment in urban planning the new settlement would become, nor were they quite ready for the implications on what had been a mostly agricultural, low-intensity-development world up to that point.

The Grid, she told the assembled listeners, was serviceable, made particularly so by some clever autonomous-function software and precision laser-com systems developed in Tanusha itself over the last few decades. But even now the systems were not equipped to the overlapping second- and third-level redundant sensitivity required to provide adequate protection from stealth raiders, who, given adequate advance knowledge of the Grid layout, could slip between the gaps. And further still, the passive sensory systems on the buoys overly relied upon doppler-effect measurements to monitor target velocities, which were notoriously unreliable in the face of phase-shifting attacking craft headed in-system carrying high-V from jump . . . which did a number of things to Einsteinian physics of light that she didn't pretend to entirely understand, except to say that it could render elements of the doppler-effect misleading . . . supra-light technologies could do that, especially on the later-model vessels in either the League or Federation fleets, something about wave effects and bending light from jump fields . . . anyhow, she waved a hand dismissively, she was not a physicist, just an ex-grunt, and she was certain that Callayan engineers could give a better explanation of the systems that were needed for an upgrade than she could herself.

"You never had to deal with the technical complexities of such things yourself, Ms. Cassidy?" asked a Union Party rep.

"Not really, sir. The physics of space combat are an extraordinarily complex business that require all Fleet officers to spend four years and hundreds of hours of tape-teach to understand with any degree of practical certainty. As a special forces commander I had the luxury of allowing them to worry about the technicalities while I concerned myself with operations within the target environment. I'm more interested with the practical implications of *what* the equipment does than how."

"You were involved in space battles yourself?" Space battles. He managed to make it sound like a VR simulation game.

"Yes, sir. My operational environments varied from stations and other space-based facilities to ships and planet-bound targets. Planets are still something of a novelty to me, actually . . . I'd guess something like seventy percent of my life has been off-world, either on stations or being transported from place to place on ships."

"And how does it feel to be now living on a planet? Do you miss your old environment?"

"Not even a little bit."

Dead silence from the gallery behind. As if they dared not breathe, lest they missed some vital clue from her lips. A clue to what, she was not sure.

"That's hardly the response I'd expect from a veteran spacer."

"I'm not a veteran spacer, sir. I never had much to do with the hour-by-hour operations of spacecraft or stations. They were a platform from which I operated as a League soldier. On military facilities you didn't even get much of a view, viewports weren't a high priority in the designers' schematics." She shrugged faintly. "I welcome the space down here. And the sunlight. And the weather. Weather's wonderful. My best friend claims the greatest present threat to my life is lightning, she's always dragging me inside when a storm front comes through. Lightning's amazing."

"Please, Mr. Selvadurai," said Chairman Hassan, "allow Ms. Cassidy to finish her presentation. There will be plenty of time for questions later."

Then came her notes on local network security systems, which were difficult to translate for a nonexpert audience, but she tried as best she could, detailing several of the more notoriously gaping holes, and outlining precisely why it had been so easy for FIA operatives to remain undetected on the system for as long as they had. Then emergency response systems . . . several of the biggest problems were glaring, most notably the lack of training for serious emergencies. The debacle at the Derry riverside had demonstrated that clearly enough, and from the reluctant nods and wry expressions of several members along the benches, she knew she'd struck a chord.

And then there was CSA and SWAT itself . . . there was the whole event on Park Street, with its masses of people to stand around, make notes and pour tea, yet somehow still a shortage of weapon-trained forces to clear neighbouring buildings, and a police force that didn't read CSA priority reports, which significantly reduced its ability to assist on CSA-run operations because it was largely out of the procedural loop on extra-irregular protocols. And of course there was SWAT procedure and training, inter-operational communication between the various CSA departments, the undersupply of airborne vehicles and certain unnecessary procurement delays that cost money, time, and valuable manpower. And then of course there were recommendations . . . not that she had any specifically planned, of course, as all things needed to be carefully planned in advance before suggestions could be made, but would the panel care for a general overview in advance?

Glazed looks from the congressors. She noted the time . . . 12:30, she'd been talking for better than two hours now. No one had said how long she should speak for, she'd been told to demonstrate her thorough knowledge of relevant security systems in need of an upgrade, and she'd done that. But maybe she'd been a bit long on technical detail?

"Well . . ." said Hassan, a little wearily, ". . . Ms. Cassidy . . . perhaps, I feel, a list of recommendations would be more well-suited to another time . . . and perhaps a panel more expert on such matters than this one, for them to judge the merit of your proposals. But I . . . thank you greatly for your insight here today . . . it has given us all much food for thought, I'm sure everyone will agree."

Much shifting and coughing from the gallery. Passing lunchtime now, and no food allowed in the hearing room. Doubtless, it occurred to her, they'd been hoping for something considerably more sexy than what she'd just delivered. Good. As a public figure, she didn't want to be sexy. She wanted to be dull, bland, and sensibly utilitarian.

"I would convene the hearing for lunch," Hassan

resumed, shifting back to a properly upright posture in his big leather chair, "but given the . . . pressing nature of everyone's schedules at this time, I feel we should perhaps proceed immediately to questions, if there are no objections?"

"Ms. Cassidy," a Union Party rep said immediately from the left end of the long double row of benches, "you are technically under suspension at this moment, are you not?"

Silence descended once more upon the shifting, coughing gallery.

"Yes, ma'am." No one used that feminine anachronism in the League, nor in the CSA. But here in the grand houses of Parliament, it remained, she'd been informed, the required mode of address to powerful women.

"Why are you under suspension?" Seated on the very far left of the front bench. Sandy had to turn her head across to look at the woman directly. Distractingly, numerous of the gallery across that side began to lean forward, seeking a better view of her face.

"There was an incident." And thought to glance across at Rafasan. Rafasan nodded for her to continue. "The bombing on the Derry riverside two nights ago. I caught the bomber. The SIB thought I took unnecessary measures in doing so, and placed me under suspension on a technicality of my Callayan citizenship conditions, pending further review."

"You *caught* the bomber?" someone else asked. All twenty-six pairs of eyes across both rows of benches fixed unerringly upon her, with a mix of incredulity and surprise.

"Yes, ma'am."

"How?"

"I'm afraid," Rafasan intervened, leaning forward to her microphone, "that that information remains classified for now . . ."

"Isn't it true," said the first Union Party woman, "that you shot and wounded a pair of SIB investigators in the process of this . . . apprehension?" Dead silence. Sandy looked at Rafasan. The President's senior legal advisor gave a long, dark look in the direction of the Union Party woman. And then shrugged to Sandy, helplessly. A go-ahead.

"After they opened fire on me in an attempt to kill me for failing to stop when they said stop," Sandy replied. "I disobeyed because I was chasing the bomber, who was getting away. Upon coming under what I perceived to be an attack intended to be lethal, I responded by aiming to wound both of my pursuers, which I achieved, whereupon I resumed pursuit of the bomber and caught him."

Another, building wave of murmuring from the gallery. It had been on the news, she knew. Lots of eye witnesses. The news media hadn't guessed it'd been her in pursuit, however, and the CSA had done a good job of confusing the issue, claiming multiple agents in pursuit . . . technically true, but not exactly clarifying. Thankfully most people had been too confused or frightened, and the media too wrapped up in sensationalism, to get very close to the truth . . . although that too would have been just a matter of time, even for the Tanushan press. The Union woman stared hard at her for a moment. Evidently it didn't correlate with what she'd been told.

"Alita Bhattacharya," Rafasan leaned over to whisper in Sandy's ear, "Union Right." Sandy nodded, knowing what that meant. Religious groups and extreme, anti-League positioning. In this city, her ideological worst enemy. Doubtless the Senate Security Council had been talking to her.

"You can corroborate your story?" asked Bhattacharya, with extreme disbelief.

"It's on tape," Rafasan replied for her. "CSA protocols have recovered traffic-control sensors which recorded the event. It correlates with Ms. Cassidy's recollection of events entirely."

"And why haven't you released this tape?" Bhattacharya replied suspiciously.

"Because the CSA and the Administration," Rafasan replied frostily, "are more concerned with performing the task circumstance has assigned to us, in accordance with the laws governing security restrictions and nondisclosure, than we are with scoring political points. Instead we are faced with a circumstance where one of this world's finest assets has been suspended for doing her job with excellence, while the SIB has been rewarded for doing its job extremely badly."

"Speaking personally, Ms. Rafasan," said a man sitting two seats along from Bhattacharya, "I find this incessant CSA bashing of the SIB and its agents extremely disturbing, particularly under these circumstances, where a couple of SIB agents have actually been *shot*, to apparently very little remorse from the person who shot them, or the CSA, or indeed the Neiland Administration in general."

"Sir," Rafasan said very coldly, nervous fingers clasping hard together on the table as she leaned forward, "if you care to examine my own personal record of statements in legal and academic arenas, you will find that my own attitude toward the SIB has generally been extremely positive for a great many years. As the President's senior legal advisor, you can trust that I have frequently supported the SIB's procedures on many things, often against the President's own feelings, or that of her various other advisors or ministers. I felt that the SIB possessed a degree of intellectual, academic sophistication worthy of the city that Tanusha, and the planet of Callay, was aiming to become.

"Recent events have come as something of a shock to me, I now most readily confess. They have revealed stark flaws in the SIB's operating procedure, most notably that its links to the Senate, and particularly the Senate Security Panel, have held its agenda hostage to narrow, often extremist and unrepresentative interests that in this case have sent it on the most disgraceful witch hunt that I have ever had the disgust to observe in all my years in the legal profession. The degree of extremist xenophobia . . ."

"Ms. Rafasan . . ." the chairman said loudly.

". . . and the accompanying dangerously irrational attempts to interfere with legal government process," Rafasan continued, her accent lilting in a pronounced, angry rush, "have as far as I can see worked only to the detriment of law-abiding people across this planet . . ."

"Ms. Rafasan, if you please . . ."

". . . and to the broader security circumstance in general, much to the endangerment of everything that all law enforcement agencies upon this world should hold dear and sacred in the extreme."

"Thank you, Ms. Rafasan, I believe your point has been made . . ."

"Ms. Rafasan," from the Union side, "I really can't believe what I'm hearing here . . ."

Sandy glanced across at the senior legal advisor, who sat flushed and angry, her jaw set at a stubborn angle. She'd gotten to know Rafasan reasonably well over the last month of consultations on one legal matter or another, but she'd never seen her this worked up. Demure South Asian femininity indeed . . . quite against the popular media images of delicate Indian beauty queens and assorted glamour princesses, she'd always thought Indian women among the most formidable people in Tanusha. Whenever they opened their mouths, that was.

"Please, please, people," cut in Chairman Hassan wearily before Rafasan could reply to the Union congressor's disbelief, "this hearing was not convened to discuss the strengths and failings of the Special Investigations Bureau, but rather to hear a presentation and ask questions of Ms. Cassidy here, who is doubtless extremely busy, as are we all . . ."

"Ms. Cassidy," spoke up another man from the Union side, "my name is Aramel Afed, I am a member of what you will know as the Union Left." A narrow-faced, dark-skinned man. North African, Sandy guessed. "I feel this might be an opportunity for us, the elected representatives of Callay, to actually get to know you, at least a little . . . after all, we've heard so much about you, but until now have had no opportunity to attach a face, or indeed a personality, to this person of whom we've been hearing. So if you will allow me, I will begin by asking you to tell us all a little about yourself. What are your first memories, if I could begin at that early stage of your life?"

Sandy looked at Rafasan. Rafasan nodded encouragingly. Union Left. Neiland's support base, them and the Centrists . . . most of the trouble came from the Right. And she suspected immediately that this man, this Congressor Afed, was most likely offering a planted question—a prearranged strategy worked out with members of the Neiland Administration to steer the hearing in a desirable direction. So. This, she realised, could take quite some time. She settled herself more comfortably into her seat, stretched her ankles more firmly out beneath the table, and began to tell them about her life.

It was another three hours before she departed via the guarded side entrance, achingly stiff despite the comfortable chair and repeated, subtle attempts at stretching during the questioning. Parliament staff had somehow arranged lunch, plates of sandwiches, falafels and samosas for herself, Rafasan and the twenty-six elected reps, while the gallery had sat on in silence, and those who hadn't brought a packed lunch no doubt wished they had. Someone had even brought herself and Rafasan tea, which the congressors did not get, doubtless there was a staff shortage of such things, but the harried young intern had left them a teapot with milk and sugar lumps . . . assuming, of course, that she *did* drink tea, common enough assumption in Tanusha, addictive Indian habit that it was.

"Well, I think that went quite excellently," Rafasan was saying as they walked side by side down the hallway, kept largely empty of pedestrians for security purposes, Sandy guessed. Agent Odano walked two steps behind, and a pair of Parliament security behind him, in addition to the two who walked before them, leading the way. "All things considered, that is. You are a very good public speaker, I did tell the President that I thought it would be a good idea to get you to talk to the Party, I did believe you would make an impression, and now I honestly think you have."

"I'm glad you think so." Not prepared right now to argue the point that only recently, most had not thought it a good idea at all. But things had changed, evidently. Many things were changing very, very fast . . . for all she knew, the next suggestion would have her running for public office. She sincerely hoped not.

It had been enough just to sit before that double row of elected representatives and recount to them in broad terms, and occasionally specific ones, the general course of her life. The reasons she'd left the League. The things she still liked about League-side, and the things she'd grown to dislike. Her combat operations. Her combat history, from ever-changing locations across the broad, ever-shifting "front" of the League-Federation conflict. The battles she'd engaged in that they might have heard of. The majority of small engagements that they never would have. Her escape to the Federation, her impressions of the Federation, her first job, her first pay cheque, her first decadently "civilian" experience (dancing to African rhythms in a street party, she'd remembered . . . only she'd left out the bit about flirting with a very handsome young dancer for the better part of an hour's exertion, and ending up in his hotel bed for the night for some equally energetic exertions). Her perspective on Callayan, and especially Tanushan, politics. Her feelings about the CSA, the SIB, the recent events, and the direction of Article 42.

She felt tired, and more than a little drained. As if she'd poured out something of herself in that hearing room, leaving the space it'd come from somehow empty.

"Where to now?" she asked Rafasan.

"Upstairs," said Rafasan brightly, her stride light, heels clacking upon the smooth floor. "We promised some of the congressors that we'd let them meet you in person. Of course the Progress Party reps wanted to meet you, but a lot of our Left do too . . . especially now, after that performance."

"How many people?" With that familiar sinking feeling she got when being manoeuvred around by political people for political reasons into things she hadn't agreed to in advance because she hadn't been told about them. It was becoming a depressingly accustomed feeling.

"Oh, don't worry," Rafasan said dismissively, waving a be-ringed and bangled hand, "it's not so many, everyone's busy, so they'll just come in when they're available—you just need to shake their hand, say hello and be generally agreeable. I'm quite sure you can manage that for another hour or two."

She wanted to complain that she was beginning to feel like a zoo exhibit . . . but she didn't see any point in complaining to Rafasan, there was nothing she could do about it. In fact, there was nothing anyone could. Neiland needed her here, and she owed Neiland . . . well, everything. She only hoped the persuasion her presence worked upon the wavering middle-ground of Parliament actually came to something positive. For everyone.

The upper corridor was broad and more well-travelled, with large, stylish wooden doors to either side, and many people going by who looked curiously as they passed.

"The chambers are just up here a ways," Rafasan said, and they walked to an exquisitely decorated intersection with carved wooden panels to match the seamless patterned tiles on the floor . . . turned left, and found the big double doorway upon the right wall almost entirely blocked by a chaotic gathering of people engaged in animated argument with officials in suits. Several more white-shirted Parliament security hovered warily on the perimeter. "What in the name of . . . ?"

The agitators, Sandy observed as she held determinedly to her stride despite Rafasan's surprised pause, did not appear your typical Tanushan political power group. They wore robes of wildly varying colours, though saffron and cotton-white predominated. Some had long, wild hair and, among the men, tangled beards. Most, it appeared, were barefoot, or clad in no more than simple leather sandals. She counted twelve in all, at least half of whom were currently engaged in a heated, hand-waving argument with suited or uniformed officialdom, which appeared to be trying to remove them from their place before the big double doors.

Then several saw the new arrivals, and there was more commotion, and much loud, rapid talking in a language that sounded distinctly Indian but was not immediately recognisable as one of the five or six she could usually identify by sound alone. A young, sari-clad, barefoot woman was tugging hastily upon the shoulder of an old man, who was shuffling away from the confronting officialdom to observe, through the gathered crowd, what new arrivals came upon him down the hallway.

"Oh no," said Rafasan, hurrying to keep up and sounding much aggrieved, "it's Swami Ananda Ghosh . . . how on Earth he got over here from the Senate building I've no idea . . . Sandy, I don't know if you should go over there, I'll get someone to remove them . . ."

"Nonsense," Sandy said calmly, observing the group with interest as they stopped. The two lead security guards walked to their compatriots guarding the doors, and asked them, no doubt in polite, low voices, what the hell was going on. "What language are they speaking?"

"Them?" Fidgeting with familiar nervousness at her side. "Oh, that's Sanskrit, it's the Swami's organisation, Sandy, I forget the Sanskrit name, but it means "guiding light," he has everyone in the group talking in Sanskrit so they can better understand the ancient texts."

"Sounds nice. I've only seen it written before, not heard it spoken." As the discussions continued, she eyed the distance between herself, her group, and the group of traditionally, but shaggily, attired people blocking her way. All arguments had ceased, and all those before her were still, waiting patiently for the security discussions to end. Not all of them were Indian, Sandy noted. Only half, in fact. Two were European, one African, and the other three looked East Asian . . . though it was not a huge leap, she'd gathered, from Buddhism to Hinduism, the Buddha himself having been a Hindu once. "Sounds a bit Arabic, only smoother."

"It's actually, um, closer to Farsi, Urdu and Pashtun, it's one of that family from Egyptian and Arabic carrying on across to northern India—that was all a civilisation once, or a series of civilisations. The birthplace of civilisation itself, actually. Most of the old Hindu texts and stories are written in Sanskrit, you could say it's the equivalent of what Latin is for the Europeans."

Sandy spared Rafasan an intrigued glance. "You speak any?"

"Oh yes, I was rather fluent back in my student days . . . it's been far too long now, of course, I can't remember half of it." Sounding almost wistful. "I'll get back to it one day. There are poems in Sanskrit that are like . . . like nothing else I'll ever . . ."

She broke off as the Swami began to walk forward. He was an old man, and it seemed he had disdained the youthful effects of biotreatments, for his gait was slow and he walked with a large, stout cane in one gnarled hand. The young sari-clad woman walked at his other hand, holding his arm. The Swami's face was mostly hidden behind a long, flowing white beard, and an equally long torrent of wispy white hair. Security stood to the side and said nothing, and the Swami stopped before her, clad only in an old white dhoti that wrapped up between his old, bare legs and over one shoulder, leaving the other bare. He looked at her, equal to her in height, and his eyes were dark and beady amid a maze of wrinkles in weathered brown skin. Sandy realised he was smiling, although she could barely see his mouth through the beard. But the eyes wrinkled up in joyful good humour.

"Hello, Mr. Ghosh," she said pleasantly. "I'm very pleased to meet you finally." The Swami laughed, a breathless, triumphant little laugh, and half shuffled about to look back at his gathering and point to her in knowing humour. As if amazed that she spoke. Sandy raised a quizzical eyebrow. Rafasan sighed and fidgeted. As if slightly embarrassed, Sandy thought. Embarrassed, it occurred to her, like Vanessa had once been embarrassed at the prospect of her meeting a particularly eccentric aunt of hers. And she realised in a flash that Rafasan was actually quite fond of the old man, as were most of his detractors, even some of those commentators who referred to him as one of the Senate's "lunatic fringe." But people had voted for this man—in the Senate, at least. And however cynical those commentators were about the Tanushan population's appetite for lunatics, Sandy determined that the recipient of those votes had at least earned the right for her audience, at least for the moment. The Swami shuffled back around to face her, the young woman at his elbow aiding him with practised skill.

"I saw you talking." The accent was very pronounced, and very melodic. The beady dark eyes gleamed at her through the profusion of facial hair—lively with humour and energy—and he waggled his head for emphasis as he spoke. "You talk very well, for an inorganic construction." Again the short bark of laughter.

Rafasan covered her mouth with a hand. Sandy just gazed at him for a long moment, eyebrow still raised. Took a deep breath.

"Thank you very much. I think."

Another bark of laughter. "Don't be offended. I am merely poking fun. I did not live this long by taking life so seriously, you know." Smiling broadly beneath the beard. And Sandy found that, somehow, it was impossible to be offended.

"Can I ask how old you *are?*" she asked. "And why you haven't allowed any life-extension treatments?"

"Oh, but I have, but I have. I am one hundred and sixty-two standard Earth years, Ms. GI, and I have had many life-extension treatments. Many many. And you know what? They work! Haha!"

Rafasan's hand went back to her mouth, very fast. Sandy smiled, the raised eyebrow now turned somewhat incredulous. One hundred and sixty-two? She knew it happened, but the odds were very low, most people didn't get past a hundred and thirty. For a man to take life extensions and live long enough to look like a very old man . . . he must be very old indeed.

"I'm fifteen," Sandy replied. "You have me at a disadvantage."

"Indeed, indeed." Nodding agreeably. "But how can you measure what you cannot define, yes? And what is a number to you? A GI, with your tape-teach and preconstructed knowledge? Life should be measured in experiences, not in flawed human time. Time is another thing we should not measure, for it, too, we cannot define, yes?" Nodding again, eyes seeking her comprehension. "Only God knows. And he's not telling."

"And you have come all the way over here to see me?"

"Oh, it is not so far. Not when I have such a helpful and devoted personal staff to attend to me. And to meet you, I thought it well worth the effort for even this old man and his creaking bones."

"Why?"

"Why?" In great surprise. And he laughed again, and the laugh turned into a loud coughing. "Why?" As he recovered, and met her eyes again. "You have come waltzing into this city and caused such trouble, young lady. Such mayhem accompanies you, life here has been turned upside down and the ground has fallen away beneath so many people's feet, and you ask me why?"

"I'm sorry if I caused trouble." Calmly. "The cause of the trouble was already here, however. I did perhaps trigger the trap, but the trap was set well before I arrived. But I'm sorry all the same for the upset, it was never my intention."

"Upset? Oh no no, I am not upset. It has been my great pleasure to see this calamity befall this city, young lady." Sandy blinked in astonishment. The Swami beamed happily. "This city has been in the greatest need of a great calamity for a very long time now, people have grown lazy in their minds and lazy in their hearts. They worship but they do not comprehend why, they talk but they have nothing to say, they listen but they know not what they are hearing. All this . . . this progress . . ." He rapped his stick hard upon the smooth floor. ". . . hah, so shameful that it should be called 'progress' at all. No, we were not progressing, we were walking backward, moving further and further away. Not progress. RE-gress. And do you know what from?"

Sandy found herself held strangely still, a slow, prickling sensation creeping up her spine. The usually noisy hallway was held as if paralysed by some foreign aura. The Swami's cheerful dark eyes bore into her, and in that abrupt, single instant she truly thought she did know what he was talking about.

"Truth," she said quietly. The Swami laughed again, his head bobbing with great, evident pleasure. Reached his free arm from the young woman's supporting grasp to pat Sandy briefly on the arm, then returned it to the supporting grip once more.

"Truth, truth, truth," he said, still bobbing, as if in momentary prayer. "A most precious thing, truth. Never to be found, only to be sought, and then found in the seeking but never to be held in one's hand. Do you understand this meaning?"

She gazed at him for a long moment. "No. I'm not sure I do."

"And do you not understand, then, why it is that I came to see you?" She shook her head. "Ms. GI, you have brought us much truth to this city. Some of it has been most painful, but that is often the nature of truth, particularly that truth which is most unlooked for. And I also do believe, young lady, that I have found much truth in you." Gazing with a great, joyful intrigue into her eyes. She didn't know who was more fascinated. His hand trembled upon his stick, and she doubted it was a result of age. He seemed positively brimming with emotional enthusiasm.

"Please," she said softly, in that deep, paralysed hush that surrounded, "tell me what you mean."

"For such a long time," he said happily, "many humans have been so very conceited. We believed that we alone had souls . . . even," waggling a gnarled forefinger, "even we

Hindus, who believe in the souls of animals and all living things all joined together in the greater expanse of the universe before God . . . even we Hindus did not always see, though many suspected. Our scientists tell us that all matter is by itself inanimate, do they not? And that all of the molecules that make up a human being, or an animal, were formed only in the hearts of stars, for that is where carbon was first born, is it not so? And so many have theorised that the soul is for some cosmic reason connected to the carbon molecule, and to the natural processes of organic lifeforms, be they carbon or be they otherwise.

"But now we must look at you. You, Ms. GI, who are not at all organic, who is made of artificial parts from the highest technology laboratories, whose entire being is inanimate, inorganic and not at all even *alive* by the terminologies used by a great many scientists and spiritual leaders before the coming of GIs, and GI technology, from the League."

He shuffled forward another step, reaching for her with that one free, frail hand . . . Sandy looked quick askance at the young woman, who gestured, and Sandy took his hand in hers. Felt the worn old fingers clasp upon her own with surprising strength. He smelled, she thought, of the old wood carving oils she'd smelled in craft shops, a strangely musky smell. This close, she could see his age, and count the wrinkles around his dark, smiling eyes.

"I came here to look into your eyes." A thousand wrinkles crinkling with an emotional, beaming smile. "I came here to see for myself that you are alive, and that you have the energy, and the soul, the spirit of a living being . . . Ms. GI, do you not see what this means?" Taking that gnarled old hand from her grasp and placing it upon her shoulder.

"The organic is alive." With a look of joy as pure as she had ever seen. "The inorganic is alive. The carbon and the non-carbon are alive. The soul of life resides in all things. *Everything* is alive. The whole universe, the very walls about us, this floor, the wind, the earth and the suns. The universe is all of one consciousness and life is nothing more than the dreaming of that single oneness. And you, Ms. GI, *you* are the final, the scientific, the spiritual proof of it all."

She was still feeling light-headed a half hour later, walking a private meeting room and shaking those hands that were offered to her. She conversed on automatic, thankful that most of those who'd come to see her (and, inevitably, each other) were already somewhat favourable to President Neiland, and at least not totally opposed to her presence within the CSA. They wished for the brief reassurance of a face-to-face contact after the hearing, that was all—a chance, as the Swami had done, to look into her eyes, and know this GI, this killing machine on legs, for a real person. It satisfied whatever human emotional requirements needed satisfying, she reckoned, to convince them that Neiland wasn't completely insane to be trusting her as much as she had. But she found herself paying little attention to any of it, in the lingering daze of her confrontation with the Swami.

She knew the basic philosophical concept. It was as old as philosophy and theology themselves. But she'd never expected to become regarded by a senior theologian philosopher, on a world known for producing such noted people, as the key and singular proof of such a concept. Rafasan had found the development exciting. So had Presidential advisor Rani Bannerjee, who was hovering around the meeting room somewhere, in discussion with one visiting rep or other. The Swami, Bannerjee informed her, though highly eccentric, was a leading light of religious and philosophical thinking on Callay, and commanded much respect throughout the Federation among people who followed such things. Such a vote of confidence could only be a bolstering support among a demographic of Federation citizens whose support had been sorely lacking to this point.

Sandy wasn't sure what to make of it at all. She knew Hindus and Buddhists had generally been less opposed to scientific progress, and biotechnology issues in particular, through the ages than the more dogmatic religions of Islam and Christianity . . . it helped to explain in part the long Indian embrace of technology and science through modern times, and their spectacular successes thereof. But why the Swami had chosen to uphold *her* as the example that proved the rule, she could not guess—artificial intelligence had been around in various forms for nearly three hundred years now, from the first computer based AIs in the mid-2200s to the first advances in artificial synapse-replication in the early 2300s, to the first truly synthetic brains in the late 2300s. That had been made possible by advances in quantum mechanics, and thus in nano-construction, enabling the creation of entirely new materials and processes, from individual electrons upwards, that severely blurred the old dividing line between "organic" and "artificial." League science, that had all been, product of the brash, youthful idealism of a new State that truly believed that its unrestricted science policies, and its utter faith in the combined systems of capitalism and scientific innovation, would utterly transform the future of all humanity for the better.

Debates over the nature of sentience, and the legal, moral and ethical ramifications thereof, had only multiplied ever since, and while the scientifically minded had generally been quick to adopt a broad-minded definition of what constituted a self-aware, intelligent being, many religious groups had been far more reluctant. Hindus, however, had been the most progressive of those, believing as they did that the body was only the vessel for endlessly reincarnated souls, and seeing little reason why a soul could not take up residence in a vessel of artificial construction as easily as an organic one. So why hadn't those Hindus been quicker to reach the conclusions of the Swami, given that it was the basis of what most Hindus believed anyway?

Perhaps, she thought, it was her intelligence. Not in terms of pure IQ, for AIs possessed levels of intellectual function in specific areas that extended far beyond her own, or that of any non-silicon sentience. But more in her ability to think laterally, and to be more than her physical form appeared to readily dictate. AIs rarely took much interest in the outside world, and lived mostly in the networks and databases of cyberspace—a psychological condition imposed upon them by their physical nature. Lower model GIs designed for combat were mostly ill-equipped, psychologically speaking, to do anything other than soldiering— also a condition imposed upon them by the design function of their artificial bodies. Their souls were not free, but were bound by physical constraints. And such was the Tanushans' fear of her. Physically, she was lethal. Tanushans feared that her psychological nature would follow the physical as logically as the tail would follow the snake. And yet she preferred civilianisms to simple soldiering, and refused to have her ideology dictated to her by her original masters and creators. A free soul.

Perhaps the Swami was not so much impressed that she was sentient, for that in itself was no big deal to any resident of the modern human galaxy. Perhaps the Swami was impressed that she was freethinking, creative and independent. That the universe was alive was a staple, commonly recurring belief of many Asian religions. That it was *intelligent,* and possessed intent, and meaning . . .

Meaning. A human invention. A sentient invention, that cynics said had no place in the cold, uncaring universe outside of human awareness. But if *she* possessed free thought, and she wasn't even human, wasn't even organic . . . was that what had so excited the Swami? Proof that meaning wasn't just a human invention, but something inherent to the most basic structures of the universe, to be found in organic and inorganic structures alike? How often had she heard that old, philosophical civilianism, the "meaning of life"? Was what the Swami thought he'd found really that significant?

Her dazed wanderings were interrupted by a newly arrived trio, who introduced themselves as the ministers for Transport and Agriculture, and the Chief of the Central Modelling Agency. There followed a remarkably civil discussion about politics, trade, and the increasing resentment among the sixty-three million Callayans who did not live in Tanusha at how all Callayan affairs had become even more Tanushan-ised in the present crisis—the Agriculture Minister was from Cavallo, capital city of Argasuto, the biggest of the southern continents, and grower of most of the planet's foodstuffs—on the broad, treeless plains of the south where environmental disruption was least, and transgenic technologies made light of the infertile soil. The Agriculture Minister declared that his constituents had put up with Tanushan dominance until now because of the politics of Federation-League conflict, which had until recently papered over so many regional concerns with greater ones. Now, he opined, the war had ended, and people were questioning the old status quo.

"Isn't that kind of their own fault?" Sandy asked him. "I mean, from what I've heard, the whole idea of Tanusha was partly because the other settlements were all so busy squabbling about who should have the centre of power that they thought they'd have to build a new city to accommodate it, and partly because none of them wanted that kind of high-tech, mega-city development to take place in *their* comfortable, sleepy little settlements. Having decided that, isn't it a bit much to start complaining about the consequences now?"

"Absolutely," agreed the Transport Minister, a Tanushan native. "And now none of them have to contend with terrorist attacks, paralysing security and mass street protests, either. There are advantages to being sleepy little backwaters, too."

From another side of the room, a civilised commotion of persons gathering about a monitor screen placed upon a small, ornate table . . . several were shushing others, and several calling colleagues across to view.

"Is Neiland on already?" asked the Transport Minister. "She's a half hour early . . . Ms. Cassidy, please excuse me, it was a pleasure to meet you in person and I must definitely watch this announcement."

They departed, adding to the gathering crowd about the monitor, lesser aides and bureaucrats hastily making room . . . Sandy walked to a convenient spot by the rear wall, depositing her empty juice-glass and trading it for a full one from the table there. She leaned against a decorative wall panel with a good view of the carpeted space, where all occupants were now clustered about one side. She opened a mental uplink, accessed the Parliament vid-feeds . . . difficult coding, but she broke it down, gained access, and a picture flickered to life across her internal vision, overlaying the room with that comfortable shift to near-focus.

President Neiland, standing behind a podium. Callayan and Federation flags cross-draped behind her . . . the press room, she recognised from similar previous broadcasts. Neiland was making some kind of official announcement. The ministers had evidently expected it . . . early, they'd said. Why the hurry? And why the timing, when all Parliament media were so obviously focused upon her own presentation in the Hearing Chamber, despite their lack of broadcast-access to the feed? She sipped at her juice, and listened in.

". . . a long time in arriving at this consensus," Neiland was saying, "and I can assure you it took many, many long hours of negotiation with all the involved parties." The suit was the most formal Sandy had seen her wear— dark, collared, and with only a pin upon the lapel, and a small white flower, to lighten the severity. The flower, Sandy remembered, had been a gift from a family member of one of the victims of the Parliament Massacre a month ago. The original flower had doubtless long since died, but was continually replaced anew by Neiland herself to remind all viewers, and political opponents, of the stakes in this most dangerous of political games.

"It has been no secret to many of you in the media for some time now," the President continued, "that ongoing debate over Article 42 has been hitting many roadblocks up to this point in time." On an abrupt impulse, Sandy switched to a wider uplink camera angle, and saw a full crowd of seated media, and a further phalanx clustered along the press room walls. That was an awful lot of media. The word had evidently spread that something was going down. An unscheduled announcement from the President. Something her closer cabinet members had apparently been aware of in advance. While she . . . she herself had been stuck in the Hearing Chamber for the last five or six hours, cut off from outside happenings. No one had briefed her . . . The timing was most coincidental.

Her glass had stopped just centimetres from her lips, eyes unsighted in the gathering cold chill that ran up her spine. And now she was up here, neatly sequestered away in a meeting and function room, while the real business went on in the central Administration quarter of the Parliament building. Not the first time she'd been kept in the dark of late. Ari hadn't wanted her chasing after Ramoja in the Zaiko Warren—had attempted to send her in the wrong direction. He must have suspected Ramoja would know something he didn't want her to find out . . . what, then? Who did Ari work for? Ibrahim. Who did Ibrahim work for? Sure as hell not Ben Grey, not lately.

Neiland. Click, click, click, the pieces were falling into place with frightening, overwhelming speed, as she stood tense and utterly immobilised against the wall, staring into space. Neiland inviting her to speak before Parliament. Now this unscheduled announcement. It all led back to Neiland, all this mad goose chase after Sai Va, the anarchist hacker who'd broken into Lexi and stolen information . . . Weren't Lexi a major player in the whole debate over Article 42? Big biotech firms had to be negotiated with, they held huge political clout, surely Lexi's top people had been in negotiations with the Neiland Administration itself, and maybe even Neiland personally . . . Oh shit, what did Sai Va steal? Something Neiland hadn't wanted stolen? Something she'd told Lexi's top brass in those secret negotiations? Something so important she directed Ibrahim to put his best, least visible agent onto it, and to recruit the walking killing machine herself for extra fire-power to make sure it got done, whatever nasties they ran into? And now here was Neiland in front of the full plane-tary media, saying something about a big new consensus deal? What deal could possibly be so big?

She rushdialed Ari's implant, came up negative as per usual. And discovered she was now quite mad and just a little bit frightened. Overrode the local codings with her best infiltration package, managed to acquire a partial lock on the local network's com functions, mutated a seeker function to Ari's mode of receptor software and sent it out . . . Parliament alarms flared, somewhere deep in the system, but she didn't care. Came up positive on a location a millisecond later, hacked that room with even less sub-tlety, which started even more alarms, got a reading on the receptor location, seized control of that room's transmission systems, hacked, opened and sent. No reply, receiver resisting . . . she locked the sender signal into a blank channel and sent him a blast of raw static on maximum bandwidth, and got an immediate sense of startled, hurried replies shooting out, trying to patch the various local and system-wide alarms she'd triggered in the security-inten-sive system. She nailed one of his patches with her most lethal League attack function and watched it disintegrate . . . "*. . . fucking hell, Sandy, WHAT!!! What do you WANT!!!*"

"You're in the damn building," she formulated coldly, "I thought so."

"*Well, clever you, what are you trying to do, get arrested?!*"

"I'm trying to get the truth, Ari. What did Sai Va steal? What was it that you didn't want me to find out, and what's it got to do with what Neiland's announcing now?"

"*Sandy,*" warningly, "*I don't have time for this right now, I'm trying to monitor something important here . . .*"

"You'll tell me or I'll fry your damn circuitry so it melts into your eardrum. What did Lexi know that Sai Va stole, Ari?"

"*Sandy,*" very firmly, and without a trace of the usual irreverence, "*don't be a spoilt child. I don't have time. This is*

*more important than your petty concerns, I'm trying to monitor
something of crucial importance and if you don't get out of my frequency right now I'll get security to your location and have you
tranqued and arrested in that order."*

He cut off. Agent Odano was suddenly at her side.

"Cassandra," with an urgent whisper, leaning close,
"someone just breached transmission frequency! Was that
you?"

"Yes." And to his baffled, alarmed look, "Watch the
damn monitor."

". . . announce here today," Neiland was saying, "a new
public amendment to the Article 42 process, an amendment I sincerely hope will assist in moving the entire
process forward, and resolve many of the great obstacles
facing not only Callay, but the entire Federation, and all of
its members."

Sandy realised she was holding her breath. The entire
room was utterly still, only the alarm frequency blinking
in the lower corner of her overlaid net-vision.

"I announce here before you today Amendment
number 15. The proposal put forward in Amendment 15 is
not merely to address the nature of the present Federation
system of governance, but rather to change it. And by
change, I mean really *change* it." Staring out into the gleam
of lights and half-visible spectrum-flash strobes of the cameras, green eyes piercing beneath sternly arranged red hair.
"Amendment 15 is a proposal to change the location of
Federation governance. To move the centre of power of the
Federation from the planet Earth, and to relocate it out
into the vast and growing colonies, from where it can
better represent the increasingly diverse and ever-changing
needs and interests of this great experiment in collective,
representative human governance we call the Federation."

From somewhere amid the crowd around the monitor,
someone dropped a glass. No one seemed to notice. Sandy
knew how they felt. Speech failed her. Thought did. She
was stunned.

"Amendment 15 does not merely shift the location of

the Federation Grand Council, however. Amendment 15 is a proposal to relocate the entire bureaucratic apparatus of central Federation governance—the bureaucracy, the Federal Bank, Fleet Command and the associated military apparatus, everything. All such branches need to communicate in realtime, with no time delays for interstellar travel, and as such all must be located upon the same world—if one moves, all must move.

"It is the collective opinion of the vast majority of Federation worlds that the present debacle of Federal Intelligence Agency powers running rampant over the rights of individual member worlds is a direct result of the corrupting influence of certain Earth-based powers that continue to run the affairs of the Federation according to their own unrepresentative agendas. Such agendas were formed during the war against the League, which is now ended, thus ending the legitimacy and relevance of many of those groups and their interests. It is time to return those powers to the people of the Federation, and to return them to the people directly, not have them wielded from a distance by committee and via request, but have them within the direct grasp of our hands.

"Furthermore, it is also the proposal of Amendment 15, a proposal arrived at once again after exhaustive consultation with the senior delegates from all Federation member worlds, that the Federation world whose infrastructure and star-lanes most suit it to becoming the recipient of all Federation bureaucracy is . . . Callay."

Another glass dropped. That didn't surprise her either. Neither, given the rest of it, did the last part of the announcement. Callay *was* the most logical choice, not only was it the best located, the best equipped and the most powerful, but also the most recently and seriously wronged. The political message was clear. As to who would buy it . . . God, she needed to sit down. That didn't happen to her often. Grand moments in history were things she'd read about. She'd never thought to be caught up in one so personally.

Move the centre of governance from Earth to Callay? Might as well shift Earth itself, all of Sol System, relocate it a convenient few hundred extra light-years closer to the vaguely defined Federation "centre." Her eyes shifted to the group gathered about the monitor, mostly stunned and silent, but for the sombre, meaningful stares of the ministers who'd known what was coming, and had no doubt been in on the consultation. A big secret, those consultations. Lots of people consulted, but no leaks. Or almost. Lexi! the thought struck her. Was *that* what Sai Va had stolen from Lexi without knowing it? News of ongoing negotiations to take the seat of Federation power away from the motherworld? Well of *course* they'd had to keep it secret. The moment the various Earth delegations got wind of that, there'd have been pandemonium—claims and counterclaims, concerted attempts to try and scupper the emerging Federation-wide consensus Neiland was claiming to have achieved in this convenient gathering of Federation-wide decision makers in the one single spot . . . The media uproar alone could have derailed the talks at that early stage of the negotiations.

And she realised she owed Ari an apology. He had needed her to catch Sai Va, the bullet holes strewn through the Zaiko Warren and the Cloud Nine gangster-club were proof enough of that. But, of course, he wasn't allowed to tell her. She wasn't cleared for that kind of knowledge—she was a soldier, she knew what rank meant, she knew that some information was classified for a reason. Not to mention the precarious political situation that existed where she was concerned. He'd tried to keep her in the dark because those were the rules. She knew rules. She just hadn't learned much respect for Tanushan rules yet. Until today she hadn't been given much reason to.

"What does that mean?" Odano was saying. Incredulity and puzzlement colliding upon his young face. "Callay's going to become the centre of the Federation? Where will they put the Grand Council? Tanusha's crowded enough as it is!"

Sandy shrugged faintly. "There'll be room on the periphery."

"City planners don't like surprises."

"I think they'll come to terms with this one pretty quickly." Which struck her as a surreal conversation . . . the trials and tribulations of Tanusha's various officious planning departments were the least of their problems right now. And she looked up as Rafasan came striding quickly over, heels muffled on the carpet. Sandy half expected her to be jubilant, her lawyer's soul seemed to rejoice at moral victories, however bureaucratic in nature. Instead, her elegant face was drawn and worried.

"Cassandra," she whispered, leaning close, "you do realise what this means? For security implications, I mean?" It was, Sandy recalled, her job. Or had been, until the SIB had put it on hold.

"Earth aren't going to like it," she replied in similarly soft, sombre tones. "Not one bit. Most of the business and political factions probably never realised how important access to the Grand Council was to them until faced by the threat of it being taken away." There was, she knew, a strong historical precedent for that, involving the United States of America and the United Nations—the USA had nearly come to blows with the European Union in 2040 when a mass UN assembly had voted to remove the UN headquarters from New York City and relocate it to Tbilisi, Georgia, in the Caucasus between the Black and Caspian Seas. Power-neutral territory, they'd said, midway between the Pan-Arabic Alliance, Europe and Russia, and mid-distant from China and the USA . . . as well as being pretty. No one had wanted the UN left in the demographic "possession" of the then increasingly isolationist, xenophobic Americans, who they feared were already holding the whole UN hostage with threats of power cuts, traffic blockages and complications with the leasing arrangements on the property.

In hindsight, one of the better things that had happened to the USA, Sandy knew. It had removed one of the last remaining veils from the truth that politicians in the USA had found so frightening at the time—that their nation was no longer the world's most powerful, and could no longer simply tell foreign cultures, in which they'd never invested any effort in trying to understand, how they had to act. That reality had only sunk in after a thirty year withdrawal from the United Nations following the Great Relocation of 2040, during which time they'd discovered just how much they'd never realised they needed it, and had finally begun to reenter the world arena with some sense of respectful decorum.

Maybe, she had to think, this would be a similar lesson for Earth. So many years of taking the colonies for granted. So much neglect and disregard. The assumptions of unchallenged supremacy, of Earth as humanity's so-called indispensable world, a phrase its leaders never stopped using in their speeches. And in many ways it was true. Humanity would always need Earth. But Earth needed the rest of humanity just as much, something it appeared to have forgotten of late. This was the wake-up call.

"The Federal Intelligence Agency will fight tooth and nail, Cassandra," Rafasan whispered intently. "That's the Old Earth backroom club, newer Federation powers like Callay just don't have *access* to that system. We're not represented, our desire to stay out of the war's more clandestine activities made it so . . . our fault too, of course, and since then we've been paying for it. All Earth-centric businesses, lobbies and power groups will fight like crazy to stop this from happening, they profit too much from the system being structured the way it is now . . ."

"What about the Fleet?" Sandy asked.

Rafasan frowned. "The Fleet? Cassandra, I'm just the legal expert. Military matters are hardly my speciality . . ."

"Well shit, I hope someone's put some thought into it. Fleet admirals are all elected through an Earth-based appointment process. I read about it in League Intel reports, the FIA has its fingers stuck into that too."

"I'm sure the relevant experts have taken all of that into

account." But she continued to look somewhat alarmed. Behind them, the group clustered about the monitor had begun to depart, a gathering momentum that threatened to break into a stampede for the doors. Her network uplinks showed a surging rush of transmission traffic, in multiple encryptions and emergency priority codings . . .

"Maisie," Sandy said sharply, grabbing Rafasan's attention with the nickname, "why did the President want me in the Hearing Chamber now?" As the room rapidly cleared of people, and bewildered security stared about in confusion.

"You were the final obstacle, Sandy," said Rafasan. "Certain of her own party were demanding to see you personally before supporting this amendment . . . she needed those last few votes to get a majority in the Union Party, Cassandra. A lot of them are still very opposed, she just needed those last, wavering few. They *wanted* to support this amendment, but claimed they could not be seen by their constituents to be siding with an administration harbouring a League GI unless they'd met the GI personally and allayed their fears, at least a little. They're covering their backsides for supporting this amendment, Sandy, it's just politics . . . You must understand that this was all very rushed, the President wanted these negotiations to continue for another several weeks at least to finalise support. Instead circumstances have forced her to rush it through before our opponents got wind of it and released it unannounced to the press, and she had to improvise your appearance here on the spur of the moment, particularly following the incident with the SIB and your subsequent suspension. That matter needed to be cleared before certain of her own party would support her on the amendment . . ."

"The media didn't know before this?" She didn't know why it was important. She just suddenly felt that it was. Extremely so. Rafasan blinked.

"Not that we are aware of."

So Sai Va hadn't told the press . . . who would he tell, once he'd realised how many people were after him for what he knew, or what they thought he knew? Once he'd broken that particular piece of most highly classified encryption and discovered this world-shaking piece of information?

She dialled Ari again, and got a reply immediately.

"I take it you have a mature, practical concern this time?" Sounding harried and distracted. Ari was the point man on tracking down the runaway leak, that being Sai Va. Doubtless he had resources watching numerous potential hotspots in the expectation that someone would try something immediately upon having heard this announcement.

"Ari, what happened to Sai Va?" Not bothering silent formulation this time, wanting to share this conversation with Rafasan and the wide-eyed Agent Odano.

"He's dead." Shortly. *"FIA. Somehow they tracked someone who tracked someone who found him, dragged him off the street in broad daylight at about nine this morning, hacked his implant in an alley and then shot him. Digital rape, very nasty."* Only half serious, he sounded ragged with lack of sleep. *"The amendment announcement was due for tomorrow, once the FIA had Sai Va's info we had to push it forward to today."*

So the FIA knew. What was the first thing they'd do? Protect themselves? Wasn't that always the FIA's first impulse? What was their greatest Achilles' heel right now? With all the legal jurisdictions threatened with rearrangement?

"Ari, where's Governor Dali?"

"Um . . . no, Sandy, we thought of that, he's under full guard in maximum security isolation . . ."

"Yeah, that's what I was scared of . . . Ari, I know you didn't have time to listen to my presentation, but I did spend a good fifteen minutes just now talking about precisely why that's not adequate against the FIA, with the resources they've still got floating around in Tanusha, especially with the Earth delegations here. They've infiltrated every damn one of them . . ."

"Shit, you don't need to tell ME about that . . . I had someone check on Dali just five minutes ago . . ."

"Send a TEAM, Ari . . . and get me transport right NOW. Alert security at Gordon Spaceport and put a SWAT team on standby, preferably SWAT Four . . . he was in detention at the Leguna HQ, right? That's the priority site for maximum security isolations? Top floor?"

"*Sandy . . .*" A brief, exasperated pause. "*. . . I'm rechecking that last message coding right now, it looks fine, all the protocols are there . . .*"

"If I had time for war stories, Ari, I'd tell you of FIA operations out of places that make Leguna HQ look like a kindergarten . . . we didn't know the prisoner was missing until twelve hours after they'd left. We can't afford it, Ari!"

Ari cut off, not wasting further time arguing . . . "We," she'd said, she realised abruptly. Had she meant "we" as in Tanusha? As in Callay? Or even just "the CSA"? Well yes, she supposed she had. To any of those possibilities.

"Sandy?" Odano asked. Rafasan was staring, wide-eyed and anxious.

"Dali was the FIA's big appointment to overthrow Neiland's Administration last month," she explained. "He's got information to reveal complicity in FIA dark ops right up to the Federation Grand Council . . . if Neiland's amendment goes through, we can just keep him here and they can't extradite him back to Earth at all. We can try him *here*, this will *be* Federation jurisdiction, and we'll make damn sure we make him answer every question the FIA don't want answered, because we'll have our fair share of the judicial appointments and procedures . . ."

Rafasan's hand had gone to her mouth in shock.

"You mean they'll try and kidnap him?" Odano exclaimed.

"Or if that doesn't work, maybe just kill him. But the FIA knew Neiland was going to do this in advance. They've got inside knowledge on the encryption Lexi would have used to keep it secret . . . they've got plants all the way through the biotech industry. They'll have decrypted it immediately. My bet is Dali's already gone."

Dammit, she *should* have had security upgraded, she

hadn't been exaggerating at all when she'd threatened him yesterday with what the FIA were capable of. But the FIA were keeping a low profile at the time, and she simply hadn't seen this coming so soon . . . if only someone had told her, she could have prevented it. Instead, Ari had moved Dali directly to the highest security government enclosure available, which the FIA would have predicted in advance, with what they'd gotten from Sai Va . . . and for all Ari's strong points in intelligence, he was *not* trained in military-grade dark ops, he just followed procedure and expected the apparatus to work. In a contest of FIA security apparatus against compromised Callayan Government apparatus, Sandy was going to bet on the FIA every time . . .

"To the spaceport?" Odano guessed. Sandy nodded. "Then what are we waiting here for?"

"Ari has to find us some transport. We don't know what pad it'll use, we don't want to waste time going in the wrong direction. Stay calm, Agent. Use your head."

Odano blinked several times. Then straightened, adjusting his lapels with a deep, measured breath.

"Agent, my weapon and badge, if you please."

He didn't even hesitate, reached into his jacket pocket and withdrew both. Sandy checked the weapon over, and settled it comfortably into her empty holster, and the badge in her inside pocket. The room security saw, but did nothing. She guessed it didn't seem the time. They walked across the empty meeting room floor and stopped in the outer hallway.

"Cassandra," Rafasan said breathlessly, "I really must get back to the President—well done today, and please take care of yourself." And leaned forward for a brief, farewell kiss on the cheek . . . Sandy gave it, after an initial delay of surprise, and gently berated herself, as Rafasan scurried off, for always forgetting to anticipate those trivial yet significant civilian rituals. A brief moment of relative silence, the hallway strangely empty after the initial rush of commotion—everyone retreated to their uplinks and vidcoms in times of crisis, and physical movement generally stopped.

"What'll happen if they've gotten him to the space-port?" Odano asked her. Doing a good job of appearing calm. A faint shift of visual spectrum showed her the pulse in his throat, and the faint sweat upon his brow.

"We'll have to stop them from taking off." Waiting patiently for Ari's word on which way to go, faced with two equally attractive lengths of empty corridor up which to sprint. "There's at least six or seven ships in orbit or docked to station that belong to Earth factions. Tough to stop them once they're in space—we don't have any military assets—and we couldn't exactly blast them, anyway, if they refused to stop, that'd be an act of war."

"Are they likely to . . . um . . . shoot at us?"

Sandy gave a mild shrug. "Almost certainly. Probably with military-grade weapons, the FIA don't do things by halves."

Another brief silence. Electronic flurries raced across her various uplink channels, a mass of interconnecting electronic information. Nothing she could monitor effectively without breaking even more security protocols. A brief switch to a news channel . . . visual flash of people talking, heated arguments, shouting. Others of people cheering. Excited faces. Angry faces. Some dancing in the streets, others overturning cars. Oh, what a city, she thought sourly, the excitement never ended.

"I don't suppose *you're* very frightened," Odano half laughed, very nervous and trying to cover it. As if the very concept of a frightened GI was unthinkable. Sandy smiled.

"This is my life," she said simply. Then Ari's signal showed them a flyer descending toward a rooftop pad on the left wing, and they ran like hell.

CHAPTER 11

The flyer coming down was an FT-25, a smaller version of the FT-750 transports that made up the larger portion of the SWAT fleet. Sandy half-crouched against the backwash, jacket and hair blasted back as the mobile four-poster came in fast, wobbling in the swirling uplift of ground effect off the pad, then hovered as the lower-rear access ramp descended . . . Odano ran, followed by the other two security agents who'd been assigned to Parliament that day but were now following her to the latest flashpoint—they'd been assigned to her, she was realising, and not having received any new orders were going to stay with her indefinitely. Her responsibility, it seemed, for the moment.

She ran last, her habit in groups, not liking to be hemmed in, ducking fast beneath the thrashing blast from the smaller, directional rear nacelles to the ramp that hovered just above the landing pad . . . and paused to see another pair of dark figures leaping up the short ramp-side ladder, then running toward her against the backdrop of broad, grassy Parliament grounds. Dark jackets blew out behind in the gale of engine-wash, exposing heavy, side-holstered weapons. She waited, reluctantly, giving them a long, dark look as they stopped. One look at Ari's dark expression and she knew Dali was gone—and that this mad scramble was no longer just an inconvenient precaution.

"Don't you have your own transport?" she yelled at them. "It's going to be crowded in there, there's three already on board plus me and these three, 25s are only rated for eight, and we've got equipment on board!"

"I'm not taking an aircar against the FIA!" Ari yelled back. "I'd rather go with you!"

"What if I don't want you?"

"That's not your decision!" Kazuma shouted with a pleasant smile.

"Great." She sprang up the ramp, the flyer's rear shifting about, compensating for the new load. Uplinked to the pilot's frequency . . . "Nine on board, you're free to go." Balancing herself past the heavy storage lockers as the wind from the rear decreased and the engines thrummed like swarming insects. Ducked under a suspended armour brace, then into the main passenger hold, a cramped enclosure of heavy-braced seats and built-in tactical displays and linkups. Some small portholes in the sides for a view, and an open space through to the cockpit beyond, a glimpse of green gardens and buildings falling away as they climbed.

"Tactical please," she announced, and one of the security agents clambered quickly enough from the seat, grasping a support brace as the flyer banked, picking up speed. Sandy climbed in, did the straps, activated screen and assistant functions, secured the light headset over one eye and ear and jacked it into the socket at the back of her head . . . all with the ease of long, effortless familiarity with many different kinds of equipment. Except that her hair was now much thicker and she had to clear a path with one hand before insertion. The data-wall hit her with a familiar rush, an abrupt interface with headset vision and sound, multiple data screens arranged before the chair . . . "So who found Sai Va?" she asked Ari, who was hanging over her shoulder from behind.

"I did," came Kazuma's voice from the other side. "Got real close. The FIA got closer. Silly fool didn't realise how many people he'd upset."

"Well," said Ari, "since anarchism itself is based upon

. . . um, a flawed perception of society, the one thing you can always count on anarchists for is mistakes."

"Yeah, well, I'll deal with the socio-graphic analysis later," Sandy replied, scrolling rapidly through the data-feed of happenings, locations, involved units and their operating codeworks. "Sec-Gov was guarding Dali?" That was Government Security, they did all major government or other public sector buildings or installations.

"Yes." Sounding more than a little angry, Sandy reckoned. She wasn't in a mood to be charitable.

"Dammit, Ari, they're not much more than private sector squibs, what were you thinking?"

"I put in a priority request for maximum lockdown a week ago. Non-rescindable. Only some bureaucrat redirected a third of those personnel just yesterday to guard some bureaucrats in the Foreign Office, and didn't consult me. It didn't occur to me to check they were all still there, I only just found out about it." A glance from Sandy's peripheral vision showed Kazuma lounging in a seat across the aisle, looking faintly amazed at the screw-up, but only a little.

"I'd have an investigation done into who did that reassignment and why," Sandy told him, flipping up full schematics on Gordon Spaceport, a racing scan across multiple levels of groundplans and security infrastructure. "FIA still have resources through the bureaucracy, it could have been more than a bureaucratic stuff up."

"Already done it. I've got three department seniors under interrogation."

"My, my," Kazuma mused, "don't we get embarrassed easily, Ari?"

"If nothing else," Ari continued, unperturbed, "it'll get the message out that priority assignments from the CSA are not to be messed with."

Sandy took it all in past the racing flood of data, analytical reflexes processing in about five different directions at once. Ari's measures were draconian, by Tanushan standards. They were also necessary, at a bare minimum.

There'd been talk of a complete sweep of Tanushan civil services for some time now, no one thought for a minute they'd gotten all the FIA plants in these places . . .

"They didn't kill anyone," Ari added, dark frustration tempered with relief. "All nonlethal weaponry. I'm guessing Dali might have refused to go with them if he'd seen his guards splattered all over the walls—he's an arse-hole, but he's no killer."

"No," said Sandy, "he gets other people to do it for him."

"Still don't know what happened, there's some kind of strange lockdown virus in the local network I've never even seen before, it got control, let them in and got Dali out. No clue where they went . . . you're sure it's Gordon?"

"PINS is useless in Tanusha, Ari, I just spent several hours in the hearing explaining that, and now Dali's escape proves it." PINS—Public Infrastructure Network Security. "Everyone in this city is so network dependent, they're blind without it. Effective security needs to operate inde-pendently from central command—decentralisation always comes with a force multiplier effect, whether it's in mili-tary systems, bureaucracy, economics or whatever. Central-isation is a weakness in any system. I'm amazed everyone's forgotten that here."

"You think Gordon's PINS is vulnerable?" Kazuma asked.

"Public infrastructure is government systems. With the amount of infiltration the FIA have done on Tanushan government systems, I'd be surprised if they hadn't written software precisely for case-by-case scenarios to infiltrate every major piece of public infrastructure in the city if they needed to . . ."

"They can't take control of the whole damn spaceport, surely?"

"No, that'd be a waste of effort. Just the bits they need . . . Ari, I'd like to establish a tactical command network, we need a com-frame in place, we can't afford overlapping operations here . . ."

"I've already got you an Ops team from HQ," Ari replied, "they're setting up your com-net basics now, we've got net-ops tracking flightpaths and all available systems between here and Gordon. If they went that way they had good cover, we can't find anything yet . . ."

"I don't think they will." Finishing her detailed sweep of Gordon's systems, and switching to broad overview . . . Stared for several long moments at the massive span of spaceport, three major runways in a triangular configuration and a web of interconnecting taxi-ways, a big five-runway complex to the south of the spaceport for atmospheric flights . . . that was a different system, thank God. The spaceport had a full forty operational shuttle bays, six more under construction in the new east wing. There were broad passenger halls, interconnecting transportation services with separate freight processing junctures on the lower levels, a traffic control wing, multilevel high-security com-net—everything highly automated but still a twelve-thousand-strong workforce—fully operational at the moment, it seemed, traffic was normal, no alarms raised, flights coming and going.

She'd hooked into the flight-data systems before she'd even realised it, checking flights and schedules. Immediately found a shuttle registered as Federation-licensed on the old north wing thoroughfare, scheduled for departure at 4:50, in half an hour's time, headed up to Grenada Station . . . where, it so happened, the Federation vessel *Capetown* was docked. *Capetown*, she knew from previous checks of the registry, was a charter vessel, under current lease of the combined delegations of numerous Earth East-Asian nations, most notably Indonesia, Japan, and the Philippines, in that order of economic significance. The laws of jurisdiction in combined leases, she knew further—from a CSA Intel briefing paper—were tricky, and had room for loopholes as to exactly who was allowed on the vessel and in what capacity. CSA Intel had had *Capetown* under close surveillance by operatives on Grenada since it had made dock, but hadn't spotted anything particularly suspicious . . . although the FIA were nothing if not sneaky, and well-experienced in dodging such surveillance measures.

"Berth 15," she said, "north wing, one of *Capetown*'s own attached shuttles, I think. Departure at 4:50."

"Plenty of time," said Kazuma.

"If they're hooked into flight control they could go early," Ari warned.

"So land a flyer in front of them," said Kazuma, "they're not going anywhere."

"Not yet," said Sandy. "Ari, I want you to put the best person HQ has available on a network scan. Focus on the PINS fire-grid. I don't want to do it myself, these guys will know my patterns too well."

A brief pause as Ari sent that out. Then . . . "They're on it."

Kazuma was staring at her from across the aisle. "You don't think that . . ." and was interrupted by an incoming frequency whose access-pattern Sandy recognised immediately.

"Hey, Ricey, I hope you've had enough sleep."

"Hey, gorgeous. What have you got for me, and do I finally get a chance to shoot at that silly bastard Dali?" Her tac-display showed the signal source, a SWAT FT-750 headed out from CSA HQ, still some thirty Ks away but converging toward Gordon on an intercept that would get them there perhaps three minutes behind Sandy.

"I think that's entirely possible, though if it comes to shooting him, his own FIA people might just beat you to it if we get them surrounded."

"Yeah, I got that much already, genius . . . who has the spaceport?"

"Good question, all appears basically functional now, I'm suspecting a localised infiltration for effective cover." With full fire-grid defensive systems schematics unfolding across her forward screen, familiar specifications indeed. "My bet would be the fire-grid, I don't want anyone unauthorised flying into spaceport airspace until we know for sure."

"Yeah, I kinda already thought that when you said Gordon

. . . I'm looking at the schematic now. That's a five-point fire system, overlapping fields of fire, the only blindspots are in among the terminal buildings themselves but you'd never get in that close without neutralising at least one firepoint, preferably two."

A feed from HQ abruptly surfaced on the B-screen . . . a realtime overhead visual, presumably someone at high altitude. A shuttle was landing, transport vehicles moving, aircraft on the adjoining airport taxiing, everything looked as usual. Massive flow of civilian traffic on the main road plus the maglev line . . . no aircars, thank God. Spaceport regulations prohibited civilian airborne transport near the flightpaths. Gordon was busy at the quietest of times, which this was not. Damn, this was going to be tricky . . .

"I'm thinking a ground assault on two adjoining firepoints, they won't hit ground targets . . ."

"I want a look at the protocols close up first, Ricey. They might override the safeties and mow you down as you go running toward them . . . that's a two kilometre run from minimum safe distance, we can't use missiles because of the micro-defensive units about the macro-emplacements, and the CSA doesn't have any airborne projectile weapons with that kind of range."

Damn, what she'd give for a single Viper assault flyer with dual AP gauss cannon mounts . . . those defensive systems were good, but they couldn't shoot down supersonic, finger-sized projectiles. But what need would Tanushan SWAT ever have for such weapons? The fire-grid itself was a fifteen-year-old system, installed in a fit of rare political awareness, she'd gathered, when FIA reports had circulated through the media explaining just how vulnerable key Callayan infrastructure was to armed atmospheric attack from League assault teams . . .

"Security reports a high-level delegation team just went through the north wing," came an HQ report on the net, *"carrying plenty of gear, bypassed customs. Another report shows several vehicles commandeered, the local officer responsible was upset about a protocol breach but wasn't sure if he'd get in trouble for reporting it . . ."*

"Oh great," Ari muttered, and on reply frequency ordered, "*Tell them, 'Do nothing, act as if everything's normal. Quietly put a withdrawal procedure in place for all personnel, to be activated on direct command from CSA or in an emergency.' This is a CSA job and we don't want overlapping jurisdictions here.*"

"Hello, HQ, this is Snowcat," Sandy added, "that's the last communication I want put out on secure-net, I want tac-net set up ASAP. This will be a SWAT-red operation if it does go down, command will be local. We'll need all command infrastructure prepped and ready."

"*HQ copies, Snowcat, Ibrahim has been alerted. We are establishing secure communications between relevant units, the link to Gordon Central could take a bit longer. As of this moment SWAT Four has command. Lieutenant Rice, prepare for tac-net establishment, matrix in thirty seconds.*"

"*Cancel that, HQ,*" came Vanessa's voice back immediately. "*This is a military operation, military-grade weapons and tactics are in evidence, strongly recommend that command is issued to Snowcat, over.*"

Sandy barely felt herself react, having half expected it. It was the most sensible option, and she was most qualified. Especially if those fire-grids were operational. The brief pause for consultation ended.

"*HQ copies, SWAT Four—Snowcat has command. Snowcat, tac-net matrix in twenty seconds, standby to receive.*"

"Snowcat copies. All units, remain on standard flight-paths, we don't want to let them see us coming." Disconnected audio briefly to shout over her shoulder, "Everyone suit up! Gear's in the back, full kit please, make it fast!" Fast visual switchback to their present position, now over midwestern Tanusha, headed due west toward where Gordon's sprawling complex lay twenty Ks beyond the megatropolis's westernmost perimeter. Low overhead sky-lane, a straight line above the heights of scattered mega-rise, cruising at a touch over five hundred kph . . . ETA just over fifteen minutes. Plenty of time. She realised abruptly she was suddenly back in the old mode—Dark Star mode,

Captain Cassandra Kresnov, on yet another assault mission. Reflexes so familiar she'd barely even noticed she was doing it. It fit like an old glove. And she found the time to be faintly amazed that she'd actually missed them.

The countdown hit zero, tac-net reception . . . the new codings jarred when she accessed them, then unfolded in a rapid rush across internal visual, interlocking graphical lines and angles—her position, the flyer's position, SWAT Four's flyer, command uplinks—a good, solid matrix layout, everything she needed in a rapidly evolving situation. Of course, it was nothing as complex or multilayered as the tac-net matrixes she'd used in Dark Star, straights couldn't process that much network information that quickly . . . but when she overlaid her own matrix-reception over the existing centralised system . . . a whole new level of complexity unfolded to her. The full Gordon layout, physical and network systems, all realtime in massive information overload. Her vision blurred, reddening in automatic combat reflex. Things seemed further away, time slowed. Central reaccessed her link, and the recognition codes seemed to take whole moments to access and unfold into an audible linkup . . .

"Snowcat, your uplink shows you receiving at a factor of ten beyond optimum . . . are you having a difficulty, or is this standard?"

"Standard, thanks, HQ." Her own voice sounded slow and ponderous to her ears. "Don't call every time you're surprised, I'll be busy." This, of course, was why Vanessa had given command over to her. She was made for it. Literally. Now she only needed to remember not to abbreviate her commands too much (that was always the reflex in this state), to keep them stringing out for what seemed like an age. Her old Dark Star team had understood her shorthand, too—CSA operatives would not. "Can someone get me that fire-grid feed, please?"

Another flash of visual data as the feed came through, a massive, multilayered system that she broke down and analysed with reflex mental speed . . . it looked military, all right, a big three-dimensional gridwork with various interconnecting bits and pieces clearly intended for armscomp, separate parts for fire control and acquisition, sensory grid, target processing, spatial awareness and field coordination . . . she raced through it, found and isolated the safety lock-outs for closer examination . . .

"SWAT Four, this is Snowcat . . . forget charging the emplacements on the ground, Ricey, they've overridden the old settings. Projectiles are still self-terminating at four Ks, so we have a safety range, but fire capability is now downward of horizontal, they can shoot up anything on legs or wheels now. The whole system is frozen, we're locked out—that's good in that it means they can't reset them again, but it also means no one from outside can get in and put them back."

"*So they've clearly got the fire-grid?*"

"It certainly looks that way. The one bit I can't see from this probe is how they're controlling it—I'm guessing a manual, realtime uplink to someone's portable, they can assign threat-ID-positive there from the sensor-grid, which will mean anyone they don't like the look of."

"*Can we hack that control link?*"

"Not a chance, it's buried, all the surrounding net infrastructure is frozen and we just can't break through what isn't interacting—that control point is connected between point A and B, we're at point C. We've no way of accessing unless we can hack their portable, and that's just not going to happen."

"*Will they target civilians as a hostage threat to hold off an assault?*" Although not in command, Vanessa certainly knew how to ask all the right questions. Threaten to blow one of those civilian shuttles out of the sky? Jesus. It *was* the FIA, she wouldn't put it past them—not considering the damage Dali could cause if they got him to spill what he knew about their collusion in just about everything Neiland's new allies found so annoying about the Federation Government right now.

"We'll put everyone into a holding pattern before we go in. First thing, someone get onto FS *Mekong* in geo-stationary communications orbit and ask them to begin the protocols for a live-fire mission, coordinates to follow." A brief pause.

"Uh . . . Sandy? You're not going to call down an orbital-fire mission on Gordon Spaceport, are you?"

"Firebird OMS is a very effective piece of hardware, Ricey, as I've had the opportunity to see for myself from the wrong end . . ."

"It's also a military-graded weapon for use in times of war, Sandy, I'm not sure the protocols allow for . . ."

"That's why I'm asking now, to give them some time to think about it," Sandy said with forced patience. "Give me some credit, it's just the first option." It also occurred to her that FS *Mekong* was a Second Fleet cruiser, based in Sol System, and its captain may well owe his or her appointment to certain connections within the Earth-based Federation bureaucracy . . . in the name of relocating which, she was now asking that same captain to open fire with an Orbital Missile System, against the interests of those who would surely like to prevent such a relocation. "Okay, Vanessa, options. We can't destroy the fire-grid emplacements because SWAT don't have the weaponry from outside the four K safe-range. We could fool the sensor-grid into thinking we're friendly, there are civilian shuttles, ground traffic and the occasional official flyer or aircar on the main highways going through constantly as we speak, but the sensor-grid is good and we certainly shouldn't think the FIA's stupid."

"We could land and catch the train?"

"Takes a half hour from the nearest stop, they'll be gone in twenty minutes—the data-feed I'm getting shows engine start-up in Berth 15, we just don't have the time. Ditto commandeering a truck. I'm not going to ask local security to intervene on our behalf, they'll just get slaughtered and achieve nothing. I'd ask a local aircrew to land a flyer or aircar in front of the damn shuttle, but there's no fireshadow within fifty metres of that spot, the fire-grid will get them. And even if they landed, self-terminating projectiles allow for the precision destruction of a landed vehicle, the shuttle could just roll over the wreckage, there wouldn't be that much left, and we'd have just murdered our friendly civilian flyer-crew. I won't do it."

"*Me neither. Ditto any intervention from ground crew, they'll have armed personnel covering the shuttle's departure, anyone getting in the way will be dead.*"

Amazing they could do it in broad daylight like this, in a busy civilian spaceport. It just showed that if you had the right systems, and the ability to access and control them to your advantage, you could do anything. From the flyer's rear came the clack and rattle of heavy armour and weapons, the murmur of voices running through system checks . . . even ordinary CSA personnel could operate in armour when needed, which was rarely. But she much preferred SWAT.

"Aside from all that, there's a whole arms bank of jamming and cloak gear I've operated with that could work over these distances, but of course CSA has none of it. I change my mind, I'm all out of options. Any suggestions from anyone that don't involve us getting blown out of the sky?"

A static silence on the com. The Tanushan outer perimeter was approaching—if she'd had time to look out the right-side porthole, she'd have seen nothing but green forest and the odd, winding river or transit route cutting through. Well beyond, the broad, open expanse of the mega-spaceport-airport complex. Now surrounded by a highly selective four kilometre exclusion zone that would cut them from the sky with the precision of a laser-scalpel if they crossed it. Above, a blue and sunny sky. That, too, was deceptive. At night, when the stations and ships went over in bright, metallic gleams against the light-washed city sky, you could see just how deceptive. Now, beyond the bright, glaring blue, there was nothing.

"Okay," she said, "get me a direct link to the captain of *Mekong*. Right now." Vanessa was right—it was a crazy option to be considering upon Tanusha's major infrastructural asset. But Sandy didn't care about that, all she knew was that it appeared to be her last option left, and she was going to take it.

"*Hello, Snowcat,*" came a new voice from HQ, "*we appear to have another seven outbound bogies in the traffic grid headed for Gordon, five appear to be media-registered, the other two are SIB.*"

If it weren't for the response-deadening effects of combat reflex, she was sure she would have muttered several very choice phrases to inform all with ears of her very severe displeasure.

"Highlight please," she said instead, and the tac-net matrix abruptly swung focus back to midwestern Tanusha, and to several red dots amid the masses of afternoon traffic flowing there. Specific detail sprang to visual. She scrolled through fast . . . five media and two SIB, like HQ said. Both SIB vehicles were breaking lanes on emergency protocols, very obvious and not the kind of thing she wanted to see with an opponent who wasn't supposed to see them coming . . .

"Someone please talk them into their lanes," she snapped, "or else I'll . . ." The command-SIB was transmitting and she cut into the frequency . . .

". . . *this is an illegal operation,*" came the clear, female voice, "*we monitor that Snowcat has been given charge of this mission, it is our duty to inform you that the individual 'Snowcat' is presently under legal suspension from duty by direct order of Special Investigation Bureau . . .*"

"*I don't fucking believe it,*" came someone's unidentified response on tac-net. The SIB couldn't hear that, they weren't hooked into tac-net, no non-CSA personnel could be unless directly authorised to—they didn't have the software. How they'd monitored enough to know that "Neiland's GI" was in charge was anyone's guess—leaks in CSA command was her own bet, it was a common enough rumour, either among personnel or net-systems. And then another call was coming in . . .

"Someone deal with them," Sandy announced, "I'm busy." And linked onto the other, broader, encrypted channel . . . "Hello, Captain Reichhardt." The accompanying text message on internal visual informed her of the captain's name and other details. "I'm sorry to disturb you, have you been following the present situation down here?"

"*Yes, yes I have.*" With that faintly tinny, static-wrinkled interface that spoke of greater distances and many relays in between. "*Your Director Ibrahim contacted me personally, and I am fully appraised of the situation regarding Governor Dali. I understand I am speaking to the famed Tanushan GI, and that you are in command of this operation at present.*"

"That is correct, sir." Scanning text furiously—the captain's age, marital status, university, degrees, military record (an accumulated twelve years' frontline service against the League as captain, another fifteen as a lower ranked officer) . . . anything that might give her an idea of the man's leanings. It was of course a political decision she was asking. In this environment, everything had a political ramification. What this particular ramification would be for herself if it happened, she had no idea. "Our present situation is that Dali will escape our custody if we cannot stop him. The FIA have now acquired complete control of the Gordon Spaceport fire defence grid. If we venture within the four kilometre exclusion zone, we will be destroyed, and we have only perhaps nineteen minutes before the shuttle leaves its berth. I am asking you, sir, to commit an OMS launch against the five defensive fire-grid emplacements to allow us to prevent Dali's unlawful escape from justice. As you will know, I am an ex–Dark Star captain. I am well versed in the operation of such weapons systems, I can safely act as your fire-control officer at this end to ensure zero collateral damage. I await your prompt reply, sir." A brief pause. Too long to be transmission delay. Then a faint, crackling sound that sounded like . . . a chuckle.

"*Ma'am, in Texas where I was born, we call that cahones . . . no matter your gender, it's still cahones.*" Texas. USA—or Los Estados Unidos—people from there were called LEUs for short. Lots of Spanish slang. Far more LEUs in the League, generally speaking. LEUs weren't generally known for their love of political chicanery, either. Her confidence level abruptly leapt . . . she might, MIGHT just have a chance here, because the USA had been one of the most vocal in speaking out *against* Federation centralism precisely *because* of FIA heavy-handedness . . . independently minded, League-sympathetic if not exactly friendly, and still sometimes accused of isolationism, the USA remained somewhat suspicious of their bigger Chinese and Indian partners that dominated the Federation Grand Council alliance, and most recently, it seemed, with damn good cause . . .

"Now I do suspect, ma'am, that you are as well aware of the Federation-wide regulations against the operation of such military-grade weapons systems in a civilian environment as I am, particularly as it's now peacetime and all."

"Yessir. There will be no peace if Dali is allowed to escape, his removal will hide from the various off-Earth governments of the Federation much of the truth about the degree of the Grand Council's complicity in covert, illegal FIA operations . . ." And she decided to take a great, great chance, ". . . operations, sir, that I greatly suspect have caused you and your colleagues in Fleet command much anger and frustration for many years past. I'm sure many Fleet captains who served against the League were greatly outraged by many instances of the FIA's conduct in that conflict, and feel the greatness of their cause diminished by those actions. If you want to let yet another of those illegal acts fly straight off this planet and into the black hole of Grand Council justice, you can simply do nothing. Or you can assist in their lawful apprehension, for the greater good of all the Federation, and in the hopes of the smooth and democratic operation of Federation democratic political process, and launch the OMS on my fire mission. I'll make sure they only hit what they're supposed to, it will not be in any way a dangerous or reckless act. What is your response, sir? We're running out of time."

"I make no comment to you upon my feelings toward the FIA, Ms. Kresnov." Ibrahim had told him her name. Her hopes sank. *"Except to say that I've already had the fire mission locked in from the moment I understood the situation, launch will commence in approximately twenty seconds from now, and y'all go*

have y'rself a good next half hour down there, y'hear? Fire-control observer protocols will follow, Mekong *out."*

She didn't even hesitate. "All units, this is Snowcat, fire mission is on its way, I have observer protocols, please now take all measures to clear all civilians away from the fire-grid points. If I do need to detonate a round short of the targets, all units be prepared to improvise advance-and-evade flightplans around the surviving fire-grid point."

It was messy, this ad-hoc collection of civilian units and operating procedures ... communicating in a language everyone could understand was a challenge, and a long way from the jargon brevity of Dark Star familiarity. But if people misunderstood, they were going to get killed. ETA showed three minutes now until the kill-zone ... and if the shuttle's start-up sequence was where she thought it was from the displays, they'd be rolling in about eighteen. Somewhere up in high geo-stationary orbit, *Mekong* was now firing, high-V shell-casings accelerating at bone-crushing Gs, hitting atmosphere in two minutes, shell-burnoff for another two, flight activation, target acquisition ... they'd come straight in at many times terminal velocity, a mere five minutes twenty-three seconds from first firing. Giving them about twelve minutes between now and the shuttle departing. Well, at least they could get close enough then to wing the shuttle while it was still on the ground ... although that too could prove tricky, given the variables.

"All units," she announced, "switch lanes to a kill-zone parallel." With a quick flash of mental illustration to show what she meant, flight paths selected that ran alongside the kill-zone perimeter, attempting to look innocuous. She didn't think it would work, but it might keep them guessing. "We're going to get about twelve minutes once the grid goes down, I'll get you your landing points when it happens. It's a fluid situation, be prepared to improvise."

"Copy that," came Vanessa's reply, calm and unworried. And she suffered her first flash of worry—"Don't trust me too much, Vanessa, I'm not perfect. I can't monitor every-

thing you're doing realtime like I would a Dark Star team-mate through direct neural linkups, I'm relying on you to use your own brain." But she *knew* she couldn't waste time worrying about that, for everyone's sake, so she forgot about it, realigned the tac-net channel to remote, unplugged herself, unbelted and swung up from the chair into the cramped aisle and headed for the rear . . . the data-flow was less intense, without the direct linkup, but only marginally, and the complete, stable, tac-net picture remained constant in her head.

The four security agents were already arming up, a tight cluster of armour harnesses, light gear in various pieces and stages of attachment, nothing like the heavy grunt-gear SWAT used, just enough for light protection with full augmentation . . . She flattened herself past Odano and one of the sec agents, keeping balance in a rough piece of air with practised ease, double-handle twisted the grips on the first available locker and the doors swung open . . . there were six basic sizes of suit, precise fits were superior but it looked like everyone was going to find a size close enough. Hauled off her jacket and hung it, sent the shoulder holster after it—a tight wriggle as an armoured body squeezed past toward the front—and took calm note of the ongoing tac-net conversation with the SIB, who had neither adjusted lanes, nor slowed down. Nor, just as alarmingly, had the media vehicles. And more were highlighted . . . like carrion birds headed for a fresh carcass, they grew to a swarm by following each other's lead.

She got a hold of the overhead handles and slapped her-self back-first into the torso armour. A quick, reflex fas-tening of straps, feeling the auto-measurements rearranging for her size and shape, and snapped the chestplate down, then worked her way down to stomach, pelvis and thighs, each time the familiar snap-whine of connection, and the tightening adjustment to a firm fit. The sec agents cleared the rear, leaving room for Ari, Kazuma, and Odano, who scrambled into their gear with somewhat less than her own rapid grace. Bank as the flyer continued course along the kill-zone perimeter. The SIB didn't seem to be slowing . . .

". . . *Snowcat not to be taken as reliable*," the leader was saying as she tuned in directly, ". . . *Dali could not have escaped without CSA fore-knowledge, CSA is attempting to allow Dali to escape . . .*" Sandy couldn't believe that. She just couldn't. And hacked quickly onto their channel . . .

"This is Snowcat to all SIB and accompanying units, this is a CSA operation, SIB is not within CSA tac-net. If you proceed within the four kilometre exclusion zone about the spaceport the fire-grid will fire upon you . . ."

"*All SIB units are operating under Senate Security Panel authorisation Meta-Niner-Alpha, direct instruction to apprehend Dali personally. There has been no infiltration of fire-grid, SIB sources indicate otherwise . . .*"

"SIB units, your sources are wrong, stand down immediately." That was Ibrahim's voice. Ibrahim knew of the SIB's "special sources"? And who would be talking to the SIB behind everyone's backs? And could the SIB honestly be stupid enough to listen to them?

"SIB units," she tried again, but . . .

"*Listen, you little piece of shit,*" Vanessa cut in, "*on your present flightpath you have approximately twenty seconds left to live. Worse, you're going to put them onto us. We're not going to waste breath warning you again.*"

No reply.

"Oh shit," said Kazuma breathlessly, "I have to see this." Sounding uncharitably excited as she hastily fixed her helmet into place out of sequence, hooking up the feed and getting the visor down . . . Tac-net showed the lead two SIB vehicles headed straight at the kill-zone. Sandy switched to a visual feed, clear vision of both SIB cruisers, five-person aircars, government issue, but hardly combat-worthy . . .

"They wouldn't?!" exclaimed Odano. Sandy watched her feed with as much incredulity as combat reflex allowed to surface. Both aircars kept going, the second perhaps naught-point-two klicks behind the first. Multiple fire-tracks registered on tac-net from the firepoints about Gordon. The lead car shattered to fragmented pieces barely a second later, exploding in flames almost as an afterthought as the combustibles ignited. The second car took wild evasive action, vis-feed tracking from an external camera . . . shots ripped out to it as it plunged and twisted, shells exploding in rapid unison a hundred metres beyond as if hitting an invisible barrier. She could see it was going to make it, the fire patterns fixed in her head, the ranges from various batteries, the speed at which they adjusted, shells chasing, then detonating alongside in fiery bursts, then out and clear, trailing smoke and left-side low as the mayday call went out, and panicked, incredulous exclamations burst across the broader net. Barely two hundred metres inside the invisible kill-zone, a long, black plume of smoke rose from the thick forest like a funeral pyre.

"That," Ari said mildly, "is possibly the silliest thing I've ever seen."

"I wouldn't say that, personally," Sandy replied, bending to finish her final leg-adjustments, "but it definitely makes my top five."

"You've seen four things crazier than that?" said Kazuma. No doubt about it, she looked almost cheerful in her incredulity. "Girl, you must have seen some weird shit."

Sandy shrugged. "*Mai pen rai*," she said, ignoring the helmet to go instead for the light headset . . .

"*Mai pen* what?" said Kazuma.

"Thai," Ari informed her, working once more on his own armour attachments with intense concentration. "Means 'whatever.' An old Thai friend once told me Tanusha was a '*mai pen rai* society.'" Sandy finished settling hair and headset into place, snapped up, checked, loaded and activated the Tanu-55 assault rifle with a series of rapid moves, and shoved off to mid-aisle, directly confronting Ari.

"Okay, greenpea, what did you test in armour?"

"Mean average eight-point-three," Ari told her, wincing as the thighplate clacked in and the whole leg assembly tightened on auto. Apparently calm, but for the brief, flickering glance of dark eyes in her direction . . . worried, she reckoned, past the typical Ari Ruben deadpan. She didn't think the armour suited him. Too official. "Authority." Not a good look for an underground fringe-dweller.

"What about you?" she asked Kazuma.

"Eight-point-nine," Kazuma said smugly. Further progressed in her suit-up than Ari. Had more practice, Sandy reckoned. It seemed to be Kazuma's thing, and the little gunslinger seemed to enjoy it. Sandy distrusted that implicitly.

"You'll do what I tell you." Gazing firmly at Kazuma. Half expecting a smart arse remark.

"Yessir," Kazuma said smartly, meeting her gaze with total honesty. Unwaveringly loyal. She didn't trust that either.

"Sandy," said Ari, recatching her attention. "No hard feelings? I couldn't tell you what Sai Va had, Ibrahim put me onto it personally, straight from Neiland . . . when it's connected to the President like that, I just couldn't tell you, you're not cleared for that information. It'd be political suicide for her if people found out you'd been told . . ."

"I understand perfectly," Sandy told him calmly. Just when did you start picking sides and protecting politicians, Ari? she wanted to ask him. Just when did you decide that something mattered enough for you to get involved? But she didn't have the time. "You're also going to do what I tell you. Everyone on this flyer is in the rear, SWAT Four gets the serious work, you get that?"

"No argument here."

"There's a chance we'll get some space to make a flanking manoeuvre up the left. If that happens I'll go first and you'll cover me. That's all you'll do. Everyone belt in tight, approach should get a little rough." She shouldered the rifle and hand-over-handed her way up the narrow aisle, past equipment, supports and waiting armoured agents, and stopped in the open space behind the cockpit . . .

"Sandy, where's the damn missiles?"

"Two minutes, Ricey, I'll get you a countdown in thirty."

Gordon continued to function, net traffic was alarmed. She could see security lights in places, crash trucks on the tarmac, some gatherings of people who'd come out to stare in horror at the plume of smoke from beyond the forest perimeter, some who were just standing stunned, shocked by the sight and sound of the fire-grid in operation, rapid staccato thumps from out on the perimeter followed by the angry, buzzing rush of projectile fire overhead. And she added "civil panic" to the list of probable circumstances she'd have to contend with, and hoped like hell the local security had removed all civilians from the north wing . . . tac-net wasn't clear on that, local security were evidently in a state, there were no clear reports available.

There *was* a new shuttle in Berth 14, however, right alongside the FIA's craft . . . the schedule showed it was new, only having docked twenty minutes ago. There were no records of disembarkation. Neither was there a name, or a registration.

"HQ, I want full details on the shuttle in Berth 14, I'm getting nothing on it."

"Roger, Snowcat."

She was in no mood for further surprises. It wasn't leaving again immediately if it had only just gotten in— shuttles took a few hours at least to turn around. But the proximity and the blacked-out ID were too much coincidence for her liking.

"I don't like that one, Sandy," came Vanessa, reading her mind. *"I think I might blow the access early, keep them inside."*

"Could do, let's see . . ." And saw tac-net highlight red as someone else broke the perimeter, accompanied by alarmed calls of "Someone's in!" and "Who the fuck is it?"

A fast mental zoom-and-highlight . . . "Media cruiser," she announced. "Broadcasting civilian press ID on every frequency, don't talk to it, you could trigger an attack, it's too late now."

Aghast silence from on the net. They'd completed nearly a half-circuit of the complex now, and Sandy stared out the right-side windows. She had a broad, clear view back across the crisscrossing of runways, terminal and building complexes, to the looming towers of Tanusha beyond . . . and a small, lonely dot that grew as she magnified it, wandering out into that lethal space above the spaceport.

"What in the prophet's good name are they doing?" muttered the pilot.

"Trying to win 'journalist of the year.' And betting the FIA won't fire on media." So far it was working. Another minute and the OMS would take out the emplacements. There was a shuttle coming in for landing too—that was safe, she'd discovered on a separate scan, fire-grid *couldn't* fire on civilian shuttles, visual verification was hardwired and wouldn't allow it—and thank God for the common-sense genius who'd written that protocol into the software. Another was circling. Worse news, three were on the tarmac awaiting take-off, one just now lining up . . . traffic control were under supervision from CSA HQ, they knew what was going on, she had to hope they'd stay rational. "SWAT Four, change course, reverse circuit, we might need to come in from different angles."

And watched the SWAT flyer comply, banking completely around to head back the other way along the kill-zone perimeter . . . and then she saw something moving by one of the fire-grid emplacements. Zoom-and-focus on tac-net, an overwhelming rush of data . . . and found a vehicle, grounds maintenance, zooming out along a service way toward the low, squat, ferrocrete bunker that housed the cannon mount . . .

"HQ, I have a civilian vehicle at grid-point three, please remove them *immediately.*" Impact ETA thirty seconds. "SWAT Four, grid-point three may survive impact, project fireshadow . . ." And whacked her own pilot on the shoulder. His hands moved, the horizon banking sharply and Gs shoved down hard . . . dammit, grid-point three was due north, they were presently west-headed-north in their circuit of the spaceport, now they had to get ninety degrees back south to give them a covered approach from that fire-point. Still the civilian vehicle approached. A hundred metres . . . too close, it'd singe their eyebrows. Stopped at fifty metres, just beyond the ground perimeter fencing.

"*Snowcat, this is HQ, vehicle is not responding, must be a bad com.*"

"Fuck it," she said, and mentally sent the termination signal. A bright flash high, high above . . . she barely looked, she'd done it all before too many times to remember. Fire-grid control panicked, rapid projectile fire ripping from five consecutive points, converging in an apex of shredding tracer above the spaceport's east wing . . . the media car disintegrated like tissue paper in a hailstorm, pieces spinning to earth in violently random directions.

"No 'journalist of the year' for you," muttered the pilot, throttle wide open, engines howling at the flyer's maximum, the treetops rushing ever closer as they lost altitude. The other four target points were clear. She gave the missiles a final OK . . . final safeties went red, warheads primed, and she spared herself a brief, upward glance. Thin white contrails in the clear blue sky. Headed in and downward at incredible velocity.

Th-th-th-thud, four rapid impacts, fireballs climbing skyward from four widely spread locations across the broad expanse of spaceport grounds, laden with debris.

"*We're in,*" said Vanessa, SWAT Four already in nearly perfect position south of the spaceport and banking hard inward, barely ten metres off the treetops.

"Four strikes," Sandy said calmly, watching the fireballs rise as yet more confusion unfurled across the tac-net schematic of Gordon, emergency calls, com traffic and general chaos—"Live fire from north of Gordon is still imminent, SWAT Four is inbound, Snowcat is inbound in . . ." Rush of schematic data, topography calculations showing the fire-blindspots and calcing that with their present trajectory. ". . . fifteen seconds when we acquire fireshadow, everyone stay low and keep the chatter down." And flicked channels. "Vanessa, you've got no angle on the north wing with that firepoint still active, I want you to get down behind north wing, check tac-net V-18Q, disperse and secure the building with two shooters high, I'm coming in at V-15R for rearguard, you right flank secure through to main baggage, we hold and pivot, you push, establish contact and hold, then I'll push the left flank and trap them." With mental illustrations across the tac-net display of the spaceport schematic, visual backup to the verbal shorthand.

"*Gotcha, Snowcat,*" came Vanessa's laconic drawl.

The pilot banked hard left—again the Gs shoved down, Sandy holding position comfortably, braced and standing behind the cockpit seats with a good view out the front . . .

"Under fire!" the copilot yelped as the north grid-point flared . . .

"Hold steady," Sandy said loudly, "they can't hit us . . ." Even as fire ripped perhaps twenty metres over them with snarling, angry velocity. ". . . we're in the west wing shadow, they're trying to scare us." Pause in fire, greenery rushing by below, then an abrupt break into open ground. Barely a kilometre to their left, thick, black smoke roiled skyward, bits of debris raining down, pieces of what had formerly been a very expensive, very efficient defensive gun emplacement. Sandy found time to wonder wryly if some fool on the Senate Security Panel would try and bill her for damages. "Five metres lower, we've got a brief gap coming up."

The flyer edged lower . . . damn slow machine, turbine-propelled and labouring at barely seven hundred and fifty kph, but at ten metres off the deck it looked plenty fast enough. The northwest to southeast runway was two Ks ahead, access roads, drainage runoffs and observation posts shot past below . . . fire from the emplacement and "CLIMB!" she yelled, the Gs smacking them down as the ground fell away, and the burst of fire through the fire-shadow gap between west wing and main terminal buildings ripped past below instead of hitting them . . . "Down down down, back on the deck." And the nose plunged once more, fire retargeting their new position, gathering from the full eight kilometres of the spaceport's far north end in glowing, ponderous clusters, then snapping by overhead at blurring velocity.

"That's it, well done." The pilot, she noted, was sweating profusely, a vision-shift showed her a vastly elevated respiration and body temperature . . . the copilot wasn't much better. For SWAT pilots a hotzone approach typically meant a few small arms—this was something they'd never trained for nor expected. "Don't look at the groundfire," she warned them both, "that's electro-mag fire, nearly five Ks a second, you look straight at it and you lose spatial perception and your flight track. Trust your flight sense, evade in future-time—real-time is too late, it's too fast."

"I have it," murmured the pilot, breathless as the runway came closer up ahead, then abruptly shot past below . . . the terminal complexes growing larger ahead by the second. "By the prophet I have it." His voice strained, breathing hard.

"Allah is with us," Sandy said firmly. "Trust in Allah."

"Allahu Akbar," the pilot agreed in a stronger tone, and entrusted them to a hard right bank at seven hundred and fifty as he readjusted their approach track, the right nacelle barely five metres off the hurtling ground. Sandy wondered if too much trust in Allah couldn't be a dangerous thing.

The spaceport proper was looming up, the SWAT Four flyer already pulling into a close, decelerating hover low past the left side of south terminal . . . the size of it struck her as she watched the buildings loom through the armoured windshield, the sprawling southern terminal with multiple wings and covered shuttle bays, layout-graphics indicating a ten thousand passenger per hour rating for each of the four main terminals. That was forty thousand people per hour all up, north, south, west and east terminals adjoining to the massive central complex, where highway connections looped into multilevel avenues of departures and arrivals, and the maglev connected underground . . . And she recalled with a brief flash of memory her own arrival here from Rita Prime nearly two months ago, through customs with fake ID and scant baggage, cavernous, gleaming architecture and masses of people arriving and departing, to and from all corners of the Federation . . . and no clue at all of how her life would have changed when she next revisited this massive, bustling, vital juncture that connected half of Callay's population to the rest of the Federation.

They hurtled in low past the broad viewing windows of the southern terminal, glimpses of staring faces, civilians gathered on viewing platforms and staring incredulously at the pair of armoured SWAT flyers that howled low past their heads in the aftermath of heavy weapons fire and massive artillery strikes on the perimeter . . . and visual enhancement through the windows showed flaring emergency lights, and uniformed staff attempting to herd hundreds of frightened passengers into convenient directions . . . pity the tourists who'd just arrived for their holidays to discover that all the worst stories they'd heard of the "Tanushan troubles" paled to insignificance next to the reality . . .

Past the southern terminal, then, and onto the central hub, ducking low past one towering side where automated traffic piled into immobile jams along the elevated departure zones, crowds of panicked people swarming the roads, emergency vehicles with lights flashing, staff directing frantically, parents clutching children and baggage . . . it all hurtled past to their right, north terminal looming ahead, Vanessa's flyer already down and unloading atop the furthest edge of the terminal roof, behind the elevated restaurant/observation deck that her schematics had shown her created a fireshadow that the remaining firepoint could not penetrate, a faint glimpse of armoured figures pouring from the flyer's rear . . .

The pilot took them low and left, passenger avenues shooting past below through decorative trees, Sandy staring leftwards where the west terminal sprawled northwards in a long passenger wing, shuttle berths breaking the length . . . that was where the crossfire would come from, Berth 15 was one of the line of berths up ahead on the west side of north terminal, completely exposed to cover-fire from the west terminal. Gordon schematic showed her passenger evacuation proceeding out of the terminals and back into central, where they would no doubt create an unholy crush. The broad tarmac appeared clear of the usual spaceport personnel and activity, empty vehicles littered across parking zones, shuttles left abandoned in their bays. Berth 11 loomed ahead, a great, cavernous shadow filled with a shuttle's thruster-heavy rear end, Berth 11 connected directly to the north terminal building, then 12 to 14 extended from there in a line along the narrow, extended north terminal wing, 15 at the far end, and 16 to 18 down the other side. The shuttle's massive trans-orbital thrusters filled the forward view as the pilot decelerated into a howling, nose-up flare, engine nacelles re-angling forward and crushing all occupants down toward the deck . . . roar of noise and wind as the rear doors clacked open and cold air rushed in . . .

"Everybody out!" Clackbump! Hard touchdown and still rolling, she turned and went, a fast scramble down the narrow aisle. Got out just after Odano, the wind and roar of flyer engines deafening as she sprinted past the reangling nacelle for the looming shuttle-tail, quickly overtaking those ahead as the flyer lifted once more behind, and made back the way it'd come. She slowed to a steady armoured run, weapon cradled comfortably, headed under the shuttle's looming right wing, around the ground vehicles and maintenance gear, aiming for the front-right rim of the huge shed . . . it seemed empty of people, everyone having evacuated from this position, at least, loose equipment left strewn about the interior, a huge elevator platform left suspended in mid-engine-inspection beside huge undercarriage tires. Shuttles used covered berths, unlike regular aircraft, all refuelling, engineering, passenger-transfer and other servicing equipment built into the structure of the berth shelter, locking shuttle and terminal into close, mutual embrace. As she scanned about within the echoing, cavernous interior amid the steady clattering of many running, armoured footsteps, Sandy reflected that they also made for very good defensive cover.

Gunfire erupted on tac-net, numerous sources, vaguely audible to the ear through muffling earpieces and armoured helmets . . . "*Contact*," Vanessa said in her ear, and she could see on tac-net the lead elements had gotten down into the main levels of north terminal, advanced as far as the narrow north wing entrance, and immediately been pinned down by defensive positions there. Vanessa had several more on the next level up, three pairs out wide to cover the full hall and maintenance accessways, two more on the tarmac down low where the baggage vehicles docked, and two remaining up on the roof, just as she'd asked . . . that was the full sixteen. "*Main level's blocked . . . that's good defensive position, can't get that out short of cannon. Upper level's the same . . . maintenance left is booby trapped, I could run it, but I'd rather not . . .*"

"No, don't do that, not against FIA." Sandy raced for the forward, right-hand corner of the Berth 11 structure, gesturing the others to stay well back as she slammed her armoured back beside the rim. Snuck a quick look out, and to no great surprise drew fire from well up along the tarmac . . . "I'm drawing fire from Berth 13," she yelled over the thunder of rounds that clanged and sparked off the rim or smacked heavily into shuttle wheels or maintenance gear further back in the shed, her teammates flattening themselves hard to wall and ground. "Heavy-cal, looks mounted, that covers the whole west side of north wing . . . hang on . . ." And looked back at her group. ". . . Weng, take your two and Odano back to the side exit there, get up to level one, spread out and hold this flank. Don't let anyone come back around us, or you'll leave SWAT Four exposed on their left."

Weng, the senior of the three sec agents nodded once and left at a clattering run, the other three in tow . . . truth was she didn't trust CSA's security detail much from what she'd seen of them, theoretically better grunts than field agents but with a fixed, immobile conception of "defend" rather than "fight." Right now she preferred Ari and Kazuma, at least they knew what a fluid situation looked like. The fire stopped, replaced by the muffled, staccato thunder on the tac-net, more audible now to the naked ear. Berth 15 was right up the end . . . had to get close enough to damage that shuttle or otherwise stop it from taking off. Damn inconvenience that surviving fire-grid emplacement, if it was gone they could just use a flyer to do it.

"Look, Ricey, keep them occupied. Pressing too hard won't help, I'm sure they've booby trapped the whole damn floor, even if they did fall back . . . I can make up some ground out here, I'll try and get under them."

"Copy that."

She turned back to Ari and Kazuma. Ari looked very concerned beneath serious dark brows, helmet visor up for the moment. Kazuma, she was relieved to see, appeared totally businesslike. "We're going that way," she told them, pointing out around the fire-chewed rim, "if you get shot at, fall flat. If you're not getting shot at, run like hell. Follow my lead, cover each other, don't try to do what I do, because you can't. And, for godsake, watch the west wing over there," pointing left over to the line of berths two hundred metres west that ran parallel to this wing, "'cause that's where the secondary cover will be. I can't see anything yet, but there's any amount of cover, and even I can't see everything, it'll be there." A short, flat nod from Kazuma.

"That way?" Ari said with trepidation. "What about that gun?"

"What about it?" She rolled her back to the wall again, shifted firegrip to her left hand, braced, and leaned quickly out, with the rifle propped to her left shoulder. Fired a brief burst. Three hundred metres out along the tarmac, the man manning the tripod-mounted machine gun past a narrow edge of Berth 13's rim took five rounds through the chest and died. A second burst riddled the gun mount, sent it crashing heavily to the ground.

She ducked out, zagged right, cleared the corner of the north terminal building and got a good view of where the long north wing adjoined—the location of SWAT Four's firefight. Immediately did a full-spectral scan across the wing directly ahead—three main levels—the middle one for passengers, upper for maintenance—and a lower one for baggage and flight operations. Only the middle passenger level offered a clear run through to the end of the wing . . . SWAT Four were pinned down at the mouth. She headed that way at full sprint, weapon trained upon Berths 12 and 13 up ahead to the left as she ran. Hurdled some abandoned luggage rollers and flattened herself to the side wall of the terminal building behind an outcrop of airconditioning complex—back-first to observe Ari and Kazuma following at full sprint—her gaze panning to the west wing. An adjoining empty shuttle berth, accompanying ground vehicles and a lot of cover points . . . she pointed that way to Kazuma as she arrived. Kazuma smacked the wall beside her and dropped to a one-knee cover, weapon trained in that direction across two hundred metres of exposed tarmac.

Sandy ducked a glance around the corner of the aircon juncture, at the point where the long length of north wing accessway attached to the main building and created the well defended bottleneck . . . inside the main-level windows, muzzle flashes were clearly evident, already side windows were riddled in places. Further along, the one-shuttle hangar of Berth 12 opened directly toward them, the entire dark, cavernous interior exposed and presently unoccupied . . . she didn't like it. Between here and Berth 12 were more abandoned ground vehicles, a passenger bus parked just twenty metres away, some elevating platforms for accessing tall shuttle cargo bays. Tac-net showed two marks well-positioned on the roof of north wing, only one was available to cover them.

"Zago, this is Snowcat, cover please, I am advancing."

Ari arrived and slid in with a metallic clatter.

"Go, Snowcat."

Sandy slid around the corner and ran for the bus. Registered movement behind a polarised upper window even as she emerged from the other side, snapped fire upward as she ran, windows shattering, and abruptly drew fire from Berth 12 . . . threw herself behind a baggage vehicle as rounds snapped and twanged all about, and then there was fire streaking across the tarmac from the west wing, several-sourced and heavy. The baggage vehicle rocked and lost pieces violently, Sandy rolled fast, doing mental triangulation on the sources, popped to a knee and nailed a burst back across the tarmac . . . one source of fire ceased. More fire was coming from Ari and Kazuma from back behind the aircon juncture, impacts spraying across the various cover two hundred metres away, keeping heads down. She up and ran at a ready crouch, heavy fire thudding overhead from Zago on the roof into Berth 12 . . .

"No fix on the target, Sandy," came Zago's terse comment, *"I'm firin' blind."*

"Keep at it, I got no angle here . . ." Angling closer to the side of the north wing that loomed overhead, running on mag-lines where automated tarmac vehicles normally plied along the sides . . . more fire from west wing and she dropped to another roll as rounds struck the wall on her right, then up and scanning . . . movement halfway up the interior wall of the Berth 12 hangar. She fired—a body fell on a walkway, weapon clattering to the tarmac below—and flung herself right at the sound of breaking glass above, shots from overhead peppering the spot where she'd been. Kazuma swung around from behind the aircon juncture, firing above her head. Shots ceased, either hit or frightened. Sandy unflattened herself off the wall, duck-rolled again as more fire streaked across from the west wing in flat, clustered bursts, popped up and returned fire across the tarmac on a good fix this time, vision magnification saw a body flung backward and rebound from sight.

"Go go," she heard Ari's voice, *"I'm covering."* And Kazuma was sprinting from cover . . . Sandy watched it all

on tac-net, that ever-present sixth-sense that overlaid her consciousness . . . the firefight stalemate in the narrow bottleneck in the building above, and now the open path she was trying to carve up the flank here outside.

"Sandy, they just pulled two off the line here," Vanessa said, *"they know you're flankin', get ready for company . . ."*

"Got that, Ricey . . . just hold them there. Keep 'em occupied, I want to get a response and see how many they've got . . ." Behind her the bus blew up in a flaming explosion, she zagged hard left, headed for the outer rim of the Berth 12 hangar as blazing debris spattered the tarmac about her like rain. Slid into it as Ari went running for Kazuma, yelling at her, Kazuma replying groggily that she was okay . . . thunder of more weapons fire from the west wing, new position this time, it sounded like platoon support . . . she snuck a glance around, saw the flash of fire-trail and ducked back hard and covered . . . WHAM!! as the round hit the hangar wall with a force that dislocated reality and turned the world to flames and noise. Fire ripped past from her left, ricocheting from the inner Berth 12 wall in a violent confusion of lethal metal—coming from Berth 13 . . . Dammit, they were communicating, they thought they had her pinned.

She flipped the rifle about, targeted left across her body. Just the top half of the Berth 13 gunner's head was visible a hundred metres away—she blew it off, and half-spun around the corner, rifle straight-armed at almost a backward angle. Triggered a sustained burst that sent another of them spinning away in a flail of limbs from two hundred metres before the two others could duck for cover that saved their lives by milliseconds. Then she ran through the hangar toward Berth 13, knowing full well they knew exactly who she was now. It was becoming unmistakable that this one trooper headed up the tarmac outside the north wing consistently killed everyone who shot at her, regardless of range, numbers or merely human considerations of accuracy. But she didn't mind if they knew.

"*Ayako's okay!*" Ari was saying with great relief. "*She's winded . . . that was some goddamn heavy weaponry, they've got God-knows how many people over on the west wing covering for them.*"

"*Final fire-up on the shuttle,*" said Hiraki, "*we're about to run out of time.*" Sandy paused her run to crouch by the huge wheelbrace that would have secured a shuttle when the hangar was occupied—seeing movement in the shadow of the Berth 13 hangar but wary of firing in a civilian environment without a clear ID . . .

"*I got an angle on a wall here,*" Vanessa announced, "*I'm gonna try it, they're two short on this side now . . . Arvi, let's go.*"

"*Watch the wiring . . .*"

They had it covered, Sandy knew . . . fired a long burst into Berth 13 to scare whoever was there, and received the thump of an RPG in return, saw it coming on a flame-trail streaking across the tarmac and threw herself into a calculating leftward run-and-dive for the wall . . . BOOM!! the shockwave shuddered . . . fire-tracking her to the wall, riddling punctures through the broad hydraulic piping running across there, a half-blinding spray of green fluid as she pressed left shoulder to the bulkhead and returned fire . . .

Huge series of explosions from the buildings behind, tac-net flaring heat and fury before SWAT Four's position, terse shouts from Vanessa, snap-firing and an advance forward in pairs . . . suddenly the way was being cleared . . . Sandy realised something was burning on the hangar wall above her, and was not greatly surprised when the next grenade went shooting that way. She leapt right and kept sprinting, hurdling wheelbraces and access elevators for the hangar's other side as the explosion took out fuel lines on the wall in a massive fireball that set the entire wall burning . . . she smashed a foot into the side access door and went through it, confronted immediately by a cramped upward stairway of metal rails and ferrocrete, up which she exploded a flight at a time . . . booted the upper door off its hinges and plunged down the short adjoining corridor to the main north wing, obliterated that door in similar fashion and ducked a glance out . . . she was in the passenger walk-in from the waiting lounge. Ran quickly up the walk, cranked that heavy door open and was in the lounge itself, rows of empty seats behind a heavy glass partition from the main wing thoroughfare . . . like spaceports/airports everywhere, in her short experience with such things. Except that charging up the long walking hall of this spaceport came several heavily armoured SWAT troops at full sprint alongside the long pedestrian conveyor belts, weapons levelled, ignoring her as they passed, tac-net already having identified her position . . .

"Watch Berth 14," she told them, quickly hurdling rows of chairs, "I still don't have an ID on the occupant." Smashed a fist through the heavy glass, then crashed shoulder-first into the long, straight hallway, trading the old rifle magazine for a fresh one from the hip-pouch . . . quick glance back at the choking smoke obscuring all view far down the end of the main building—several more SWAT troops charging her way . . . and that would be Vanessa, bringing up the rear on short legs. Those were the FIA-fixed booby trap explosives she'd seen blow—those huge explosions from where SWAT Four had been pinned—Vanessa had found a way to detonate them herself . . . she admitted herself puzzled, she knew of several tricks but nothing with the capabilities SWAT Four possessed. But where capabilities were concerned, there was SWAT Four, there were SWAT procedures, and then there was Vanessa . . .

"Ari," she called as she broke into a run, "stay with Kazuma, keep down and don't get exposed."

"*I got it . . .*" And another call cut in over the top . . .

"*Snowcat, this is HQ, Berth 14 is occupied by a shuttle registered to the* Diligent, *currently in stand-off orbit from Markov Station . . .*"

"I copy, HQ . . . SWAT Four, hold and cover!" Ahead the running troopers dropped to skidding, clattering halts just short of where the thoroughfare ahead opened into a broad circular space. Sandy kept running, accelerating to a loping, over-accelerated gait with explosive thrusts of her legs. "Berth 14 is a League shuttle! Full caution, target left is not secure!" Marking tac-net red-hostile with a mental impulse, sliding in feet-first beside Singh, rolling at the last moment to come over face-first and rifle-braced.

The broad, circular waiting area had two berths, 14 diagonally to the left, and 15 diagonally to the right. Scan-entry consoles and service desks were deserted, security doors across the exits closed and, according to tac-net, locked. Sandy didn't trust that reading for a second. Semi-circular arrangements of waiting seats for passengers, an inbuilt cafe to the left, a display arrangement for the Tanushan tourist bureau to the right, touch-screen and interactive. Before the waiting seats a flatscreen TV displayed a realtime image from some aircar beyond the space-port perimeter . . . a newsfeed, camera focused with no doubt horrified fascination upon the various plumes of smoke rising from different locations across the spaceport grounds. To the best of her memory, it was the first time she'd ever done an op on live net-broadcast before.

Clatter-thump as Vanessa slid in beside her.

"They didn't get a berth right next to an FIA ship by accident," Vanessa said off-net, voice muffled behind the faceplate of heavy SWAT armour. "They must have finagled it."

Sandy's mind raced. Remembered Ramoja's explanations. The change of League government, the new League factions sent out to Callay to help "put things straight." *Diligent*, however, was not the ship Ramoja had arrived on . . . that was the *Rodriguez*, it and *Diligent* had come in together from League space, both military-registered cruisers, high on power, low on mass, very little crew space . . . courier vessels, as they were commonly known. Each carried its own shuttle . . . this was no doubt one, presently docked in Berth 14, its ID kept silent for security protocol reasons, the League admitting to no "official delegation" at this moment.

A new League government sent two courier ships to

address the problem the old League government had helped create on Callay. One held Ramoja, a senior and apparently trusted League Intelligence officer, plus a complement of additional GIs for extra muscle. Those GIs were Dark Star . . . military, not Intelligence. Were all of them on *Rodriguez*? What was *Diligent* doing here? And why had they only just sent their shuttle down now, and arranged for it to get a berth directly alongside a shuttle they'd assuredly know belonged to the FIA? Unless . . .

Unless they knew something was going to happen. Ramoja's stolen information from the Zaiko Warren that she'd chased him to try and uncover. Stolen from Sai Va's friends. Sai Va hadn't been able to crack the codes and discover Neiland's plan for the relocation of Federation governance. Ramoja was Intel, and however good the Tanushan underground, she doubted they quite measured up to League Intel's capabilities . . . especially given the League's longstanding underground presence in Tanusha. Ramoja had probably cracked Sai Va's information in a few hours, and discovered what Neiland was up to. That done, it couldn't have been a difficult guess for him that the FIA would want Governor Dali off-planet by any means necessary. Intel's obsession with a low profile meant he couldn't intervene directly. But now a mysterious second shuttle had come down from the second League ship in orbit and had just happened to dock beside the FIA shuttle of Dali's intended get-away . . .

Tac-net gave her no reading on the shuttle's readiness, those systems were totally closed off, except to register on basic flight control that engines were powered up and preparing to leave. It should be leaving right about now, especially when they'd hurried up the sequence. It wasn't.

"Everyone just hold," she said on tac-net, "we might be okay here." Recalled Ramoja's access codings, which she'd managed to glean from their brief contact . . . penetrated the local net infrastructure as far as the main-level grid for the north wing. Berth 15 was impenetrable, severed totally from the surrounding network. Berth 14 . . .

She sent a basic connection frequency, nothing threatening. A knock on the door. It uplinked immediately, an unfolding of multi-layered, very familiar League security protocols.

"*Cassandra Kresnov?*" asked a cool, unhurried voice in her inner ear . . . and she switched it to broadcast on tac-net so the others could hear.

"That's me," she sent back. "Can you advise me as to the present status of the vessel currently docked in Berth 15?"

"*Berth 15 has been secured by League operatives,*" came the voice. Just like that. The FIA had evidently been in too much hurry to notice the new shuttle that had docked alongside, and had left themselves wide open. And she felt a surge of temper . . . it could have saved a lot of trouble if they'd told her earlier instead of persisting with this clandestine nonsense. But then, she supposed, it appeared to have worked.

"Our thanks on behalf of the Callayan Government for your assistance," she said. "We now request that you hand over Governor Dali and any surviving FIA personnel to our lawful custody."

"*Of course. Please stand by.*" The connection broke. There was still some sporadic shooting on tac-net, Zago and Sharma were keeping the several survivors across on the west wing pinned down with well-placed gunfire from the roof, and then there were those shooters holed up in Berth 13 . . .

"Squad Two," Sandy said, "get back down to Berth 13, they're not headed north with League GIs in Berth 14. Make sure they don't get into the wing, and someone try to tell them the game's up, might be nice to interview some live ones."

A clatter as six of the surrounding, covering troopers got up and ran back down the wing. And Sandy found time to wonder if she hadn't gotten just a little too callous about the lives of Federal Intelligence Agency personnel of late . . . just yesterday she'd been agonising over the lives of terrorists, now she just felt . . . nothing.

It was hatred, cold and simple. Hatred at what they'd done to her personally, at what they stood for, the innocent lives they'd cost in pursuit of a cause founded primarily on xenophobia and intolerance. Not a violent, boiling hatred . . . rather a cold indifference as to whether they lived or died. If they got in her way, they'd die. The onus, as she saw it, was on them to stay out of her way. She'd come a long way in her new life as a civilian. But she knew she was a long, long way from becoming a pacifist.

Movement up the passenger access from Berth 15, a shift of light on her most sensitised vision.

"They're coming out. Everyone hold position, we don't know if this place is rigged." Another fast vision-scan across the broad, circular waiting room, multi-spectrum, scanning for possible tampering and finding nothing. But FIA agents were well-trained in this sort of thing, and a booby rig might just have been stuffed under a chair to blow the place apart. It would give a trigger signal, which might give advance warning of a second or two, but no more than that . . .

Figures moving up the passenger access behind the glass security door. It slid open on a signal—they were system-locked, then, patched in to that part of the network. She revised her possible scenarios, and levered herself smoothly into a compact crouch for a better firing angle over the chairs, sighting calmly along the rifle. If something went down, she knew damn well she'd be the first target. At this range, with limited possibilities for her to cover, she didn't think it would make any difference, GIs or not . . . she *was* that good, and she knew it. She hoped they knew it too.

A man walked from the open access of Berth 15, casually dressed, sports jacket and cargo pants . . . she filed a mental note about the cargo pants, it seemed every GI subjected to civvies chose them for casual wear. It was becoming a dead giveaway. Something to remember on future covert ops. He was armed, a light STZ assault weapon, common League Intel issue. A woman followed, similarly dressed and armed. Both took up alert, ready positions on either side of the open door.

"*GIs*," Sandy said, in case they hadn't figured it out . . . if the thirty-five degree body temperature wasn't giveaway enough, the coiled, effortlessly controlled poise in their stance made it doubly obvious. She looked like that herself when she moved. Each weapon was held in comfortable cross-brace, unthreatening yet ready.

The next man emerged. Ramoja. His eyes found her immediately . . . no confusion despite the line of armoured SWAT troopers levelling weapons at him from the thoroughfare entrance . . . her head was bare unlike the others, and her blonde hair under the partial headset was obvious. But she suspected he would have known anyway, as she could have picked him just as easily from a group of straights.

"Agent Kresnov," he called cheerfully across the broad space. "We meet again, and this time our weapons find common cause. I have a present for you."

And he stepped aside, giving full view of the next man to emerge from the passenger access . . . a tall, dark-skinned man with deep, sallow eyes and a nervous, trembling gait. Governor Dali. He looked very, very scared, hair dishevelled, his expensive dark suit rumpled, flanked behind by another two GIs. They hadn't even bothered to restrain him—a GI's typical disregard of any straight's ability to resist, particularly an untrained civilian.

"Where are the other FIA?" she called. "Is the fire-grid down?"

"Oh yes, there was merely one woman with a hand-comp, only able to select targets, no more subtle control than that. We have her and the second-in-command restrained, the leader and two aides unfortunately resisted with lethal force, leaving us with little choice."

Sandy nodded reluctantly . . . in close quarters even GIs couldn't always shoot to wound against trained, augmented, heavily armed opponents. No GI was immortal against modern weapons, and most were not suicidal, unless tape-trained to be otherwise. She was not, however, about to call HQ just yet and give them the all-clear. She hadn't survived this many firefights by taking things for granted.

"This space is clear," Ramoja added, "we swept it thoroughly, and FIA field combat tactics frown upon the emplacement of defensive explosives so close to operational HQ."

"I've discovered many commanders neither read nor practise field manuals," Sandy said blandly. And she got up, lowering her weapon. "Guys, check it out, full sweep. No slacking." She meant more than just booby traps. By the careful, ready way they moved out, she knew they heard her. She grasped the rifle at comfortable cross-hold, and swaggered coolly across the floor . . . the seal on the carpeted centre of the circular space, she noted, was a Federation Sunburst and Stars—the vertical outline of a Tanushan skyline emblazoned behind, "Welcome to Callay" in curving English above, and again in Sanskrit below. The ceiling above had been overlaid with an orange blaze of sunset upon a broken, cloudy sky, a striking image to confront passengers just arrived from weeks or months of travel in the cold, black void of space. She'd only just now noticed how startling the colour was that burned across the circular ceiling—in the heat-motion sensitive mode of combat vision, there were a lot of ordinary things she could no longer see. Beautiful things. Underground techies no doubt thought it wonderful to possess the sensory abilities she did. Personally, she preferred normal light. Life without sunsets held little appeal for her.

She rounded a section of waiting seats, constantly aware of the spread of her SWAT troops around her, and strolled up to Ramoja . . . Dali had collapsed wordlessly into a seat, his two guards standing over him, and was staring blankly at the wall. That surprised her, she'd expected outrage, complaints, demands for the protection or administrations of his beloved bureaucracy in one form or another. But there was none of that, just the bleak, frightened silence of a man who was perhaps only just coming to realise what he'd gotten himself into by agreeing to work hand-in-glove with the FIA in their little biotech laboratory project in Tanusha . . . and what it ultimately might end up costing him.

It had nearly cost him his life . . . Ramoja and his GIs must have been good, Sandy had no doubt the FIA would have killed him if they'd realised they were about to be overrun. A better option than leaving him on Callay, perhaps to be subject to full, independent investigation by independent bodies once Callay, and not Earth, became the legal, bureaucratic and administrative centre of the Federation. No hiding what he knew. No more friendly faces from old, Earth-appointed bureaucracies to sweep things under the carpet, to keep the old power structures safe and intact from unwanted questions and unwelcome questioners. They'd find the connections implicating the FIA in the appointment of federal governors to member worlds, and in the workings of secret FIA operations on those worlds . . . operations that had cost the lives, and trampled the rights, of innocent Federation citizens in the name of advancing the FIA's outdated, paranoid, xenophobic goals. They'd trace it all back to senior power figures in the Federation Grand Council, manipulated behind the scenes by powerful people on Earth, to serve Earth's own narrow, conservative interests rather than those of the broader Federation.

Dali stared now at the wall with the stricken look of a man whose entire world had just fallen in upon his head. Well, it had. And Sandy wasn't certain whether the fear in his eyes was from the fright of a recent brush with death, or from the greater fright that he was still, inconveniently, alive. She stopped before Ramoja. He stood calmly expectant, smiling the faint, measured smile of a man very, very pleased with himself.

"Nice job," Sandy said, with a glance to Dali. "Why do it?"

Ramoja's smile spread a little wider across his handsome black face. "I told you, Cassandra, I'm here to fix things. The days of League complicity with secret FIA plans are over. The new League Government wishes to reestablish friendly relations with the Federation. You can take this as a gesture of our good intentions, and our desire to see lawful conduct reign within the broader Federation."

"That would be nice," Sandy agreed. "Maybe we could then export some of that lawful conduct back to the League."

"I should definitely hope so."

"How are you here? Your shuttle only just arrived, this area was cleared when we realised Dali was missing."

"It was I who called the shuttle down early," Ramoja replied. Very pleased with himself indeed, Sandy thought sourly. "I came out here just as early to meet them—dodging the security evacuation was not difficult. I could not be sure the FIA would move as it did, but there were oh-so-many of its agents scattered throughout the various Earth delegations . . . the major transnational, planetary delegations are particularly vulnerable, Cassandra, the United Nations, Earth Gov, the Grand Council itself. In the mishmash of overlapping security procedures of such enormous organisations there is much room for infiltration and dark ops, individual national delegations like the Indian or Chinese delegations are far tighter by contrast."

"We know. Intel had already figured this might happen, but hardly anyone knew what Neiland was planning. Someone who didn't know overrode Intel's orders to put Dali under special protection . . . typical bureaucratic stuff up. There's so many of them here—this place was made for business not security ops, public sector infrastructure here stinks."

"I've always said an emaciated public sector was death for any civilisation," Ramoja agreed mildly. "Though, as soldiers both, it is perhaps predictable we should reach such a conclusion."

"No shit. Vanessa . . ." as the smaller, armoured figure arrived alongside, ". . . this is Major Mustafa Ramoja, League ISO. Major, Lieutenant Vanessa Rice, Callay's leading SWAT officer."

"One does observe," Ramoja acknowledged, with a meaningful glance back down the north wing thoroughfare, rapidly obscured by more smoke than the air scrubbers were designed to readily cope with. Extended his hand, and Vanessa shook it with reflex yet unnecessary concern of her armoured grip, her faceplate visor lifted for politeness, despite the gathering smog in the air. Somewhere back down the long thoroughfare, alarms and speakers echoed above the crackling of flames and the hiss of localised fire retardant. "Federal Intelligence, my sources tell me, is no fan of yours, Lieutenant. Their casualty levels in Tanushan operations have become quite alarming. It is assuredly causing a reassessment of their operations here. Gratifying, is it not, that just one or two talented, well-placed people can change the direction of such policies, and thus the course of history?"

Vanessa nearly smiled. Sweaty and tired within the helmet, Sandy could see her eyes flash with familiar, gleaming energy. You slick bastard, she thought at Ramoja. He'd met her for all of ten seconds, and immediately pressed *precisely* the buttons to which Vanessa was most responsive. She'd never had such instinctive people skills, herself. She'd assumed all GIs would be lacking in them. It seemed she was wrong.

"Since customs went running madly in the other direction," Vanessa said, "as ranking officer here I'm going to have to ask you what's in the shuttle, and request that you show me a full manifest." Her voice gave no indication that flattery would impact upon her professionalism.

"Of course." And spared a brief glance over his shoulder as several more people came down the Berth 15 access behind him. "All of our personnel shall remain in the vicinity until customs returns and re-establishes proper procedure. Mostly, Lieutenant, we brought down personnel. GIs, for precisely this operation, when we suspected that something of this nature might occur. And I decided to play a particular ace up my sleeve that I had been saving for just such a moment. An ace I believe Cassandra will find greatly interesting."

And indicated aside to the three people exiting the Berth 15 access . . . GIs all, lean and armed, looking no less dangerous for the lack of armour. The last of the three carried a small hand recorder, military-model, onto which Sandy guessed the FIA's shuttle flight systems and comp-data had been downloaded. The woman headed for Ramoja, and stopped dead, staring at Sandy.

She stood at middling height, a lean, Chinese-featured woman with short black hair and an STZ snub rifle in her free hand, comfortably grasped with the effortless familiarity with which an orchestra conductor might wield a conductor's wand. Beautiful, in the dark, lean, dangerous way of most GIs, a lithe swagger to her poise, even standing dead still before them. Sandy stared, forgetting to breathe. The rifle slipped from her cross-hold to dangle limply in her hand, muzzle to the floor.

"Chu?" she breathed.

Chu grinned. "Hi, Cap. I *thought* I might find you here. The Major said you would be. Can't ever keep you out of a fight, he reckoned."

Sandy back-racked her rifle with one fast move, strode forward and grabbed her in a tight embrace that would have crushed a straight to mangled flesh and broken bones. Chu hugged her back, with similar force, and she felt her armour creak. She hung on for a long time.

"Um, Cap?" A happy yet quizzical voice in her ear. "Cap, that's actually starting to hurt. Come on, I'm not as big as you." Sandy lessened her grip somewhat.

"Are you the last? What about Pessivich and Rogers?" Sandy's voice struggled to work and her vision was blurred with moisture.

"No, they're gone. Bastards who took us blew 'em away when the government changed and ISO tried to take over the operation . . . see, Cap, you're not the only one who's been having adventures, I got a whole stack of stuff to tell you. I've been *busy* the last year."

"You're gonna tell me. I want to hear all of it." The ground felt unstable beneath her. In the suspicious, rational corner of her mind, she'd half expected this from the moment she'd heard of the League delegation on Callay. But it hit home like a forty-thousand-volt shock to the system. And she remembered something abruptly, released Chu and spun about to Vanessa . . . found her just on the verge of sneaking away, presumably to offer them some privacy . . . "Hey, Ricey, come here. I want you to meet an old friend."

Vanessa came over, helmet off, eyes intensely curious beneath the bedraggled, sweaty fringe. Extended a hand to the other woman. "Sandy's told me all about you. And about your friends. I'm really sorry."

"Can't be helped," Chu said with a shrug, clasping her hand. Her expression was equally curious.

"Chu, Vanessa's the best straight friend I've ever had. And one of the best straight soldiers I've ever seen." Adding the latter because she thought it probably carried more weight with Chu than the former. But . . .

"A friend of Sandy's?" Chu said quizzically. "You must be nuts too, huh?"

"Certifiable," Vanessa replied with a smile. "And you came to Callay—that makes three of us."

"Oh, man," Chu said with an amazed gleam in her eyes. "I've been following the stuff that's been going on here on the Fed-sat newscasts the ISO picks up, it's been crazy, huh? They're changing the whole Federation upside down, just like the League's gone all spaced out since the government changed. All of us here together, now everything's changing . . . League and Callay working together to kick the FIA and Old Earth's butt . . . We're gonna have some fun now, I reckon. This is gonna get interesting."

Vanessa gave Sandy a flat, quizzical smile, an eyebrow lifting slightly. Sandy sighed.

"Same old Chu. Welcome to the Federation."

ABOUT THE AUTHOR

Joel Shepherd was born in Adelaide, South Australia, in 1974, but lived in Perth, Western Australia, for many years. He now lives in Adelaide. He studied film and television at Curtin University but realized that what he really wanted to do was write stories. His first manuscript was shortlisted for the George Turner Prize in 1998, and *Crossover* was shortlisted in 1999.

Apart from writing, Joel helps in his mother's business, selling Australian books to international schools in Asia and beyond. This has given him the opportunity to travel widely in Asia and other parts of the world. Joel also writes about women's basketball for an American Internet magazine.

Crossover, the first Cassandra Kresnov novel, was Joel's first published book.